ZIONISM

THE REAL ENEMY OF THE JEWS

VOLUME II: DAVID BECOMES GOLIATH

"In this extraordinary book, Alan Hart has succeeded in elucidating for us the immediate and long term dangers involved in the unconditional Western support for Zionism and its oppressive policies against the Palestinians. ... Motivated by a genuine concern for peace in Israel and Palestine and beyond in the world at large, Alan Hart has written not only a strong indictment of Zionism, based on both research and personal experience, but also provided us with a charter for a better future..."

ILAN PAPPE
Israel's leading revisionist historian and author of The Ethnic Cleansing of Palestine

"I hope that all who are concerned about the troubles of the Middle East will read this book. It is immensely readable and a magnificent piece of work which reflects Alan Hart's close relationship with Israeli and Palestinian leaders. We are in terrible trouble in the Middle East. The book explains how we got here and how we could move forward. The tragedy is hurting Palestinians, Israelis and the rest of the world. All who wish to engage in finding a way forward will be helped by reading this book."

CLARE SHORT, MP
and International Development Secretary in Prime Minister Tony Blair's government until her resignation over the invasion of Iraq

"As a principled and historical review it is excellent, of great importance I think in terms of content, and the series when finished may even be considered heroic in effort and scope."

MARK BRUZONSKY
MiddleEast.org, founder
World Jewish Congress, first Washington Representative

"Hart's readable account of history, his obviously erudite analysis and his ability in bringing the factual conflict to life on the page ensures the reader's interest is unwavering throughout. His passion and empathy with both sides is apparent. For the Jews, the 'unspeakable fear' of another Holocaust due to Zionist manipulation and tyranny; and for the Arabs and Muslims, the anger and humiliation they are feeling every day that Palestine is being torn apart."

SAMIRA QURAISHY
Islamic Human Rights Commission

"Perhaps the biggest perplexity of the current world political scene is the acceptance by most western countries of the respectability of the State of Israel.... It is perhaps premature to expect the world to come to its senses within the near future, but writing as an Orthodox Jew I hope and pray that the Zionist State of Israel is recognised for what it is and that firm but peaceful pressure be brought to bear for the whole flawed concept to be brought to an end. A pre-requisite for this is a correct historical view and Alan Hart in his chillingly revealing and very readable account of the intrigues of the Zionist political development has made a tremendously valuable contribution to this cause."

RABBI AHRON COHEN

ZIONISM
THE REAL ENEMY OF THE JEWS

VOLUME II

DAVID BECOMES GOLIATH

BY

ALAN HART

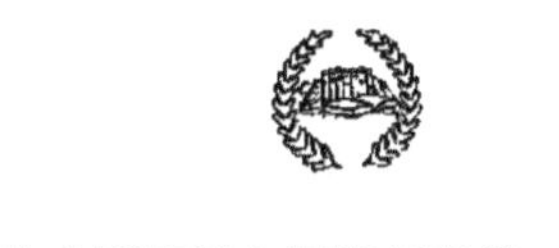

CLARITY PRESS, INC.

ISBN: 0-932863-66-3
978-0-932863-66-9

In-house editor: Diana G. Collier
Cover: R. Jordan P. Santos
Cover photo with permission from Reuters America

Library of Congress Cataloging-in-Publication Data

Hart, Alan, 1942-
Zionism : the real enemy of the Jews / Alan Hart.
v. cm.
Includes bibliographical references and index.
Contents: v.1 The false Messiah
ISBN-13: 978-0-932863-64-5
ISBN-10: 0-932863-64-7
1. Zionism--History. I. Title.

DS149.H41245 2009
320.54--dc22

2008054300

First edition published in hard cover in the United Kingdom in 2005 by World Focus Publishing.

Clarity Press, Inc.
Ste. 469, 3277 Roswell Rd. NE
Atlanta, GA. 30305, USA
http://www.claritypress.com

An epic story dedicated to everyone working for justice and peace in the Middle East

TABLE OF CONTENTS

VOLUME II

DAVID BECOMES GOLIATH

1

THE ANNIHILATION MYTH

An honest summary of the situation in Palestine on the eve of Israel's unilateral declaration of independence is this. By 14 May, Zionism's military forces—the Haganah and the Palmach, with the assistance of the two terrorist organisations, the Irgun and the Stern Gang—had secured control of most parts of Palestine which had been allotted to the Jewish state of the vitiated partition plan, and had captured important positions in the areas allotted to the Arabs. In addition the expulsion of the Palestinians from their homeland was underway. Zionism's pre-war priority had been cleansing the Arab territory allotted to the Jewish state of its Arab inhabitants.

The proclamation of Israel's unilateral declaration of independence was followed by the entry into Palestine of elements of the armies of five Arab states—Egypt, Lebanon, Syria, Iraq and Transjordan; and the first Arab-Israeli war was underway.

According to the first draft of history as written by the winners, and which became implanted in the public mind of North America and Europe as truth, the Arab Goliath had both the intention and the ability to destroy the Jewish state.

If you looked at a map of the region, the notion of the Arabs as Goliath was plausible. The land area of the Arab states was 200 times larger than Israel. And the combined population of those Arab states was tens of millions and rising fast. The number of Jews in Israel at the time was about 700,000. On the face of it, and especially if you played the total numbers game (as Zionism's propaganda maestros did and continue to do), the odds against the Zionist state surviving a concerted Arab attack seemed to be great.

But as we shall now see, the prospect of Israel being annihilated was not a real one except in Zionist mythology, which was able to present itself as truth to the Western world because of the ignorance of public opinion and the bellicose rhetoric of some Arabs, and this against the background of the Nazi holocaust.

The first revelation of the war was to the Palestinians.

When elements of the Arab armies entered Palestine the first thing they did was to disarm the Palestinians. Among the first to be disarmed—he might have been the first—was a student by the name of Yasser Arafat. (As a student leader he had risked his life, many times, to buy ancient rifles and ammunition from tribes in the Egyptian interior for smuggling into Palestine).

Looking back I can say that never in my many conversations with Arafat over the years did he speak with such intense but controlled feeling as when he described to me what happened when the incoming Egyptian army reached Gaza. Arafat did not, in fact, give emphasis to any of his words on this occasion. He spoke in a quiet, flat voice and as though he was still finding it difficult to believe that what he was describing had actually happened. I think all of his words are worthy of emphasis.

When elements of the Arab armies entered Palestine the first thing they did was to disarm the Palestinians.

> *An Egyptian officer came to my group and demanded that we hand over our weapons. At first I could not believe what my ears were telling me. The officer said it was an order from the Arab League. He gave me a receipt for my rifle. He said I could have it back when the war was over. In that moment I knew we had been betrayed by the Arab regimes. I was myself touched by their treachery. I can't forget.*[1]

A slightly different perspective was given to me by Khalad Hassan who became the intellectual giant on the right of the authentic (as opposed to Arab puppet) PLO and who, with his younger brother Hani, was to be for many turbulent years the crisis manager of Arafat's stormy relations with those Arab leaders who mattered most. Looking back, Khalad said: "To call the Arab regimes traitors is not completely fair. To be a traitor you must *want* to betray. The truth is not so much that the Arab regimes of the day wanted to betray our cause. They did what they did because of their circumstances."[2]

The circumstances included the fact that Egypt, Iraq and Transjordan were entirely dependent on Britain for their arms and ammunition. Transjordan had the best and most effective Arab army—the Bedouin Arab Legion. It was commanded, and had been fashioned into the elite and mechanised fighting force it was, by a Lawrence-like Englishman, John Bagot Glubb. And most of the Arab Legion's senior officers at the time were British.

Egypt, Iraq and Transjordan were entirely dependent on Britain for their arms and ammunition.

In the Zionist version of history which, like most Western correspondents, I took as read (accepted without question) throughout most of my ITN and Panorama reporting days, Israel really was facing the prospect of annihilation. Eventually exposure to the other side of the story, the Arab side, made me realise that to have an opinion worth having about whether or not the survival of the Jewish state was actually at stake in 1948, it was necessary to have some basic background understanding of two things:

- the difference between Arab rhetoric and Arab military capability and, in that context, the difference between Arab and Zionist preparations for war; and

- the real, as opposed to the publicly stated, intentions of the frontline Arab leaders, the most important of them being, as it turned out, Transjordan's King Abdullah.

On the Zionist side, advance planning for the war was switched into overdrive following Golda's success in raising the $50 million in America. *Though his judgment might have been different if Golda had failed to raise the necessary funds, nobody was more pleased than Ben-Gurion when the Arabs rejected partition.* (The reasons why will become clear in due course).

Ben-Gurion's strategy of securing the ammunition, weapons and other military hardware needed to guarantee victory if the Arabs opted for war was brilliantly conceived and executed—*chutzpah* at its clandestine and magnificent best.

Directed by Ben-Gurion himself, the initial effort to turn David into Goliath was masterminded by two men, Haim Slavine and Ehud Avriel.

Three years before Israel's unilateral declaration of independence, Slavine was sent by Ben-Gurion to America. His mission was to locate and purchase the equipment needed to enable the Zionist state-in-waiting to create, under British occupation, the beginnings of an arms manufacturing industry of its own. Slavine toured America from coast to coast, visiting junkyards and factories, buying up machine tools about to be disposed of as war-surplus material. The machine tools he purchased were smuggled out of America and into Palestine where they were put to work beneath the fields of a kibbutz. By May of 1948, before the end of the British occupation, they were producing hundreds of submachine guns a day and the armour plating for homemade tanks and personnel carriers.

Avriel was sent to Europe by Ben-Gurion the day after the rigged vote on partition at the UN. His mission was to set up a clandestine network to handle the purchasing and shipment of ammunition and the heavy-duty weapons and military hardware the Israelis-to-be could not then manufacture for themselves. The priority was artillery and above all, literally, aircraft—fighters, bombers and transporters. They were to include Czech-made Messerschmitt 109s, English-made Spitfires, American Flying Fortresses, Constellations, C-46s and Dakotas.

Avriel's crowning glory was the acquisition of a complete airbase. It was located in the little Czech town of Zatec. It had previously been a Luftwaffe base in Nazi-occupied Sudetenland. Ariel persuaded his Czech friends to rent it to him; and under his direction a largely American-staffed airfield came into being. It was to be the vital link in the supply chain to Israel.

One of Avriel's most celebrated agents was the handsome,

aristocratic-looking Yehuda Arazi. He had started Zionism's clandestine arms procurement in Poland in 1936 by stuffing a steam boiler bound for Haifa with rifles. His great achievement early in 1948 was to get himself named—in return for a bribe of US$200,000—as a special ambassador of Nicaragua to the governments of Europe charged with the responsibility of procuring arms for the Nicaraguan army.

On the supply side, and in advance of the war, Avriel and his network had just about solved all of Ben-Gurion's outstanding problems of ammunition, weapons and other military hardware. The remaining problem was actual delivery or, to be more precise, *the timing of the delivery.*

There was no way the Zionists could take deliveries from Zatec or anywhere else until the British were gone and Israel had declared itself to be in existence. Obviously it would take some days after that to get a bare minimum supply service to Israel going, and probably a week or two or more for a supply that was adequate and sustainable enough to assure Israel of victory. On the face of it the implication was this. If the Arabs launched their attack as soon as the Jewish state declared itself to be in existence, and if the Arab attack was well planned and coordinated, Israeli forces might be hard pressed, initially, to hold even the territory that had been allotted to the proposed Jewish state of the partition plan.

Ben-Gurion was, however, totally confident that his forces would contain the Arab offensive while they waited for the supplies from Zatec and elsewhere to come on stream, supplies that would enable the Israelis to turn the tide of war in their favour. His confidence was reinforced by his knowledge that Transjordan's King Abdullah was not intending to join in any Arab attack on the Jewish state of the partition plan.

A promise to that effect had been given by Abdullah himself to the then acting head of the Jewish Agency's Political Department—Golda Meir (Myerson, as she then was). The promise was made to her when, on 17 November 1947, 12 days before the vote in the General Assembly on the partition resolution, she and Abdullah had the first of two secret meetings. It took place in a house at Naharayim on the Jordan River where the Palestine Electric Corporation ran a hydroelectric power station. Many years later Golda's own account of her first secret meeting with the Hashemite monarch included this:

Ben-Gurion knew that Transjordan was not intending to join in on any Arab attack on the Jewish state in territory provided for it by the vitiated partition plan.

> We drank the usual ceremonial cups of coffee and then we began to talk. Abdullah was a small, very poised man with great charm. He soon made the heart of the matter very clear: he would not join in any Arab attack on us. He would always remain our friend, he said, and, like us, he wanted peace more than anything else.[3]

Abdullah did, in fact, tell Golda much more about his intentions than she ever acknowledged in public.

The Hashemite monarch hated the exiled Palestinian leader of the time (Haj Amin Husseini, the mufti of Jerusalem) and feared what he represented—Palestinian nationalism. Abdullah's plan, he told Golda, was to prevent the mufti and his supporters getting control of the parts of Palestine that had been assigned by the partition plan to the Arabs. *To that end, he told Golda, he was intending to take the Arab parts of Palestine and attach them to his own kingdom.* And he asked Golda what the Zionist response to his plan would be.

The essence of Golda's reply was set down by Avi Shlaim in *The Iron Wall, Israel and the Arab World*, a remarkable Jewish deconstruction of Zionist mythology. (A Professor of International Relations at St. Anthony's College, Oxford, Shlaim was born in Baghdad and grew up in Israel). Golda told Abdullah the Jews would view his plan in a favourable light especially if Abdullah did not interfere with the establishment of a Jewish state and avoided military confrontation with it. The understanding the two of them reached was that he would take Arab Palestine, the Jews would set up their own state, and, after the dust had settled, the two parties would make peace.

As Shlaim noted, that first Golda-Abdullah secret meeting did not commit either side formally to a particular course of action in advance of the vote at the UN on the partition plan. "But it did result in a meeting of minds and laid the foundations for a partition of Palestine along lines radically different from the ones eventually envisaged by the United Nations."[4]

The main points were that Transjordan was not going to war against the Jewish state of the partition plan and it would welcome Abdullah's effort to close the file on Palestinian nationalism.

Golda also recalled that Abdullah told her they should meet again, after the vote on the partition resolution at the UN. My speculation is that when she said goodbye to Abdullah, she was entertaining in her own mind a comforting thought. If the decision at the UN went against partition and the creation of a Jewish state, the Zionists could still do their own partition deal with Abdullah.

According to one interpretation of history that still finds favour with many historians, Abdullah was the only Arab leader who was ready and willing to accept the Jewish state of the UN partition plan. In fact Abdullah's real position was not so clear-cut. His own representation of his thinking was in an article he wrote for *The American Magazine* published in November 1947. I presume it was written before his first secret meeting with Golda Meir. It was an appeal for understanding by the people of America and it was headlined AS THE ARABS SEE THE JEWS. Because of King Abdullah's critical role in the events as they happened, I decided that the text of the whole article should be included here.

> So many billions of words have been written about Palestine—perhaps more than on any other subject in history—that I hesitate to add to them. Yet I am compelled

to do so, for I am reluctantly convinced that the world in general and America in particular, knows almost nothing of the true case for the Arabs.

We Arabs follow, perhaps far more than you think, the press of America. We are frankly disturbed to find that for every word printed on the Arab side, a thousand are printed on the Zionist side.

There are many reasons for this. You have many millions of Jewish citizens interested in this question. They are highly vocal and wise in the ways of publicity. There are few Arab citizens in America, and we are as yet unskilled in the technique of modern propaganda.

The results have been alarming for us. In your press we see a horrible caricature and are told it is our true portrait. In all justice, we cannot let this pass by default.

Our case is quite simple: For nearly 2,000 years Palestine has been almost 100 per cent Arab. It is still preponderantly Arab today, in spite of enormous Jewish immigration. But if this immigration continues we shall soon be outnumbered—a minority in our home.

Palestine is a small and very poor country, about the size of your state of Vermont. Its Arab population is only about 1,200,000. Already we have had forced on us, against our will, some 600,000 Zionist Jews. We are threatened with many hundreds of thousands more.

Our position is so simple and natural that we are amazed it should even be questioned. It is exactly the same position you in America take in regard to the unhappy European Jews. You are sorry for them, but you do not want them in your country.

We do not want them in ours, either. Not because they are Jews, but because they are foreigners. We would not want hundreds of thousands of foreigners in our country, be they Englishmen or Norwegians or Brazilians or whatever. Think for a moment: In the last 25 years we have had one third of our entire population forced upon us. In America that would be the equivalent of 45,000,000 complete strangers admitted to your country, over your violent protest, since 1921. How would you have reacted to that?

Because of our perfectly natural dislike of being overwhelmed in our own homeland, we are called blind nationalists and heartless anti-Semites. This charge would be ludicrous were it not so dangerous.

No people on earth have been less "anti-Semitic" than the Arabs.

The persecution of the Jews has been confined almost entirely to the Christian nations of the West. Jews, themselves, will admit that never since the Great Dispersion did Jews develop so freely and reach such importance as in Spain when it was an Arab possession. With very minor exceptions, Jews have lived for many centuries in the Middle East, in complete peace and friendliness with their Arab neighbours.

Damascus, Baghdad, Beirut and other Arab centers have always contained large and prosperous Jewish colonies. Until the Zionist invasion of Palestine began, these Jews received the most generous treatment—far, far better than in Christian Europe. Now, unhappily, for the first time in history, these Jews are beginning to feel the effects of Arab resistance to the Zionist assault. Most of them are as anxious as Arabs to stop it. Most of these Jews who have found happy homes among us resent, as we do, the coming of these strangers.

Abdullah: In the last 25 years, the Arabs have had one third of their entire population forced upon them. This was unwanted, not because they are Jews, but because they are foreigners. The equivalent for the US would be the forced acceptance of 45 million people.

I was puzzled for a long time about the odd belief which apparently persists in America that Palestine has somehow "always been a Jewish land." Recently an American I talked to cleared up this mystery. He pointed out that the only things most Americans know about Palestine are what they read in the Bible. It was a Jewish land in those days, they reason, and they assume it has always remained so.

Nothing could be farther from the truth. It is absurd to reach so far back into the mists of history to argue about who should have Palestine today, and I apologize for it. Yet the Jews do this, and I must reply to their "historic claim."

I wonder if the world has ever seen a stranger sight than a group of people seriously pretending to claim a land because their ancestors lived there some 2,000 years ago!

Abullah: "I wonder if the world has ever seen a stranger sight than a group of people seriously pretending to claim a land because their ancestors lived there some 2,000 years ago!"

If you suggest that I am biased, I invite you to read any sound history of the period and verify the facts.

Such fragmentary records as we have indicate that the Jews were wandering nomads from Iraq who moved to southern Turkey, came south to Palestine, stayed there a short time, and then passed to Egypt, where they remained about 400 years. About 1300 BC (according to your calendar) they left Egypt and gradually conquered most—but not all—of the inhabitants of Palestine.

It is significant that the Philistines—not the Jews—gave their name to the country: "Palestine" is merely the Greek form of "Philistia."

Only once, during the empire of David and Solomon, did the Jews ever control nearly—but not all—the land which is today Palestine. This empire lasted only 70 years, ending in 926 BC. Only 250 years later the Kingdom of Judah had shrunk to a small province around Jerusalem, barely a quarter of modern Palestine.

In 63 BC the Jews were conquered by Roman Pompey, and never again had even the vestige of independence. The Roman Emperor Hadrian finally wiped them out about 135 AD. He utterly destroyed Jerusalem, rebuilt under another name, and for hundreds of years no Jew was permitted to enter it. A handful of Jews remained in Palestine but the vast majority were killed or scattered to other countries in the Diaspora, or the Great Dispersion. From that time Palestine ceased to be a Jewish country, in any conceivable sense.

This was 1,815 years ago, and yet the Jews solemnly pretend they still own Palestine! If such fantasy were allowed, how the map of the world would dance about! Italians might claim England, which the Romans held so long. England might claim France, "homeland" of the conquering Normans. And the French Normans might claim Norway, where their ancestors originated. And incidentally, we Arabs might claim Spain, which we held for 700 years. Many Mexicans might claim Spain, "homeland" of their forefathers. They might even claim Texas, which was Mexican until 100 years ago. And suppose the American Indians claimed the "homeland" of which they were the sole, native, and ancient occupants until only some 450 years ago!

I am not being facetious. All these claims are just as valid—or just as fantastic—as the Jewish "historic connection" with Palestine. Most are more valid.

In any event, the great Muslim expansion about 650 AD finally settled things. It dominated Palestine completely. From that day on, Palestine was solidly Arabic in population, language, and religion. When British armies entered the country during the last war, they found 500,000 Arabs and only 65,000 Jews.

If solid, uninterrupted Arab occupation for nearly 1,300 years does not make a country "Arab", what does?

The Jews say, and rightly, that Palestine is the home of their religion. It is likewise the birthplace of Christianity, but would any Christian nation claim it on that account? In passing, let me say that the Christian Arabs—and there are many hundreds of thousands of them in the Arab World—are in absolute agreement with all other Arabs in opposing the Zionist invasion of Palestine.

May I also point out that Jerusalem is, after Mecca and Medina, the holiest place in Islam. In fact, in the early days of our religion, Muslims prayed toward Jerusalem instead of Mecca.

The Jewish "religious claim" to Palestine is as absurd as the "historic claim." The Holy Places, sacred to three great religions, must be open to all, the monopoly of none. Let us not confuse religion and politics.

We are told that we are inhumane and heartless because do not accept with open arms the perhaps 200,000 Jews in Europe who suffered so frightfully under Nazi cruelty, and who even now—almost three years after war's end—still languish in cold, depressing camps.

Let me underline several facts. The unimaginable persecution of the Jews was not done by the Arabs: it was done by a Christian nation in the West. The war which ruined Europe and made it almost impossible for these Jews to rehabilitate themselves was fought by the Christian nations of the West. The rich and empty portions of the earth belong, not to the Arabs, but to the Christian nations of the West.

And yet, to ease their consciences, these Christian nations of the West are asking Palestine—a poor and tiny Muslim country of the East—to accept the entire burden. "We have hurt these people terribly," cries the West to the East. "Won't you please take care of them for us?"

We find neither logic nor justice in this. Are we therefore "cruel and heartless nationalists"?

We are a generous people: we are proud that "Arab hospitality" is a phrase famous throughout the world. We are a humane people: no one was shocked more than we by the Hitlerite terror. No one pities the present plight of the desperate European Jews more than we.

But we say that Palestine has already sheltered 600,000 refugees. We believe that is enough to expect of us—even too much. We believe it is now the turn of the rest of the world to accept some of them.

I will be entirely frank with you. There is one thing the Arab world simply cannot understand. Of all the nations of the earth, America is most insistent that something be done for these suffering Jews of Europe. This feeling does credit to the humanity for which America is famous, and to that glorious inscription on your Statue of Liberty.

And yet this same America—the richest, greatest, most powerful nation the world has ever known—refuses to accept more than a token handful of these same Jews herself! [As we saw in Volume One, initiatives by Presidents Roosevelt and Truman to give substantial numbers of Europe's uprooted Jews a safe haven in America were frustrated and effectively sabotaged by hardcore Zionists and their supporters].

I hope you will not think I am being bitter about this. I have tried hard to understand that mysterious paradox and I confess I cannot. Nor can any other Arab.

Perhaps you have been informed that "the Jews in Europe want to go to no other place except Palestine."

This myth is one of the greatest propaganda triumphs of the Jewish Agency for Palestine, the organization which promotes with fanatic zeal the emigration to Palestine. It is a subtle half-truth, thus doubly dangerous.

The astounding truth is that nobody on earth really knows where these unfortunate Jews really want to go!

You would think that in so grave a problem, the American, British, and other authorities responsible for the European Jews would have made a very careful survey, probably by vote, to find out where each Jew actually wants to go. Amazingly enough this has never been done! The Jewish Agency has prevented it.

Nobody on earth really knew where the unfortunate Jewish refugees wanted to go. When preparations were made to poll the desires of the Jews in German camps, the Jewish Agency stopped them.

Some time ago the American Military Governor in Germany was asked at a press conference how he was so certain that all Jews there wanted to go to Palestine. His answer was simple: "My Jewish advisors tell me so." He admitted no poll had ever been made. Preparations were indeed begun for one, but the Jewish Agency stepped in to stop it.

The truth is that the Jews in German camps are now subjected to a Zionist pressure campaign which learned much from the Nazi terror. It is dangerous for a Jew to say that he would rather go to some other country, not Palestine. Such dissenters have been severely beaten, and worse.

Not long ago, in Palestine, nearly 1,000 Austrian Jews informed the international refugee organization that they would like to go back to Austria, and plans were made to repatriate them.

The Jewish Agency heard of this, and exerted enough political pressure to stop it. It would be bad propaganda for

Zionism if Jews began leaving Palestine. The nearly 1,000 Austrians are still there, against their will.

The fact is that most of the European Jews are Western in culture and outlook, entirely urban in experience and habits. They cannot really have their hearts set on becoming pioneers in the barren, arid, cramped land which is Palestine.

One thing, however, is undoubtedly true. As matters stand now, most refugee Jews in Europe would, indeed, vote for Palestine, simply because they know no other country will have them.

If you or I were given a choice between a near-prison camp for the rest of our lives—or Palestine—we would both choose Palestine, too.

But open up any other alternative to them—give them any other choice, and see what happens!

No poll, however, will be worth anything unless the nations of the earth are willing to open their doors—just a little—to the Jews. In other words, if in such a poll a Jew says he wants to go to Sweden, Sweden must be willing to accept him. If he votes for America, you must let him come in. Any other kind of poll would be a farce. For the desperate Jew, this is no idle testing of opinion: this is a grave matter of life or death. Unless he is absolutely sure that his vote means something, he will always vote for Palestine, so as not to risk his bird in the hand for one in the bush.

In any event, Palestine can accept no more. The 65,000 Jews in Palestine in 1918 have jumped to 600,000 today. We Arabs have increased, too, but not by immigration. The Jews were then a mere 11 per cent of our population. Today they are one third of it.

The rate of increase has been terrifying. In a few more years—unless stopped now—it will overwhelm us, and we shall be an important minority in our own home.

Surely the rest of the wide world is rich enough and generous enough to find a place for 200,000 Jews—about one third the number that tiny, poor Palestine has already sheltered. For the rest of the world, it is hardly a drop in the bucket. For us it means national suicide.

We are sometimes told that since the Jews came to Palestine, the Arab standard of living has improved. This is a most complicated question. But let us even assume, for the argument, that it is true. We would rather be a bit poorer, and masters of our own home. Is this unnatural?

The sorry story of the so-called "Balfour Declaration," which started Zionist immigration into Palestine, is too complicated to repeat here in detail. It is grounded in broken promises to the Arabs—promises made in cold print which admit no denying.

We utterly deny its validity. We utterly deny the right of Great Britain to give away Arab land for a "national home" for an entirely foreign people.

Even the League of Nations sanction does not alter this. At the time, not a single Arab state was a member of the League. We were not allowed to say a word in our own defence.

I must point out, again in friendly frankness, that America was nearly as responsible as Britain for this Balfour Declaration. President Wilson approved it before it was issued, and the American Congress adopted it word for word in a joint resolution on 30th June, 1922.

In the 1920s, Arabs were annoyed and insulted by Zionist immigration, but not alarmed by it. It was steady, but fairly small, as even the Zionist founders thought it would remain. Indeed for some years, more Jews left Palestine than entered it—in 1927 almost twice as many.

But two new factors, entirely unforeseen by Britain or the League or America or the most fervent Zionist, arose in the early thirties to raise the immigration to undreamed heights. One was the World Depression; the second the rise of Hitler.

In 1932, the year before Hitler came to power; only 9,500 Jews came to Palestine. We did not welcome them, but we were not afraid that, at that rate, our solid Arab majority would ever be in danger.

But the next year—the year of Hitler—it jumped to 30,000! In 1934 it was 42,000! In 1935 it reached 61,000.

It was no longer the orderly arrival of idealist Zionists. Rather, all Europe was pouring its frightened Jews upon us. Then, at last, we, too, became frightened. We knew that unless this enormous influx stopped, we were, as Arabs, doomed in our Palestine homeland. And we have not changed our minds.

I have the impression that many Americans believe the trouble in Palestine is very remote from them, that America had little to do with it, and that your only interest now is that of a humane bystander.

I believe that you do not realize how directly you are, as a nation, responsible in general for the whole Zionist move and specifically for the present terrorism. I call this to your attention because I am certain that if you realize your responsibility you will act fairly to admit it and assume it.

Abdullah: "I believe that you do not realize how directly you are, as a nation, responsible in general for the whole Zionist movement and specifically for the present terrorism."

Quite aside from official American support for the "National Home" of the Balfour Declaration, the Zionist settlements in Palestine would have been almost impossible, on anything like the current scale, without American money. This was contributed by American Jewry in an idealistic effort to help their fellows.

The motive was worthy: the results were disastrous. The contributions were by private individuals, but they were almost entirely Americans, and, as a nation, only America can answer for it.

The present catastrophe may be laid almost entirely at your door. Your government, almost alone in the world, is insisting on the immediate admission of 100,000 more Jews into Palestine—to be followed by countless additional ones. This will have the most frightful consequences in bloody chaos beyond anything ever hinted at in Palestine before. It is your press and political leadership, almost alone in the world, who press this demand. It is almost entirely American money which hires or buys the "refugee ships" that steam illegally toward Palestine: American money which pays their crews. The illegal immigration from Europe is arranged by the Jewish Agency, supported almost entirely by American funds. It is American dollars which support the terrorists, which buy the bullets and pistols that kill British soldiers—your allies—and Arab citizens—your friends.

We in the Arab world were stunned to hear that you permit open advertisements in newspapers asking for money to finance these terrorists, to arm them openly and deliberately for murder. We could not believe this could really happen in the modern world. Now we must believe it: we have seen the advertisements with our own eyes. I point out these things because nothing less than complete frankness will be of use. The crisis is too stark for mere polite vagueness which means nothing.

I have the most complete confidence in the fair-mindedness and generosity of the American public. We Arabs ask no favours. We ask only that you know the full truth, not half of it. We ask only that when you judge the Palestine question, you put yourselves in our place.

What would your answer be if some outside agency told you that you must accept in America many millions of utter strangers in your midst—enough to dominate your country—merely because they insisted on going to America, and because their forefathers had once lived there some 2,000 years ago?

Our answer is the same.

And what would be your action if, in spite of your refusal, this outside agency began forcing them on you?

Ours will be the same.

King Abdullah's own preferred solution to the Palestine problem was the one he had advocated in 1938—the creation of a United Arab Kingdom of Palestine and Transjordan with, of course, himself the master of it all. In the United Arab Kingdom of Abdullah's vision the Jews would administer themselves in Jewish districts and serve in the cabinet of a federal government. (That, minus Transjordan, was in essence the solution to which Britain committed itself in the 1939 White Paper when it ruled out the creation of a Jewish state).

What Abdullah became with the passage of time and events was an ambitious pragmatist. When he met with Golda for the first time he was already reconciled to the fact that, with or without the sanction of the UN, the Zionists would have their state. He was thus prepared to accept Zionism's *fait accompli* when it happened. But...

There was much more to Abdullah's thinking than loathing of the mufti of Jerusalem and fear of Palestinian nationalism. He understood Zionism. He was fully aware of its ambitions and that it would not, could not, settle for a state as small as the one of the proposed UN partition plan.

Annexing the parts of Palestine assigned by the UN to the Arabs was therefore the only credible way of preventing Zionism from gobbling them up. From that perspective Abdullah was prepared to do what he could to contain Zionism.

Through various channels Ben-Gurion's Jewish Agency had long been in contact with Abdullah. So even before Golda's first secret meeting with him, Ben-Gurion and his leadership colleagues knew that Abdullah despised his brother Arab leaders because they were urinating into the wind.

As Golda noted, Ben-Gurion was cautioned by his advisers that while Abdullah was "certainly sincere" in his expressions of friendship, he would not necessarily be bound by them in the event of war.

Despite that caution Ben-Gurion was thrilled by Golda's report of Abdullah's promise. If the Arab Legion—the best and most effective fighting force in the Arab world—did not participate in the coming war, the task of containing the Arab offensive until Israel was completely organised and armed for victory would not be so daunting. Even more exciting was the prospect of capturing all of Jerusalem, quickly and without too much trouble.

What of the Arabs? How did they prepare for war? At leadership level, and with the exception of Transjordan, the frontline Arab states matched Zionism's *chutzpah* with complacency and incompetence.

In December 1947, shortly after the rigged vote at the UN to partition Palestine, eight Arab leaders met in the Egyptian Ministry of Foreign Affairs. Seven of them (prime ministers and foreign ministers) represented the seven nations of the Arab League as it then was—Egypt, Lebanon, Syria, Iraq, Yemen, Saudi Arabia and Transjordan. The eighth man was Abdurrahman Azzam, the organisation's Egyptian Secretary General.

Though bound together by common ties of language, religion and history, the Arab states were then (as they were to remain) *deeply divided about almost everything*. Who was to have most influence in the region? In order to compete with Egypt and Saudi Arabia, Syria wanted Lebanon; Iraq wanted Syria; and Abdullah, who wanted both Syria and Iraq, was intending to annex parts of Palestine that had been assigned to the Arabs in the partition plan.

The greatest hypocrite of them all was Iraq's leader, Nuri as-Said. Short and stubby with a little white Chaplinesque moustache, he had ridden with Lawrence and had cast his destiny with the British whom he truly admired. In public no Arab leader was more ready than Nuri as-Said to do the Jews verbal violence; but in private, between visits to the London clubs of which he was a member, he told his British Foreign Office friends that he would accommodate a Jewish state for a price. The price was Britain's support for his annexation of Syria to Iraq, to enable him to realise his dream of a fertile Arab crescent from the Mediterranean to the Persian Gulf.

Unfortunately for the Palestinians, these Arab rivalries and the plots and conspiracies that were part and parcel of them, resulted in all Arab League leaders but the Saudis viewing Palestine as a card in their own power game. As a consequence their intentions with regard to Palestine were determined in large part by their perceptions of how playing the Palestine card would serve their own interests—individual and national—to the disadvantage of their rivals. And as a consequence of that they were incapable of the unity and coordination needed for even the conception of a credible military or political strategy for confronting Zionism.

In reality none of the frontline Arab leaders wanted to commit their armies to war in Palestine. But at the December meeting in Cairo only Mahmoud Nokrashy dared to say so behind closed doors. He was the prime minister of Egypt, the Arab country with the biggest army and, by definition, the country that would have to commit the most men, weapons and resources of all kinds in the event of war. Nokrashy's greatest concern was Britain's continuing occupation of the Suez Canal. He was seeking to get the British out in order for Egypt to have complete independence, and he did not want a crisis with Britain over Palestine.

The Arab League policy as agreed by the seven leaders was set down in the first paragraph of a four-page memorandum stamped SECRET. It was prepared by Azzam on the basis of their discussions over several days. "The Arab League", the document stated, "is resolved to prevent the creation of a Jewish state in Palestine and to conserve Palestine as a united, independent state."[5]

None of the divided leaders of the Arab League wanted to commit their armed forces to war in Palestine. In the face of British disapproval, they could only propose setting up a guerrilla force, the Arab Liberation Army—which would not include any Palestinians.

How were they going to do that when none of them wanted to commit their armed forces to war in Palestine?

Their answer was to set up a guerrilla force to be called the Arab Liberation Army. The representatives of the seven countries around the Cairo table pledged to provide the League a total of 10,000 rifles, 3,000 volunteers and £1 million sterling, to enable guerrilla operations in Palestine to begin as soon as possible.

Just about the only thing the seven Arab leaders agreed on without dispute was that *the volunteer force, the Liberation Army, should not and would not include Palestinians.*

As we have seen, the power that was pulling most of the strings of the Arab League, Britain, *did not want Palestinian nationalists to be armed and capable of determining their own destiny*. For their part the Arab regimes—Egypt, Iraq and Transjordan especially—could not afford to cross Britain on this matter and, anyway, Palestinian self-determination was not an item on their own agendas.

It was, in fact, Nokrashy who set the parameters within which the Arab League would act. As the host of the Cairo meeting the Egyptian prime minister had spoken first. He said and repeated with emphasis that while he was prepared to provide arms and money to prevent a Zionist takeover of Palestine, *he would not commit Egypt's armed forces*.

That was good music to Transjordan's ears but not what Lebanon and Syria wanted to hear. Their leaders knew that without the participation of Egypt's armed forces, war to defeat the Zionists—a war and a victory they had promised their people—was unthinkable. But as the leading advocates of guerrilla action, Lebanon and Syria were to some extent mollified by Nokrashy's commitment to a proportion of the rifles, volunteers and money for a Liberation Army.

As Azzam worked on drafting the document that would define the Arab League's intentions, he knew the meeting would not end with an agreement demonstrating a token show of unity if the final document did not pay lip-service to preparations for war. Thus it was that the four-page document stamped SECRET concluded with the statement that the Arab League would assign to an Iraqi general the responsibility of preparing a contingency plan, for the coordinated intervention of the Arab armies in the event of a declaration of independence by the Jews.

The Iraqi general was Ismail Safwat, the man who subsequently rejected Abdul Khader's appeal for arms and ammunition, and to whom the Palestinian resistance leader said, "The blood of Palestine and its people shall be on your head."

The man chosen by the Arab League to lead the Liberation Army, and to be its recruiting sergeant, was the red-haired Fawzi el Kaukji, described by some as looking more like a Prussian major than an Arab chief.

Born in northern Lebanon, Kaukji was a mercenary with a touch of class. He had served his military apprenticeship in the Turkish army fighting the British. Then, when the Ottoman Empire began to crumble, he spied on the Turks for the British. Subsequently he spied on the French for the British, on the British for the French and then on the French and the British for the Germans. As an admirer and lover of all things German, he had married a pretty German girl more than 30 years younger than himself during World War II. On one of his nightly rounds of the cabarets in wartime Berlin, as recounted by Collins and Lapierre, he had won the girl's admiration by ordering for her two of the rarest commodities in the Nazi capital—a bottle of Veuve Clicquot champagne and a packet of Camel cigarettes. The couple became inseparable so perhaps real love was also a part of the chemistry.

As a fighter Kaukji had distinguished himself and won admirers during the Arab revolt against the British in Palestine. For the Arab League Kaukji's greatest value was in the presumption that he would do whatever he was told to do so long as it rewarded him better than any other potential paymaster.

At Syria's insistence Kaukji and the Liberation Army was to be headquartered in Damascus. This for two reasons. The first was that it would enable Syria's leaders to claim a disproportionate share of the credit for any of Kaukji's successes. The second was that it would enable the Syrian regime to monitor his every move and telephone conversation. Syria's leaders lived with the fear that Kaukji might be ordered to lead a revolt against them. (At leadership level the Arab who trusted another Arab was, as he still is, very rare).

On what turned out to be his last visit to Damascus, to beg Safwat for arms and ammunition, it was Abdul Khader's sight of the weapons that were being stockpiled for Kaukji that led the Palestinian resistance leader to tell Abu Gharbieh that they, the Palestinians, had been betrayed.

The time was coming when Safwat himself could be forgiven for thinking that he, too, had been betrayed.

Of the seven Arab leaders who sat around the Cairo table with Azzam in that December of 1947, only one of them had in his head a credible strategy for preventing the creation of an independent Jewish state.

That one man was Prince Feisal, Saudi Arabia's foreign minister. Feisal was the only Arab leader with *chutzpah*. In the privacy of his own mind, his logic went something like this. The Zionists have awesome influence in America because of Jewish money for election campaign funds and the organised Jewish vote. The Zionists are playing their cards ruthlessly. We should play our only card—our oil—with equal ruthlessness.

Feisal had discussed use of the oil weapon with his father; but Ibn Saud refused to consider such a strategy. "The problem is Palestine not petroleum," he said.[6]

Apart from the fact that he had given his word to President Roosevelt, Ibn Saud was not prepared to risk an interruption to the escalating flow of money from oil that was enabling him to develop his country and create a ruling dynasty that none would ever be able to challenge. The founding father of Saudi Arabia had many strengths and virtues; *but he did not possess Feisal's understanding of how cards had to be played in a world in which politics was concerned only with interests, and short-term interests at that.*

Feisal believed that Saudi Arabia's wealth generation would not be put at risk because, almost certainly, the Arabs would not have to go as far as actually cutting off supplies of oil. All they would have to do to oblige the Truman administration to cut Zionism down to size was to make a credible threat—that the Arabs *would* resort to use of the oil weapon if Zionism was not required to accept a solution on terms Arab leaders could just about sell to their peoples. Such a solution would not have given Zionism the independent Jewish state it was demanding, but it would have provided for a self-governing Jewish entity as part of a unitary Palestine.

My own interpretation of events is that Feisal was right. If the Arabs *had* made a credible threat to play their oil card, the views of the U.S. Departments of State and Defence, together with those of the American intelligence community, would have prevailed; and Zionism would have been required to accept less than an independent Jewish state. (If the boot had been on the other foot—if the Zionists had been the Arabs—they *would* have played the oil card. In private conversations with me over the years, a number of Israeli leaders said so).

With use of the oil weapon ruled out by his father, Feisal was reduced to being an impotent bystander as the leaders of the frontline Arab states plotted and schemed, more against each other than the Zionists.

The most pragmatic and also the most farsighted of the plotters and schemers was Transjordan's King Abdullah. His plan to annex the parts of Palestine that had been allotted to the Arabs by the partition resolution was approved at a secret meeting in London in February 1948. Those present were Ernest Bevin, Britain's Foreign Secretary, Tewfic Abu Hoda, Abdullah's prime minister, and John Glubb, the Arabic-speaking English commander of Abdullah's Arab Legion. Glubb was there as translator. Neither Abdullah nor Abu Hoda had wanted to trust a fellow Arab with the task of translating.

The ground had been well prepared. In Transjordan some weeks earlier Abdullah himself had run the idea past the British ambassador, Sir Alec Kirkbride. "What would be London's response if I annexed those parts of Palestine assigned to the Arab state?" the Hashemite monarch had mused aloud.[7] It was, he knew, a question that could not be answered there and then. Abdullah's purpose in asking it was to cause Kirkbride to inform the Foreign Office about the way the king's mind was working.

So by the time Bevin received Transjordan's prime minister, the Foreign Office mandarins had considered Abdullah's proposition and made their recommendation.

When Abu Hoda formally presented his master's annexation plan, he stressed that Abdullah would never undertake such a major action without the approval and support of its principal ally (Britain).

"It seems the obvious thing to do", Bevin told Abu Hoda.[8] *With those seven words Britain sanctioned the betrayal of the Palestinians and the dismissal of their claim and their rights to self-determination.* It was the moment in history when, effectively, the Palestinians were required to accept their lot as the sacrificial lamb for slaughter on the altar of political expediency.

If British ministers and mandarins had a conscience about what they were sanctioning, they might have squared it by telling themselves that the Hashemite annexation plan was the best and probably the only way to contain Zionism—prevent the Jewish state expanding beyond the partition plan borders. The British knew, of course, that Zionism's zealots in Palestine were hell bent on creating a much bigger state than had been allotted to the Jews by the partition plan. If Zionism could be contained, the danger for the region and the world of unending conflict between the Arabs and the Jewish state would be eliminated—*assuming that in the future the Arab regimes would play their part in preventing a regeneration of Palestinian nationalism.* (As I noted in the Prologue, Arafat's crime was making that happen).

Bevin's approval of Abdullah's annexation plan was accompanied by two instructions. The first was "Don't go and invade the areas allotted to the Jews."[9] The second was to the effect that under no circumstances should Transjordan involve itself in any action that would change or seek to change the status of Jerusalem as envisaged by the partition plan. It was critical that neither the Arabs nor the Jews should be the master of the Holy City and that it become an international city administered by the UN.

On behalf of his king, Transjordan's prime minister gave Bevin categorical assurances on both counts; but his assurance with regard to Jerusalem was to be compromised by events, and to cause him at a moment of great crisis to question Abdullah's wisdom.

Glubb's work in London was not finished. With Bevin's green light his task now was to see to it that the Arab Legion was fully capable of executing Abdullah's annexation plan.

Under Glubb's leadership the Arab Legion, consisting almost entirely of illiterate but fierce Bedouin tribesmen, had been turned into an elite mechanised force. By 1945, and because of its participation in World War II on the side of the British and their allies, the Arab Legion had grown from 2,000 to 17,000 men. To have said that the Arab Legion was feared by all likely to find themselves in confrontation with it would have been an understatement. But after the war, and mainly because Britain could no longer afford to subsidize it, the Arab Legion had been allowed to run down. When Bevin approved the Hashemite annexation plan, it was down to 4,000 men. That was not enough for Glubb to guarantee success. As a matter of urgency he wanted to build it up to 7,000 and to expand its mechanised regiment to a division by purchasing 50 to 75 armoured cars. His other needs were related to the fact that the Arab Legion had always relied on the British Army in Palestine to provide its maintenance support. All that, workshops and logistics, would have to be replaced by the time the British withdrew. (The end of the Mandate was now only three months away).

Britain gave the green light to Transjordan's annexation of the Arab state of the partition plan, and upgraded its Arab Legion, with a view to enabling Abdullah to confine Zionism to its partition plan borders—and extinguish for all time the fire of Palestinian nationalism.

Glubb argued his case in London and, following a threefold increase in Britain's subsidy, seemed to be getting everything he wanted.

At this point I think it is worth re-stating that Britain was upgrading the Arab Legion not to enable it to oppose the coming into being of a Jewish state, *but to enable Abdullah, by annexation, to play the leading role in confining Zionism to the borders of the partition plan and, in the process, to extinguish, hopefully for all time, the fire of Palestinian nationalism.*

From the British perspective it might have seemed that an Arab-Israeli conflict was now unlikely. Abdullah was not going to fight the Jews. And, as the British knew, Egypt's Prime Minister Nokrashy was not intending to commit his country's armed forces to war in Palestine. The others—Lebanon, Syria and Iraq—would not even think of going to war unless Egyptians and the Arab Legion's Bedouin were going to do most of the fighting and the dying. All things considered, it might well have seemed to the British that the Palestine problem was about to be fixed without a war. So what went wrong? How was it that the frontline Arab states found themselves propelled to war?

The short answer is Arab rivalry.

A large part of the problem lay in the fact that Egypt was ruled by a royal buffoon. King Farouk. In his own extravagant and incompetent way he was the symbol of everything that was rotten in the leadership of much of the Arab world. And it was the combination of his vanity and naivety that gave those Arab leaders who talked most about the need for war, and how they would destroy a Jewish state, the opportunity to influence the course of events. The man who knew best how to manipulate Farouk was Riad Solh, Lebanon's prime minister. He was a spellbinding talker and it was his task, representing the interests of his Syrian friends as well as his own, to persuade Farouk to overrule his prime minister and commit Egypt's armed forces to war in Palestine.

The critical conversations between Farouk and Solh took place in April, less than a month before the termination of Britain's Mandate for Palestine. The meetings were arranged by Antonio Pulli, Farouk's Minister of Personal Affairs. He owed his position to the fact that he was the procurer-in-chief of the women for the king's harem. (I once had the pleasure of viewing Farouk's preserved bedroom. The women in his harem were represented by numbers in the headboard above his bed. There was a gold tassel attached to each number which Farouk pulled according to the number he fancied. Minutes later a big, black eunuch would deliver the lady). For a man as out of touch with reality as Farouk, the scenario outlined by Solh was a breathtaking one.

When the British left Palestine the Arabs would sweep in and restore that land to Arab sovereignty. What a tragedy it would be for the Arab world, and for Egypt especially, and Farouk above all, if the Arabs' largest army was not present at that "historic rendezvous." If Egypt remained aloof from the coming conflict, Solh said, the only ones to profit would be his enemies—Abdullah and his British masters. (It was not a secret that Farouk despised and loathed Abdullah every bit as much as the Hashemite

If Egypt remained aloof, there was not the remotest prospect of the Arabs going to war.

monarch despised and loathed the Egyptian king). There was no doubt, Solh insisted, that destiny was calling. Palestine would soon be under an Arab crown. It was for Farouk to decide whether it would be the crown of Egypt or the crown of the Hashemites. If Egypt's armed forces went to war in Palestine, Farouk would emerge as the undisputed leader of the Arab world.

If Farouk had not been totally blind to reality he would have seen the obvious flaw in Solh's logic. If Egypt remained aloof there was not the remotest prospect of the Arabs going to war. Solh's vision of what would happen without Egypt's participation was pure fantasy.

But Farouk was persuaded and did not consult anybody. Egypt would go to war. And that decision put Nokrashy on the spot. He was still opposed to Egypt going to war but did not dare to say so out of fear of offending his king and losing his job. From here on the inevitability of catastrophe for the Arabs was assisted by the fact that the Commander-in-Chief of the Egyptian Army, Mohammed Haidar, was a fool. A genial man by all accounts, but a fool. It was said that he owed his position to the fact that he made Farouk laugh.

Resigned to Egypt's participation in the war in order to keep his job, Nokrashy questioned Haidar about the state of the army's readiness. Was it really prepared for war? In response to Nokrashy's questions—they were more a plea for reassurance than a prime minister's necessary due diligence, Haidar uttered the words which confirmed in retrospect his status as the court jester. "*There will be no war with the Jews. It will be a parade without any risk whatsoever.*" The Army, Haidar concluded, "*will be in Tel Aviv in two weeks!*"[10]

Shortly after receiving Haidar's comfort, Nokrashy granted an audience to Sir Ronald Campbell, Britain's ambassador to Egypt. According to the prime minister's minute of their conversation, Britain's position was the following. It did not approve of, and would not encourage, a clash of arms in Palestine. Furthermore, Britain was resigned to accepting partition. If Britain was asked for counsel by any of her Arab friends, she would advise them not to go to war and to accept partition. But... If Egypt decided to go to war, Britain would not oppose her efforts nor hinder the movement of her forces.

"And what would be Britain's position on the matter of the supply of ammunition and arms?" Nokrashy had asked.

His Britannic Majesty's ambassador was more than ready for that. Should Egypt decide to go to war and find herself in need of additional ammunition and arms, Britain was prepared to allow the Egyptian Army access to her Suez Canal supply depots on two conditions.

The first was "discretion". Britain could not afford to be seen to be making arms and ammunition available to the Egyptian Army.

The second was that their two nations would continue to make satisfactory progress in discussions about the problem "which most concerns us". *The problem was not Palestine but the Sudan*. In war and peace, and in between, there was a price for everything. (Modern Sudan—brown Arabs in the north, black Africans in the south—was the largest country in Africa.

Its capital, Khartoum, was at the confluence of the two great life-giving rivers—the Blue Nile coming from Ethiopia and the White Nile flowing from Lake Victoria in the south. The Sudan was the vital corridor between Egypt and the central and southern African chunks of the British Empire. Since its reconquest—a most bloody affair—by Anglo-Egyptian forces under Lord Kitchener in 1898, the Sudan had been ruled by a British-Egyptian Condominium. Britain needed Egypt's cooperation to go on denying the Sudanese any meaningful form of self-determination).

By the time the British ambassador departed, Nokrashy was more relaxed about Egypt's participation in the coming war, so much so that he ordered his aides to lift the restrictions he had imposed on Egypt's newspapers.

Up to this point, to assist his strategy of keeping Egypt's armed forces out of war, Nokrashy had required editors to play down the Palestine story. But from here on Egypt's newspapers were ordered to whip up support for war on the promise Haidar had made of quick and easy victory, a promise Nokrashy thought had been given additional substance by Britain's assurance of additional ammunition and arms if they were needed. There is nothing in the record to suggest that Egypt's prime minister considered the question of what might happen if Britain for one reason or another failed to deliver on her assurance.

There were some Egyptian journalists who tried to urge caution. Among them was Mohammed Heikal, who was to emerge under President Nasser as the most influential and respected editor in the Arab world. Heikal had been to Palestine and the caution he injected into his reports included the observation that the Jews were "courageous" and "organised". But such truth had no place in the script Egypt's political and military leaders were now writing. Heikal was summoned to Nokrashy's office and told that he was undermining morale.

Those with most reason to hope that Egypt's commitment to war was the guarantee that Zionism would not prevail were the leaderless Palestinians, especially those who had already fled or were fleeing their homeland in the face of Zionist terrorism and Allon's whispering campaign. Without exception they expected to be back in the homes they had abandoned and were abandoning within a matter of weeks at the most. Two weeks if Egypt's Commander-in-Chief was right. They would not be refugees for long. The logic of what was happening appeared to them to be irrefutable. If the Arab armies were really going to intervene, the Jewish state, if it came into being, would be annihilated.

There were two reasons why Egypt's proclaimed commitment to war did not dent Ben-Gurion's confidence that his forces could hold an Arab attack until the Jewish state was sufficiently well armed to turn the tide of war in its favour.

One was that Ben-Gurion's intelligence gatherers already knew what Egypt's fighting forces would not discover until the war was underway—

that most in the High Command of Egypt's Army (and for that matter the High Commands of all the frontline Arab armies with the exception of Transjordan's Arab Legion) were as incompetent as they were complacent. Haidar was not the only jester in a military uniform at Farouk's court. The point? *The Arab armies minus Transjordan's Arab Legion were unlikely to put up a fight that would be beyond Israel's capability to manage.*

If you want to win a war the first rule is *know your enemy*. The Zionists in Palestine did know the enemy (at least in terms of its military capabilities). But with the main exception of King Abdullah, the frontline Arab leaders, politicians and generals, were not even close to understanding who and what they would be confronting

The other reason for Ben-Gurion's continuing confidence was that Golda had kept in touch with King Abdullah. Through his personal surgeon in Jerusalem, Dr. Mohammed el Saty, she could communicate directly with the Hashemite monarch. When Arab newspapers reported that Transjordan was about to follow Egypt and commit to war against the Jews, Golda sent Abdullah a short message. "Is this indeed so?" she asked.[11]

Many years later Golda's recall of the prompt reply from Amman included this: "King Abdullah was astonished and hurt by my question. He asked me to remember three things: that he was a Bedouin and therefore a man of honour; that he was a king and therefore a doubly honourable man; and, finally, that he would never break his word to a woman. So there could not possibly be any justification for my concern."[12]

Reassessment and conclusion: Abdullah, it seemed, really was intending to honour his promise that Transjordan would not be part of a concerted Arab attack on the Jews; so there was not too much for Ben-Gurion and his leadership colleagues to be seriously worried about.

But events were now moving quickly and in a way that would put a question mark over Ben-Gurion's confidence.

An Arab League meeting of politicians and generals took place in Amman, Transjordan's capital. Item one on the agenda was persuading the Hashemite monarch to follow Farouk and commit his forces to war against the Jews.

After that gathering Golda received a message from Abdullah. It said he was in need of what she described to her colleagues as a "concession"—something from the Jewish leadership that would enable him to persuade his Arab brothers to consider the advantages of pursuing peace instead of war.

Against the background of the Arab League meeting, and Arab newspaper reports of it, Ben-Gurion and his leadership colleagues concluded, wrongly, that Abdullah was as good as saying he could not keep his promise and had, as Golda was subsequently to put it, "thrown his lot in with the Arab League."[13]

In fact Abdullah had done no such thing. When he received Arab League leaders in his spare throne room, Abdullah's position could not have been more delicate. He could not tell them he was reconciled to accepting partition and therefore a Jewish state. To do so, he knew, would cost him his throne and probably his life. For the same reason he also could not tell them that the only purpose of the military action he intended to take was to annex the parts of Palestine that had been assigned to the Arabs in the partition plan. What could he say to his brother Arabs?

He decided that attack was the best form of defence.

"Before plunging into war," the Hashemite monarch said, "my advice is—stop shooting at the Jews and demand an explanation from them. Has anyone even tried this, just to find out what possibilities it offers?"[14] He also told them the Haganah was "perfectly trained and equipped with modern weapons." And he asked them to consider what was happening on the ground while they were talking. The Arabs were fleeing as the Jews advanced. He went on: "Tomorrow (he meant soon, after the Jewish state came into being) the Jews will arrive by the thousands. They will push along the coast to Gaza and up to Acre. How will the Arabs stop them? Yes, let the Arabs try to confront them and thrust them back after the English leave, and say to them 'We don't recognise you', and then God will do as he wills."

Then he gave his Arab League guests a most prophetic warning:

"I swear to you, if tomorrow groups of Arabs coming from Jaffa, from Haifa or someplace else come forward and miserably demand an understanding with the Jews; *the reins of this affair will have escaped the Arab leaders, the Arab states and the Arab League*."

For those with ears to hear Abdullah was saying that his Arab brothers were seriously underestimating the many strengths of the Jews; that the Arabs could not defeat them in war; and that if the Arabs did not come to an understanding with the Jews instead of resorting to war, the Arabs were likely to remain, perhaps forever, at the mercy of Zionism and its American champion.

But... To protect his back, Abdullah did give his assembled Arab brothers what they took to be a commitment. Should fighting be necessary, he would be "among the soldiers fighting at the front."

Believing, apparently, that the Arab League had secured Abdullah's promise to commit his Arab Legion to war against the Jews, Secretary General Azzam suggested they should call in the generals they had brought with them. The time had come for them to discuss and hopefully agree on a plan for the invasion of Palestine.

Because of their rivalries, a joint military command and supreme commander could not be established. Unable to agree, the Arab states decided to fight separately.

At some point they could not avoid discussing the most difficult problem facing their coalition—the selection of a joint military command and a supreme commander. Because of their rivalries there was never the possibility of agreement. Farouk was never going to allow Egypt's armed forces to be under the command of a non-Egyptian. Abdullah was never going allow the Arab Legion to be commanded by anybody but Glubb and, anyway, he had his own secret agenda. And the Syrians and the Iraqis were never going to allow their forces to be commanded by other Arabs.

Unable to agree, they decided to fight separately. It was, to say the very least, a decision that guaranteed inefficiency on the battlefield. The only concession they made to the reality of their own situation was an agreement that each of the five nations would appoint a liaison officer to a joint operations centre. It was to be at the Arab Legion's base in Zerqa, outside Amman.

In reality Abdullah was not intending to break his promise to Golda. He had to be seen to be going through the motions because of the pressure of his frontline Arab brothers at leadership level and, also, the popular mood for war that was now manifest in the Arab states including his own. But he was still intending to put on only a "semblance" of war; and Glubb knew what he meant. Not attacking Jews in territory allotted to the Jewish state of the partition plan, but resisting Jewish attempts to capture land assigned to the Arabs and which Abdullah was going to annex. Such a strategy was consistent with his promise to Golda. But he wanted to do more than honour it. He was still hoping to find a way to talk his brother Arab leaders out of war. To have even a chance of success he needed some assistance from the Zionist leadership. And that was why he had sent Golda what was effectively a "talk to me" message.

How did the Zionist leadership in Palestine respond? Many years after the events Golda revealed this much:

> ...for all of his assurances, Abdullah had, in fact, thrown his lot in with the Arab League. We debated the pros and cons of requesting another meeting before it was too late. Perhaps he could be persuaded to change his mind at the last minute. If not, perhaps we could at least find out from him just how deeply he had committed himself and his British trained and officered Arab Legion to the war against us. A great deal hung in the balance, not only was the Legion by far the best Arab army in the area, there was another vital consideration. If, by some miracle, Transjordan stayed out of the war, it would be much harder for the Iraqi army to cross over into Palestine and join in the attack on us.[15]

Ben-Gurion decided that Golda should seek another meeting with Abdullah. But it was not to be for the purpose of exploring the possibility of an accommodation with the Arabs.

For her second meeting with Abdullah, Golda was required by the Hashemite monarch to take all the risks. Through their intermediary he said it was too dangerous for him to meet with her in Naharayim. He was not intending to travel to any halfway meeting point. If she wanted a face-to-face discussion, she and her companion, Erza Danin, would have to make their own way to Amman and talk themselves through the Arab Legion checkpoints on the roads. Given the circumstances as they were, Abdullah had said, he could not be expected to alert the Arab Legion to the fact that he was awaiting Jewish guests from Palestine. He was, he had emphasised, taking no responsibility for what might happen to them on the way.

When the two Zionists set out for Amman by car on the evening of 11 May, three days before the termination of the British Mandate for Palestine, Golda's only personal security was her disguise as a Muslim wife—"dark and voluminous" robe and veils. She could not speak Arabic but she was unconcerned on that account. Muslim wives were required to know their place and keep their mouths shut. She also knew that her "Muslim husband" was a most dependable man. He was one of the Jewish Agency's top experts on the Arabs. He spoke Arabic fluently and could easily pass for an Arab. Golda was later to say that she had "perfect faith" in Danin's ability "to get them through enemy lines safely." And she was, anyway, much too concerned with the outcome of her mission "to think about what would happen if, God forbid, we were caught."[16]

They made it safely to the rendezvous point in Amman. Waiting for them there was the man in whose home the meeting with Abdullah would take place. He was a Bedouin the Hashemite monarch had adopted and raised since childhood.

The only firsthand account of the secret meeting is Golda's.

When Abdullah arrived he was "very pale and seemed under great strain."

With Danin interpreting they talked for about an hour. Golda said she started the conversation by going straight to the point. "Have you broken your promise to me, after all?" she asked. Abdullah was much too polite to object there and then to such an approach—scolding mother to naughty child.

According to Golda, Abdullah replied: "When I made that promise, I thought I was in control of my own destiny and could do what I thought was right. But since then I have learned otherwise... Now I am one of five." From what subsequently happened it is perfectly clear that Abdullah, whatever he actually said, was not meaning "and now I have to do what the other four want." He was meaning only that his position was extremely difficult and that his room for maneuver was smaller than it had been previously. But he still believed, Golda quoted him as saying, that war could be averted. According to Golda, Abdullah said: "Why are you in such a hurry to proclaim your state? What is the rush? You are so impatient!"

Golda replied that she didn't think that a people who had been waiting 2,000 years should be described as being "in a hurry".

Then, in her best scolding mother tone, she said: "Don't you understand that we are your only allies in this region? The others are all your enemies."

According to Golda, Abdullah agreed that was so.

Then she said: "*You must know that if war is forced upon us, we will fight and we will win!"*

According to Golda, Abdullah sighed and said: "Yes, I know that. It is your duty to fight. But why don't you wait a few years? Drop your demands for free (unlimited) immigration. I will take over the whole country and you will be represented in my parliament. I will treat you very well and there will be no war."

Golda said she tried to explain to him that his plan was impossible. "You know all that we have done and how hard we have worked", she said to Abdullah. "Do you think we did all that just to be represented in a foreign parliament? You know what we want and to what we aspire. If you can offer us nothing more than you have just done, then there will be a war and we will win it. But perhaps we can meet again—after the war and after there is a Jewish state."

At this point Danin said to Abdullah: "*You place too much reliance on your tanks. You have no real friends in the Arab world and we will smash your tanks as the Maginot Line was smashed!*"

When they took their leave of the Hashemite monarch there was, Golda would later say, "no doubt left in my mind that Abdullah would wage war against us."

She was wrong. As events were to prove, Abdullah was still committed to honouring his promise to her and had no intention in any circumstances of being part of any Arab attack on the Jewish state as envisaged by the partition plan. But...

Abdullah was to be drawn into war with the Jews on the Jerusalem front. As we shall see in the next chapter, it happened only because Ben-Gurion, in defiance of the will of the organised international community, was determined to capture and keep the Holy City, to create facts on the ground in order to prevent the implementation of that part of the partition plan that had called for Jerusalem to become an open city administered by the UN.

Ben-Gurion was determined to capture and keep Jerusalem by creating facts on the ground, in defiance of the will of the organised international community for it to become an open city administered by the UN.

From information not available at the time, it is possible to construct a very clear picture of Abdullah's thoughts about how to achieve a necessary accommodation with the Jews in Palestine. The complete picture suggests that Golda's summary account of her second meeting with Abdullah was a considerable misrepresentation of what might very well have been available to the Jews if Ben-Gurion had not been hell bent on war.

To avert war Abdullah believed that a manageable solution to the problem of Palestine had to begin with agreement to create a unitary Arab state, effectively federal in structure, in which the Jews would administer their own affairs in their own areas. In time, and provided the Jews of Palestine demonstrated intent to live at peace with their Arab neighbours, there was no reason why the self-administered Jewish entity of the federal structure should not evolve into an independent Jewish state, one accepted and recognised by the Arabs.

That is what Abdullah had in mind when he said to Golda "Why don't you wait a few years?"

The implication was this: A Jewish state could have been created without setting in motion an escalating and unending conflict if... If the Zionists had been prepared to wait a few years and seriously explore a political way forward, initially with King Abdullah.

If such a judgment was only my own, I would not be entirely comfortable with it (even though it was endorsed in private conversations with me by Abdullah's grandson, King Hussein, and other Arab leaders of his generation). I am entirely comfortable because of the conclusion in retrospect of one of Zionism's own giants, Dr. Nahum Goldmann.

When Goldmann died in 1982 he was given a state funeral in Israel because he was one of the five former presidents of the WZO. (He was also the first president of the World Jewish Congress, WJC. Encouraged by Rabbi Wise, Goldmann founded the WJC after being disgusted and disillusioned by the WZO's refusal to confront Hitlerism). It can be said without fear of contradiction that no individual worked harder and to better effect than Goldmann to unite world Jewry after the Nazi holocaust and to secure American support for the Zionist enterprise and to bring Israel into being.

It was the same Nahum Goldmann in the November–December 1974 edition of the *New Outlook* magazine published in Jerusalem, who wrote the following:

> If we had invested in the Arab problem a tenth of the energy, the passion, the ingenuity, the resourcefulness which we developed to gain the support of Britain, France, the US and Weimar Germany, our destiny in the development of Israel may have been quite different... *We were not ready for compromises; we did not regard it (the majority Arab presence) as a major problem... We did not make sufficient efforts to get, if not the full agreement of the Arabs, at least their acquiescence to a Jewish state, which I think would have been possible. That was the original sin.*

On the one occasion I met and talked with Nahum Goldmann, I was moved by the way he was trying to handle the guilt he felt on account of the enormity of Zionism's crime, the injustice done Palestinians. And it was obvious that he was shocked to the core of his being by the way in which, for daring to speak the unspeakable, he had been vilified by the defenders of Zionism right or wrong. He was never to be forgiven by hardcore Zionists for refusing to suppress for all time his own moral sense of what was right and wrong. That he fought and won the battle with his own conscience made him, in my view, a man worthy of respect without limit by people of goodwill, everywhere.

Nothing better illustrates the contempt Zionism's zealots had for Goldmann's goodness than Prime Minister Begin's response to his death. Begin could not avoid giving permission for a state funeral and Goldmann's burial on Mount Herzl; but he did refuse to attend the funeral. In his place Deputy Prime Minister Simcha Ehrlich said: "We regret that a man of so many virtues and abilities went the wrong way."[17] There could not have been a more callous epitaph for the man who was owed so much by Israel and all Israelis.

So far as Zionism's zealots were concerned, there was much more to Goldmann's "wrong way" than daring to suggest that Arab acquiescence to the creation of a Jewish state could have been secured in time without resort to war.

In his advancing years Goldmann had advocated the need for the creation of a Palestinian state. And he became the leading and most influential Jewish critic of Israel's continuing occupation of Arab land taken in 1967 and the illegal settlement of it. *He utterly rejected the claim of Zionist bigots who insisted that Jews had to make the Greater Israel project a reality because God had promised them the land. Goldmann called this thesis "a profanation."*[18]

Nahum Goldmann, the first president of the World Jewish Congress, advised Carter that it would be necessary to "break the back" of the Zionist lobby in America if he was serious about peacemaking in the Middle East.

There was also a moment during Begin's first term as prime minister when *Goldmann advised President Carter to "break the back" of the Zionist lobby in America.*[19] The President had to do that, Goldmann said, if he was to have the freedom to be serious about peacemaking in the Middle East. Nobody was more qualified than Goldman to give such advice because he was as much as any the founder of the lobby.

Near the end of his life, and deeply troubled by the fact that the Zionist lobby had broken President Carter's back, (as we shall see in due course), Goldmann gave this warning:

> Blind support for the Begin government may be more menacing for Israel than any danger of Arab attack. American Jewry is more generous than any other group in American life and is doing great things... But by misusing its political influence, by giving the Begin administration the impression that the Jews are strong enough to force the American administration and Congress to follow every Israeli desire, they lead Israel on a ruinous path which, if continued, may have dire consequences.[20]

In passing, Goldmann blamed the Zionist lobby for U.S. failures to bring about a comprehensive settlement in the Middle East. "It was to a very large degree because of electoral considerations, fear of the pro-Israel lobby and the Jewish vote."[21]

Then, putting the flesh on the bones of his warning, he said this:

> It (the Zionist lobby) is slowly becoming a negative factor. Not only does it distort the expectations and political calculations of Israel, *but the time may not be far off when American public opinion will be sick and tired of the demands of Israel and the aggressiveness of American Jewry.*[22] [Emphasis added]

I think I know precisely what it was that inspired Goldmann to express such a thought. On visits to America over the years I had private conversations with a number of Congressmen and women, who told me they were sick and tired of having to be stooges for Zionism because of the power of its lobby and the pork-barrel nature of the American democratic system. And I got the clear impression that a day might come when the stooges turned and became Israel's most influential and worst enemies and that, as a consequence, anti-Semitism might erupt and even run wild in America. A vision of such a future was, I believe, the fear that inspired Goldmann's warning.

Goldmann went to his grave knowing that the lobby in America had become a monster and was, in association with Zionism's zealots in Israel, a threat to the best interests of Jews everywhere and even to Judaism itself.

If there is a spiritual life beyond the grave, I can imagine Goldmann's first words to Ahad Ha-am: "If only we had had listened to you...`

When Goldmann said publicly in 1974 that he believed an accommodation with the Arabs would have been possible without war, he was, in fact, only repeating what he had said behind Zionism's closed doors in 1947.

After the rigged vote on partition at the UN General Assembly, Goldmann took the lead in arguing against a unilateral declaration of Jewish independence; and up to virtually the moment of the actual declaration he continued to urge Ben-Gurion to delay, for the sake of at least trying to reach an understanding with the Arabs. He was subsequently to describe Ben-Gurion as being "organically incapable of compromise."[23]

Goldmann was also deeply troubled by the fact that a unilateral declaration of Jewish independence would amount to—actually would be nothing less than—a Jewish declaration of war against the Arabs. Knowing that U.S. Secretary of State Marshall was pressing hard for a truce to halt the fighting between Zionism's military forces and the Palestinians who were being assisted to some degree by the Arab League's mercenaries led by Kaukji, Goldmann believed that the Arab armies could be stopped from crossing into Palestine, thus averting a war, if only Ben-Gurion would agree to a truce and signal that he was ready for serious discussions with the Arabs, initially with Abdullah.

Why did Ben-Gurion and enough of his leadership colleagues insist on war when a political solution either was available or, to say the least, might very well have been available—i.e. if the Arabs had been put to the test of serious discussions as Goldmann and even some of Ben-Gurion's leadership colleagues wanted?

Why did Ben-Gurion insist on war when a political solution was available if the Arabs had been engaged in serious discussions and negotiations?

The question has its own special context, beginning with what happened after Golda's return from Amman on 12 May.

Ben-Gurion had fixed that Wednesday as "D" day, the day when the Zionist leadership in Palestine, after one more review of the entire situation, would take the final, irrevocable decision—to go ahead or not with a unilateral declaration of Jewish independence the moment the British Mandate expired.

Ben-Gurion's prospects of getting what he wanted, war, had been much improved by the reduction of the number of those who would be called upon to make the decision. He had created the Council of Thirteen. This replaced the much bigger Executive of the Jewish Agency and was to be the provisional government of the Jewish state. The evidence suggests that Ben-Gurion would not have got his way if the decision had been left to the larger body.

On the fateful day, the Council of Thirteen was actually the Council of Ten—nine plus Ben-Gurion. Three members of the provisional government-in-waiting were absent. There would have been a fourth absentee if Ben-Gurion had not taken an extraordinary precaution. He sent the Jewish Agency's precious Piper Cub from Tel Aviv to besieged Jerusalem, a short but extremely perilous air journey, to extricate an orthodox rabbi whose vote he knew he could count on.

What they were actually going to vote on, at Ben-Gurion's insistence, was not "Do we go ahead with a unilateral declaration of independence—yes or no?" but "Do we accept or reject the call by Secretary of State Marshall for a truce?"

If they accepted Marshall's call for a halt to the fighting they would obviously have to postpone a unilateral declaration of independence; a postponement Marshall wanted, to allow more time for the General Assembly to reconsider the problem of what to do about Palestine, and more time for diplomacy, driven by the U.S. State Department and the British Foreign Office, to come up with a solution that would avert a major war—a war that Marshall and Forrestal (and others) feared would light a fire in the Middle East that nobody would ever be able to put out.

Marshall had made a personal plea to Moshe Sharret, the man destined to become Israel's first foreign minister and, all too briefly, prime minister when Ben-Gurion stood down for a while. (As we shall see in due course, Sharett was by far the most rational and wise of all of Israel's leaders). Sharett had met with Marshall in Washington, and the Secretary of State had underlined his call for a truce with a warning that the Zionists might lose everything if they provoked an attack by the Arab armies. Marshall indicated that the Zionists in Palestine would be making a terrible mistake if they were assuming that American forces would go to the aid of a unilaterally declared Jewish state in trouble on the battlefield.

How explicitly Marshall made his point has remained a secret, but his message, if only by implication, was to this effect: "If you think your friends in this country have sufficient influence to cause this administration to send American troops to Palestine—you are wrong. It isn't going to happen." Because Sharett understood and accepted that the U.S. had interests of its own, it might also have been that there was a good enough chemistry between them for the Secretary of State to have said something like: "Even if we had the troops to send, we would not do so because it would be against America's own best interests, given the opposition to the Zionist enterprise throughout the entire Arab and Muslim world." In other words, Marshall might have added, "The U.S. is not going to war with the Arab and Muslim world on behalf of Zionism." (Half a century later, when George "Dubya" Bush was in the White House and being influenced far too much by the Zionists around him, such a possibility seemed to some to be a real one).

Sharett's report of his conversation with Marshall was one of the main items for consideration by the Council of Ten on 12 May. Another was Golda's report on her meeting with Abdullah. After both reports had been presented there was a final military briefing by Yigael Yadin, the Haganah's chief of operations and Yisrael Galili, its *de facto* commander-in-chief. The assessment of both men was that the Jewish state would have a "50-50" chance of surviving a concerted Arab attack. As Yadin put it, "We are as likely to win as we are to be defeated."[24]

In fact that "50-50" assessment was much too pessimistic. It was made on the worst case scenario including the wrong assumption that Abdullah was going to break his promise and join a concerted Arab attack on the Jewish state of the partition plan. If the reality of Abdullah's position had been factored in, the assessment of Israel's ability to survive would have been much better than 50-50: perhaps 70-30 or even 80-20.

If the vote had been taken then, it would have gone against what Ben-Gurion wanted. The unilateral declaration of Jewish independence would have been postponed and war would have been averted, at least for a while. But Ben-Gurion had not yet spoken. *It was the moment for him to reveal his secret—the amount and quality of ammunition, weapons and other military hardware his agents had purchased and stockpiled in Europe and elsewhere*. The summary details were contained in two files which he proceeded to open. He was about to tell them what Marshall did not know.

Slowly and dramatically Ben-Gurion read out the contents of the files, pausing to let each figure make an impression on his audience. From File One: 25,000 rifles; 5,000 machine guns; 58 million rounds of ammunition; 175 howitzers; and 30 airplanes with options on more. From

File Two: 10 tanks; 35 anti-aircraft guns; 12 120-millimeter mortars; 50 65-millimeter canons; 5,000 rifles, 200 heavy machine guns, 97,000 artillery and mortar shells of assorted calibres; and 9 million rounds of small-arms ammunition.

The point, Ben-Gurion said, was that only by declaring their independence and becoming a sovereign state would they have the freedom to bring that ammunition and those weapons on stream.

It was true, Ben-Gurion admitted, that it would take some time to get the weapons he had stockpiled in Europe and elsewhere flowing; and that meant, obviously, that if the Arab armies attacked the moment the Jews declared their state to be in existence, they, the Jews, might suffer "shocks and severe losses." Initially. But they would be able to turn the tide and go on to victory.

Ben-Gurion also had good news for them on the manpower front.

At the time they were speaking, the Haganah had only 18,900 men fully mobilised, armed and in a position to resist an Arab offensive. But it also had available in Palestine a trained manpower pool of 60,000 awaiting only the ammunition and the weapons to fight. In addition there were 28,000 Jewish immigrants, many of them of military age, waiting in Britain's detention camps on Cyprus for the boats that would deliver them to Israel as soon as the Mandate expired. Others were already in vessels and on their way from Europe. In addition there were in many countries—America, Britain, South Africa and Australia to name only four—fully experienced Jewish combat pilots (and senior Jewish military officers of all kinds) waiting to join the armed forces of the Jewish state as soon as it declared itself to be in existence.

Prospect? Though it might be hard pressed in the opening days and possibly the first week or two of the war, the Jewish state could look forward to a quite early moment in the conflict when its armed forces—trained and increasingly well equipped—would number between 85,000 and 100,000.

On decision day Ben-Gurion could not have known that the total number of men the Arab armies would commit to war in Palestine would be only 21,500. But he did know that the regular fighting strength of the combined Arab armies totalled only 80,000 men. And you did not have to be a genius of any kind to work out that the frontline Arab rulers, in constant fear of being toppled from within, would not even dream of committing to war in Palestine more than a portion of their regular forces. Fighting the Jews might be quite important, but protecting their own backs at home was much more important.

By the time Ben-Gurion had finished making his case for Marshall's call for a truce to be rejected, he might well have felt that the vote in favour of what he wanted, war, would be unanimous. If he did he was in for a shock. When he called for the vote, four of the nine hands were raised in favour of accepting the truce Marshall wanted. *It was by only one vote that the decision to reject a truce and declare the coming into being of the Jewish state was taken.*

Amazing but true. The region and the world was, finally, set on course for a catastrophe that is still unfolding before our eyes by just one vote.

The answer to the question of why Ben-Gurion was hell bent on war is in two parts.

The first is that he knew enough about the true balance of military power in the region to be confident that a Zionist victory was inevitable; not least because there would come a point when the fighting Jews would out-number as well out-gun the fighting Arabs.

But what drove Ben-Gurion was not only the prospect of a first victory over the Arabs.

Ben-Gurion was uncompromising and therefore a complete and true political Zionist. True political Zionism could not even think about being satisfied with a Jewish state as small as the one of the vitiated partition plan. Why not?

As I have previously noted, political Zionism was by definition a philosophy of doom. Its underlying assumption, reinforced by the Nazi holocaust, was that the Jewish state had to be big enough in terms of land to be capable of becoming the refuge of last resort for all the Jews of the world.

From that perspective the issue for Ben-Gurion and those who thought like him was simple and straightforward—a bigger Jewish state than the one of the vitiated partition plan had to be fought for and won.

On that fateful May Day in 1948 Ben-Gurion's trump card was actually not the information he revealed about why it was reasonable to "dare to believe in victory". The trump card was the one the Arab regimes had given Zionism—rejection of partition; and nobody knew better than Ben-Gurion how to play it. That the Arabs had international law and most if not all of the moral right on their side was not the point. Not so far as the uncompromising and true political Zionists were concerned. Arab rejection enabled Ben-Gurion to assert that because the Zionists had accepted the partition plan despite their reservations, the Arabs by their rejection had "forfeited their rights". Arab rejection, Ben-Gurion said, had "changed everything." The Jews now had "the right" to take what they could get by war. The borders of the Jewish state would now be determined by arms, not by a United Nations resolution. The point? *A bigger Jewish state than the one envisaged by the partition plan was the prize now available for the taking. And there was nothing the international community could do about it.*

Arab rejection of the partition plan, even though they had international law and moral right on their side, enabled Ben-Gurion to assert that the Arabs had thereby "forfeited their rights", giving the Zionists the right to determine Israel's borders by force of arms.

One of the four who had voted in favour of accepting Marshall's call for a truce suggested that if there was to be a unilateral declaration of independence, it (the actual declaration) should put the Jewish state in the best possible standing with the international community by indicating that its borders were those of the partition plan. That, of course, was a bright red rag to Ben-Gurion's bull. He angrily rejected the suggestion and pointed out that the Americans had not announced the frontiers of their state in their Declaration of Independence.

There is only one word that properly characterises Ben-Gurion's assertion that Arab rejection of partition gave Zionism "the right" to take what it could get by war. That word is *self-righteousness*. It was to become, with the arrogance of military power, the Zionist state's hallmark; and it, self-righteousness, was subsequently to be identified by Harkabi as the biggest threat to the Jewish state. He put it this way [emphasis added]:

> The Jewish people has traditionally seen itself as a chosen nation, but generally understood this to mean *additional obligations, not as permission for immoral behaviour.* The new moral permissiveness breeds self-righteousness and self-congratulation. But self-righteousness is the main source of national mistakes. *Dazzled by its self-righteousness, Israel cannot see the case of the other side*. Self-righteousness encourages nations no less than individuals to absolve themselves of every failing and shake off the guilt of every mishap. *When everyone is guilty except them, the very possibility of self-criticism and self-improvement vanishes...* [25]
>
> But self-criticism is imperative in order to counterbalance the tendencies to self-righteousness and self-pity that stem from basic Jewish attitudes, from the historical experience of persecution and from the ethos fostered by Menachim Begin. *No factor endangers Israel's future more than self-righteousness, which blinds us to reality, prevents a complex understanding of the situation and legitimises extreme behaviour...* [26]
>
> I believe it was a damaging error on Menachem Begin's part to insinuate that criticism of Israel is a manifestation of anti-Semitism. There is a recklessness in the grandiose assertion that 'the whole world is against us.' If indeed the whole world is against Israel, its future is very bleak. Only those intoxicated with their own greatness can believe that they can succeed in overcoming the entire world. But in any case it simply is not true that the entire world is against Israel... *In my opinion, self-righteousness is a greater danger to Israel than anti-Semitism."* [27]

It was after reading Harkabi on this subject that I felt more at ease with my own analysis—that the name of the global power game was and is saving Israel from itself. I did, in fact, ask Shlomo Gazit if he would object to me putting the proposition in such a way. He said he had no objection. That was the name of the game.

What of the Arab regimes when the crunch came?

With the exception of Transjordan's King Abdullah, the leaders of the frontline Arab states opted for war in large part *to save their faces*. They had made so many extravagant promises to their people about how they were going to prevent a Zionist takeover of Palestine that they were, in effect, trapped into going to war by their own stupid rhetoric.

Given their extravagant rhetoric to their peoples about how they were going to prevent a Zionist takeover of Palestine, leaders of the frontline Arab states opted for war in large part to save their faces and governments.

Though it was hidden from public view at the time, Arab disarray on the eve of the war was great. If the situation had not have been so tragic for the Palestinians, it would be amusing in retrospect.

There was no Arab military co-ordination.

At the Arab Legion's Zerqa base, Glubb, committed with King Abdullah to only a "semblance" or pretence of war, confessed to "not having the vaguest notion about what the Syrians and the Egyptians are going to do."[28]

When Arab League Secretary General Azzam arrived at the Arab Legion's base, where the liaison officers of the five Arab armies were to do their coordinating, the place, he said, "brewed with confusion."[29] The brigadier sent by the Egyptians as their liaison officer appeared to have no idea of what his army's movements would be. And the Iraqi had not shown up.

The Iraqi was Ismail Safwat, the man the Arab League leaders had appointed months previously to draw up a co-ordinated contingency plan for a possible Arab invasion of Palestine, and who was going to be the overall coordinator of the Arab military effort. The reason for Safwat's no-show was explained by the man himself in a cable to the Arab League, sent from Damascus to Azzam in Zerqa. It arrived at noon on 13 May.

Safwat's cable read: "FIRMLY CONVINCED THAT THE ABSENCE OF AGREEMENT ON A PRECISE PLAN CAN ONLY LEAD US TO DISASTER I SUBMIT MY RESIGNATION."[30]

Like Abdullah, but much, much later than Abdullah, the Iraqi general who had had to juggle the rival interests and hypocrisies of the frontline Arab leaders had seen the predictable future. (He might also have been responding to a request from Britain to pull the plug).

But even Safwat and Abdullah could not have foreseen the extent of the disaster to come when Britain, under irresistible pressure from the U.S., declined to supply the outnumbered and out-gunned Arab armies with so much as a single bullet while the Israelis were importing everything they needed for victory.

As we shall now see, the greatest threat to Jews in Israel during the war of 1948 was the consequence of Ben-Gurion's insistence that Zionism's priority was to capture and keep Jerusalem, in defiance of the will of the organised international community.[31]

2

"GO SAVE JERUSALEM!"

Given Ben-Gurion's priority when the first Arab-Israeli war started, King Abdullah's crisis was not long in coming. It was as inevitable as the midnight strike of the clocks in Palestine on 14 May. That was not only the moment the British Mandate ended and the Zionist state came into being, it was also the moment for which the Haganah's Jerusalem commander, Shaltiel, had been waiting. To launch Operation Pitchfork.

That was the code name of the first offensive military operation the provisional government of the new state authorised, as a matter of extreme urgency. Its objective was the conquest of Jerusalem—the whole lot including the Old walled (and mainly Arab) City containing the Muslim Quarter, the Christian Quarter, the Armenian Quarter and the Jewish Quarter; and the symbols sacred to each of the faiths.

Ben-Gurion's priority was not only to create facts on the ground but to have them created with maximum speed, to enable the self-declared Jewish state to say to the organised international community: "We have taken all of Jerusalem. It's our eternal capital. The question of it becoming an international city under the trusteeship of the UN is no longer for discussion. That idea is now dead and buried. Forget about it."

Shaltiel allowed himself to entertain a comforting thought. If Abdullah's Arab Legion did not intervene, his prospects for taking all of Jerusalem quickly and with minimum casualties were good. Why so? The Old City's only Arab defenders were the resident Palestinian fighters who had been led by the late Abdul Khader Husseini plus a number of Arab irregulars or volunteers. Not too much in the way of opposition could be expected from such a disparate, undisciplined and leaderless rabble.

While elements of the regular Arab armies were entering Palestine, the Arab League ordered Kaukji's irregular liberation forces to withdraw—even from the Latrun slopes, key to holding Jerusalem!

Shaltiel's early confidence had been boosted by the Palmach's discovery of a most amazing thing. While the Arab armies were entering Palestine, the Arab League's so-called Liberation Army led by Kaukji was making its exit!

Kaukji had been ordered to take his irregulars out of Palestine, to leave the fighting to the regulars of the incoming Arab armies.

In the final countdown to war, several hundred of Kaukji's irregulars had occupied and held the hilltop positions that controlled the most important crossroads in Palestine. The Latrun slopes. Below them, in the wheat fields and vineyards of the Valley of Ayalon, the principal roads from the north, south and west joined to form the highway that ran up to Jerusalem through the gorge of Bab el Wad. *Since Biblical times, the fate of Jerusalem had been decided by whoever controlled the ridgelines of Latrun.*

During the first day of Israel's existence, a unit of the Palmach's Givati Brigade had fired a couple of probing mortar shells into Kaukji's Latrun positions. Surprised by the lack of response, the Palmach unit advanced cautiously up the slopes. Unbelievably, or so it seemed to the advancing Israelis, they met no resistance. There was no opposition. As ordered by the Arab League, Kaukji's forces had withdrawn. Because Kaukji was in it only or mostly for the money, he had obeyed his orders without question.

Incredibly the road to Jerusalem was now open to the Israelis—provided they occupied the positions from which Kaukji's irregulars had withdrawn. (Abdul Khader must have been revolving in his grave). Even more incredible was that the fighting Jews did not occupy the Latrun slopes when they were there for the taking. It was to be their biggest mistake of the war.

And Shaltiel was in for a nasty surprise, too.

The late Abdul Khader's Palestinian fighters in the Old City launched an offensive of their own—to capture the Jewish Quarter. And they were making progress. The battle with the Quarter's outnumbered Haganah defenders was desperate. Street by street. House by house. And sometimes room by room.

By the end of the first day's fighting the Palestinians had brought almost a quarter of the Jewish neighbourhood's surface area under their control. In panic and fear the residents of the Jewish Quarter crowded together and recited psalms. And then they decided to do what Golda on her fundraising tour of America had vowed that Jews in Palestine would never do. In a message addressed to the Haganah men who were guarding them, they chanted in unison: "Surrender. Wave a white flag. Save our souls." (Most of the words spoken by the characters in this chapter are taken from the Collins and Lapierre account in *O Jerusalem!* as referenced in the chapter's Notes).

This was followed by a direct appeal, the first of many, to their Haganah protectors. "We have lived in peace with the Arabs. If we surrender we can live in peace with them now."

The expression of that sentiment was first and foremost a response to immediate danger, but it was rooted in the view Palestine's religious Jews had always held—that political Zionism was morally wrong and bound to be the cause of conflict. The future they had long feared was now the present. Thanks to Zionism.

Not surprisingly, the pleas for surrender and the gains the Palestinians made in one day's fighting for the Jewish Quarter undermined the morale of the local Haganah force and its commander, Moshe Russnak. His messages throughout the day to Shaltiel at his headquarters in the New City had grown increasingly urgent. At a point Russnak had radioed: "The situation is desperate. They are breaking in from all sides." Later: "Send help immediately otherwise we will not be able to hold out."

Russnak's own moment of crisis came when he was confronted by Rabbis Weingarten, Mintzberg and Hazan. They wanted his agreement for them to open surrender negotiations. Russnak was appalled by the idea of assuming personal responsibility for fate of the Jews, 1,700 or so, in the Old City. He was also disheartened by what he felt was a lack of understanding and guidance from Shaltiel's headquarters in the New City. Eventually, in a whisper, Russnak said to the three rabbis, "Alright, go ahead."

Rabbi Weingarten then telephoned an Italian priest, Alberto Gori, to ask him to find out what the Arabs' surrender terms were.

Meanwhile, at his headquarters in the New City, Shaltiel was about ready to renew his assault on the Old City. With still no sign of any intervention by Abdullah's Arab Legion, he was confident that he could save the Jewish Quarter from surrender and complete his conquest of all the Old City. Within two or three days of the birth of the new state, Jerusalem would be its undivided and eternal capital. The diplomats at the United Nations could huff and puff but the Zionist *fait accompli* would be irreversible.

Operation Pitchfork was now benefiting from the fact that the late Abdul Khader's largely untrained fighters were suffering from their usual problem. They were running out of ammunition. They had appealed to the Arab Legion for assistance, but no help had been forthcoming. Glubb had no intention of making his precious ammunition available to the Palestinians or of involving the Arab Legion in any action to change the status of Jerusalem as envisaged by the UN partition plan. He had given his word on that in London and it was in accordance with his orders from Abdullah.

Then it was that King Abdullah came under great and eventually irresistible pressure to break the undertaking his Prime Minister, Abu Hoda, had given to British Foreign Secretary Bevin.

At four o'clock on the morning of Monday 17 May, Abdullah was beginning his new day as usual, with prayers in his bedroom. For the Hashemite monarch it was a personal dialogue with the God of whom one of his distant ancestors had been the messenger.

An invasion of Abdullah's privacy in that place and at that moment could mean only one of two things—the arrival of an assassin or a messenger with seriously urgent news. The messenger was Hazza el Majali, the king's *aide de camp*. He had been propelled to action by a telephone call from Jerusalem. The caller was Ahmed Hilmi, one of the few members of Haj Amin Husseini's Arab Higher Committee still in the Old City.

Majali was aware that his master would sooner spit on Haj Amin's grave than assist his enterprise (Palestinian self-determination), but Hilmi's telephone call was only one of many the *aide de camp* had received from Jerusalem that night. Each and every one of them had been a desperate plea for help. Most callers had spoken through their tears. Majali had not been brave enough to wake the king from his slumber but now in all conscience he had to deliver Hilmi's message, his second of the night.

Hilmi, the *aide de camp* informed the king, had begged for the Arab Legion "to come to our assistance and save Jerusalem and its people from a certain fall."

Abdullah's emotions were touched by the plea but his overriding consideration of the moment was still what was best for his own survival.

As a pragmatist he was reconciled to the partition of Palestine and, like Ben-Gurion, he had not been in favour of Jerusalem becoming an international city under UN trusteeship; but he had succumbed to immense British pressure to agree that Jerusalem should not be part of either the proposed Arab or Jewish state. Continuing British support including money was vital for the survival of the Hashemite dynasty. In short Abdullah knew that offending his only ally might well cost him his throne.

While Abdullah took himself off to reflect further about his decreasing room for maneuver, a great drama was taking place at Zerqa.

The Arab League leaders assembled there had also received telephone calls from Jerusalem throughout the night. Azzam himself had been woken by an Egyptian volunteer who had been fighting in the city. (Not all of Kaukji's men had been willing to withdraw and leave the fighting to the regular Arab armies. Some, after abandoning the Latrun slopes, had made their way to Jerusalem to continue fighting there). The Egyptian told Azzam the Arabs were desperately short of ammunition and that Jerusalem would fall to the Jews if the Arab Legion did not intervene. "One concerted Jewish attack", he said, "and all of Jerusalem will be theirs!"

In pyjamas the Arab League leaders assembled at Zerqa did the thing they were best at. They squabbled among themselves. The air was thick with recriminations (on only the second night of the war).

Eventually an emotional Azzam had had enough. He turned to Iraq's Crown Prince Abdul Illah and said: "If you don't go immediately and convince your uncle to send troops to Jerusalem, and if Jerusalem falls for want of them, I will tell the world the Hashemites are traitors even if I hang for it!"

Iraq's Crown Prince was impressed by the threat but not brave enough to go to Abdullah alone. So, after washing and dressing, they all set out, uninvited, for an audience with Abdullah.

Abdullah meanwhile had gone visiting. His destination was his prime minister's home. Abu Hoda was still rubbing the sleep from his eyes when he bowed to the king in his own living room.

The purpose of Abdullah's visit was to find out if he had any room for maneuver with Britain, given that events were moving beyond his ability to control, and given also that Israel had started its life by challenging the will of the international community with regard to the Holy City. Was it possible, Abdullah wondered aloud, that, without provoking the wrath of the British, he could commit at least some troops to Jerusalem, to prevent a Jewish takeover? Would the British be understanding if not actually supportive?

Abu Hoda's advice was unequivocal. Any interference in Jerusalem would constitute a breach of the agreement he had concluded in London with Bevin.

When Abdullah left his prime minister, he was still of the view that his own interests would best be served by not offending Britain. The British had screwed his father. He was not going to give them the opportunity to screw him. He would not commit the Arab Legion to the struggle for Jerusalem.

Abdullah's initial decision not to intervene to prevent the Zionist conquest of Jerusalem was dramatic proof of his total dependence on British political support, arms and money.

Abdullah knew better than anybody that a Jewish conquest of Jerusalem would have a disastrous effect on his prestige. The fact that he was still not prepared to intervene in Jerusalem, to prevent a Jewish takeover, was therefore dramatic proof of two things—how alone he was and his total dependence for his own survival on British political support, British arms and British money.

When he returned to the palace the Arab League delegation was waiting for him. And it was Azzam, perhaps because he did not trust Iraq's Crown Prince to be explicit enough, who did the talking. To Abdullah's face the Secretary General of the Arab League repeated the threat he had made at Zerqa. That was the bad news. The good news for Abdullah was in what Azzam said he would do personally if the Arab Legion saved Jerusalem. "I will not oppose declaring you king of Jerusalem and I will put the crown on your head with my own hands, even though my own sovereign (Farouk) will oppose it!"

Abdullah replied, "You will not be disappointed."

So far as the Arab League delegation was concerned, Abdullah was now resolved to fight the Jews for control of Jerusalem. But that was not quite what the Hashemite monarch had in mind.

The Arab Legion received its orders on red slips of paper. The first red message, addressed to its commander, Glubb, said: "His Majesty the King orders an advance towards Jerusalem from Ramallah. He intends by this action to threaten the Jews in order that they may accept a truce in Jerusalem."

Glubb ignored the order.

Half an hour later he received another red message. "His Majesty is extremely anxious to ease the pressure on the Arabs and incline the Jews to accept a truce for Jerusalem... His Majesty is awaiting swift action. Report quickly that the operation has commenced."

Glubb was still determined to keep the Arab Legion out of Jerusalem. Quite apart from his assurance to London on that account, there were two other considerations on his mind. His Bedouin were desert warriors, open-country fighters. They were not trained to fight in cities. They might not perform well in Jerusalem's streets. They might even come to grief. Glubb also chose to believe that the situation in the Holy City was not as bad for the Arabs as they were making it out to be. But he had to do something. He could not go on defying Abdullah.

Elsewhere his plan in accordance with Abdullah's wishes to wage only a semblance of war had gone well to this point. *The Arab Legion had been inside Palestine for 48 hours without an engagement of any consequence. Some of his regiments had not fired a single shot.*

That was on the plus side so far as the Glubb-Abdullah grand strategy was concerned. But there were things on the minus side.

The proud Bedouins of his Arab Legion wanted more than a semblance of war and relations between Glubb's commanding British officers and their Bedouin subordinates were becoming strained. Worse still, Glubb had received reports that Arab women were jeering his Bedouins, calling them cowards. At least one Arab Legion unit was close to mutiny.

After quickly reviewing the situation Glubb concluded that he could remain true to his promise to London and satisfy Abdullah's needs with only a token show of force on the Jerusalem front. He believed that if he fired a few shells into positions held by the Haganah, that would be enough to cause Shaltiel, out of fear of the Arab Legion going all the way, to halt his assault on the Old City. There would then be a truce and that would save Glubb from having to commit the Arab Legion to fighting in Jerusalem.

In retrospect that tells us Glubb was completely unaware of Ben-Gurion's intentions with regard to Jerusalem and somewhat naïve, and the same could be said of Abdullah himself.

The eight artillery shells Glubb lobbed into Jewish Jerusalem had no impact on Shaltiel's thinking, not least because he was under immense pressure from Ben-Gurion to breach the walls of the Old City and capture it. Through the Belgian Counsel, Israel's provisional government had received the first indication that the Jewish Quarter Shaltiel was supposed to be saving was negotiating its surrender.

In fact the surrender negotiations had stalled. Rabbi Weingarten was insisting that his Jews would surrender only to the Arab Legion because they did not want to entrust their safety to Palestinian and other Arab irregulars. That may well have been the rabbi's own idea; but subsequent developments suggest it could also have been a tactical ploy, conceived by somebody close to Ben-Gurion and imposed on the rabbi, to win time for Shaltiel to breach the walls of the old City and prevent the surrender.

The Palestinian and other Arab irregulars resumed their attack on the Jewish Quarter. If they had not run out of ammunition they would have captured all of it. Probably.

As they started to run out of ammunition the initiative was once again with Shaltiel's Haganah forces and the Palmach. And now it was the turn of the Arabs of Jerusalem, all of them, to panic. From her switchboard in the Rawdah School, Nimra Tannous called the royal palace in Amman. To her astonishment she got through to the king. "Your Majesty, the Jews are at the gates! In a few minutes Jerusalem will be theirs!"

The Jews were at the gates but Shaltiel's strategy for breaking into the walled Old City was not going quite according to plan. On two of Pitchfork's three prongs his attack was close to stalling for a number of reasons. Some of the Haganah's improvised explosive devices had not performed to expectation and some had not worked at all. There were tactical differences between the Haganah and the Palmach. And the fighting Jews had a communications problem—their language. Israelis now they all were, but from so many different homelands, speaking in so many different tongues, that orders were frequently not understood as well or as quickly as they needed to be.

The fighting Jews suffered from a communications problem—coming from so many different homelands and speaking so many different tongues, orders were frequently not understood as well or as quickly as needed.

Meanwhile... There was one young Arab Legion officer the Palestinians knew to be sympathetic to their cause. His name was Tell. Major Abdullah Tell. The unit he commanded was based at the police station in Jericho. Tell was sleeping when a deputation of desperate Palestinians arrived from Jerusalem. Wide-awake in seconds, Tell instructed his orderly to make tea for his Palestinian guests. And then he listened to their report. They were weeping and shaking with fear as they spoke. Their fighters were out of ammunition and were exhausted. The Arab inhabitants of the Old City were in a state of complete panic. There was nothing now to prevent the Jews conquering all of Jerusalem.

Tell didn't need time to think. "You must go at once to Amman." He picked up the telephone and spoke to the palace. "I'm sending a deputation of Palestinians. His Majesty must receive them."

At 2.00 a.m. the call was incoming. Tell's orderly came to attention and handed the telephone to the major. "It's our master."

"Ya habibi" (Yes, my dear), King Abdullah said. "I saw the Palestinians you sent me. *We cannot wait any longer. Go save Jerusalem!*"

Alone, but no doubt in consultation with his God, Abdullah had taken two monumental decisions.

The first was to ignore his army's chain of command. He had decided to bypass Glubb because he knew the Englishman would again raise objections on account of the assurances that had been given to Britain; but Arab pride and emotions could no longer be ignored as prime factors in the equation. And for Abdullah personally the prospect of the Israeli flag flying over the mosque in which his father was buried was too much to bear. Glubb now had a choice, to go with the action and give Major Tell whatever support he needed or resign.

Abdullah's second monumental decision was about strategy. His intention now was not just to threaten Jerusalem for the sake of inducing the Israelis to accept a truce. Abdullah's objective now was the same as Ben-Gurion's—conquest of the Holy City. The self-righteous Ben-Gurion had gone too far. In response Abdullah was going to match him.

Major Tell was as incisive as any Israeli officer. (Which made him a quite rare and remarkable regular Arab soldier). Within an hour of his receipt of the king's command, his advance party was moving slowly down the Mount of Olives toward the Garden of Gethsemane and St. Stephens's Gate. At 3.40 a.m. a lime-green flare illuminated Jerusalem's black skyline. Though Glubb was still unaware of what was happening, the flare was the signal that men of the army he had wanted to keep out of Jerusalem were on the ramparts of the Old City. In less than 24 hours there would be over 1,000 Arab Legionnaires in the city; with their armoured cars and artillery.

Confronted with Abdullah's *fait accompli* in ordering Major Tell to Jerusalem, Glubb pretended that the decision had been his. In a cable to his senior British deputy, Brigadier Norman Lash, who was headquartered in Ramallah's Grand Hotel, Glubb said he had decided to intervene in force in Jerusalem.

Glubb then had a meeting with the British ambassador to explain that he had no choice and to ask for his thoughts. Sir Alec Kirkbride studied Glubb's map and said: "You've had to go into Jerusalem and it seems to me that what happens there is going to be decided in Latrun. You'll have to go down there."

The English Commander of the Arab Legion did not reply for some time. He was still coming to terms with the uncomfortable fact that it was no longer possible for him to put on only a semblance of fighting a war. He was also acknowledging to himself that placing the Arab Legion in strength on the Latrun slopes would present Israel's military forces with a challenge they could not ignore. They would have to drive the Arab Legion off those heights or lose Jerusalem.

Eventually, in a very quiet voice, Glubb replied: "You're right, but you realise that if I move into Latrun we're going to have a real war on our hands."

The truth was that if Ben-Gurion had not defied the will of the organised international community, Transjordan would not have gone to war with Israel over Jerusalem; and Abdullah would have been able to keep Abu Hoda's promise to Bevin. In taking on the Israelis in order to defend Jerusalem, Abdullah was not breaking his promise to Golda because the Holy City was not a part of the Jewish state of the partition plan.

For the first week or so of the war on all other fronts, the main problem for the new Jewish state was the domination of its skies by the Egyptian and Iraqi air forces. Unchallenged, Egyptian planes bombed Tel Aviv every night. They did some damage. One bomb, for example, fell on the city's bus depot and killed 41 people. But the main impact of the air raids was psychological. And, anyway, Arab domination of the skies was short-lived. On 20 May, the sixth day of the war, Israel took delivery of the first of its stripped-down fighter planes from Zatec, a Messerschmitt 109.

From the moment they crossed into Palestine the Arab armies proclaimed great victories, leading the Arab masses to believe that the destruction of the Jewish state was at hand. But most of the land the regular Arab armies were taking was that which had been assigned by the partition plan to the Arab state: land coveted by Zionism's child but not yet in Jewish hands. In reality there were no great Arab victories.

Once into Palestine, the Arab armies proclaimed great victories to their peoples. But most were in the sector assigned by the partition plan to Palestine but not yet in Jewish hands. In reality there were no great Arab victories.

While the Haganah, the Palmach, the two Zionist terrorist organisations and armed Jewish settlers were fighting to check the Arab armies, and waiting for Ben-Gurion's stockpile of ammunition, weapons and additional manpower to come on stream, the most threatening Arab advance was in the south from two advancing Egyptian columns. One was a regular Egyptian army column, the other was composed mainly of Muslim Brotherhood volunteers. The combined strength of the two columns was about 10,000 men supported by 15 fighter planes, a regiment of Sherman and British Matilda tanks, and 25-pounder field guns.

Of the 27 Jewish settlements in the Egyptian area of operations, only five had more than 30 defenders. Supporting the Jewish settlements, deploying here and there as necessary, were two Haganah brigades totalling fewer than 4,000 men without a single anti-tank weapon except mines and Molotov cocktails. Initially on this front the fighting Jews were outnumbered and out-gunned. But apart from the promise of the ammunition, weapons and additional manpower that would enable them to turn the tide of war in their favour, they had one thing going for them that the soldiers of the regular Arab armies lacked. *Motivation.* In the history of warfare, no combatants before or since were better motivated than the fighting Jews of Palestine that became Israel in 1948.

Some Arabs, most likely Shukairy was the first of them, had boasted that the Arab armies were going to "drive the Jews into the sea." The fact that the intervening armed forces of the Arab states did not have the capability to make good such a threat was of no relevance whatsoever. All that mattered was that the fighting Jews believed they were facing the prospect of annihilation. *They believed it because of their history of persecution which had climaxed with the obscenity of the Nazi holocaust. They believed it because they took Arab rhetoric at face value. And they believed it because they were conditioned to do so by their own leaders; leaders who, at the top level, knew there was a vast difference between Arab rhetoric and Arab military capability.*

Allon was later to write: "As a whole, the Israeli forces were... superior in organisation, discipline, fighting spirit, unity and the sense of no alternative. 'Either you win the war, or you will be driven into the Mediterranean—you individually along with the whole nation'; this was the meaning of no alternative, a phrase widely used at this time by troops and civilians alike to express the nation's consciousness that it was fighting for its survival."[1] The significance of the silly and actually empty threat of some of the Arabs to "drive the ZIonists into the sea" is impossible to exaggerate. Apart from motivating the fighting Jews to perform in almost superhuman ways, it gave Ben-Gurion everything he needed in political and propaganda terms to justify the war he wanted. It enabled him to make public opinion in the West, in America especially, believe that he was speaking nothing less than the complete truth when he asserted that the Jewish state really was fighting for its survival and had had no alternative but to fight.

The empty, rhetorical threat of some of the Arabs to "drive the Zionists into the sea" played into the hands of the Jews in a multitude of ways.

Many years later Arafat offered me a most interesting observation on the lack of motivation of most ordinary Arab soldiers in 1948. He said that when the ordinary soldiers who formed the vast bulk of any army had contempt for their ruling elites, and little or no respect for their commanding officers, motivation was not an issue. It simply could not and did not exist. I was not recording this particular conversation with Arafat or taking notes of it, but I recall him saying something like this: "Imagine yourself as an ordinary soldier in the army of a country with a corrupt, incompetent and repressive government, which did not give a damn about improving your lot and that of your family... Would you be well motivated to fight and die for such a regime?"

The best-motivated officer on the Arab side was Major Tell. Assisted by the Arab Legion's success in preventing Ben-Gurion's forces from capturing the Latrun slopes and opening the road to Jerusalem, he did precisely what his king commanded. He went and saved the Holy City.

The Jewish Quarter of the Old City was completely besieged and its inhabitants were facing the prospect of starvation. Their daily food ration was down to 900 calories, only 200 calories more than the Belsen concentration camp inmates had received. And the price of water on the black market was US$2.65 a quart. And for the Jews of the Old City the situation could only get worse.

Tell's strategy was to squeeze the Jewish Quarter methodically from all sides. As each Jewish strongpoint was captured, he ordered it to be destroyed, to prevent the Israelis reclaiming it in the event of a counterattack. It was a slow and deliberate approach designed to save the lives of his men. Tell was as aware as Glubb that the Arab Legion had not been trained for street fighting. The imperative to protect his men was all the greater because the warrens of the Old City were much less than streets.

As one Haganah position after another fell to Tell's men, its local commander, Russnak, could not have been surprised by his next encounter with the rabbis to whom he had previously given permission to open surrender negotiations. This time they had a different request. They wanted him to surrender the Jewish Quarter. "We have been saying psalms all the time," one of the rabbis said to Russnak, "yet still the battle continues."

If that dreadful thing called reality had been the overriding consideration, Russnak might well have agreed to their request. His ability to prevent Tell's Arab Legionnaires taking the Old City's Jewish Quarter was effectively at an end. Only the frequently promised breakthrough by Shaltiel's men could save them from disaster.

Conditions in the Jewish Quarter could no longer be described as desperate. They were hopeless. The religious Jews under the protection of Russnak's men were now huddled together in three synagogues. The Quarter's limited space had been reduced to half its original dimensions. There was no electricity. The water was almost gone. The sewers had stopped working and the air in Quarter's alleys was heavy with the stink of human excrement. Unable to bury their dead, the Quarter's doctors had ordered the bodies to be wrapped in old sheets and stacked in the courtyard behind the hospital. The smell of bodies decomposing in the May heat was spreading.

All of Tell's company commanders were now giving him the same message. One concerted push and the Jewish Quarter would be theirs. Tell now felt that the risk to his men was small enough for him to put his armoured cars into the very heart of the Jewish Quarter. They now went where before, from time immemorial, the only forms of transportation had been mules and goats.

One of the Haganah defenders was later to say, "We didn't know what hit us."

Without a single anti-tank weapon in his armoury, Russnak ordered some of his men to the rooftops, to snipe and drop Molotov cocktails. He was not going to surrender. With Ben-Gurion now making all the decisions, even the military ones, surrender was not an option whatever the situation. *Ben-Gurion had let it be known that any Jew who attempted to surrender would be shot.*

By dawn on Friday 28 May, Rabbi Hazan had decided that if Russnak wanted to stop him surrendering to the Arab Legion, the Haganah would have to kill him.

The rabbi, less frail than his 70 years suggested, emerged from his synagogue with a white flag raised high. But he did not make it, the first time, to the Arab Legion's most forward position. The Haganah opened fire on him, wounding him in the leg. In what has to have been one of the most dramatic moments in the history of the Jews, Rabbi Hazan looked at those who had fired on him and said: "It makes no difference who kills us! The situation is hopeless!"

Unwilling when the crunch came to kill the rabbi, Russnak decided to use him to play for time. If only he could keep the Arab Legion talking, Shaltiel surely would make the breakthrough to save them. So yes, Rabbi Hazan could approach the Arab Legion, but he was to ask for a ceasefire only for the specific purpose of removing the dead and the wounded.

Before the rabbi had finished making his request as instructed by Russnak, Tell realised what the Haganah's game plan was. Politely but firmly Tell ordered Rabbi Hazan to re-cross the six metres of no-man's land, now all that separated the two sides. He was welcome to return but only if he was accompanied by Rabbi Weingarten (who was 83) and a Haganah representative.

Russnak delayed for as long as he dared and then ordered an Arabic-speaking officer, Shaul Tawil, to return to the Arab commander with the two rabbis.

Tell had used the interval to make arrangements for two witnesses to be in attendance. One was the Red Cross's Otto Lehner, the other was the UN's Pablo de Azcarte. The latter would later report that Tell had conducted himself "without a single word or gesture which could have humiliated or offended the defeated leader in any way." Tawil for his part was, according to Azcarte, "calm, strong, showing not the slightest sign of submission or resentment."

The business of arranging the Haganah's surrender was evidently to be done in a gentlemanly way but Tell was not prepared to have a discussion about his terms. All able bodied men would be taken prisoner. As an aside Tell said he was fully aware that there were women in the ranks of the Haganah but he was not intending to take any women as prisoners. The women, children and the aged would be sent to the New City. Depending on the extent of their injuries, the wounded would be held prisoner or returned to their own authorities.

The Haganah had until four o'clock to accept Tell's offer.

Russnak was still looking for a negotiating strategy. If he could negotiate about something, anything, and if he could keep the talking going until nightfall, there was still hope. Did he really believe in miracles? Given where he was, why not. The miracle he was praying for was the arrival of Shaltiel's men in the place most sacred to all the world's Jews.

What happened next was truly inspiring, but it was not the miracle on which Russnak was counting.

Word that the surrender delegation had returned with a deal reached the Jews huddled in the cellars of the Rabbi Jochanan ben Zakai Synagogue. Suddenly, spontaneously, with shrieks of joy and thanksgiving, they rushed past their Haganah guards and into the street. Arabs and Jews, old friends made enemies by Zionism, were embracing through tears of relief. Tell's Arab Legionnaires moved out of their positions and mingled with the men of the Haganah. Jewish shopkeepers opened their stores and were soon serving the Arabs with cakes and coffee. That was particularly galling for Russnak because they were the same Jewish shopkeepers who, for the past two weeks, had signalled their antipathy to Zionism by giving his men glasses of water only begrudgingly.

A sad and somewhat embittered Russnak realised that surrender was already a *fait accompli*. All he could do now was to make it official. He assembled his men; only 30 had survived unscathed, and took a vote. Only the Irgun's representative was opposed to the formal surrender.

When the deed was done, Tell walked down the line of the assembled Haganah men and said to Russnak: "If I had known you were so few we would have come after you with sticks, not guns."

The joy of the Old City's Jews was on account of their belief that surrender meant only an end to the fighting and that they would be allowed to go on living, protected by the Arab Legion, in the most sacred of Judaism's holy places. But that was not in accordance with Tell's terms.

When they realised they were being required to move out, the Old City's Jews, almost as one, were gripped by a terrifying conviction that they would be massacred. Their fear was not of the Arab Legion or even the Arabs of the Old City with whom they had been neighbours and friends before the war. Their fear was born of the knowledge that the Old City's population was now swollen by Arab refugees who had been driven from their land by the Haganah and the Palmach with the assistance of the Irgun and the Stern Gang. How might these Palestinians, themselves traumatised by what had happened at Deir Yassin (and other places) take their revenge? If the gathering Arab mobs turned against them, their prospects of getting out of the Old City alive were not good.

Tell read this fear in Jewish eyes and, to his everlasting credit, he walked among them, quietly seeking, with a word here and a gesture there, to reassure them. And in the hours to come this Arab officer would see to it that his men displayed in victory a quality that most Israelis seemed (and still seem) not to possess—magnanimity or, if not quite that, at least concern for the safety of the vanquished.

The exodus of the Jews from the walled Old City was through Zion Gate. As they filed through it to the New City, flames from the first of their fired buildings were lighting the night sky. Their departure marked the end of almost 2,000 years of a continuous though small Jewish presence in the Old City. Did some of the departing religious Jews find themselves wondering about how different things would have been if Zionism had not had its way? Probably.

As the Old City's Jews stumbled through the narrow passageways so familiar to them on their way to Zion Gate, Tell's Legionnaires protected them with their bodies, holding back the excited Arab crowds. They also assisted the aged and carried bundles or children for overburdened women. And they drove back Arab mobs with their rifle butts and arrested those who tried to pelt the Jews with stones. On one occasion the Legionnaires fired over the heads of an Arab mob to keep it at bay.

Tell's triumphant day ended with a telephone call from King Abdullah. Congratulations for a job well done.

For Ben-Gurion and those who shared his Messianic view that seizing Jerusalem in defiance of the will of the organised international community was the priority, the loss of the Old City was an unthinkable calamity, one that just had to be reversed.

But the news for Ben-Gurion was not all bad. Far from Israel and what was still left of Palestine decisions had been taken that would enable David to become Goliath.

The decision which most determined the outcome of the first Arab–Israeli conflict was taken on 22 May. On that day Britain withdrew her veto on the Security Council's order for a ceasefire. It was to include an embargo on ammunition and arms to both sides, with severe sanctions against any of the combatants who did not keep to the rules of the ceasefire once it was in place.

The British had been fully aware that Ben-Gurion wanted war in order to grab more Arab land by fighting than he could get from diplomacy; and when the war started Britain's unstated but real position was that events should be allowed to take their own course for a while. London's hope was that the Arab armies would be competent enough to prevent the Israelis taking territory that had been allotted to the proposed Arab state of the vitiated partition plan.

Why on 22 May, the eighth day of the war, did Britain change its position and remove her veto on the Security Council's call for a ceasefire and arms embargo?

The short answer is that Washington told London that Britain could forget assistance for economic recovery if it did not fall into line on the Middle East. In the years to come *British diplomats would recall with great bitterness the pressures exerted by America to prevent Britain supplying the Arabs with a single bullet while the Israelis were importing everything they needed to impose their will on the Arabs—not just the Palestinians, but the Arabs.*

The US threatened to withdraw its economic aid to Britain if it did not stop supplying arms to the Arabs, while the Israelis were importing everything they needed for victory over not just the Palestinians, but the Arabs.

As ever the Arab League was divided and initially rejected the Security Council order for a ceasefire. When that happened Britain took the initiative of placing before the Security Council a resolution for a 30-day truce.

The man with the responsibility on behalf of the United Nations for negotiating the truce into being and then putting together a proposal for permanent peace was Count Folke Bernadotte, a nephew of Sweden's King Gustav V. In his own right he was a distinguished soldier, humanitarian and diplomat. During World War II he had headed the Swedish Red Cross and was credited with saving some 20,000 inmates from death in Nazi concentration camps. On 14 May, after President Truman had made a nonsense of the UN's proceedings and thrown the world body into confusion by recognising the unilaterally-declared Jewish state, the General Assembly had passed a resolution authorising the appointment a mediator "to promote the peaceful adjustment of the future Palestine". The 53 year-old Bernadotte was named on 20 May.

Ben-Gurion's first response to the Security Council's insistence on a 30-day truce was to poll his military commanders and advisers. They were aware that their supply situation was improving. True it was that things were happening more slowly than they had hoped, but what had been stockpiled in Europe and elsewhere was beginning to come on stream. Five more

Messerschmitts had been flown to Israel and the first major shipment of arms to arrive by sea had been unloaded at Haifa. The view of Ben-Gurion's military commanders and advisers was however a unanimous one. A 30-day truce was much to be desired. Why?

The Haganah had come into being as an underground or clandestine force for the purpose of defending new Jewish settlements in Palestine. *The need now, if the Zionist project was to proceed as intended, was for Israel to go on to the offensive, to take the war to the Arabs.* That required much more than a different mindset. What now had to be created, with maximum possible speed, was a truly national armed service as appropriate for a sovereign state—a proper army, air force and navy. A 30-day truce would enable Israel to put its military act together with due attention to organisation, training, discipline and co-ordination, with a top-to-bottom chain of command. There was also need to end the rivalry between the Haganah and the Palmach. That would happen when the Palmach was absorbed into the new Israeli Army, which would be the land force component of the IDF (Israel Defence Force) when it came into being. During the truce.

Ben-Gurion's own priority was still Jerusalem, the need to open the road to it in order, first, to lift the Arab siege of the New City and its 100,000 beleaguered Jews, now including the religious Jews expelled from the walled Old City. Naturally the victory he anticipated would see the conquest of the Old City, too. Tell's triumph would be very be short-lived. Or so Ben-Gurion believed when he demanded a second attack to break the Arab Legion's hold on the Latrun slopes.

For his part Major Tell was intending to push into the New City and he had started the softening up process with an artillery barrage. His expectation was that a daily pounding would make life impossible for its Jewish residents and bring about their surrender.

Behind the scenes a great political drama was taking place in Washington, London and Amman.

As part of his secret preparations for war, Ben-Gurion had secured in principle the services of a number of very experienced and celebrated American officers. They were pledged to travel to Israel as soon as Israel declared itself to be in existence and President Truman had recognised it. The most senior of them was no less a figure than Brigadier General Walter Bedell Smith. He had been Eisenhower's chief of staff in Europe during World War II. Ben-Gurion had pencilled him in to be the advising architect of the IDF.

The drama started in Washington when Defence Secretary Forrestal formally banned all officers from travelling to Israel to assist the Zionist enterprise so long as they remained on the Pentagon's payroll. The only senior American officer to defy Forrestal's veto was Colonel David Marcus, a veteran of the Normandy landing and the holder of both American and British decorations. He had been marked for promotion to very high rank but he walked away from the Pentagon in order to answer Ben-Gurion's call.

Behind closed doors Ben-Gurion was incandescent with rage. If the Truman administration would not allow American officers to serve with Israel's military forces, the U.S., he insisted, should demand forthwith, and using whatever pressure was required, that Britain withdraw its officers from Transjordan's Arab Legion.

On that, Ben-Gurion had his way.

As a result of tremendous American pressure the British War office informed Transjordan's prime minister, Abu Hoda, that all British officers seconded to the Arab Legion were to be withdrawn "immediately" across the Jordan River. They were to take no further part in engagements in Palestine—engagements in which the only intention was to occupy Arab land allotted to the Arab state of the vitiated partition plan, in order to prevent Israeli forces grabbing it.

When Forrestal denied Ben-Gurion the use of American officers for the IDF, Ben-Gurion demanded and got, through U.S. pressure, the withdrawal of all British officers who were directing the Arab Legion's efforts in Palestine and an embargo on British arms sales to the Arabs.

At a stroke Glubb was deprived of more than two-thirds of the officers who had made his Arab Legion the effective fighting force it was. He was given the news by Abu Hoda in what he would later describe as "one of the most painful and humiliating" interviews of his life.

"Is this the kind of allies the British are?" Abu Hoda asked.

So far as both men were concerned, they were on the receiving end of an almost complete reversal of British policy. Though he did not say so at the time, Britain's ambassador in Transjordan, Sir Alec Kirkbride, agreed. He would later say: "After waving the green flag for weeks we suddenly started sawing the branch off on them."

Privately Glubb described Britain's change of policy as "absolutely catastrophic." But there was worse news to come.

A second message from the War Office in London informed Abu Hoda that Britain was imposing an embargo on arms to the Middle East. The seriousness of Britain's intention was underlined by the statement that Britain's subsidy to the Arab Legion would be reviewed if Transjordan was found to be defying the United Nations. *Only Israel would be allowed to do that and get away with it. In 1948 and thereafter forever*

While the political drama was being played out, the Israelis made their second attempt to take the Latrun slopes from the Arab Legion. The second attack was masterminded and directed by the American Colonel Marcus. On his arrival in Tel Aviv, Ben-Gurion had appointed him commander-in-chief of the Jerusalem front with the rank of *alufo*. That made Marcus the first general of a Jewish army since the Maccabean revolt. Ben-Gurion evidently believed that the only missing ingredient in the plan for the conquest of Jerusalem was experienced military leadership. His own inexperienced military commanders were not up to the job. General Marcus would get it done. The prospect of making the Holy City the eternal capital of the Jewish state, and telling the non-Jewish world to go to hell, was still a real one. In Ben-Gurion's mind.

But the strategic advantage the Arab Legion forces enjoyed from their occupation of the Latrun slopes (and which the Israelis could have had) proved to be too great for even General Marcus to overcome. And the second Israeli attempt to capture them failed.

While their ammunition lasted, Tell's men continued to threaten the New City, and it was to be the plight of the beleaguered Jews there that obliged Ben-Gurion to accept the 30-day truce.

By the end of May the fledgling Israeli Air Force (IAF) was in action; and it was about to give the Arabs notice that their domination of the sky would soon be ended.

Israel's first blood in the air was the shooting down of two Egyptian DC-3's. Then, on 1 June, Ben-Gurion ordered two of his Messerschmitts to bomb Amman, to give King Abdullah's capital its first taste of what Tel Aviv had experienced in two weeks of nightly raids by Egypt's Air Force.

But it was the rapidly deteriorating situation on the ground in Jerusalem that changed the immediate course of events by giving Bernadotte some negotiating leverage with the Israelis.

On 4 June, a Friday, the eve of the Sabbath, Dov Joseph, Ben-Gurion's trouble-shooter in Jerusalem, sent a desperate plea to his boss. It was by far the most alarming of Joseph's messages to date. If the already inadequate bread ration was reduced from 200 to 150 grams, he would have enough flour to supply Jerusalem's beleaguered Jews with bread for five more days. "We can't rely on miracles", Joseph warned, "I ask you to order the transportation of bread in any way possible...Try to send it by jeep or camel."

But it was not only food and medicines that were required if New (Jewish) Jerusalem was to be saved from surrender. The Haganah forces in and around the New City, under siege and shellfire, were down to their last reserves of ammunition. The problem was not a lack of ammunition in the Jewish state. What had been stockpiled in Europe was coming on stream. On a nationwide basis, the Haganah (on paper and with the Palmach now the official army of the IDF) had more than enough ammunition for its needs. The problem, as with food and medicines, was how to get ammunition to Jerusalem when the Arab Legion still had complete command and control of the only road in.

Yitzhak Levi was Shaltiel's intelligence officer. His calculations, almost to the last bullet, invited only the "blackest" of conclusions. Their reserves of ammunition might get them through only 24 hours of intense fighting. "Clearly", Levi told himself, "we have to be re-supplied and re-supplied quickly or we're going to collapse."

In Levi's assessment the few cases of munitions that were being delivered by Piper Cub or parachuted from a DC-3 would not be enough to save them. To Shaltiel he said, "If we are not re-supplied we are doomed!"

Levi then proposed that, somehow, he should get himself to Tel Aviv to tell Ben-Gurion personally about their supply situation and warn him that a catastrophe was imminent. "Go" Shaltiel said.

Ben-Gurion had only one question. "Will we be able to hold Jerusalem or will it fall?"

Levi replied: "The fate of Jerusalem does not depend on food this morning. It depends on ammunition. If there is a serious Arab attack we will simply run out of ammunition." Pause. "We will be overwhelmed."

In Zionism's version of history the Jewish state was in danger of being "overwhelmed". That was never the case. As it actually happened, it was only the Haganah's forces in besieged New Jerusalem that were in real trouble. If they had surrendered there would still have been a Jewish state but one without Jerusalem as its capital. The body without the soul in Ben-Gurion's thinking but still the Jewish state as proposed by the vitiated partition plan. *In other words, it was not Israel's existence that was at stake but the Jewish state's ability, in defiance of the will of the organised international community, to take and keep Jerusalem.*

In Zionism's version of history, the Jewish state was in danger of being "overwhelmed". That was never the case.

Collins and Lapierre made this observation on page 523 of *O Jerusalem!:*

> Jerusalem's Jewish population would not easily forget that the centres of Western Christianity, which had clamoured for their city's internationalisation, now ignored their agony. The Vatican, the Church of England, the councils of orthodoxy, the governments of those nations that had supported internationalisation did not see fit to launch a storm of protest over what was happening to them in New Jerusalem. To the city's besieged residents, it seemed that the outside world was more interested in saving Jerusalem's Christian stones than in saving its Jewish inhabitants.

I think such an observation requires comment. *The plight of the 100,000 Jews in the New City would not have been nearly as desperate as it was, in fact they would have been in no danger to speak of, but for Ben-Gurion's determination to take all of Jerusalem in defiance of the will of the organised international community.* To say nothing of international law, and the Palestinians' rights of ownership and self-determination. If King Abdullah had not been placed in an impossible position by Operation Pitchfork, the Arab Legion would not have been ordered to fight the Jews for control of Jerusalem.

Ben-Gurion's last words to the departing Levi were: "Tell Shaltiel to hold on. We'll organise things from here. We'll open a new road to Jerusalem!"

Levi was one of the very few people who knew why Ben-Gurion's idea was perhaps not as crazy as it sounded.

Out of a mixture of the curiosity born of desperation and *chutzpah*, the Palmach and the Haganah had discovered that it was possible, just about, to travel by jeep between Tel Aviv and Jerusalem without taking the road on which the only certainty was death from the Arab Legion's guns on the Latrun slopes.

The first part of the discovery had been made by a young Palmach officer, Amos Chorev, while he was driving General Marcus and Chaim Herzog in the direction of Jerusalem from Tel Aviv. (Herzog, from Belfast, was in the process of establishing Israel's Directorate of Military Intelligence).

About 12 miles from Tel Aviv, Chorev had turned his jeep off the road. That was the start of an incredible and exhausting journey, the jeep bouncing and skidding and protesting as he drove through the wadis and across steep mountain slopes leading up to the Judean heights.

Time after time Marcus and Herzog had to jump out of the vehicle to lighten its load and, in the moonlight, guide it from rock to rock. They reached the crest of the Judean ridge by pushing the jeep up the last few yards. From the top they could make out the road to Jerusalem. The passage they had negotiated was roughly parallel with it. Completely exhausted, they decided to grab some sleep under the stars.

They were woken by the sound of an approaching vehicle, this one coming up the other side of their ridge. Astonished, they grabbed their Sten guns and crept forward to investigate. And then they watched, their hearts pounding with excitement, a virtual re-play of their own gruelling journey up their side of the ridge. The approaching vehicle was a Palmach jeep. One Palmachnik driving, the other, just as Marcus and Herzog had done for Chorev, guiding him through the rocks. At the top the five Israelis celebrated. Three had set out from Tel Aviv. Two had set out from Jerusalem. And they had met roughly in the middle.

Chorev, Marcus and Herzog returned to Tel Aviv to give Ben-Gurion the news. The possibility of building a new road to Jerusalem to lift the siege was a real one. The decision to go ahead with such a daunting project was taken by Ben-Gurion as he had listened to Levi and, most critical of all, because of Levi's presence. The jeep in which he had travelled from besieged Jerusalem to Tel Aviv was the first Israeli vehicle to make the whole journey.

As he listened to Levi, Ben-Gurion had said to himself, "If one jeep can make it, many jeeps can." In the Israeli leader's mind there was suddenly the prospect of re-supplying Jerusalem with ammunition and food and thus averting the need for him to accept a truce. Ben-Gurion knew better than anybody else that in the event of a truce, his scope for defying the wishes of the international community with regard to the future of Jerusalem would be much reduced. If there was a truce before Israel conquered all of Jerusalem, and if the truce led to a permanent ceasefire, the Old City would remain under Arab control. That was unthinkable.

In the moment of their discovery at the top of the Judean ridge, Herzog had asked Marcus if he really thought it would be possible to build a new road. The American had replied: "Why not? We got across the Red Sea, didn't we?"

By Monday 7 June, Dov Joseph, in besieged Jerusalem, was more than desperate. He was convinced they were "coming to a perilous end" and he sat down to draft a doomsday message to Ben-Gurion.

For his part Major Tell was convinced that he would soon be taking the surrender of the Haganah in New Jerusalem. The only cloud on his horizon was a report he had received from an Arab villager. "The Jews are building a secret way to Jerusalem." Tell was concerned enough to convey the report to Colonel Habes Majali. He was the commander of the Arab Legion's Fourth Regiment, the master of the Latrun slopes. Tell's message confirmed what Majali was already suspecting. He had heard with his own ears the noise of the engines of what he now presumed to be Israeli bulldozers at work, and he had seen with his own eyes the columns of dust they were creating as they advanced.

Majali knew that he could quite easily disrupt the work. All he had to do was open up with his 25-pounder guns. If he laid down an intense enough barrage, the Israelis would have to abandon their new road project. But before he could do that, Majali needed the permission of his English brigade commander, Colonel T.L. Ashton. So it was that Majali despatched his adjutant, Captain Rousan, to brief Ashton and obtain his permission for use of the 25-pounders.

For Rousan the English colonel put on a show of indifference. "The terrain is too tough. It's too mountainous. They'll never get a road through there."

But that was not really the point. Ashton now knew that when the Arab Legion had exhausted its reserves of ammunition, there would be no more. London was going to be very serious about the embargo. No doubt about it. So Ashton's reply to Majali was in the form of a handwritten order he gave, sealed, to Rousan. The order said: "Under no circumstances are you to waste your 25-pounder ammunition in the sector Beit Jiz-Beit Susin" (where the Israelis were at work on their new road).

Joseph's cabled message to Ben-Gurion contained his anger as well as his concern. "Do we have to be satisfied with only hopes and possibilities? I've been warning for weeks that there is need to send food supplies and nothing has arrived. I suggested a few ways and you didn't respond. You managed to send other things, why not food? Why not draft those hundreds who are sitting in cafes in Tel Aviv for Jerusalem's sake." One of Joseph's earlier suggestions had been for a long march—the transportation of essential supplies to Jerusalem by foot if all else failed.

When he was drafting his S.O.S. to Ben-Gurion, Joseph was aware that the Haganah was preparing a third attempt to take the Latrun slopes from the Arab Legion. He made reference to it in his last paragraph, the doomsday part of his message. "I ask you what will happen if, God forbid, the operation doesn't succeed. If we do not receive flour by Friday (11 June), there will be starvation in the city!"

Ben-Gurion now had no choice. If he was to prevent the surrender of the Jerusalem Haganah and the Arabs from taking control of New as well as Old Jerusalem, he had to accept the 30-day truce. But he was still going to play for time.

In his dealings with the UN mediator up to this point, Israel's leader had neither accepted nor rejected the Security Council's demand for a truce. Instead, and in the hope that he would not have to agree to a truce until his forces had broken the siege and conquered all of Jerusalem, he had haggled about the terms of the truce as they would apply to Israel.

In the Bernadotte truce plan as originally presented to the warring parties there was to be an embargo not only on the shipment into the area of weapons but, also, a ban on the shipment of men of military age.

Ben-Gurion was not concerned about the arms embargo. Unlike the Arabs, and because of his forward planning, Israel was not dependent for its supplies on any government. Israel was well positioned, quietly and without making a fuss about it, to defy the arms embargo.

But with regard to the proposed ban on the shipment into the area of men of military age, Ben-Gurion had dug his heels in. Such a proposal was unacceptable and if Bernadotte insisted on it, even with Security Council backing, there would be no truce. For Ben-Gurion it was a matter of principle as well as the IDF's need for recruits. The Jewish state had not come into being, and was not fighting for its independence in order to continue Britain's policy of appeasing the Arabs by denying Jews from anywhere their right to emigrate to it.

Bernadotte was over a barrel. He knew there was no prospect of persuading the Arabs to accept a truce unless he could tell them Israel had said "Yes". So he gave in to Ben-Gurion. Men of military age would be allowed into the area during the truce provided they had not been formed into military units before the truce. That proviso was no more than diplomatic face-saving on Bernadotte's part.

Apart from what was happening in and around Jerusalem, the Israelis had contained the unprepared and ill-equipped Arab armies in less than a month of fighting.

Apart from what was happening in and around Jerusalem, *the Israelis had contained the Arab armies in less than a month of fighting.* They had driven the Lebanese back across their own border. They had chased the Syrians out of most of Galilee. They had seen off the Iraqis who, when the crunch came, did not have the stomach for war and were on that account a total disappointment to their Arab brothers, and most important of all, they had stopped the Egyptians 25 miles from Tel Aviv.

And there were already indications of big trouble to come for the Egyptians. When they came upon a well-defended Jewish settlement they tended to go around it rather than fight. Such a strategy assisted their early advance but it left them vulnerable to attack by armed Jewish settlers from the rear.

And Egyptian soldiers and junior officers were in the process of discovering how unprepared and ill-equipped their army was for war—thanks to the incompetence of the high command and its bottom-licking subservience to a corrupt and stupid king and his rotten regime. The men fighting in the desert were running out of everything, not just ammunition but water, food, medicines and fuel. Rifles were jamming and grenades were exploding prematurely in men's hands. And the collapse of morale was assisted by the sight of senior officers sheltering from the heat in their tents instead of being part of the experience of war with their men.

Ben-Gurion was later to say that in the first week of June 1948 Israel was "at the end of its rope." That was true only with regard to the situation in Jerusalem—a potential disaster of his own making—and it was to prevent a disaster there that the Israeli leader sent a cable to Bernadotte accepting his truce plan.

Bernadotte was then in a position to turn the diplomatic heat on the Arab League. And the stage was set, when its leaders met in Amman, for a very dramatic confrontation between Egypt's Prime Minister Nokrashy and Secretary General Azzam.

Because they had most to lose—their land, their homes and their rights—the leaderless Palestinians were bitterly opposed to the idea of a truce. They feared it would lead to a loss of Arab military momentum. The Syrians and the Lebanese were also opposed to a truce for the same reason. And so was Azzam. But he had done some serious thinking.

In his own mind the Arab League's Secretary General had balanced the two most critical considerations. The first was that the Arabs would not be resupplied with ammunition and weapons during the truce. The second was that the Israelis would find ways to get around the arms embargo and, more to the point, would be assisted to do so because of the sympathy the fighting Jews enjoyed, in America especially, on account of the Nazi holocaust. Conclusion. If the Arab armies stopped now, all would be lost.

But when the Arab League leaders met in Amman to consider their response to Bernadotte, there was only one man whose view mattered. Nokrashy, Egypt's prime minister, was in a position to call the policy shots because (apart from what was happening in and around Jerusalem) his country's army was carrying the main burden of the war effort; and nearly one month into the fighting it was, more or less, the only Arab army still fighting. The Lebanese and the Iraqis were as good as out of the war, and the Syrians, though still willing, had been contained.

Nokrashy was also free again, to some extent, to be his own man, to speak his own mind. He had this freedom because his corrupt and stupid king had already lost interest in the war. Farouk had been promised a quick victory and when it did not materialise he had effectively washed his hands of the Palestine Problem.

To his brother Arab leaders Nokrashy said: "We went into this war when we never should have. It is time to accept the United Nations ceasefire and use the four weeks to improve the state of our armies. Then perhaps we can hope to win the war."

Azzam exploded. "You are talking nonsense! Your army is only 25 miles from Tel Aviv. You haven't been defeated and you want to catch your breath. What do you think the Jews will do with a ceasefire? Do you think they will do nothing? They will use it, too, and you will find them twice as strong as you afterward."

Nokrashy was deaf to Azzam's arguments. "My decision is based on the advice of my Chief of Staff. I'm not going to take your advice over my soldiers."

Azzam could not contain his rage. "You're getting your advice from the most ignorant man in Egypt when it comes to warfare!"

Though he did not say so, Azzam was convinced that Nokrashy was intending to take Egypt out of the war. And he was right. Because Farouk had lost interest, Nokrashy, if he was to survive as prime minister, had to have a way of extracting Egypt from the mess. The truce was the way.

The Secretary General of the Arab League was now desperate. If he was to change Nokrashy's mind about the wisdom of accepting a truce, he had only one card to play. Arab public opinion and, in particular, Egyptian public opinion. Prior to the war it had been fed a diet of bellicose propaganda. The Jewish state would be annihilated if it came to war. No doubt about it. Then, during the first three weeks of the fighting, the Arab masses had been led to believe that their glorious armies were making good on their promise. If now the Arab regimes ordered their armies to stop fighting—i.e. when victory was, allegedly, so close—it would not be all that difficult to inspire the masses to revolt by charging that their cause had been betrayed.

When it became clear that Nokrashy's insistence on a truce was going to carry the day, Azzam played his last card. He grabbed a piece of paper, angrily wrote his resignation and threw it across the table. On his feet he said he was going to denounce the men who had forced a ceasefire on the League. And then, as if to make good on his threat, he stormed out of the room.

For a moment Nokrashy remained seated, white-faced and stunned. Then, suddenly, he was on his feet, running after Azzam. When he caught up with the Secretary General he tugged at his sleeve. "Azzam, do you know what you're doing? You're killing me! If I go back to Cairo with your resignation and a ceasefire, I will be assassinated!"

Azzam studied the prime minister's face and drew breath. "All right", he said, "I'll accept the truce. *But the Arab people will never forgive us for what we are about to do.*"

In silence Azzam returned to the meeting room and tore up his resignation.

Despite their profound difference with regard to strategy, Azzam and Nokrashy were old friends who had shared many a trial and tribulation.

One interpretation of what happened is that Azzam simply could not bear the thought of being responsible, even indirectly, for putting the life of his friend at risk. Azzam knew that the possibility of Nokrashy being murdered by the Muslim Brotherhood in the event of his return to Cairo with both a ceasefire and his resignation was a very real one. The implication is that Azzam changed his mind and went along with a decision that he believed would have disastrous consequences for the Arabs in order to protect his friend. Perhaps. But I think there is another and more straightforward explanation for Azzam's apparent volte-face. His threat to denounce those who insisted on accepting the truce was a bluff. He was hoping that making the threat would be enough to cause Nokrashy to reject the truce. Effectively Azzam's bluff was called.

With the agreement of both the Zionist state and the Arab League secured, Bernadotte was now in a position to fix the starting date and time of the four-week truce. For Ben-Gurion, and because of the certainty of the loss of New Jerusalem if the fighting continued, the truce could not now come quickly enough.

When Friday 11 June dawned, Major Tell believed he was only days away, and perhaps hours, from obliging the Jerusalem Haganah to surrender; and he was not aware that ten o'clock that morning had been fixed as the time for the truce to come into effect. His confidence had been boosted by news of the Arab Legion's success in defeating the Haganah's third attempt to capture the Latrun slopes. There was no possibility of the Israelis lifting the siege of the Holy City. The Arab Legion now had all of Jerusalem in its grasp.

In fact the situation in Jewish Jerusalem was worse than Tell could have known. The New City's 100,000 inhabitants, many of them recent arrivals, legal and illegal immigrants, were on the brink of actual starvation. Leon Angel, one of the two bakers still producing bread, later remarked that "death was stalking the city." All the shutters were closed and the silence was more eloquent than any words. Angel presumed that the hunger-weakened population was "probably staying inside, trying not to move to save energy."

Joseph and Shaltiel had already agreed they would have to confront the question of who to stop feeding first, the civilians or the soldiers.

At eight o'clock Tell answered the telephone. It was His Majesty, calling to tell him that "hudna" (a truce) had been agreed and would take effect in two hours time. Abdullah had decided to call the young Major personally because he realised that imposing a ceasefire might test his authority to its limits. His men would be far from happy with the decision.

As Tell listened his face was a picture of shock and disbelief. At the first opportunity he said: "Your Majesty, how can I stop these men? They feel victory is within reach."

Abdullah's rasping reply was loud enough to be heard by an Arab reporter who was listening at Tell's shoulder. "You are a soldier and I give you an order. You will execute it. You must order a ceasefire at ten o'clock!"

The king then informed Tell that he was intending to come to

Jerusalem for noon prayers in the Mosque of Omar. That was Abdullah's way of saying, in effect: "My presence will require that you have the situation under total control". In other words: "Do whatever has to be done to see that nobody on our side breaks the truce." If that meant shooting Arab objectors who caused trouble, Palestinians or even Legionnaires, so be it. Tell got the message.

If Jerusalem had been the most beautiful and desirable woman in the world and the love of the Major's life, and if King Abdullah had been her father announcing that his daughter was off limits to him, Tell could not have been more heart-broken than he was. When he replaced the receiver there were tears in his eyes. He dabbed them with edge of his *kaffiyeh*. And there was anger in his heart. He believed that his king was betraying the Arab cause. But Tell would obey. Without saying a word he rushed into the street and gave his men an order. They were to open fire with everything they had and keep firing until ten o'clock. After that they were not to fire a single shot, except as directed, if the need arose, to take out any armed Arab who sought to keep the fighting going.

By four minutes past ten on Friday 11 June the first truce of the first Arab-Israeli war was in being in Jerusalem and then on all fronts.

In private Ben-Gurion was about to speak the words that haunt Arab leaders to this day.

As the guns fell silent Ben-Gurion was studying the latest report from Avriel. A third shipload of arms was ready to leave Yugoslavia. It included 100-millimeter mortars purchased in France. The Czechs had agreed to train pilots, paratroopers and weapons experts for the IDF. Best of all, Avriel now had planes that could fly stockpiled ammunition and weapons and men non-stop from Prague to Tel Aviv. Ben-Gurion knew that if Bernadotte was to prevent Israel breaking the terms of the truce, he would have to arrange for those planes to be intercepted and turned back or shot down. And that, the Israeli leader could be sure, was not going to happen. In the wake of the Nazi holocaust, the governments of the Western world would not dare to contemplate such action against Jews.

The arms embargo was to have meaning for only the Arabs. In Ben-Gurion's judgment, the Arabs had made "a fateful mistake".

The arms embargo was to have meaning for only the Arabs. Ben-Gurion's judgment was that his Arab enemies, by accepting the truce, had made a mistake, "a fateful mistake."

Many years after the events Allon wrote the following about the state of the military play when the truce came into effect. "Not only had the enemy been held back in most areas, but considerable territorial gains had been made."[2]

In Ben-Gurion's retrospective assessment of the first round of the war, their real problem had not been a shortage of weapons and ammunition and other supplies but "a lack of discipline." He said: "If we had had one army instead of a number of armies, and if we had operated according to one strategic plan, we would have had to show more for our efforts." (It was presumably the lack of one strategic plan, and the fact that Ben-Gurion was a disaster as the commander-in-chief, that accounted for the failure of the fighting Jews to take the Latrun slopes when they were there for the taking.)

Bernadotte's task now was to prevent a resumption of the fighting and develop a peace proposal for discussion with the warning parties.

The early omens on the Arab side were good. *At government level neither Egypt nor Transjordan wanted the fighting to be resumed.* Abu Hoda, Transjordan's prime minister, told Glubb that he and Egypt's prime minister were determined not to let the war break out again. "There will no more fighting and no more money for soldiers" Abu Hoda said.

Glubb was delighted. His analysis of the situation was very perceptive. The main problem as he saw it was in the fact that "you had a modern European population opposed to a much more numerous local population which was without technical knowledge and modern skills, and which was uncontrollably excitable and emotional." *Glubb felt that until the Arabs produced more mature societies, economies and populations, they would never be able to compete with the Jews, in war or peace.* (More than half a century on, the same could still be said). In Glubb's judgment a continuation of the fighting was most definitely not in the Arab interest.

While Glubb and Abu Hoda were talking, Ben-Gurion was meeting with all of his senior military commanders. His cup of confidence was running over because he knew he could deliver on his promise—to supply them with all the weapons and reserves of men they needed to take the offensive when the truce ended.

Israel's policy henceforth would be not only to defeat the Arab armies but to capture and keep more Arab land, and insofar as possible, to cleanse it of its indigenous inhabitants.

Israel's policy from here on would be not only to defeat the Arab armies but to capture for keeping more Arab land and, to the maximum extent possible, cleanse it of its indigenous Arab inhabitants.

The certain prospect now—provided the Arabs were stupid enough to continue the war—was for a Zionist state that would be significantly bigger than the one of the vitiated partition plan. From here on Israel's confines would be determined not by any UN resolution, not with respect for international law, not with regard for the rights of the Palestinians, but by military might. And the instrument of its application was to be the IDF. With every passing hour of the remaining 29 days of the truce, its three arms—army, air force and navy—would become stronger. The formality of declaring the IDF to be in existence had actually taken place with ceremony on 31 May.

As it happened the most serious threat to the well-being and stability of the Jewish state came not from the Arabs but, during the truce, from Begin and his Irgun terrorists. Begin had denounced Ben-Gurion for accepting the truce and, before it, had condemned the Haganah's surrender of the Jewish Quarter of the Old City as "shameful". With reinforcements on their way by sea in a ship named Altalena, Begin was determined that his Irgun would succeed where the Haganah had failed. Truce or no truce he was intending to take the Old City. A Jewish state without Jerusalem including the Old City as its capital was unacceptable.

Whether or not Begin entertained the idea of overthrowing Ben-Gurion before the *Altalena* affair brought the two of them into confrontation is a good question.

In the vessel's holds, funded by American money for Zionist terrorism, were 5,000 rifles, five half-tracks and 300 Bren guns. Plus 900 men. Those were the weapons and reinforcements with which Begin was intending to capture the Old City.

Not surprisingly Ben-Gurion viewed the imminent arrival of the *Altalena* as a challenge to his government's authority. He gave orders for the arms on board the vessel to be landed and placed in government warehouses. Begin was determined to prevent that happening. He ordered the *Altalena* to unload at Kfar Vitkin on 20 June. Ben-Gurion responded by sending 600 men of the Alexandroni Bridge to surround the Irgun's unloading party. Firing broke out and the *Altalena* hastily set sail. Dodging Israeli Navy ships sent out to intercept the *Altalena*, her captain headed south with the intention of running the vessel aground on the beach at Tel Aviv. He almost made it. Barely 100 yards from the beach the *Altalena* grounded itself on the submerged wreck of an immigrant ship the British had sunk. And that set the stage for the showdown between Begin and Ben-Gurion. *The Irgun was ordered to mobilise to "take over the government."*

In Tel Aviv Ben-Gurion called an emergency cabinet meeting. He said, and it was true, that the city around them, their capital for the time being, was "in danger of falling to rebel forces." More than that, Ben-Gurion told his Cabinet colleagues, the Irgun's move "endangers the very existence of the state."

The man chosen by Ben-Gurion to take on the Irgun was Yigal Allon, the commander of the Palmach until its absorption into the IDF, and the man designated to be the IDF's first commander. To him Ben-Gurion said: "Your new assignment may be the toughest one you've had so far. This time you may have to kill Jews!"

In the brief but brutal struggle for control of Tel Aviv the forces commanded by Allon were outnumbered and if he had not been prepared to kill rebel Jews, Ben-Gurion's government might have fallen. For a few bloody hours Tel Aviv was in the Irgun's hands. In that time 83 fighting Jews on both sides were killed and wounded. Allon's victory was assisted by an artillery strike which set the *Altalena* ablaze and deprived the Irgun of the weapons and equipment with which Begin was planning to liberate the Old City. (One consequence of the Irgun's defeat was that Begin had to wait 29 years to get his hands on the levers of power by democratic means.)

But there was much else for Ben-Gurion and his military commanders to celebrate. Before the truce was two weeks old, supplies of ammunition, weapons and military hardware of all kinds were pouring into Israel, and not just from the secret stockpiles in Europe and Cyprus.

Most impressive of all was the speed and efficiency of the preparations to give the Israel mastery of the skies. During the truce the Israeli Air Force took possession of 20 Messerschmitts, five P-51 Mustang fighters, four Beaufighters, seven Sansons, three B-17 Flying Fortresses, three Constellations, 15 C-46s, two DC-4s and 10 DC-3s.

During the truce the embargo-busting priority was to get ammunition and weapons to Shaltiel in besieged Jerusalem. And that was now possible because a miracle had happened. The secret road by-passing the Arab Legion's guns on the Latrun slopes had been completed. In three weeks. Thanks to the truce and the sweat and skills of Israel's engineers. On 19 June the inaugural convoy along it—the Israelis named it their Burma Road—consisted of 140 trucks, each carrying a three-ton load of ammunition and weapons for Shaltiel. Dynamite. Rifles. Sten guns. Czech machine guns. Hand grenades. And mortars of every size. As he watched the approach of that first convoy through his field glasses, Shaltiel was almost speechless with joy. The only words that came out of his mouth were "Oh, my God! Oh, my God!"

In that moment Shaltiel might well have been the happiest feller on Earth. Not only was the Arab siege of the Holy City being broken before his eyes. He knew that when the fighting was resumed he would be able to pound the Arab Legion on the Latrun slopes with murderous canon fire of his own.

There were UN truce supervisors on the ground whose task was to check vehicles for the purpose of preventing arms and ammunition reaching Jerusalem, but they were in the wrong place. They were stopping and searching Israeli convoys carrying food along the road that had been a no-go route during the fighting. The convoys along the Burma Road were not challenged. They also carried food and within a week Joseph's warehouses had received an incredible 2,200 tons, enough on minimum rations to last New Jerusalem's 100,000 Jews four months. And the convoys kept on coming.

Like Ben-Gurion, Shaltiel was praying that the Arabs would be stupid enough to reject the peace proposal Bernadotte was preparing. It was essentially a re-working of the vitiated partition plan.

But what if the Arab League accepted Bernadotte's proposals? Assuming Ben-Gurion would then have no choice but to accept them, there would be weeks and probably months of negotiations to tidy up the situation on the ground—adjusting borders here and there. And the fighting Jews would be denied the opportunity to take more Arab land and conquer all of Jerusalem. The body of the Jewish state would be without its soul. *On the Israeli side the prospect of peace then was too awful to contemplate.* If the Arabs rejected Bernadotte's proposals, war would be resumed at the stroke of midnight on 9 July because the Israelis were not intending to wait for the Arabs to fire the first shot. In that event Shaltiel would not have too much trouble capturing the Old City. Or so he believed.

The first man to discover how seriously Britain was committed to the embargo on arms and ammunition to its Arab clients was Glubb. Though he was hoping the war would not be resumed, he decided that he had to take some precautions for defensive purposes. He flew to Suez to beg his old friend who commanded British forces in the Middle East to let him have some shells for his 25-pounder guns. It was, of course, a private and unofficial request. Nobody would ever know about it. As Glubb himself later revealed, the response he got was not the one he expected. "His feelings were with me but his orders were blunt and unequivocal—not one cartridge." Prior to the truce the Egyptian Army in the Suez Canal Zone had been allowed, discreetly, on the "q.t.", to draw ammunition from the British Army's stocks. Usually at midnight. That practice was ended when the truce came into effect.

There were a few Arab attempts to get around the arms embargo but none succeeded. The most notable failure was that of Colonel Fouad Mardam, a Syrian agent. He did succeed in acquiring some Czech-made arms. His problem was transporting them. He was eventually referred by the proprietor of his hotel to the Menara Shipping Agency on the Via del Corso in Rome. For quite a large amount of money it arranged for him to charter a 250-ton corvette, the *S.S. Arigo*. Relieved by the news that this vessel was on its way to Alexandria with his arms on board, Mardam cabled Damascus. The cable reached the Syrian capital but the *Arigo* did not get to Alexandria. Its cargo was unloaded in Tel Aviv. The Menara Shipping Agency was a front for Israeli intelligence agents. They probably tracked Mardam's every move.

On 27 June, Arab League prime ministers met in Cairo to consider Bernadotte's peace proposals. Before Abu Hoda left for the Egyptian capital Glubb said to him: *"We have no ammunition. For God's sake, no matter what happens, don't agree to resume fighting."*

The Arab leaders were trapped by their own propaganda. They couldn't tell their peoples the truth—that they were too weak and too dependent on foreign powers to do anything to prevent the creation of a Jewish state in Palestine.

If Egypt's prime minister had not reversed his "no more war" position, he and Abu Hoda might just have changed the course of history. But when Nokrashy said he was prepared to resume hostilities, Abu Hoda thought it would be unwise for Transjordan to be isolated. So it was, in just one session, that the assembled Arab League leaders, with "deep sorrow", unanimously rejected Bernadotte's proposals. The official statement said the Arab League could "not accept these proposals as a convenient basis for negotiations."

Why did the Arab League leaders decide to fight on? It was not because they believed they had anything to gain on the battlefield. They knew they were in a military mess and had already lost more Arab land than the partition plan had wanted them to give away. And they knew things could only get worse when the fighting was resumed. As Collins and Lapiere put it, "They had again been trapped by their own propaganda."

That is a fair judgment but there was more to it. The only alternative to just letting things happen was truth-telling. And that would have required Arab leaders to say something like the following to their peoples. "We believe, as you all do, that the creation of a Jewish state in Palestine is unfair and unjust, but there is nothing we can do about it—because we are too weak militarily and too dependent, because of history, on Britain and France who, in their turn, are too dependent on America." Complete honesty would have required them to add something like: "Painful though it is, we must now accept a small Zionist state in our midst in the hope that by doing so we can create the conditions that will make it impossible for that state to take more Arab land."

Arab leaders, frightened of their masses, opted for a resumption of the fighting to protect their own short-term survival interests.

A more rounded judgment, I think, would be something like this: Arab leaders, frightened of their masses, opted for a resumption of the fighting to protect their own short-term survival interests. In other words, they were playing politics—I mean politics without principle—and that made them no different from their pork-barrel American counterparts, the perfidious British and the French charlatans.

I think the "deep sorrow" of the Arab rejection was genuine, at least so far as Nokrashy and Abu Hoda were concerned. Egypt's prime minister had reversed his "no more war" position out of fear that, if he insisted on an end to the war, the Muslim Brotherhood would assassinate him.

Ben-Gurion and most of his leadership colleagues were delighted by the Arab League's rejection of Bernadotte's peace proposals. It saved Israel from having to say 'No' to the UN mediator.

Israel's rejection was transmitted to Bernadotte on 5 July. The grounds of it were that Bernadotte's proposals violated the provisions of the partition resolution. Given Israel's position on matters territorial this was pure humbug. Because the Arabs had started the war Ben-Gurion was insisting that Israel had the right to keep land which had been assigned to the Arab state of the partition plan and which Israeli forces had occupied in the fighting; but Ben-Gurion was also insisting that the Arabs should be required to withdraw from territory which had been assigned to the Jewish state of the partition plan and which they had occupied.

In his reply the following day, Bernadotte took Israel's humbug head on. In diplomatic language he said that whatever the legal status of the partition resolution, it was all they had to work with; and that none of the parties were free to accept those parts of the resolution which they liked and reject those parts to which they objected. Bernadotte's main point was that

Israel could not have it both ways. On the one hand it was saying that the partition resolution was its birth certificate and thus the source of the Jewish state's legitimacy. On the other hand, by keeping captured Arab land beyond the partition plan borders, it was denying that the partition resolution was also the birth certificate of an Arab state. In other words, Bernadotte was saying, the partition resolution was either the birth certificate of two states or it was nothing. By effectively denying the Arab state its birth certificate, Israel was also denying its own. (It bears repeating that partition plan proposal, before it was vitiated, had no status in international law because the UN had no right to give any part of Palestine away without consulting its inhabitants).

Even the Truman administration supported Bernadotte's reading of the riot act to Ben-Gurion. But Ben-Gurion was not willing to move an inch from his rejectionist position.

With only three days to go before the truce ended at midnight on 9 July, Bernadotte made one last attempt to prevent a resumption of the fighting in terms of full-scale war. (Both sides had violated the truce but the Israelis had gained much more than the Arabs from their violations). To give himself more negotiating time, Bernadotte called for both sides to accept a prolongation of the truce.

Ben-Gurion, with every fibre in his body, wanted to tell the UN mediator to go to hell. But the need of the moment was for good public relations. Ben-Gurion was persuaded by some of his leadership colleagues that if he said "No" to Bernadotte on this occasion, there was a danger of Israel being condemned by the whole of the international community as a pariah state. So Israel's leader said "Yes", he was willing to accept a prolongation of the truce.

Two decades later Ben-Gurion confessed that his only fear at the time was the Arabs would also say "Yes" to a prolongation of the truce.

Two decades later, Ben-Gurion confessed that his only fear at the time was that the Arabs would say "Yes" to a prolongation of the truce.

In private the Arab League informed Bernadotte that the Arab armies would not be ordered to resume the fighting when the truce ended; and that was the message the UN mediator passed to the Israelis. With the IDF poised to take the war to the Arabs one second after midnight on 9 July, Ben-Gurion could have responded by saying, "Let's wait and see if the Arabs mean what they said to Bernadotte." Instead he chose to take the Arabs' reluctance to say publicly that they were not intending to resume the fighting as the justification he so desperately wanted to re-start the war.

During the truce the Israelis added 60,000 men to the IDF's fighting strength. When the war was resumed it was no contest. Some 90,000 well-armed Israelis were taking on not more than 21,000 Arab regular soldiers who were without the ammunition and the weapons to offer more than token resistance. From here on, it was the Arab (Palestinian) state of the partition plan that was in danger of annihilation. Not the Jewish state.

The vision of Israel gobbling up what was left of Palestine, including the Old City of Jerusalem, provoked real alarm in the Truman administration, especially on the part of those in executive positions who had always believed that the creation of a Jewish state in the face of Arab opposition was not in America's interests. And there was real panic in the Security Council. On 14 July it issued a demand to all the warring parties for "an immediate and indefinite end to the fighting".

Arab League leaders responded almost immediately. In a short cable to UN Secretary General Lie they now said (for all the world to hear) "Yes."

This time the speed of the Arab response was not at all to Ben-Gurion's liking. But the Israeli most bothered by it was Shaltiel in New Jerusalem. On the morning of 15 July he reckoned he needed three to four more days to defeat Tell's forces and capture the Old City. And then he learned he had only 48 hours. Bernadotte had fixed the ceasefire in Jerusalem for 5.00 a.m. on Saturday 17 July, two days before it was to take effect in the rest of the country—Israel and what was still left of Palestine.

Shaltiel assembled his staff. His message was brief, to the point and emotional. The second cease-fire would almost certainly end the war. What they did not get in the next 48 hours, actually less, might be lost for years and perhaps for generations to come. He had no need to remind them of the historic importance that the conquest of the Old City would have for the state of Israel and all Jewish people, but he did. "What glory will fall upon us if it is we who conquer Jerusalem for our generation and all subsequent generations of Jewry."

At sundown that evening Shaltiel assembled his staff again. This time, for them to listen to him rehearsing his victory speech. It began: "I have the supreme honour to announce that the forces of the city of Jerusalem have liberated all of the city and we hand it over to the people of Israel with pride!"

In the Old City, Tell was fully aware that he and his Bedouin defenders were about to be hit with everything Shaltiel now had, including, no doubt, heavy artillery. But the Arab commander had also prepared a text for the moment. Not a victory speech but an order of the day. He had it radioed to all of his positions. *"Let every true Believer resolve to stand or die. We shall defend the Holy City to the last man and the last bullet. Tonight there will be no retreat!"*

In three hours, with thanks to Ben-Gurion's embargo busters, Shaltiel poured more than 500 shells into the Old (Arab) City. That was as much in an hour as the New (Jewish) City had received in a day when the Arab Legion was shelling it.

But when the ceasefire in Jerusalem came into effect, the Old City was still in the Arab Legion's control. More than a few of the attacking Israeli officers and men wanted to ignore the ceasefire and capture the Old City, but Shaltiel said "No". So Jerusalem was divided and was to remain so for another 19 years.

The second ceasefire came into general effect on 19 July and lasted until 15 October. Before it ended, Bernadotte was assassinated by the Stern Gang. (Why has its context in the next chapter.)

About what Israel might have achieved but for the "imposition" of the second cease-fire, Allon was later to write this:

> ...the Israeli offensive might have continued more or less unabated, shifting the main effort from one front to another until a complete destruction of the enemy, or at least his withdrawal from the entire territory of Mandatory Palestine had been achieved.[3]

That was something of an understatement. If Ben-Gurion had had his way in cabinet, the Jewish state that emerged from the first Arab–Israeli conflict might very well have been in existence on virtually the "entire territory of Mandatory Palestine". In other words, Zionism's Greater Israel project would not have been put on hold.

On 26 September, for example, Ben-Gurion proposed to the cabinet a major military offensive to capture much of the West Bank. This despite the fact that King Abdullah had honoured his promise not to attack the Jewish state of the partition plan, a promise he had made on the understanding that Israel would respond favourably to his annexation of the territory assigned to the Arabs including, obviously and especially, the West Bank. With his proposal to the cabinet Ben-Gurion was indicating his desire to screw the Hashemite monarch as well as the Palestinians. The IDF could have captured the entire West Bank. All it needed was the order to move. The cabinet was evenly divided, split. Six ministers voted for Ben-Gurion's proposal and six voted against it. As a consequence Ben-Gurion shelved his proposal, but not before he described the decision as a cause for "mourning for generations to come."[4]

Shlaim's conclusion was that whatever his motives for shelving his proposal and not bringing it up again, "Ben-Gurion bore the ultimate responsibility for the political decision to leave the West Bank in the hands of King Abdullah."[5] (As we shall see, the 1967 war was all about Israel's hawks doing what Ben-Gurion had failed to do in 1948).

With the West Bank option effectively vetoed by some of his cabinet colleagues, Ben-Gurion then turned his mind to the Egyptian front. *As he was doing so, Israel received a peace feeler from King Farouk*. The Egyptian monarch had not only lost interest in Palestine, he was desperate for a way out. Through his emissary, Kamal Riad, he was offering Egypt's *de facto* recognition of Israel in exchange for a strip of territory in the Negev. Most of it had been assigned to the Jewish state of the partition plan and a part of it was still occupied by Egyptian forces. Farouk's message to Ben-Gurion was effectively this: "Help me to save face by keeping just a little bit of the Negev, and I will recognise the Jewish state."

The wise Moshe Sharett, Israel's first foreign minister, wanted to explore this offer but Ben-Gurion brushed it aside. Then, on 6 October,

Ben-Gurion presented the cabinet with a proposal to renew the war against Egypt. This time Ben-Gurion got his way. And on 15 October, Israel broke the ceasefire and launched an offensive against Egyptian forces in the south. It was to lead to tensions in the Truman administration and a moment of crisis in Britain's relationship with America.

Forrestal's diary entry for 31 December included this: "Palestine. Lovett said [at a cabinet meeting] that Israeli troops had apparently invaded Egypt. Specifically, they were reported to have attacked an airfield within the Egyptian border; that it was reported the British would notify us that the failure of the Israelis to withdraw promptly would automatically bring into operation the Anglo Egyptian Mutual Defence Pact."[6]

Advancing Israeli forces had entered Egyptian territory (Sinai) on 28 December. One small mobile task force penetrated to within 40 miles of the Suez Canal, then still in British hands. Allon's subsequent account of the events included this:

> The entire Egyptian army had in fact been cut off from Egypt (Egypt west of the Suez Canal) and it seemed that it was about to be finally defeated. The main Israeli task-force was standing at the gates of El-Arish, ready for the last blow when the government, acting under American political pressure, ordered the advance to be stopped and all troops to be withdrawn from Sinai. The order was deeply resented by the troops; but their discipline was such that they nevertheless complied with it, and by 5 January the last Israeli soldier had left Sinai.[7]

Without British pressure on the Truman administration, the Israelis would have been free to cut the remnants of the trapped and bedraggled Egyptian army to pieces.

A week after Israel broke the ceasefire and launched its offensive to destroy the Egyptian army in the Negev and, Israel's military hawks hoped, the whole of the Sinai peninsula, Forrestal had expressed his thoughts about what was happening in the Middle East to a meeting of the NSC. He had just learned of an unexpected request from the State Department for 6,000 American troops to be used as a "guard force" in Jerusalem, apparently to assist the implementation of Bernadotte's peace plan. With some bitterness Forrestal said the request was another example of "the disconnection in our policy-making", and of how the Palestine situation "has drifted without any clear consequent formulation of United States policy by the NSC."[8] He also repeated his long held view that America's Palestine policy had been made for "squalid political purposes."[9] He concluded by saying that he hoped, some day, to be able to "make my position clear on this issue."[10]

The implication is that if Forrestal had lived, he would have written an insider's book about the corruption of American foreign policy making and the need to clean it up—if those with Executive responsibility for protecting

U.S. interests and security were to be allowed to do their jobs to the best of their professional ability, and in a way the people of America had a right to expect. (As I write, my thoughts return to the question of Forrestal's apparent suicide. Did he jump or was he pushed?)

The first Arab-Israeli war was brought to a formal end by a series of Armistice Agreements—with Egypt on 24 February (1949); with Lebanon on 23 March; with Transjordan on 3 April; and with Syria on 20 July.

As a consequence of the first Arab-Israeli war the name of Palestine was erased from the map. On the ground there was no entity left that could be called Palestine. The partition plan had assigned 56.4 percent of it to a Jewish state. Israel ended up with nearly 80 percent. And the parts of Palestine the Israelis did not take were annexed: the West Bank by Transjordan—after which the extended Hashemite kingdom became Jordan with a majority Palestinian population; and the Gaza Strip by Egypt. The only downside for Zionism—a big one emotionally but without military significance—was that the Old City of Jerusalem was beyond its grasp. For the time being.

As a consequence of the first Arab-Israeli war, the name of Palestine was erased from the map. On the ground, there was no entity that could be called Palestine.

And nearly 800,000 Palestinians were refugees, homeless and stateless, most of them existing on the margins of life, mainly in squalid camps in the frontline Arab states. Yitzhak Rabin was one of the Israeli officers who directed the shellfire that drove terrified Palestinians from their homeland in the last phase of Israel's ethnic cleansing programme.

If Israel, the big powers and the governments of the Arab States had had their way, the signing of the Armistice Agreements would have been the end of the Palestine problem. The Palestine file was closed. And it was to remain closed. There was NOT to be a regeneration of Palestinian nationalism because, if there was, a confrontation with Zionism might be unavoidable. And nobody at leadership level anywhere, including the Arab regimes, wanted that.

The main point being made here is critical to real understanding of what really happened after the first Arab–Israeli war. *The Arab regimes did not want a regeneration of Palestinian nationalism.* Though they could never acknowledge in public the reality of the Arab situation, they knew what it was. A continuing fight would not be with Israel alone but with Israel and America—not America actually, but America effectively, because of its support for Zionism right or wrong. *And that, Arab leaders told themselves behind closed doors, was a fight they could not win.*

In the years to come the main problem for everybody in authority almost everywhere, Arab leaders especially, was Yasser Arafat. He was determined to make the regeneration of Palestinian nationalism happen. The evidence is that it could have been prevented from happening—Arafat and his leadership colleagues could have been stopped from developing enough momentum to press their claim for a minimum amount of justice for their people—if Israel, the real Goliath, had been willing to make peace with the frontline Arab states. It could not because it was a Zionist state, not a Jewish state.

3

BERNADOTTE'S ASSASSINATION

Such hope as there was that Zionism's territorial ambitions could be contained by diplomacy was invested in Count Bernadotte, the UN Mediator. Because he was acting for the organised international community, he was not without some real influence and political clout. If the U.S. did not veto his proposals, it was likely that whatever he proposed would become UN policy.

By the middle of September 1948, two months into the second ceasefire and one month before Israel broke it to get more of what it wanted by military means, Bernadotte had completed and submitted to the Secretary General a 35,000-word report on the situation. And he was on a tour of the Arab world, Israel and Jerusalem. Though his report and its recommendations were not then in the public domain, all the major players were aware of what he believed had to happen if there was to be peace after protracted negotiations. For starters, all the parties had to agree that the partition resolution, whatever its actual legal significance and status, had to be the basis for discussion. That meant:

- Israel and the Arabs would have to be satisfied with something very like the vitiated partition plan borders. "Something like" implied that in negotiations, and subject to the agreement of the parties themselves, Israel and the Arabs could swap land, but that neither the Jewish state nor the Arab state should have in total more land than had been assigned to them by the partition plan.

- Jerusalem, undivided, had to be an international city under UN trusteeship.

- Israel had to allow the Palestinian refugees to return to their homes. At the time, and because Israel's main offensive to expel Palestinians was still in the near future, there were about 300,000 refugees.

Everything the UN Mediator represented (with the support of the international community) was an anathema to Ben-Gurion, most of his leadership colleagues, the IDF and, especially, those who had contributed to the creation of the state of Israel and the Palestinian refugee problem by playing the terror game.

For Friday 17 September, Bernadotte had two engagements in his diary: a conference with Palestinians in Ramallah and a meeting in New or Jewish-controlled Jerusalem with Dov Joseph, who by then had the title of Military Governor.

As Bernadotte was preparing to leave Ramallah, somebody told him that cars were often shot at and that it might be safer for him to travel to the Jewish area by a roundabout route, entering it at the last possible moment instead of passing through it to his meeting point.

According to General Lundstroem, the Head of the UN Truce observers, who was travelling with Bernadotte, the UN Mediator replied: "I will not do that. I have to take the same risks as my Observers, and moreover, I think that no one has the right to refuse me permission to cross the line."[1]

Thus it was that the man in whom hope for peace had been invested by the organised international community set out for Jewish-controlled Jerusalem in a small convoy. Three cars. Two flying the UN flag and one a Red Cross flag.

The lead car in the convoy was driven by Major Massart (a Frenchman) with Captain Moshe Hillman, an Israeli Army Liaison Officer, sitting beside him in the front seat. The rear passengers were Miss Barbara Wessel, Bernadotte's personal secretary, Lt. Col. Flachs and Major DeGreer, all Swedish.

The second car was driven by Colonel Frank Begley of the UN Secretariat with Commander Cox, an American, sitting beside him in the front seat. The rear passengers were General Lundstroem, the UN Mediator himself and his assistant, Colonel Serot.

They had a late lunch at the Y.M.C.A. in the neutral Red Cross zone and then, with the afternoon advancing, crossed into Jewish controlled Jerusalem. What happened at five minutes past five was later described to UN staff by General Lundstroem.

> In the Katamon Quarter we were held up by a Jewish Army type jeep placed in a road-block and filled with men in Jewish Army uniform. I saw a man running from the jeep, but I took little notice because I thought it was merely another checkpoint. However, he pushed a Tommy gun through the open window at my side and fired point blank at Count Bernadotte and Colonel Serot.
>
> I also heard shots fired from other points and there was considerable confusion. The Jewish Liaison officer told Begley to drive away as quickly as possible. In the meantime the assailant was still firing. Colonel Serot fell

> in the seat towards me and I saw immediately that he was dead. Count Bernadotte went forward and I thought at the time he was trying to take cover. I asked him, 'Are you wounded?' He merely nodded and fell back. I helped him to lie down in the car and I saw that he was seriously wounded as there was a considerable amount of blood on his clothes, especially around the heart.[2]

General Lundstroem then ordered Begley to rush them to the Hadassah Hospital, which they reached in a few minutes. There, and as the account in *The Palestine Post* put it, "doctors could only confirm that both men were dead."[3]

Bernadotte had taken three bullets, two of them just above his heart.

Ben-Gurion's government pledged that it would do everything in its power to "track down the murderers and their accomplices and bring them to justice." But as so often was to be the case with Israel's words, they were not matched by deeds. Though the names of the Stern Gang's hit-team were known to Ben-Gurion, they were never brought to justice. And nor was the operation's mastermind—the man who targeted Bernadotte and sanctioned his assassination.

In 1977, an Israeli, Dr. Michael Bar Zohar, writing in the U.S. under the name of Michael Barak, told a press conference marking the publication of a new book on Ben-Gurion that one of the three assassins, Yehoshva Zeitler, was a "best friend" of Israel's founding father. Zeitler himself was quoted as saying: "We executed Bernadotte because he was a one-man institution who endangered the status of Jerusalem by his declared intention of turning her into an international city. He was hostile to Israel from the moment the state was established and actually laid the foundation for the present UN policy of supporting the Arabs."[4]

According to those who ought to know, the mastermind, the one who targeted Bernadotte and sanctioned his murder, was the Stern Gang's director of operations, Yitzhak Shamir, who, when he emerged from the shadows many years later, would become Begin's foreign minister and then his successor as prime minister. During his later years in the shadows—the 1960s and the early 1970s especially, Shamir was the chief adviser to, and perhaps even the director of, the department of Mossad that was responsible for the assassination of scores of Palestinians across Western Europe.

UN General Assembly Resolution 194 enshrined the right of Palestinian refugees to return to their homes or to receive compensation for loss of their property.

Bernadotte's insistence that Israel had to allow the Palestinian refugees to return to their homes did not die with him. It was enshrined less than a month after his murder in another resolution of the UN General Assembly—number 194 of 11 December 1948. *It was to become famous on account of Israel's contempt for it.*

Article 11 of that resolution stated:

> The General Assembly of the United Nations" Resolves that the refugees wishing to return to their homes and live in peace with their neighbours should be permitted to do so at the earliest practicable date, and that compensation should be paid for the property of those choosing not to return and for loss of, or damage to property which, under principles of international law or in equity, should be made good by the Governments or authorities responsible.

For a particular purpose Israel said it would accept its obligations as set down in UN resolutions, including 194; but, as events were to prove, it had absolutely no intention of doing so.

The purpose was Israel's admission to the UN. *The membership application required Israel to say that it would implement the resolutions of the world body. If the Jewish state had not been willing to give that undertaking, its application could not have been considered.*

Israel's application was considered and approved and, on 11 May 1949, the formal invitation to the Jewish state was in the shape of another resolution—273 of the General Assembly. It noted the declaration by the State of Israel that it "unreservedly accepts the obligations of the United Nations Charter and undertakes to honour them from the day when it becomes a Member of the United Nations." Because its undertaking was accepted in good faith, the resolution also declared Israel to be "a peace-loving state."

But within three weeks, punctuated by Forrestal's suicide, the notion of Israel as "a peace-loving state" which "unreservedly" accepted its obligations was to be questioned by no less a person than President Truman.

When Israel broke the second ceasefire and launched its offensive on 15 October (1948), it was intending not only to destroy the remnants of the Egyptian army in the south and tidy up the situation on the ground with the Syrians in the north. *It was also determined to escalate military activities that were designed to put to flight, expel, as many as possible of the indigenous Arab inhabitants from all the land the IDF had then occupied and the additional land it was intending to occupy* (nearly 80 per cent of Mandatory Palestine by the time of the Armistice agreements).

It was as a result of that final ethnic cleansing push that a further 500,000 Palestinians became refugees, taking their total to about 800,000. For many years Zionism's story—the Palestinians departed in answer to the calls of their absent leaders to leave clear fields of fire for the Arab armies—was widely believed by the general public of the Western world. Today, and due in part to the belated truth-telling of some Israelis who participated in the expulsion of the Palestinians, Zionism's story is widely seen for what it was—not simply a propaganda lie but an outright perversion of the truth.

Among those who played a leading role in the final ethnic cleansing push of 1948 was the man destined to become the principal architect and, one might also say, the structural engineer and on-site manager of Zionism's "Greater Israel" project—Israel's one-eyed warlord, Moshe Dayan. (That he also became Israel's most illustrious and respected critic of Palestinian terrorism is more than a touch ironic). On 11 July 1948 Dayan and his IDF force attacked the Arab town of Lydda, today the location of Tel Aviv airport. In their book *A Clash of Destinies* published by Frederick A. Praeger in 1960, Jon and David Kimche, pro-Zionist writers, described what happened. "Dayan drove at full speed into L*ydda shooting up the town and creating confusion and a degree of terror among the population... Its Arab population fled or were herded on the road to Ramallah. The next day Ramleh also surrendered and its Arab populous suffered the same fate.*" [Emphasis added]

President Truman, whose starting concern had been the plight of Jewish refugees in Europe, became increasingly disturbed by Israel's policy of forcing the Palestinians out—creating Arab refugees. The more he received reports of what was actually happening, the more his relations with the Zionists of America and Israel cooled.

By 28 May, six days after Forrestal's death, which must have shaken him, Truman was so troubled that he sent a strong and angry note to Israel.

It expressed his "deep disappointment at the Israeli refusal to make any of the desired concessions on refugees and boundaries."[5] It demanded that "Israel withdraw to the boundaries of the partition plan." It urged Israel "to allow Palestinian refugees to return to their homes." And, remarkably, Truman said he interpreted Israel's attitude as being "in opposition to the General Assembly's resolutions" and "dangerous to peace."[6]

Even more remarkably, Truman warned that if Israel continued in her attitude, "the U.S. will regretfully be forced to the conclusion that a revision of its attitude toward Israel has become unavoidable."[7]

It might have been that as he was composing or approving the text of his note to Israel, the President recalled Lovett's advice that he should not recognise the Jewish state until they had some idea of what kind of state it was going to be—a state worthy of U.S. recognition or "a pig in a poke".

Ten days later, in a formal note of reply, Israel rejected Truman's demand and his urgings. "The war", the Israeli note said, "has proved the indispensability to the survival of Israel of certain vital areas not comprised originally in the share (of Palestine) of the Jewish state." So far as the Palestinians refugees were concerned, they were "members of an aggressor group defeated in a war of its own making."[8]

Translated, Israel's message to Truman with regard to the Palestinian refugees was effectively: "They fought and lost and have thereby forfeited any rights they may have had. They can go to hell as, frankly Mr. President, can you if you persist with your attitude."

Most Israeli leaders were incapable of considering (as Nahum Goldmann had done) the possibility that war might very well have been avoided if Ben-Gurion had not been so determined to have it.

At the State Department Israel's reply to Truman was analysed by Dean Rusk, then deputy undersecretary. He wrote: "With regard to the refugees, the note repeats the familiar arguments blaming the Arab states for the plight of these people..." Rusk also underlined Israel's continued rejection of any territorial settlement and pointed out that "the basic positions of the United States and Israel thus remain unchanged and there is no reason for the United States to abandon the firm position it has taken as regards Israel."[9]

While Rusk was writing those words, Truman was coming under great and mounting pressure from Niles and Clifford to back away from any confrontation with Israel and its supporters in America. Two days later, still apparently confident that President Truman would stand firm, the State Department sent him a top-secret memorandum. It recommended the action to be taken to press Israel, in accordance with the UN resolutions which were the basis of U.S. policy, to agree to withdraw to the partition plan borders, to allow Palestinian refugees to return to their homes and to accept that Jerusalem would become an international city.

The steps recommended were:

> 1. Immediate adoption of a generally negative attitude toward Israel. This would include refusing Israeli requests for U.S. assistance, such as the training of Israeli officials in this country and the sending of U.S. experts to Israel, maintenance of not more than a correct attitude toward Israeli officials in this country and toward American organisations promoting the cause of Israel, and failing to support the position of Israel in the various international organisations.
>
> 2. Export-Import Bank loan. The Export-Import Bank should be immediately informed that it would be desirable to hold up the $49 million as yet uncollected of the $100 million earmarked for loan to Israel.
>
> 3. U.S. contributions to Israel. The time is appropriate to undertake exploring as to whether it is proper, now that the Jewish state has been established as an independent foreign country, for U.S. contributions to the United Jewish Appeal and to other Jewish fundraising organisations to continue to be exempt from income tax as having been made for charitable purposes. Such contributions are now of direct benefit to a sovereign foreign country.[10]

The memorandum added that a reply to the Israeli note would be drafted "answering the points made and re-iterating the U.S. expectation that Israel will take action along the lines suggested by the U.S."[11]

Zionism then launched its counterattack against the State

Department. James G. McDonald, by now the U.S. Ambassador to Israel, cabled Clifford, not the State Department, to inform him that President Truman's personal note to Israel had "embittered Israeli opinion." As a consequence, McDonald's cable said, Prime Minister Ben-Gurion and Foreign Minister Sharett might be forced "despite their will and better judgment to resist demands." On the other hand, "Israeli concessions with refugees are possible if request for these is not again put in form of demand..." [12]

On President Truman's watch there were no more attempts to put pressure on Israel. And it was to be McDonald himself who, as Lilienthal put it, "later reported the subsequent U.S. retreat." In his own book, *My Mission to Israel*, McDonald wrote: "The next American note abandoned completely the stern tone of its predecessor... More and more Washington ceased to lay down the law to Tel Aviv."[13]

The reality thereafter was that Tel Aviv was more and more laying down the law to Washington.

It was to be many years before the State Department's proposals for the U.S. to get tough with Israel were deemed to be fit for consumption by the general public. When the State Department's top-secret memorandum was de-classified in 1977, it made the front pages of Israel's newspapers. Over a story by Wolf Blitzer, its correspondent in Washington, the headline in *The Jerusalem Post* was U.S. PRESSURED ISRAEL TO WITHDRAW IN 1949. In fact the headline and the story missed the point. *The State Department had wanted Israel to be pressured, but it never happened.*

President Truman had wanted to get tough with Israel, but he concluded, as almost all of his successors in the White House were to do in their turns, that, beyond a point, putting pressure on Israel was likely to be counterproductive with regard to developments in the Middle East—i.e. would cause Israel to be more, not less, intransigent, and would result in too much political damage on the U.S. home front because of the awesome power of the Zionist lobby and its allies.

At a point Ben-Gurion did sanction the making of an Israeli offer to allow up to 100,000 Palestinian refugees to return to their homes. But that was to be Israel's contribution to a once-and-for-all settlement of the Palestine refugee problem. Ben-Gurion knew the offer would not be acceptable and that he would not have to deliver on it. He would not have made the offer if he had thought otherwise.

Between 1948 and 1973, 385 Arab villages, most including cemeteries and tombstones, were erased from the face of the earth.

Thereafter Israel's policy was to see to it that the Palestinian refugees had no homes to return to.

Prior to Israel's unilateral declaration of independence and the first Arab–Israeli war it triggered, there were 475 villages in Arab Palestine's 15 districts. That essential fact of real history was established by Dr. Israel Shahak, a survivor of the Nazi death-camps and the founder of the Israeli League for Human and Civil Rights. His report, *Arab Villages Destroyed in Israel*, was first published in mimeographed form in February 1973. It had to be smuggled out of Israel for printing in London and Washington.

Introducing the details in his report, Shahak wrote:

> The truth about Arab settlements in the area of the State of Israel before 1948 is one of the most closely guarded secrets of Israeli life. No publication, book or pamphlet gives either their number or their location. This is done on purpose so that the accepted official myth of an 'empty country' can be taught in schools and told to visitors."

The story that emerged from the clinical details was that between 1948 and 1973, 385 Arab villages, three-quarters of the lot including cemeteries and tombstones, had been destroyed, erased from the face of the earth by the Israeli authorities. As the bulldozers had gone about their work in one place after another, passing visitors had been told by Israeli demolition experts, Shahak reported, "That was all a desert."

On 4 April 1969, the Israeli newspaper *Ha'aretz* quoted Defence Minister Dayan as telling students of the Haifa Technion School: "There is not a single Jewish village in this country that has not been built on the site of an Arab village."[14]

When Israel came into being it was promulgated not as the state of people living on a particular chunk of land but as the state of the "Jewish people"— Jews, everywhere, this despite the fact, as I noted in Volume One, that few if any of the Jews who went to Palestine in answer to Zionism's call had any biological connection to the ancient Hebrews and were thus without a valid hereditary claim to the land. (In fact, and as stated by Israeli journalist Tom Segev in his review of a book published in Hebrew by Resling in 2008 with the title *When and How Was the Jewish People Invented?*, "There never was a Jewish people, only a Jewish religion." The author of the book Segev reviewed for Ha'aretz is Tel Aviv University scholar and professor, Shlomo Sand. His purpose is to promote the idea that Israel should be "a state of all its citizens"—Jews, Arabs and others—in contrast to its declared identity as a Jewish state). It was therefore entirely logical from the Zionist perspective that Israel would enact a Law of Return. It did so in 1950. While nearly 800,000 Palestinian refugees were denied their right of return to their land and homes from which most of them had been expelled by Zionist terrorism and more conventional applications of Zionist military might, the Law of Return granted to foreign nationals of any country in the world, provided only that they were Jewish, the right to

The Israeli Law of Return granted to foreign nationals of any country in the world—provided only that they were Jewish—the right to citizenship in Israel, while denying displaced Palestinians their right to return to their land and homes.

emigrate to Israel and, instantly upon arrival, to become citizens of it, with all the rights that conveyed.

Initially only a small number of Jews wanted to emigrate to Palestine that became Israel. Somebody with authority in Israel was so concerned by the apparent lack of enthusiasm that Israeli agents were given a very delicate assignment. They were required to pose as Arab terrorists and plant bombs to scare Iraqi Jews into going to Israel to swell the numbers; and set a precedent for Jewish citizens of other Arab lands and Iran to follow. (Today informed Israelis know that is what happened).

By the early 1970s, the Jews in Israel were from 102 countries and spoke 81 languages.

From the moment of little Israel's birth, those of its political and military leaders who were hell-bent on further territorial expansion were, of course, aware of what had to happen if they and their heirs and successors were to have a free enough hand to do it, and get away with it—the it being the creation of Greater Israel. The imperative was for the Jewish state to be perceived in the Western world, in America especially, as being in constant danger of annihilation, when in reality, as we are beginning to see, Israel's existence was never in danger from any combination of Arab military force. Only then, when there was the perception in the Western world of the Jewish state's very existence being in danger, would Israel have the necessary political and propaganda scope to portray its aggression (in pursuit of more land and teaching the Arabs to be subservient) as self-defence.

From its beginning Zionism was about deception, deceiving even the Jews of the world about what had to be done in Palestine if it was to become a refuge of last resort for them. In due course the Zionist state would be allowed by the Western world not only to interpret UN resolutions as it wished and reject them at will without any sanction—beyond, sometimes, a slap on the wrist from Washington. With the complicity of the mainstream media, the Zionist state would also be allowed to give new and opposite meanings to important concept words and phrases—as in the claim of self-defence when the reality was aggression. This was a remarkable tribute to two things: the fear almost all Western politicians have of offending Zionism and inviting its wrath, and being accused of anti-Semitism; and the genius, and also the ruthlessness, of those who masterminded and executed Zionism's propaganda campaign.

But it was the Nazi holocaust that gave them the cards for a winning hand. In Zionism's mind it justifies everything including assassination and state terrorism.

4

ISRAEL SAYS "NO" TO PEACE

When the first Arab-Israeli war was ended by the signing of the four Armistice Agreements between February and July of 1949, the most important question waiting for an answer was this: Could Israel be a *normal* state—one that abided by the rules of international law, complied with UN resolutions and generally behaved in a reasonable and responsible way?

Events were to demonstrate that the answer was no.

The most important question awaiting an answer was: Could Israel be a normal state—one that abided by the rules of international law, and generally behaved in a reasonable and responsible way?

An explanation of why was provided by the illustrious Abba Eban on 20 November 1974, by which time he was a former Israeli foreign minister. On that November day he addressed an audience of American students and professors on the campus of the William Patterson College in Wayne, New Jersey. He said:

> *Israel could never be a normal state because its memories are not normal—with six million wiped out, centuries of persecution.*[1] [Emphasis added]

The implication was that the behaviour of Zionism's child, however outrageous (not to mention counter-productive), had to be excused and accepted in that context. Eban was not saying he believed that whatever Israel did was justified by centuries of persecution and the Nazi holocaust. His meaning was that most Israelis and far too many Jews of the world did so believe, not overtly in most cases but covertly—in their sub-consciousness.

There was one Israeli leader (Eban's first boss) who wanted Israel to become a normal state and make the earliest possible peace with the frontline Arab states. That man was Moshe Shertock who became Moshe Sharett. He was Israel's first foreign minister from 1949 to 1956; and for an all-too-brief period, 1953 to 1955, he doubled as foreign minister and prime minister while Ben-Gurion was resting.

Essentially there were two kinds of Israeli political and military leaders—doves and hawks. (In the simple-minded American approach to labelling, Arabs could call the doves "the good guys" and the hawks "the bad guys.") Sharett was the founding father of the dovish tendency at mainstream leadership level.

I think Shlaim's most perceptive summary of Sharett and his significance is as close to the truth as one can get.

> Sharett was a balanced man in unbalanced times, a man of peace in an era of violence, a negotiator on behalf of a society that spurned negotiations, a man of compromise in a political culture that equated compromise with cowardice. His temperamental incompatibility with Ben-Gurion had been apparent for some time. But their recurrent clashes over policy had deeper roots in their outlooks on Israel's place in the world. Ben-Gurion was a great believer in the Jewish revolution. His principal tenet was self-reliance. He strongly believed that the revived Jewish nation in its historic homeland could be guided by its own, unique code of morality. Sharett put the emphasis on Jewish normality rather than Jewish uniqueness. His principal tenet was international co-operation and the peaceful settlement of disputes. He strongly believed that international law and the prevailing norms of international behaviour were binding on Israel, and it was his ambition to turn Israel into a respectable and reasonable member of international society.[2]

The quality of Sharett's insight into what would be in store for Israel if the hawks had their way was indicated by his diary entry for 12 October 1955, shortly before Ben-Gurion reclaimed the dual role of prime minister and defence minister. In just one short sentence Prime Minister Sharett expressed his Forrestal-like sense of despair. "*What is our vision on this earth—war to the end of generations and life by the sword?*"[3]

This Chapter and the next two tell the story of how Sharett and all he represented—a non-violent solution to Israel's problems with the Arabs—was destroyed by Ben-Gurion and his protégé, Moshe Dayan; and how as a consequence Zionism's child took its first confident steps along the road to "war to the end of all generations."

In Zionism's version of history, victorious Israel wanted peace and the leaders of the defeated Arab states did not. Arab leaders, Zionism's version of history insisted, were committed to the destruction of the Jewish state and, as a consequence, there was nobody on the Arab side for Israel to talk peace with.

The truth? As Shlaim said in his revision of Israel's history: "*The files of the Israeli Foreign Ministry, for example, burst with evidence of Arab peace feelers and Arab readiness to negotiate with Israel from September 1948 on.*"[4] [Emphasis added]

There were two main reasons why Zionism got away with telling its lies virtually without challenge for so many years.

One was to do with the fact that Arab leaders did not want the truth known (which is why this book will require a courageous publisher, if it is to be released in Arabic in the Arab World). Simply stated, *Arab leaders, particularly those of the frontline states, did not want their peoples to know that they had been prepared in the aftermath of defeat to engage with the Jewish state in a constructive dialogue for peace*. The Arab record of these efforts was not for publication because Arab leaders feared, with good reason, that they and their regimes would not survive the truth-telling in the face of Israeli rejectionism.

The truth about Israel's responses to the first Arab peace initiatives remained locked away from public scrutiny for decades. For their part the regimes of the frontline Arab states didn't want their own peoples to know they had been seeking an accommodation with Israel and had been further humiliated by Israeli rejectionism.

After Israel's victory on the battlefield, the humiliated Arab masses were much more hostile to the Jewish state than in the days when it was only a concept. Because of the passions of the Arab "street", doing business with Israel required two things on the part of Arab leaders—real courage and an investment in Israel's good faith, an investment which Arab leaders feared, with very good reason, would be misplaced.

The other reason for the long life of Zionism's lies was that the record of Israel's responses to the first Arab peace initiatives was locked away in classified state papers and the heads of the participating Israeli diplomats and military men. *The Iron Wall* is indispensable reading for those wanting to know in detail what really happened because Shlaim had access to that original source material and interviewed many surviving key players.

One of the endorsements on the back cover of Penguin's paperback edition of Shlaim's book is by Ethan Bronner of *The New York Times* Book Review: "Fascinating ... Shlaim presents compelling evidence for a revaluation of traditional Israeli history." And the endorsements on the first page of the same edition included this from Arnold Wesker: "I've lined up a book I'm dreading to read, *The Iron Wall* by the brilliant young Israeli historian Avi Shlaim, who I fear may scuttle some cherished views."

As I indicated in the Prologue, the thought that drove the writing of *Zionism: The Real Enemy of the Jews* is that peace will not have a chance until the "cherished views" of enough Israelis and Jews everywhere are scuttled.

As I mentioned in Chapter Two of this volume, the first Arab peace feeler—an offer of *de facto* recognition of Israel—was from King Farouk in September 1948, when the Armistice Agreements were still some way off. The Egyptian monarch's emissary, Kamal Riad, conveyed the offer in talks in Paris with Elias Sasson, the head of the Middle East Department of the Israeli Foreign Ministry and a leading dove. Sharett wanted to explore the Egyptian proposition but Ben-Gurion brushed it aside—because he was already committed in his own mind to breaking the second truce and resuming the war.

Sharett bottled his disappointment and gave priority to political forward planning. On his instruction the Middle East department in the Foreign Ministry set about the task of exploring various plans for a Palestinian government. Sharett was in favour of something very like the two-state solution of the partition plan.

Ben-Gurion responded by discouraging political planning of any kind while Israel was in a position to exploit its military advantage on the ground—i.e. before the IDF was obliged to stop fighting by Israel's signature on Armistice Agreements.

In all probability Israel would not have concluded Armistice Agreements with the frontline Arab states when it did—i.e. would have gone on fighting to take more Arab land and teach the Arabs even more of a lesson about who was the master of the region—but for the diplomatic skills and tenacity, and the inexhaustible energy, of a black American diplomat. His name was Bunche. Dr. Ralph Johnson Bunche. At the request of a desperately worried Secretary General and a deeply troubled Security Council, he had taken on the awesome task of completing Bernadotte's mission. His official title was Acting UN Mediator.

Among the moving spirits and founding fathers of the UN there were those who wondered if the world body as the maker and keeper of peace could survive the double whammy of Zionism's subversion of the General Assembly's decision-making process and Bernadotte's murder. And behind closed doors at the UN's headquarters, and all the foreign policy establishments of the Western world, there was real fear that the assessment Secretary of State Marshall had made, and which Defence Secretary Forrestal had endorsed, would prove to be correct. A fire started in the Middle East might well be one that nobody could extinguish. But there was also a belief that Bunche was the fireman most likely to succeed in putting the blaze out—assuming the arsonists and assassins did not strike again.

If today people were stopped on any street in the world and asked, "Who was Ralph Bunche?", none of them (well, hardly any of them) would have a clue. He was, in fact, one of the few truly great and good men of the 20th century. At the time he took on the job of containing Zionism—that was his real but publicly unspeakable purpose—this black American was on his way to becoming the diplomat most admired by other diplomats everywhere whose prime concern was crisis management and conflict resolution. For his success in bringing four sets of negotiations to a successful conclusion and the signing of the Armistice Agreements—actually in the face of mind-numbing Israeli obscuration and procrastination—Bunche became in 1950 the first black man in the world to be honoured by the award of a Nobel Peace Prize. In 1957 he was elevated to the post of Under Secretary General for political affairs. In that capacity he was the chief global trouble-shooter for Secretary General Dag Hammarskjold. At the time of his resignation from the UN for reasons of health in 1970, Bunche was the most influential political adviser to Secretary General U Thant and the highest-ranking American in the international organisation. But for his health he might have become the first black Secretary General.

Though not enough people are aware of it, the fact is that *the UN is not a self-standing institution with a mind of its own. It is the sum total of the hypocrisies of the governments of the member states.* And as all students of the UN and its history know, the vested interests and rivalries of the big powers that control the world body are the main reasons for its failure to deliver on the promises of its Charter. But in my analysis, which I know is shared in private by some of the organisation's most senior and respected former servants, *the greatest corrupting influence on the UN was Zionism.* Its success in rigging the partition vote of 1947, and the injustice that sanctioned, was a disaster from which the UN has not yet recovered. And perhaps never will.

The consequence of Ben-Gurion's active discouragement of political planning was that Israel's doves (realists) were increasingly marginalized and frustrated. On 2 November 1948 this frustration was given expression by Yaacov Shimoni, the deputy head of the Foreign Ministry's Middle East department. Shimoni's boss, Sasson, was in Paris conducting a dialogue with various Arab and Palestinian officials. The essence of Shimoni's complaint to Sasson was that Ben-Gurion "seeks to solve most of the problems by military means, in such a way that no political negotiations and no political action would be of any value."[5]

Ben-Gurion "seeks to solve most of the problems by military means, in such a way that no political negotiations and no political action would be of any value."

On 28 December, Egypt's Prime Minister Nokrashy was assassinated (as he had feared). He was shot as he was leaving his office. The assassins were members of the Muslim Brotherhood. It is reasonable to assume that the Brotherhood's reasons for killing him included inside knowledge that his government, at Farouk's command, was seeking not only an Armistice Agreement to end the war with Israel, but wished to make an accommodation with the Jewish state for a permanent peace.

Surprising though it may seem given all that has happened to the time of writing, and leaving aside for the moment King Abdullah's determination to make peace with Israel, it was a Syrian leader, Colonel Husni Zaim, who offered Israel its best and strategically most significant early opportunity for peace.

Unlike the Egyptian army, the Syrian army was not destroyed but the country was unstable internally. On 30 March 1949, Zaim, then chief of staff, overthrew the regime in a bloodless coup. As chief of staff he had promised his Arab brothers that Syria would fight Zionism to the finish. As president of his country he wanted to be the first Arab leader to conclude a peace agreement with Israel.

The evidence, much of which remained secret for many years, indicates that Zaim was nothing but serious. When negotiations for an Israel-Syria Armistice Agreement broke down, Zaim came up with an audacious initiative to break the deadlock. *His proposal was that Syrian and Israeli negotiators should skip the armistice talks and move directly to the conclusion of a peace treaty, with an exchange of ambassadors, open borders and normal economic relations.* In the context of an overall settlement, and to give Israel an additional incentive, Zaim also offered to take 300,000 Palestinian refugees and settle them in northern Syria. (At the time there were already about 100,000 refugees in Syria, so effectively Zaim was offering to take another 200,000 who had ended up in other Arab states). And there was more. Zaim offered to meet with Ben-Gurion face-to-face. In return Zaim was asking for a modification of the border to give Syria half the Sea of Galilee. (The Israel of the partition plan was to include all it).

Ben-Gurion rejected Zaim's overture out of hand.

Zaim refused to give up and turned to the UN (Bunche) for assistance with communicating to Israel a new and improved offer. There were three main elements to it: an Armistice Agreement based on the existing military lines (Syrian forces were still in occupation of some territory that had been assigned to the Jewish state of the partition plan); a peace settlement within three months based on the partition plan border; and the settlement of 300,000 Palestinian refugees in Syria. To make it an offer he thought Israel could not reject, Zaim, in the context of an overall settlement, had dropped his demand for redrawing the partition plan border.

It was an offer no Israeli leader could have refused unless he wanted the flexibility of no peace, with the Jewish state not being confined, at least on the Syrian front, by a recognised (legally sacrosanct) border. Put another way, it was an offer no Israel leader could refuse unless he was dreaming of a time when Israel would capture and keep more Syrian territory. A legally sacrosanct border was a most serious obstacle to territorial ambition.

Sharett was delighted when Bunche indicated his support for the view that Zaim's offer was of the greatest importance and should be taken very seriously. On his own reading of the significance of the Syrian proposal—he was particularly pleased with the offer to settle 300,000 Palestinian refugees in northern Syria—Sharett urged Ben-Gurion to respond positively to Zaim's repeated call for a face-to-face meeting to progress matters.

When Ben-Gurion again said "No", Bunche decided that it was time for him to press the Israeli leader to grant Zaim's request for a meeting. Bunche entertained the hope that, if the meeting took place, it might generate the momentum to bring about a complete regional peace. Signed and sealed by all parties.

When the chips were down, Bunche was not a man you could say "No" to unless you really believed he was making an unreasonable demand of you. Even Ben-Gurion was not going to say "No" to this UN Mediator. Instead he did what he was best at. *He said "Yes" with conditions which made the answer "No"*.

To maintain an appearance of reasonableness, Ben-Gurion said "Yes" with conditions which made the answer "No".

At a cabinet meeting on 24 May 1949, Ben-Gurion read the text of his reply to Bunche. It stated that Israel's prime minister was prepared to meet with the Syrian leader to promote peace between their two countries, but that he saw no point in such a meeting until the Syrian representatives to the armistice talks had declared their readiness to withdraw to the pre-war lines.

Bernadotte had told Ben-Gurion he could not have it both ways. Ben-Gurion was now saying to his successor, "Yes, we can." Israel would keep Arab land of the partition plan it had occupied, but the Arabs had to withdraw from every inch of the territory that had been assigned to the Jewish state.

Translated, Ben-Gurion was telling Bunche, to tell Zaim, there was no question of a meeting of the two leaders until Syria had accepted Israel's terms for an Armistice Agreement. That was an early manifestation of Israel's arrogance of power. In theory Zaim had two options.

One was to tell Ben-Gurion to go to hell because it was evident that he was not interested in peace. But that was not really an option for the Syrian leader. It would have invited a renewed Israeli military offensive and Syria could not take that.

Zaim's only other option—the one he exercised—was to instruct Syria's negotiators to resume the deadlocked discussions with their Israeli counterparts for the purpose of concluding an Armistice Agreement. A formal peace treaty with Israel, which the Syrian leader wanted, would have to await developments.

Bunche was comforted by the fact that the way was now clear for him to bring the war to an end. The Israel-Syria Armistice Agreement was the only one outstanding. But it was to take him nearly two more months of negotiating to get Israel's signature on an Armistice Agreement with Syria. *And in the course of those two months he was to learn that the Israelis were the most obdurate and impossible people to negotiate with.* (It was Egypt's President Sadat, shortly before he was assassinated in October 1981, who gave me the most revealing insight into what it was really like to negotiate with Israel. He told me that Israel's negotiating strategy was to wear you out, to exhaust you, to make you so "fed up" that, at a point, you had to decide either to walk away from negotiations and take the blame for failure, or, if you were not to go mad, to throw up your hands and say, "Okay, you win, I'll agree to more or less whatever you want.")

The evidence that even Bunche was driven to the point at which he was "fed up" with Israel's negotiating strategy and tactics is in the fact that the Israel-Syria Armistice Agreement he sanctioned was most unsatisfactory. On the ground the essence of it was the creation of a demilitarised zone (DMZ) between the ceasefire lines and the international borders. It was an agreement that failed to pin the Israelis down and left them scope for continuing disputes and the opportunity, at a time of their choosing, to provoke confrontation. But that was a problem for the future.

Three weeks after the signing of the Israel-Syria Armistice Agreement, Zaim was overthrown in a bloody coup.

Nobody can know what might have happened if that Syrian leader had remained in power. Would Ben-Gurion, pressed by Bunche, have met with him? Perhaps, but not in my opinion. In the context of all that happened my bet is that Ben-Gurion would have found a way, created a pretext if necessary, to justify a continuing refusal to meet with Zaim.

There is, however, a judgment that ought to be beyond dispute by all but supporters of Israel right or wrong. It was put into words by Shlaim. In his days as Syria's leader, Zaim

> gave Israel every opportunity to bury the hatchet and lay the foundations for peaceful coexistence. *If his overtures were spurned, if his constructive proposals were not put to the test, and if opportunities for a breakthrough had been missed, the responsibility must be attributed not to Zaim but to Israel.* And the responsibility can be traced directly to the whole school of thought, of which Ben-Gurion was the most powerful proponent, which maintained that time was on Israel's side and that Israel could manage perfectly well without peace with the Arab states and without a solution to the Palestinian refugee problem.[6] [Emphasis added]

It was on 29 May, less than a week after he gave Bunche his yes-meaning-no response to Zaim's offer to meet with him, that Ben-Gurion explained to his cabinet colleagues why time was on Israel's side and why, therefore, there was no need for Israel to have formal peace treaties with any of the Arab states. Ben-Gurion gave three reasons:

- With the passage of time the world would get used to Israel's existing borders and would "forget" about the partition plan borders. Israel would not be pressed in any meaningful way by the international community to return to them.

- With the passage of time the world would "forget" about the UN idea of an independent Palestinian state and, apart from "moral pressure" from the UN (which naturally would run like water off the back of the Zionist duck), the Jewish state would not be pressed in any meaningful way to allow the Palestinians to return or be compensated.

- With the passage of time the world would "forget" about the UN idea of internationalising Jerusalem. People, Ben-Gurion said, were already getting used to the situation on the ground there and beginning to see the absurdity of the idea of suddenly establishing an international regime over the city.

In effect Ben-Gurion was saying something like the following. "Provided we Zionists continue to play the holocaust card for all its worth, and provided we can convince the Western world that our little state is in danger of being annihilated, we can do what the hell we like in this region."

Without Judaism's moral compass, the Zionist state was on its way to becoming its own worst enemy.

Given Ben-Gurion's mindset after the signing of the Armistice Agreements, it is not surprising that King Abdullah did not succeed in his attempt to negotiate a formal peace treaty with Israel.

For the most hawkish of Israel's political and military leaders, including Ben-Gurion himself, even the signing of the Armistice Agreement with Transjordan had been too much of a "concession" to the Arabs.

The official vehicle of the extreme right was the Herut party led by Menachem Begin. He and some of his fellow madmen formed it after the "dissolution" of the Irgun. In reality Herut at birth was more or less the Irgun without its guns and bombs. It was also what could have been called the honest voice of the Greater Israel movement. It believed and said that the "Jewish people" had an "historic right" to all the land of biblical Israel, and that it was the duty of the government Ben-Gurion led to capture and keep the West Bank including all of Jerusalem.

In the Knesset on 3 April 1949, the day after the Israel-Transjordan Armistice Agreement was signed, Begin tabled a motion of no confidence in Ben-Gurion's government. King Abdullah had not yet formally annexed the West Bank so, in theory, it was still available as the truncated Arab (Palestinian) state of the partition plan. Begin was obviously aware of Abdullah's intention to annex that territory, and his motion of no confidence said Israel's signature on the Armistice Agreement was tantamount to recognising the incorporation of the West Bank and the Old City of Jerusalem into Abdullah's kingdom. Begin was, of course, right about that. The specific charge in the no-confidence motion was that Ben-Gurion's government had "abandoned" to the Hashemite Kingdom of Transjordan a huge portion of the western part of "the motherland." (The description of Israel or any part of Palestine as "the motherland" of more than a very few of the Jews who were in it in 1949 was an indication of how divorced from historical reality Begin was).

At the time the no-confidence motion was no more than a symbolic gesture. Begin was putting down a marker; but it was pregnant with meaning for the future.

The secret peace talks between Israel and Transjordan started in November 1949. On the Jordanian side the main participants were King Abdullah himself and his minister of the royal court and future prime minister, Samir Rifai. On the Israeli side the main participants were Reuven Shiloah and Elias Sasson of the Foreign Ministry. Other Israelis who sometimes attended the meetings included Walter Eytan, the ministry's director general, Yigal Yadin, the IDF's chief of staff, and Dayan. Most of the meetings took place in King Abdullah's winter palace at Shuneh near the Allenby Bridge over the river Jordan.

In *From The Wings; Amman Memoirs* nearly 30 years later, Britain's Ambassador of the time, Sir Alec Kirkbride, offered this quite fascinating observation:

> The visitor (Reuven Shiloah) used to travel down from Jerusalem in a car sent by the king, dine at the royal table with the prime minister and then retire with the latter to an ante chamber for discussions which seemed to be interminable. King Abdullah used to stay up for as long as he could keep his eyes open in the hope that some positive result might emerge. The exchange usually terminated at about three o'clock in the morning after which Shiloah went back across the lines. I marvelled at the amount of time the two participants managed to take up with their discussions.[7]

That for me is a particularly fascinating observation in the light of Zionism's historic assertion that Israel had "nobody to talk peace with" on the Arab side.

Transjordan's officials were much more cautious than their king because they feared that a separate peace with Israel, unless the terms were right and unless it could be seen as part of an all-Arab peace process, would result in Transjordan being expelled from the Arab League and isolated. And that was why King Abdullah told Israel's negotiators, again and again, that he had to have an agreement he could sell to his Arab brothers at leadership level on the grounds that it would open the door to a comprehensive peace. In other words, Abdullah needed to be able to say to his brother Arab leaders something like, "Take it from me that Israel is serious about peace on terms we can all accept."

In government on the Israeli side it was (among the heavyweights) only Foreign Minister Sharett who viewed the secret negotiations with Transjordan as being a means to an end—a comprehensive peace with all the frontline Arab states.

It was not until April 1950, when it was clear to him that Ben-Gurion's Israel was not interested in a comprehensive peace, that Abdullah formally annexed the West Bank. That had always been his intention, but his actual decision to do it was triggered by a warning from Britain, conveyed by Kirkbride. *If His Majesty did not grab the West Bank, Israel most probably would, especially if Dayan had his way.*

Ben-Gurion had said that "the boundaries of the state would have been much larger had Moshe Dayan been commander-in-chief in 1948."

Dayan was constantly questioning the value of formal peace agreements with the Arabs. And at a point when the negotiations with Abdullah were more off than on, he suggested that instead of continuing them, Israel should capture all of the West Bank up to the Jordan River.

In cabinet it was Sharett who led the fight to prevent Dayan's idea becoming policy. He said:

> The State of Israel will not get embroiled in military adventures by deliberately taking the initiative to capture territories and expand. Israel would not do that, both because we cannot afford to be accused by the world of aggression and because we cannot, for security and social reasons, absorb into our midst a substantial Arab population... We cannot sacrifice Jewish fighters, nor can we harm others in an arbitrary fashion, merely in order to satisfy the appetite for expansion.[8]

In one respect Sharett was to be proved wrong by events. Israel could afford to be accused by the world of aggression or, to put it another and more accurate way, Israel did not have to be concerned about being accused of aggression. Why not? Because the governments of the Western world were content—to avoid provoking Zionism's wrath—to allow Israel to define its aggression as "self-defence".

Israel did not have to be concerned about being accused of aggression—because the governments of the Western world allowed the Zionist state to define its aggression as "self-defence".

By February 1951 Ben-Gurion had decided that he did not want a political settlement with Jordan. (Transjordan officially became Jordan when Abdullah formally annexed the West Bank). On the 13th day of that month Shiloah came to consult with Ben-Gurion in advance of his next discussion with King Abdullah. Ben-Gurion had a question for his negotiator: "Do we have an interest in committing ourselves to such ridiculous borders?"[9] In the conversation that preceded his question, Ben-Gurion had given four reasons for why the answer was "No". And after the question he gave two more.

Because of Ben-Gurion's total lack of commitment to peace with Jordan, the negotiations were doomed. In despair Abdullah offered to go to Jerusalem and talk face-to-face with Ben-Gurion. The Israeli leader simply ignored the king's suggestion for a meeting. On this occasion there was not even a Ben-Gurion "Yes" that meant "No". Just silence.

On Friday 20 July, King Abdullah was assassinated outside the al-Aksa Mosque in the Old City of Jerusalem.

The night before, pointing to his grandson, Hussein, Abdullah had said to his prime minister: "If ever anything happens to me, it is he who must carry on the house of the Hashemites." When the prime minister protested and said there was no reason to talk of the succession, Abdullah replied, "No, I feel my end is near."[10]

Abdullah was acknowledging that his son and heir apparent, Talal, was not fit to be king on account of a genetic inheritance that made him mentally unstable. As it happened, Talal did rule for a few months until he was required to stand aside in favour of the 17-year-old Hussein. Both Talal and Hussein were at Abdullah's side when he was murdered. (One of the many privileges of my own life was knowing King Hussein and having the opportunity at critical moments to enjoy access to his private thinking). On hearing the news of Abdullah's assassination, Ben-Gurion's first thought was that it presented an opportunity for him to rectify what he had come to regard as his "mistake" of 1948. *He asked his military advisers to prepare a contingency plan for the capture of the West Bank.*

At the same time, evidence that he was fantasising in a way that only half-sane men do, Ben-Gurion was also considering an approach to Britain. Would the British allow Israel to expel the Egyptians from Sinai for the purpose—apart from expanding the territory of the Jewish state—of making Britain-and-Israel instead of Britain-and-Egypt the guardian of the Suez Canal?

Led by a prime minister who became as deluded as Israel's hawks, Britain would be prepared to enter into a conspiracy with Israel (and France) in a vain, stupid effort to keep the sun from setting completely on the British Empire—but that was not yet.

After military victory in what it called its war of independence, Israel had a choice of two futures.

One was as a small state confined to the borders of the partition plan (probably with adjustments in Israel's favour) and living in peace with its Arab neighbours, and with the prospect in time of great benefit from playing a leading role in the development of the economy of the entire region. Such a state would have been a normal one—ready and willing to honour its obligations under international law and comply with UN resolutions.

The alternative future was as a state not bound by formal peace treaties and therefore free to expand its borders by applications of superior military might. This was a future of unending conflict and perhaps, in Sharett's words, "war to the end of all generations" if the Zionists were wrong in their assumption that, at some point, the Arab will to resist Israeli expansionism would be broken by brute force. By definition such a state could not be normal because it would be committed to showing contempt for international law and UN resolutions. Such a state would also be one that, because it was without a moral compass, would become its own worst enemy. Sharett understood that. Ben-Gurion did not. Or if he did, he did not care about the consequences.

It was because Israel chose the flight path of the hawks and not that of the doves, Ben-Gurion's way instead of Sharett's way, that the myth of Israel being in danger of extermination had to be invented and promoted, to justify the aggression that would be necessary for the creation of Greater Israel.

As it happened the prospects on the Arab side for an early peace with Israel were not yet dead. There was coming a revolution in Egypt that would overthrow Farouk's corrupt and incompetent regime and produce a leader who, though he was to be demonised by Zionism and its child, and by Britain, France and America's hawks, actually wanted an accommodation with Israel. His name was Nasser. Gamal Abdul Nasser.

5

MAKING NASSER THE ENEMY, ACT I

With the exception of Arafat, no Arab leader was to be more demonised by Zionism than Nasser. That was because Egypt's leader, while not being willing to surrender on Israel's terms, wanted an accommodation with the Zionist state—an accommodation that, with the main exception of Foreign Minister and all too briefly Prime Minister Sharett, none of Israel's heavyweight leaders wanted.

In Israel the rational Sharett was the only leader who bothered to make an effort to understand the real Nasser in the context of Egypt's own tragic history.

As Anthony Nutting put it, Nasser was "the first true Egyptian to rule Egypt since the Persian conquest nearly 2,500 years before."[1] Nutting was the minister of state at the British Foreign Office when Nasser came to power. One of his responsibilities was to negotiate with Nasser Britain's final withdrawal from Egypt. Nutting was that rare thing in politics—a man of principle, which was why, at a point, he resigned in protest at the madness of British policy. His eventual book, *Nasser*, was the product of unique insight.

Egypt was the first recorded nation-state in human history. It came into existence around 3000 BC. But after a glorious beginning there were, for Egyptians, 2,500 years of taking orders successively from Persian, Greek, Roman, Byzantine, other Arab, Kurdish, Turkish, French and British proconsuls.

The consequences? "Culture and learning came to a standstill; education was confined to memorising the Koran; irrigation canals silted up and vast areas of formerly fertile lands reverted to desert; plague and famine carried off hundreds of thousands. And along the perilously narrow green line of the Nile, which from time immemorial had been the sole artery of Egypt's existence, the fellah fought or worked with his neighbour to keep his family alive and to satisfy the extortionate demands of the tax-collector and the money-lender."[2]

The length of subservience to foreigners—the British for the last 70 years—had so sapped Egyptian resistance that, at the time of Nasser's revolution, "the nationalist spirit was little more than a tiny ember in a heap of cold ashes. Subjected for so many years to foreign rule, the ordinary

Egyptian had come not only to feel, but also to accept that his country did not belong to him and that fate had relegated him in perpetuity to the status at best of a tenant, at worst of a slave, to the foreigner who occupied the throne, owned the land and ordered the life of Egypt."[3]

In that historical context the key to understanding the real Nasser—where he was coming from and where he hoped to be taking his people—was in a letter he wrote to a friend:

> Egypt... is in a state of hopeless despair. Who can remove this feeling? The Egyptian Government is based on corruption and favours... Who can cry halt to the imperialists? There are men in Egypt with dignity who do not want to be allowed to die like dogs. But where is... the man to rebuild the country so that the weak and humiliated Egyptian people can rise again and live as free and independent men? Where is dignity? Where is nationalism?... The nation sleeps like men in a cave. Who can awaken these miserable creatures who do not even know who they are?[4]

It is remarkable that Nasser was only 17 when he wrote those words. There was nothing in his family history to suggest that he could be "the man."

He was born on 15 January 1918 in a mud-brick house on an unpaved street in the Bacos section of Alexandria. His father was in charge of the local post office there. For reasons unknown, perhaps because he was an anti-British trouble-maker, Nasser's father was transferred to al-Khatatibah, a squalid Nile delta village; and that was where Gamal Abdul got his first schooling. From there young Nasser went to live in Cairo with an uncle who had just been released from a British prison and who had rooms in a building occupied by nine Jewish families.

The maturity of expression in the letter the teenage nationalist wrote was partly explained by his devotion to reading. He devoured work by philosophers of the Western tradition and he read the lives of Alexander the Great, Julius Caesar, Napoleon, Bismarck, Kemal Ataturk, Winston Churchill and Mahatma Ghandi.

After completing his secondary education, Nasser went to law school for several months and then entered the Royal Military Academy. He graduated as a second lieutenant.

In the war against the unilaterally declared state of Israel, Nasser was an officer in one of three battalions surrounded and outgunned for weeks by the Israelis in a group of Arab villages called the Faluja Pocket. Early in the fighting he was wounded in the stomach and hospitalised in Cairo, but he insisted on returning to the action. It was mainly due to a fierce counterattack he led that the Israeli pressure was relaxed enough to allow the Faluja defenders to hold out until the armistice between Egypt and Israel was signed.

In Palestine Nasser's eyes were opened to the fact that the Egyptian Army had been sent to war without planning, preparation and the means to put up more than a token fight before being defeated and humiliated. He also realised that many of the army's most senior commanders were as corrupt and incompetent as the stupid king who had sent them to war. And on reflection after the war, the debacle, he realised that what had happened in Palestine could not be divorced from what was happening in Egypt. The whole system was rotten to the core. Farouk's regime had to go.

On 23 July 1952, Nasser and 89 Free Officers staged an almost bloodless *coup d'etat*. The new ruling authority was the Revolutionary Command Council (RCC). It consisted of 11 officers controlled by Nasser with General Mohammad Naguib as the puppet head of state. For more than a year Nasser kept his own role so well hidden that not even the most informed foreign correspondents knew of his existence. Intrigue followed intrigue and then, in 1954, by which time he was already exploring in secret the prospect of an accommodation with Israel, Nasser emerged from the shadows and named himself prime minister.

Nasser's hope was that the new Egypt he wanted to create would turn its back on confrontation with Israel in order to allow him to concentrate on an "Egypt first" policy of domestic reform and development—in a word, modernisation. And that, modernisation, was one of two reasons why Nasser was to find himself in confrontation with, and in considerable personal danger from, Egypt's home-grown extremists of the Muslim Brotherhood. (They had already assassinated two Egyptian Prime ministers—Ahmed Maher in 1945 and Nokrashy in 1948).

The Muslim Brotherhood was then, as it is again today, a potent force. It was founded in 1928 by Hassan al-Banna, a Sheikh of Al-Azhar, Cairo's thousand-year-old Islamic university. With its ancient mosque the university is still the most important and respected Islamic institution in the Muslim world.

In the beginning the Muslim Brotherhood was a largely religious organisation which advocated a return to the Qu'ran and the Hadith as the guidelines for a healthy Islamic society. The Brotherhood spread rapidly throughout Egypt, the Sudan, Syria, Palestine, Lebanon and North Africa. Everywhere it set up schools, medicinal clinics and small industries. In demanding purity of the Islamic world and the protection of its spiritual/cultural norms, it rejected all direct foreign intervention and influence through Westernisation, secularisation and modernisation. Then, in the late thirties, it developed into an overtly political movement preaching jihad ("holy war" in the view of those calling for it and the inadequate translation usually provided in the West) to evict the British army, which was still occupying the Suez Canal Zone when Nasser came to power. It set up departments for military training and intelligence gathering, and it created a terrorist wing. Unlike the Egyptian army, the Muslim Brotherhood emerged from the war in Palestine with some credit, and that was one of the reasons why it insisted on being part of the new order in Egypt following Farouk's overthrow. It was when Naguib turned out to be less than a puppet and backed the Muslim Brotherhood that Nasser came close to being finished as the revolutionary leader. For the first two years his position was not secure.

Nasser had a warm, pleasant personality. In normal conversation he was soft-spoken and sounded, I thought, a bit like Liberace. I met him only twice and I had the impression that, if he had been free to do so, and in order to contain Zionism—prevent Israel taking more Arab land—he would have made peace with the Zionist state the moment he came to power. When he told the Americans he did not see war as an instrument of policy for settling differences with Israel, he meant it. And they knew he did.

Dignity, the key concept word in Nasser's teenage nationalist thinking, was to become the central theme of his early speeches as leader. Dignity was the first principle of Egyptian and Arab nationalism. Dignity required independence, and independence required the final and total elimination of all foreign occupation and interference in the affairs of Arab states.

In Egypt's case that meant Nasser's first priority, above and beyond all else, was getting the occupying British army out of the Suez Canal Zone. The problem was that Britain did not want to go. Continuing control of the canal was deemed to be vital if Britain was to have a chance of hanging on to what was left of its disintegrating empire. In theory a 1936 treaty committed Britain to withdraw its military forces from the Canal Zone in 1956; but the British in 1936 had insisted on a treaty with an option to enable it to continue its military occupation after 1956. Nasser was convinced that when the crunch came, Britain would use all and any means to exercise its option to stay. He understood that Britain's imperial elite (like its French counterpart) was terrified of the real Arab nationalism he represented. If it became the prevailing force in Egypt and then the wider Arab world, Britain's days of interfering in Arab affairs, essentially for the economic benefits that interference guaranteed, would be gone forever.

Nasser's real fear was that if he failed to secure Britain's agreement to withdraw in 1956, he would lose his ability to contain the Muslim Brotherhood (which had committed itself to driving the British out by violent means). That could lead to real conflict with Britain and quite possibly civil war in Egypt at the same time. All up Nasser could see a nightmare scenario in which Britain would have a pretext for re-imposing its authority on more of Egypt than the Canal Zone. In short, Nasser believed that his revolutionary home base was not secure and would not be until the British as masters were finally gone. (Nutting understood this).

So far as their management of the tense and dangerous situation between Israel and the Arabs was concerned, the three major Western powers—Britain, France and the U.S.—had laid down the ground rules with their Tripartite Declaration of 25 May 1950, regulating the supply of arms to the Middle East. With this declaration the three major Western powers committed themselves to action, within and without the United Nations, to resist any attempt by either Israel or the Arabs to change by force of arms the 1949 armistice boundaries Bunche had negotiated. It was a commitment, consistently reaffirmed, to act against any aggressor—Arab or Israeli. The implications for the Arabs and Israel were quite clear.

When it came to negotiations for a permanent peace, the Arabs, like it or not, were going to have to accept a Jewish state inside something like the 1949 armistice lines—which meant accepting an Israel substantially bigger than the Jewish state of the partition plan. And Israel would not be permitted to grab any more Arab land. Further territorial expansion by the Zionist state was out of the question, assuming the three big Western powers meant what they said and could deliver if they did.

Not too much imagination is required to think that the Tripartite Declaration might have been President Truman's way of saying, in effect: "Lovett's pig is out of the poke. We must try to make the pen secure."

Nasser was not stupid. He knew and accepted that Egypt and all the Arabs had no choice but to accept Zionism's fait accompli. And there was no mystery about why. The three main Western powers and the Soviet Union were committed to Israel's existence.

The Arab leaders believed they had no choice but to accept Zionism's fait accompli because the major Western powers and the Soviet Union were committed to Israel's existence.

In reality making Nasser the enemy was going to require a quite spectacular effort by Israel's political and military hawks. It was a challenge they relished and they were to succeed (with the help of a British prime minister who became deluded and America's own hawks) despite Sharett's best efforts to stop them.

In the Knesset on 18 August 1952, Ben-Gurion congratulated the Free Officers on their revolution and expressed his hope for a new beginning in Egyptian-Israeli relations. There were no grounds, he said, for any quarrel between Egypt and Israel. A vast expanse of desert (the Egyptian Sinai) stretched between their two countries and left no room for border disputes. "There has never been, nor is there now, any reason for political, economic or territorial conflict between the two neighbours."

It was classic Ben-Gurionism. Saying one thing in public while, in private, thinking about doing the opposite. But Ben-Gurion's public stance did give Foreign Minister Sharett the space he needed to try to get an exploratory secret dialogue with the RCC going. At the time nobody had any idea that it was Nasser who was pulling the RCC's strings.

In Paris on 22 August, Shmuel Divon, the first secretary of the Israeli embassy, visited the home of Ali Shawqi, the *chargé d'affaires* at the Egyptian embassy. Divon proposed the opening of a secret channel for discussions about the possibility of peace. There was no direct response but several messages of RCC goodwill to Israel were conveyed by other Egyptian diplomats and third parties.

By 1 October Ben-Gurion was explaining to his government's senior officials that while Israel's talk about peace was "not a trick", *there were limits to Israel's desire for peace*. He did actually use those words. "We have to remember that there are limits to our desire for peace with the Arabs."[5]

Peace was one of their vital interests, but it was "not the first and all-determining interest", Ben-Gurion said. "First and foremost we have to see to Israel's needs (which he had previously defined as immigration, money for development and security) whether or not this brings an improvement in our relations with the Arabs. The second factor in our existence is American Jewry and its relationship with us. The third thing—peace with the Arabs. This is the order of priorities."[6]

That really was a most extraordinary statement. The political and financial support of Jewish Americans was more important for the survival of the Jewish state than peace with the Arabs.

For Ben-Gurion, the political and financial support of Jewish Americans was more important for the survival of the Jewish state than peace with the Arabs.

But at the time he made that statement Ben-Gurion was alone in government in knowing the real significance of Jewish American money. It was already funding the super secret development of Israel's atomic bomb.

In late October, still in the shadows, Nasser made his first tentative, conciliatory move. He sent Abdel Rahman Sadeq to Paris. Officially he was there to serve as the embassy's press attaché. His more important job was to develop the contact with Divon. In due course Sadeq told Divon it was from Nasser that he received his instructions and to Nasser that he reported.

By the end of January 1953, Sadeq was telling Divon that he had been instructed by Nasser to say that he, Sadeq, was conducting the talks "in the name of the RCC"; but that for the time being Egypt could not depart from the pan-Arab position on the Palestine problem. Sadeq also stressed Nasser's insistence that their talks remain secret. If their dialogue became a matter of public knowledge, Nasser might very well have to end it.

Then came a remarkable indication that Nasser was actually looking upon Israel as a potential ally. On Nasser's instructions Sadeq requested Israel's political support for Egypt's case for economic aid from America, and Israel's moral support for Egypt's demand for the withdrawal of British forces from the Suez Canal Zone.

Prime Minister Ben-Gurion had more influence than Foreign Minister Sharett in drafting the reply to Nasser's request. It was in some respects apparently positive in principle, but on a conditional basis; and the conditions made the reply much more of a "No" than a "Yes."[7]

- Israel regretted Egypt's "unwillingness" to depart from the hostile attitude of the Arab states. (That, as Nasser would subsequently indicate, was an unfair characterisation of his position. He was signalling a willingness to lead the Arab world in the direction of peace with Israel but not yet—because of, at street level, the humiliation-driven hatred of Israel throughout the entire Arab and Muslim world. Simply stated Nasser was saying, "Give me time.")

- Israel hoped for a fundamental transformation in the relations between the two countries but Egypt could prove its good intentions by lifting the Arab ban on Israeli shipping through the Suez Canal and the Straits of Tiran which commanded the entrance to Gulf of Aqaba. (Because the balance of military power was so heavily in Israel's favour, just about the only bargaining chip Arab governments had—apart from legitimising the Jewish state through the mechanism of formal peace treaties—was the denial of freedom to Israeli shipping, and the economic and trade boycott of the Jewish state that was part and parcel of that denial).

- Israel was ready to contribute to economic development in Egypt by placing an order for the purchase of US$5 million worth of cotton and other products—if Egypt lifted the restrictions on the passage of Israeli oil tankers through the Suez Canal and the Gulf of Aqaba. (Ben-Gurion was effectively saying, "We'll buy one of your very few negotiating cards forUS$5 million.")

- Israel "sympathised" with Egypt's wish to see the evacuation of British forces from the Suez Canal Zone and was willing to support Egypt in the matter—if Egypt first improved Egyptian-Israeli relations.

With that Israeli reply there was a suggestion for upgrading the contact between Divon and Sadeq—continuing the secret dialogue with more senior representatives from both sides.

Nasser's eventual response was in the form of a letter. It was typed on official RCC stationery, addressed to Sadeq and signed by Nasser as Naguib's deputy. On 13 May, Sadeq met with Divon in the Hotel Reynolds in Paris and showed the Israeli a copy of the letter.

In it Nasser explained that because of public opinion in Egypt and the Arab world, the RCC, for reasons of "prudence", meaning self-preservation, had "to build its policy toward Israel gradually." Nasser agreed that the avoidance of aggressive statements against Israel was necessary and he pledged again that Egypt "does not harbour any belligerent intentions." And then came the most significant statement in the letter. "It was important that Israel use its influence in America to get support for Egypt's demand for the withdrawal of British forces because it, Britain's withdrawal, would make it easier for the RCC to reach a final settlement with Israel." [8] He was saying without saying, "Until Britain's occupation of my country is ended, I will not be able to take on and beat those on my own side (the fundamentalists of the Muslim Brotherhood) who are most opposed to an accommodation with Israel."

In passing Nasser added that he was grateful for the offer to buy Egyptian cotton but it was, he felt, "premature". He concluded with what he obviously thought was a demonstration of goodwill. He would see to it that the RCC examined the matter of the passage of Israeli ships and he had already taken steps, he said, to ease the restrictions. (As a first gesture of goodwill he did, in fact, lift the ban on all cargoes but oil to and from Israel through the Gulf of Aqaba provided the ships carrying them were not flying the Israeli flag).

On any reasonable interpretation by rational minds, Nasser in secret was saying, in effect, something like the following to Israel's leaders; "My first priority is Britain's final withdrawal to bring an end to 2,500 years of foreign domination of my country. When that is done I can claim a victory that will enhance my prestige in Egypt and throughout the Arab world. That will enable me to make a start developing and modernising Egypt and then, and only then, will I be secure enough to go for a settlement with Israel."

It could be said that such an interpretation of Nasser's real intentions needed a degree of goodwill on the part of those Israelis required to do the interpreting. *And it was here, on the matter of goodwill to Nasser in particular and the Arabs in general, that the differences between Sharett and Ben-Gurion were so profound.*

Sharett had spent some of his childhood in an Arab village. He spoke Arabic fluently; he had Arab friends he kept in touch with; and he was well acquainted with Arab history, culture and politics. Which meant, among other things, that Sharett had some understanding of how limited Nasser's room for maneuver was. Even more to the point, Israel's foreign minister did not look upon the Arabs as just "the enemy". He saw them as a "proud and sensitive people" with "extremely subtle understanding and delicate senses." It was true, he conceded in argument with Ben-Gurion, that "there is a wall between us and them"; but there was "a tragic development that is making the wall taller, and Israel has a sacred duty to prevent the wall getting even taller, if at all possible."[9]

Ben-Gurion on the other hand knew nothing worth knowing about the Arabs. Any of them. Arabic was not one of the six languages he spoke. He did not trust or even like Arabs. He viewed them as a primitive, wild and fanatical enemy with a hatred of modern Israel so deeply ingrained as to be unchangeable. He repeatedly stressed the alienation and the gulf between "us" and "them". As Shlaim noted, Ben-Gurion compared Israel to a boat and the Arabs to a cruel sea. His aim was to make the boat so robust that that no storm or turbulence in the sea could capsize it. The bottom-line for Israel's prime minister was in the statement he frequently made that the only thing the Arabs understood was the language of force. It was because he meant what he said on that score that he commanded the respect of Israel's military hawks.

Given their different images of the Arabs, it was entirely logical that Sharett interpreted Nasser's secret messages as an indication of his wish for an eventual accommodation with the Jewish state, and concluded that Israel's leaders should give priority to the politics of peacemaking. It was also entirely logical that Ben-Gurion could not see the emerging Egyptian leader as a partner for peace, not least because he, Ben-Gurion, had been made blind to that possibility by his ignorance and bigotry. But for Ben-Gurion the gut-Zionist there was also the hidden agenda—Greater Israel as the insurance policy for Jews everywhere.

Israel's hawks set about undermining Nasser's security, embarking on a policy of provoking confrontation to create the pretext for taking more Arab land.

Unfortunately for all concerned, it was now to be Israel's hawks who called most of the policy shots. While seeking to make Israel secure with applications of brute force—their preferred alternative to Sharett's politics of peacemaking—they set about undermining Nasser's security. They were, in short, embarked on a policy of provoking confrontation, to create the pretext for taking more Arab land.

The climax did not happen until 1967. The intervening years (from Nasser's emergence as Egypt's leader) were the foreplay.

The "tragic development" of Sharett's statement quoted above, a development that was bringing out the neo-fascist-like (some would say Nazi-like) worst in Israel's military hawks, Sharon especially, was Israel's response to the infiltration of Palestinian refugees across the armistice lines and into Israel. The bulk of the infiltrations were from the Gaza Strip (Egyptian territory) and Jordan.

With most of the nearly one million Palestinian refugees camped in the frontline Arab states, it was inevitable that there would be infiltrations. The reasons for them were explained to me by Khalil Wazir, the man at the epicentre of a political earthquake that was to be caused by Israel's mad military actions, and which resulted in the Middle East being sucked into the East-West confrontation known as the Cold War.

At the time we were talking (1980) Wazir was the commander of the PLO's military forces and Arafat's number two; and better known by his *nomme de guerre*—Abu Jihad. He was the co-founder with Arafat of Fatah, the engine of the regeneration of Palestinian nationalism. The son of a small shopkeeper, Wazir was born in 1935 in Ramleh, some ten miles to the southwest of Jaffa and Tel Aviv. That meant he was 12 when the Israelis were preparing to implement the final phase of their ethnic cleansing programme. Wazir's memories had not faded with the passage of time. (I am giving some space in this book to Wazir's personal account of the final phase of Israel's ethnic cleaning programme because it is the key to understanding the "tragic development" of which Sharett spoke, and why he believed Israel had a "sacred duty" to do everything it could to stop "the wall" between the Israelis and the Palestinians getting "taller").

Wazir's account:

> I can remember as if it was yesterday the day the Zionist forces attacked Jaffa. The Arabs there sent some cars and trucks to us in Ramleh. 'Help for Jaffa!' they cried. 'Help for Jaffa!' I remember the men and women of Ramleh getting into the cars and trucks. They had one very old pistol, a few knives and some sticks. In this time we were helping each other. We knew the Jews would come for Ramleh and Lod if they captured Jaffa. And that is exactly what happened. In one night they surrounded Ramleh and Lod and they were able to do it easily because the Jordanians withdrew without a fight. We were surrounded and alone.
>
> Our people could not fight—they had nothing to fight with. The Mayor and a delegation from the Municipality visited the Jewish commanders. The Mayor said to them: 'Okay, you can enter the city but you must not harm the people or take prisoners, and you must allow the people to stay in their homes and have their normal lives.' The Jews said 'No.' They wanted us to leave our homes—to leave our city.
>
> When we decided not to leave, the Jews put Ramleh and Lod under their artillery fire. I can't forget what happened. The top of our house was hit and we lived in the bottom. Then another shell exploded and our door was destroyed by the blast. The shells were falling in every part of Ramleh and the Mayor told all the people to take shelter in the mosques and churches. We lived in the Christian part of the city and we went to the Roman Catholic Church. On the way some of our neighbours were killed by the shells.
>
> We lived in the church for two days before the Jews entered the city. Men, women and children sleeping side by side. There was not the space to put a foot between the bodies. We had to put our legs on the bodies of others. When the Jews came I went to the fifth floor. I looked through the shutters and with my own eyes I saw Jewish soldiers shoot and kill some women and children who were still in the street. I can't forget. Then I watched as the Jewish soldiers entered our houses, kicking and breaking the doors and shooting. Sometimes they pulled people into the street and killed them.
>
> In the church people were crying. They were saying, 'Deir

Yassin', 'Deir Yassin.' We were sure we were going to be massacred. The priest made a white flag and when the Jewish soldiers entered the street of the church he went out to meet them. The priest and the soldiers entered the church. They said to all of the people, "Hold up your hands." Everyone held up his hands. Then the Jews began to separate us. They said they wanted all the youths and men from 14 to 45. And they took them away. Those of us who were left were the kids, the women and the very old men.

The next day the Jews allowed us to return to our homes and I can't forget what happened. In the night the Jewish soldiers came not less than ten times to our house. They pushed their way in and made a mess of everything. They said they were searching for weapons but really it was a part of their policy to make us feel insecure and frightened. It was their tactic to make us run away from our homes and our country. My grandmother at the time was very old and very sick, and each time the Jews came to our home they pulled the covers from her bed. When the Jews realised we were not going to leave our homes they became more and more angry.

Two days later the Jews made an announcement over their loudspeakers. They ordered us to leave our homes and assemble at certain points on the road. They said they were arranging for some buses to take us to Ramallah. We lived for three days on the roadside. At night they fired over our heads. On the second day, when the buses had still not arrived, they ordered the older men to walk to Ramallah. I was left with three of my brothers—one was still a baby—my three sisters, my mother, my grandmother and my aunt.

On the third day the buses arrived. We had some bags with us. In one there was some bread and cheese and also a new pair of pyjamas of which I was very proud. When the Jews told us we could not take our bags on the bus, I made an attempt to get the bread and the cheese and my new pyjamas. With the innocent voice of a very young boy I spoke to one of the drivers. In Hebrew I said, 'Mister, mister I want some food', and I pointed to one of our bags. He said, 'Okay, okay.' When I put my hand into the bag there was some angry shouting in Hebrew. In that instant my mother pulled me to her chest. She had seen a Jewish soldier taking aim at me. He fired several shots. I would have been hit and probably killed if my mother had not seen what was happening. The bullet missed me and entered the leg of one of our neighbours. He was from the family of Al-Marsala. Today he lives in Amman.[10]

Eventually the women and children of Ramleh were put aboard the buses and sent on their way to Ramallah. But their ordeal was far from over. The worst was still to come.

When we were more than ten miles short of Ramallah the Jews stopped the buses and told us to walk the rest of the way. They pointed and said, 'Ramallah is over there, you must pass through those hills and valleys.' So we started to walk. We had to move slowly. Some of the women were very old and very sick and they had to stop every few minutes to catch their breath and rest. Some of the other women who were more able to walk became exhausted from carrying their children.

On the second night the Jews shelled us with their artillery and mortar bombs. At first we took cover behind some rocks, then, when the shelling continued, everybody started to cry and panic... and we were running, running, running all the way to Ramallah. I can't forget what happened. Some mothers abandoned their children—they were just too exhausted to carry them further. Even my aunt told my mother to leave some children behind. My mother was carrying three children. My aunt said to her: 'You can't run while you are carrying three children. You will be killed. You must leave two children behind and we will send help when we get to Ramalah.' My mother refused. She said to me: 'Khalil you are only 12 and you are not very strong—do you think you can carry one of your sisters and run?' I said 'Yes' and I did. Some children were left behind because there was nobody to carry them. Till now I cannot forget.

There were no Arab forces in the area—no regulars, no volunteers, no Arab forces of any kind. The Jews knew who we were and where we were. It was a deliberate and calculated attack on us with only one objective. They were making sure that we arrived in Ramallah in an obvious state of panic and distress. They were hoping that our condition and the stories we would tell would cause others to be frightened and flee from their homes. It was all part of a very clever and very successful Zionist strategy to force us to leave our homeland in fear. [11]

In Ramallah, and in the bigger panic that followed, Wazir and some 50 of the women and children from Ramleh managed to find places in a truck bound for Hebron. From there they crossed into Gaza.

By then Gaza was on its way to becoming a hell-hole. The Strip was, is, about 40 kilometres long and averages just over eight kilometres in width. Prior to the final phase of Israel's ethnic cleansing programme, its population, Arab, was about 100,000. By the time the Armistice Agreements were signed, its population was 310,000 and rising. The Gaza Strip was home—they hoped and believed it would be only temporary—to nearly a quarter of a million Palestinian refugees.

By the time of Nasser's emergence from the shadows, the Gaza Strip (his Egyptian outpost) was described as resembling "a vast concentration camp."[11] That was the description of General Burns, the Chief of Staff of the UN's Truce Supervision Organisation from 1954 to 1956. In his book, *Between Arab and Israeli*, he said this of the concentration camp's inmates:

> They can look to the east and see wide fields, once Arab land, cultivated extensively by a few Israelis, with a chain of kibbutzim guarding the heights or the areas beyond. It is not surprising they look with hatred on those who have dispossessed them.[12]

Use of the emotive term "concentration camp" so close in time to the horrors of the Nazi holocaust was not politically correct, but it was justified. Contrary to Israel's propaganda claims, the RCC, from the moment of its coup, had taken steps to put the lid on Gaza. Egyptian security agents in the Strip were instructed to do whatever was necessary to prevent the Palestinians from demonstrating, acquiring weapons, organising in any way and, above all, crossing the armistice line into Israel—infiltrating. Whatever was necessary came to include brutal beatings, formal arrest and torture, and prison sentences of up to ten years. The Egyptian Army was very thin on the ground but the place was crawling with Egyptian security people. In time Wazir would attempt to organise an embryo liberation movement of his own in Gaza and was imprisoned and tortured by Nasser's security people.

Egyptian security agents in the Gaza Strip were instructed to do whatever was necessary to prevent the Palestinians from demonstrating, acquiring weapons, organising in any way and infiltrating into Israel.

The RCC's policy of brutal suppression was driven by the determination to do everything possible to prevent the dispossessed Palestinians giving Israel's hawks even the smallest pretext for further military action—reprisals. The point was not that Israeli reprisal attacks would cause the dispossessed Palestinians further great suffering, though, of course, they would do that. The point was that the post-war Arab regimes, because of the balance of military power—Israel's superiority—were not in a position to stand up to the Jewish state. *If they were attacked by it, they would be seen to be incapable of defending their own territory and peoples; and that, to say the least, would not have been good for regime survival.*

As matter of fact the governments and the security services of all the frontline Arab states were doing their best to prevent Palestinian refugees crossing into Israel. And they were all motivated by the same fear—Israeli reprisals. The Lebanese authorities effectively sealed their border with Israel and moved most of their Palestinian refugees to camps in the north—in Sidon, Tyre and Beirut. The Syrian authorities exercised strict control over their border. Jordan had the most difficult and actually impossible task because it had the longest and most winding border with the Jewish state, and some of its villages were divided down the middle by the armistice line; but the Arab Legion and other Jordanian security services were not less brutal than their Egyptian counterparts in trying to prevent their Palestinian refugees crossing the armistice line.

Yet still there were infiltrations. Wazir explained:

> It was the habit of many Palestinian refugees, at the weekends especially, to slip secretly over the border to look at their homes and their farms and their land in Israel. Usually they only looked from a distance—you can imagine what a sad experience it was for them. In those areas where the Jews were not settled the Palestinians sometimes went into their homes to see if everything was okay. And sometimes at night they used to bring fruit and vegetables from their gardens. I remember one man returned with the motor from the pump of his well. This was the habit of the Palestinian refugees in Gaza and also Jordan.[13]

Between 1949 and 1955 there were thousands of infiltrations, mainly from Gaza and Jordan. Research acknowledged by Shlaim was subsequently to show that probably 98 percent of the infiltrations were of the kind described by Wazir. In other words, most Palestinian infiltrators were motivated by social and economic concerns, not by political and military concerns. By definition most infiltrations were not incidents of hostile intent and did not constitute a threat to Israel's security. But...

The infiltrations did have the effect of undermining the morale and confidence of Jewish settlers in the border areas. Many of them were recent immigrants from Arab countries (Oriental Jews as they were called), including some of those who had been encouraged to leave Iraq by the activities of Israeli agents posing as Arab terrorists. All the new Jewish settlers in the border areas were undergoing a painful process of adjustment to their new environment. (In a sense they were the equivalent of America's cowboy settlers, troubled by the visitations, mainly at night, of the dispossessed Indians—except that most of the Palestinian Indians were not attacking). As it happened, the psychological impact on Jewish settlers of even the non-hostile Palestinian infiltrations was sufficient to cause Israel's security establishment to conclude that the settlers might lose their nerve and give up. Withdraw. If they did, the territorial integrity of the Jewish state would be in question. Conclusion—the infiltrations had to be stopped by all and any means.

Israel's first response was a "free fire" policy. It authorised the IDF, border guards and police to *shoot first and ask questions later.* As a consequence up to 5,000 Palestinian infiltrators were killed between 1949 and 1956. The vast majority of them were unarmed.

It was, however, the two per cent (or thereabouts) of hostile Palestinian infiltrations that gave Israel's political and military hawks what they wanted most—*the opportunity by escalation to teach the Arabs lessons and demonstrate who was the master.* Hostile Palestinian infiltrations—the planting of homemade explosive devices and shooting—resulted in Israeli deaths. Not many but some. And Israel's policy of massively disproportionate retaliation (still today as counter-productive as it was in the beginning) was underway.

Fear that even non-hostile Palestinian infiltrations would destroy settler morale led Israel's security establishment to embark on a "free fire" policy on infiltrators. Some 5,000 Palestinians were killed betwen 1949 and 1956, the vast majority of them unarmed.

Initially the "free fire" policy was supplemented by the razing of abandoned Arab villages—presumably they would not have been destroyed if there had been enough incoming Jewish immigrants to take them over; by Israeli patrols along the borders to prepare ambushes, lay mines and set booby traps; and by periodic searches of Arab villages whose inhabitants had not fled during Israel's war of independence.

What sometimes happened during these periodic searches was described by Shlaim. He wrote:

> From time to time the soldiers who carried out these operations committed atrocities, among them gang rape, murder, and, one occasion, the dumping of 120 suspected infiltrators in the Arava desert without water. The atrocities were committed not in the heat of battle but for the most part against innocent civilians including women and children. *Coping with the problems of day-to-day security thus had a brutalising effect on the IDF. Soldiers in an army that still prided itself on the precept of 'the purity of arms' showed growing disregard for human lives and carried out some barbaric acts that can only be described as war crimes.*[14] [Emphasis added]

When Hussein took his place on the Hashemite throne of Jordan at the age of 17 in May 1953, he confessed to not knowing much about Israeli thinking, but making allowance for that he was still puzzled, he said, by the violence of Israel's response to minor incursions across the armistice line by Palestinian infiltrators.

In conversation with King Hussein many years later, I said I thought Israel's lust for violence was not for explaining by any journalist, politician or military man. Only a psychiatrist could explain it. The king replied, "I think, sir, you are correct." (Hussein was so polite that he addressed all of his visitors, even us wretched journalists, as "sir").

Inevitably, belief in the notion that the only thing the Arabs understood was force led to further escalation—attacks by Israeli Special Forces on Arab villages in the frontline Arab states, Jordan especially. Israel justified its aggression, which it called self-defence, with the assertion that Arab governments and their security forces were aiding and abetting the border violations. It followed that Arab governments, not Israel, were the threat to the peace of the armistice agreements. Israel's assertion was completely without foundation. It was a propaganda lie, pure and simple.

General Burns offered a version of the truth.

> The wrongness of the policy was not that it sought to make the Arabs stop sending marauders into Israel, but that it was a slightly indirect method of *using military power to force the Arab states, primarily Egypt, to accept the Israeli peace terms.* [Emphasis added] That is to say, it was an attempt to settle an international dispute by military force, in complete disregard of Israel's engagements as a member of the United Nations.[15]

It was the policy of massive and disproportionate retaliation that prompted Sharett to fight in cabinet for what he believed—*the idea that a peaceful accommodation with the Arabs was possible, probably, and that the prospects for reconciliation were being sabotaged by Israel's behaviour.* Sharett and his doves argued that the policy of massive and disproportionate retaliation was doubly counterproductive. It was not actually saving Israeli lives. And it was inflaming the hatred of the Arab masses (making "the wall" taller) and making it more and more difficult for their leaders to be accommodating. The doves were, of course, right on both counts. In public Abba Eban had the job at the UN of defending Israel's line. But in private he supported his political boss, Foreign Minister Sharett, and warned that Israel's actions were not in its own best interests.

Unfortunately it was a fight Sharett was never going to win, but he fought.

It is reasonable to assume that in July 1953 Sharett entertained the hope that he could stop the madness on his own side. In that month he took over from Ben-Gurion—became acting prime minister as well as foreign minister. (Ben-Gurion was 68 and exhausted.) But within days of Ben-Gurion's departure for three months leave of absence, Sharett was considering resignation.

The cause of his concern was a Dayan project to divert water from the Jordan River in the north to the parched lands of the Negev in the South. It was an absolutely outrageous enterprise. The Jordan River, which flows southward from Syria across Israel and into Jordan, is the longest river in the world. It rises on the southeast slopes of Mount Hermon in Syria (other headstreams rise in Lebanon), flows through a deep trench flanked by high plateaus, and, having crossed the Hula Basin and traversed the Sea of Galilee, drains into the Dead Sea. The point? The River Jordan was an international waterway and, under international law, all the riparian states had rights over it. The project was all the more contentious because some of the diversion work would have to be carried out in the UN supervised DMZ—the one that put some distance between Israeli and Syrian military forces.

Nobody knew better than Dayan that Israel had no legal right to divert the water and, more to the point, that when the matter was referred to the UN the ruling would go against Israel. So Dayan invoked Israel's own first rule for the playing of the Game of Nations—the creation of facts on the ground. The bulldozers suddenly appeared and, covered by the IDF, started digging a canal in the DMZ. It was Dayan's intention to say to the outside world, in effect: "We know we should not have done this, but we've done it; and there's nothing you can do about it now."

Angry and alarmed, Sharett decided to call on Ben-Gurion in Side-Boker, the resting leader's isolated kibbutz in the southern Negev. The acting prime minister assumed that when he presented the facts, the "Old Man" would side with him against Dayan. (At the time Dayan was chief of the operations branch of the General Staff). Sharett would then give the order for work on the water diversion project to be stopped and Dayan would not dare to challenge him. Sharett's problem was that the cabinet had approved the project in principle before Ben-Gurion went on leave. At Side-Boker, with Dayan and his advisers present, Sharett argued that the manner in which the project was being carried out was "unwise, illegal and provocative," and "will bring Israel into confrontation with the UN."[16] Dayan's advisers argued that the UN had no right to interfere. That was nonsense but Ben-Gurion went along with it. *He ruled that the UN should be ignored and that the work should proceed.*

To make matters worse Sharett discovered that Dayan's people were lying to him as well as the UN. On orders from Dayan, Israel's representative on the Mixed Armistice Commission was telling the UN that work in the DMZ was confined to Jewish-owned land. When Sharett visited the area to see for himself, he discovered that was not true. And it was clear to him that Dayan had two objectives—the first to divert the Jordan River, *the second to take by stealth Arab-owned land in the DMZ.*

It might have been that Sharett did not resign because he received word from Washington that the Eisenhower administration was outraged and intended to apply pressure of its own to support his stand against the hawks. In any event, Secretary of State Dulles publicly announced the suspension of a $26 million dollar grant-in-aid to Israel. Subsequently Sharett got enough cabinet support to stop the water diversion project; but his real problems with Israel's military hawks (and Ben-Gurion as their champion) were only just beginning.

When Ben-Gurion went on leave he left a ticking time bomb in the cabinet room. It, or rather he, was Pinhas Lavon. Ben-Gurion, prime minister and defence minister, had given Lavon the defence portfolio on an acting basis. While Ben-Gurion was away Sharett, obviously, could not be foreign minister, acting prime minister and acting defence minister. Lavon would later be described by Golda Meir as one of the "most capable" but "least stable" of her colleagues.

As acting defence minister Lavon's first contribution to Israel's military madness was ordering an attack on the Arab village of Qibya in Jordan. An Israeli mother and her two children had been murdered by Palestinian infiltrators who had apparently crossed the armistice line near that village.

The IDF force assigned to the mission had been training for weeks. It was a small, special commando unit, designated 101. Its commander was Ariel Sharon, then as aggressive and as thirsty for Arab blood as he was ambitious.

Dayan's stated view—he knew it had no basis in reality—was that all Palestinian infiltrators were "terrorists", and that the frontline Arab states, unchangeably committed to Israel's destruction, were encouraging and supporting them and would continue to do so until the Arab armies were ready to launch an all-out attack on the Jewish state. In other words, infiltration was, in Dayan's stated view, both an Arab substitute for total war and part of the Arab softening up of Israel for war. So the message of the up-coming Israeli reprisal attack on Qibya was addressed to the Palestinians and Jordan in particular and the Arabs in general: "If you mess with us, you'll pay a terrible price."

When Sharon was at "Go", Sharett tried to stop the attack after learning what had happened at a meeting of the Mixed Armistice Commission. Jordan's representative had denounced the murder of the Israeli mother and her two children and promised his country's full co-operation in tracking down the killers. The Jordanian also conveyed a personal appeal from Glubb—he was still in charge of the Arab Legion—for Israel to refrain from retaliation because it was in nobody's best interests and would only make a deteriorating situation worse for all concerned.

That was more than enough for Sharett to telephone acting defence minister Lavon to say he wanted the attack on Qibya called off. The soundness of Sharett's judgment was subsequently confirmed by no less an authority than Yehoshafat Harkabi, then deputy DMI. He would later say that no proof of Jordan's complicity in the murder of the Israeli mother and her two children could be given "because no proof existed." He went on to say that having personally made a detailed study of the "phenomenon of infiltration", he had come to the conclusion that the Jordanians, the Arab Legion especially, were doing their best to prevent infiltration, which he described as "a natural, decentralised and sporadic movement." Effectively he was rubbishing Dayan's view.[17]

But Dayan, Sharon and all the gut-Zionists were not concerned with reality or truth. *The murder of the Israeli mother and her two children was too good a pretext to be passed up.* If the Jordanians were as good as their word, it might be some time before the IDF had another such opportunity to teach the Arabs a lesson and, more generally, to heat up the situation and sabotage whatever prospects there were for peace on terms that would confine the Zionist state to something very like the armistice borders.

Lavon told Sharett that he would speak with Ben-Gurion. The evidence is that he did not. Ben-Gurion subsequently said that he would have approved the attack on Qibya if he had been asked. The implication is that Dayan said to Lavon something like: "Don't bother to ask the Old Man, he will approve."

The acting defence minister had no further contact with Sharett or any member of the cabinet until the deed was done.

On the night of 14-15 October, 69 residents of Qibya, most of them women and children, were slaughtered. The 45 houses in which they lived were blown up over them. Sharon was later to claim that he believed all the inhabitants had run away and that their homes were empty when they were dynamited. It was a lie and the evidence that said so, noted by UN observers when they arrived on the scene, included a bullet splintered door with a body sprawled across the threshold. It was clear that the Arab residents had been forced to stay inside their homes by heavy gunfire.

Sharon's attack on Qibya was by any standards a war crime. It could also be described as the IDF's Deir Yassin.

The world responded to Israel's attack with diplomatic fury. And it was Ben-Gurion himself—not foreign minister and acting Prime Minister Sharett—who decided what Israel would say to the world. Though he was about to announce his retirement for good, Ben-Gurion had just completed his three months' leave and he chaired the cabinet's crisis management meeting on 18 October.

Sharett was sickened by the scale and brutality of the Unit 101's work. His proposal was that Israel should come clean and issue an official statement expressing regret over the action and its consequences. Ben-Gurion, who had congratulated Sharon, said "No". Israel was not going to admit that the IDF had carried out the action. The story Israel would tell the world, Ben-Gurion himself would draft the statement, was that Qibya was the consequence of irate Israeli villagers whose patience had been exhausted by endless murders taking the law into their own hands. And that was the substance of Israel's official statement. Endorsed by a cabinet majority.

On 24 November the Security Council passed a resolution condemning Israel and calling on it to refrain from such operations in the future. It was, as ever, Eban who put his finger on why, really, the international community was so cross with Zionism's child. Two days after the UN's condemnation he wrote to Sharett. "The thing that most distinguishes Israel from all other countries is the sending of forces across an international border. No other state acts in this way. It was this, rather than the heavy casualties, that shocked the world."

In retrospect and to illustrate the point Eban could have said something like this: "Imagine how shocked the international community would be if, in response to the murder in British Northern Ireland of a mother and her two children by the IRA, Britain sent special forces across the border with the Republic of Ireland to massacre 69 innocent Irish people, mainly women and children, by blowing up their homes on top of them."

Eban: "The thing that most distinguishes Israel from all other countries is the sending of forces across an international border. No other state acts in this way."

Though he defended his country's action in public at the UN, it was, Eban said in private, no way for any state including the Jewish state to behave.

But crossing borders by land and air—violating the territorial integrity of other nation states—was Israel's way.

One consequence of Ben-Gurion's explanation of the Qibya massacre was that lying became a norm for many of those with responsibility for making and defending Israel's policies.

It was to Aryel Eilan, an official of the Foreign Ministry, that Harkabi had said there was "no proof" of Jordan's complicity in the murder of the Israeli mother and her two children. As quoted by Benny Morris in *Israel's Border Wars*, Eilan said that whatever the truth of the matter, the fact was that Israel's leaders had repeatedly gone on record asserting Jordan's complicity, and it was therefore necessary for Israeli spokesmen to go on supporting their leaders. Eilan then said [emphasis added]: "*If Jordanian complicity is a lie, we have to keep on lying. If there are no proofs, we have to fabricate them.*"[19] He had described precisely how Zionism operates.

After the unprecedented diplomatic and public relations disaster for Israel that Qibya was, Ben-Gurion confirmed to his cabinet colleagues his intention to retire. But he was not going until he had set Israel's course.

At a special cabinet meeting on 19 October he presented his defence review. It was a detailed plan with specific proposals for strengthening the IDF and improving the country's security. The assumption on which the plan was based, an assumption Ben-Gurion said was "incontestable", was that the Arab states were preparing for war with Israel. *That was complete nonsense but it was what Israel's gut-Zionists needed their people, Jews everywhere and the Western world as a whole to believe—in order, against the ever present background of the Nazi holocaust, for Israeli aggression of the future to be seen and accepted as self-defence.*

Sharett for his part did not hold back from indicating what his strategy would be when he took over as prime minister in his own right. He would seek to forestall any Arab threat to Israel by non-military means. These would include, had to include, "activating solutions to the refugee problem by a bold and concrete offer on our part to pay compensation; restoring good relations with the great powers; and ceaseless struggle for an understanding with Egypt."[20]

Before he went into retirement on 7 December, Ben-Gurion made three appointments. He confirmed Lavon as minister of defence; appointed Dayan as the IDF's chief of staff; and promoted Shimon Peres from deputy to director general of the Defence ministry. At the time probably only three people in Israel—Ben-Gurion himself, Dayan and a scientist—were aware of what the prime responsibility of the new director general of the Defence ministry was to be... *oversight and control of the development of Israel's atomic bomb.* The scientist, a refugee from Nazi Germany and the son of one of Berlin's most influential rabbis, was Ernst David Bergmann. He was the father of Israel's doomsday weapon.

Sharett had unsuccessfully opposed the appointments of Lavon and Dayan; and Golda Meir was among the cabinet ministers who had pleaded with Ben-Gurion not to confirm Lavon. But the "Old Man" had refused to listen.

Dayan and Lavon were absolutely committed to extending Israel's borders by war. Ben-Gurion appointed them in the hope and belief that they would screw Sharett—prevent him from implementing his policy of seeking an accommodation with the Arabs in general and Nasser in particular.

When Sharett became prime minister in his own right, his cabinet was evenly and therefore deeply divided between those who wanted peace with the Arabs and those who wanted war.

The other main division was over the matter of what Israel's attitude to the outside world should be, and to the UN in particular.

Sharett and his doves believed that the UN, having played an indispensable part in the creation of the State of Israel, should be allowed to play a bigger and more effective role in regulating the Arab-Israeli conflict. Sharett also believed that international public opinion did matter and would have a bearing on Israel's well-being and security. And that in turn was why Sharett believed it was absolutely necessary for Israel to abide by the prevailing norms of international behaviour which meant, by definition, that Israel had to refrain from military actions that would damage the Jewish state's relationship with the outside world as well as fuel the fire of Arab hatred at street level. *In short, Sharett believed that what the Gentiles thought was important.*

The view of the hawks, in keeping with the tradition of gut-Zionism, had been set in a tablet of stone by Ben-Gurion. In an article on the UN he had written:

> We must wean ourselves from the preposterous and totally unfounded and baseless illusion that there is outside the

> State of Israel a force and a will that would protect the life of our citizens. Our own capacity for self-defence is our only security.[21]

Put another way, and as Ben-Gurion himself was fond of saying, the position of the hawks was this: "*Our future does not depend on what the Gentiles say but on what the Jews do.*"

But it was Ben-Gurion's protégé, Dayan the ultimate gut-Zionist, who was the most pessimistic of all the hawks. He shared Ben-Gurion's view that Jews could never again put any trust in Gentiles. He also believed, or said he believed, that the Arab-Israeli conflict was a struggle for survival between two communities whose interests were, and would remain forever, irreconcilable. From that perspective Israel had no alternative but to go on imposing its will by force. To the end of time if necessary.

The real Dayan, the one I came to know quite well, was revealed by the words he spoke at the funeral of Ro'i Rotberg. He was a young Israeli farmer and armed settler from the kibutz Nahal-Oz where he was killed by Palestinian infiltrators from Gaza. Dayan, one of the few of Israel's early leaders to be born in Palestine—in Degania near the Sea of Galilee in 1915—said this:

> Let us not today fling accusations at the murderers. What cause have we to complain about their fierce hatred of us? For eight years now they sit in their refugee camps in Gaza, and before their eyes we turn into our homestead the land and villages in which they and their forefathers have lived. We should demand his (Rotberg's) blood not from the Arabs of Gaza but from ourselves... Let us make our reckoning today. We are a generation of settlers, and without the steel helmet and the gun barrel, we shall not be able to plant a tree or build a house... *Let us not be afraid to see the hatred that accompanies and consumes the lives of hundreds of thousands of Arabs who sit all around us and await the moment when their hand will be able to reach our blood. Let us not avert our gaze, for it will weaken our hand. This is the fate of our generation. The only choice we have is to be prepared and armed, strong and resolute, or else our sword will slip from our hand and the thread of our lives will be severed.*[22] [Emphasis added]

The indication that Sharett was going to be stretched to his limits to control Dayan was not long in coming. On 31 January 1954, at Lavon's request, there was an informal meeting in the prime minister's home. Its purpose was to allow Dayan to unveil a number of plans for military action. One was to break the Arab blockade on the Gulf of Aqaba. A ship flying the Israeli flag would challenge the blockade. If the Egyptians took any preventative action, Israel would bomb the covering Egyptian airbase or attack and capture controlling Egyptian territory.

In his diary for the day Sharett quoted himself as saying to Dayan: "Do you realise that this would mean war with Egypt?"

And he quoted Dayan as replying: "Of course."

Prime Minister Sharett said "No" to the plans Dayan presented on that day and to others he put forward in the following three or four weeks. Exasperated, Dayan decided that the only way he could force Sharett's hand was by bringing Ben-Gurion into the act. Thus it was, at the end of February, that another informal meeting took place. This one in the library of Ben-Gurion's home in Tel Aviv.

This time it was Defence Minister Lavon who made the presentation with Dayan pulling his strings. It was a proposal for military action and quite probably war on two fronts: a thrust in the south to detach the Gaza Strip from Egypt; and an invasion of the DMZ in the north—along the border between Israel and Syria.

Ben-Gurion said he was opposed to provoking Egypt for the time being, *but he was in favour of invading and occupying Syrian territory*. And he agreed with Lavon and Dayan that they could tell the world a plausible enough story that would make Israeli aggression appear to be self-defence. There had just been another coup a Syria and they could claim that, out of fear of anarchy in Syria following the coup, Israel had taken pre-emptive action to protect its settlements in the north.

Ben-Gurion then put forward his own idea for not confining Israeli action in the north to such a limited objective. *What he proposed—proof that he was half-mad?—was that Israel should set about dismantling Lebanon!*

At the time Lebanon was an uneasy coalition of interests with a Christian majority and a Muslim minority; but it was evident that a day was coming when the Muslims would be the majority. The time was therefore right, Ben-Gurion said, for Israel to seize the initiative and re-make Lebanon by encouraging and assisting the Christians to set up their own state which would be allied to Israel. If that required Israeli military intervention in Lebanon, so be it. (The Greater Israel of Zionism's mad dream included a chunk of Lebanon up to the River Litani. If grabbing it could be part of the deal with the Christians, so much the better).

Ben-Gurion proposed that Israel should re-make Lebanon by encouraging and assisting the Christians—by military intervention if necessary— to set up their own state, which would be allied to Israel.

Sharett explained why he thought that re-making Lebanon was a crazy notion and why he was rejecting the Lavon-Dayan plans for military action. They were bound to unite the Western powers and the Security Council against Israel and it would end, no doubt, with a humiliating Israeli withdrawal.

For the moment Sharett seemed to be in control of events on his own side.

Though it was required by Sharett's opposition to refrain from massively disproportionate reprisal attacks, *Israel's military Establishment, led by Dayan and assisted by Lavon, was in the process of becoming a law unto itself. Operating behind the prime minister's back and lying to him when he asked questions.*

The process of undermining Sharett and all he represented started with an escalation of small-scale Israeli attacks across the border with Jordan, where Glubb on the orders of the young King Hussein had deployed four Arab Legion battalions as part of a determined effort to stop Palestinian infiltration.

On Dayan's instructions IDF spokesmen described the Israeli attacks as a new and necessary form of reprisal in the name of self-defence. They were "hot pursuit" missions. According to the IDF's version of events, all such Israeli actions started with a provocation—an infiltration incident—and Israeli patrols merely followed the fleeing infiltrators ("terrorists" all) across the border, to deal with them when they stopped running, and to punish those who supported them. More often than not the IDF's version of events was a pack of propaganda lies. And no less a figure than Dayan himself admitted as much to Jon Kimche, a friendly British journalist. Kimche then told Sharett that Dayan had said to him, "UN reports are often more accurate than ours."[23]

Most "infiltration incidents" which entailed massively disproportionate reprisal attacks by the IDF were in actuality initiated by IDF patrols without provocation, as a strategy for "terrorizing the Jordanians".

The truth was that most of these Israeli attacks were initiated by IDF patrols without provocation. They were, as Shlaim described them, "a covert and devious strategy for terrorizing the Jordanians."[24]

In a conspiracy with Dayan, Lavon's function was to conceal the strategy from Sharett and to give him false reports when incidents made news. As it turned out, even Lavon himself was not told the truth about the number and scale of the unprovoked Israeli attacks. But that did not stop him boasting to a meeting of the General Staff in July. He claimed that during his period as defence minister to date, more had been done in the military sphere than in all the previous years of struggle. And he listed the variety of operations as "acts of robbery, laying mines, destroying houses, firing on vehicles, etcetera, etcetera."[25]

As a result of Kimche's report of what Dayan had said to him, Sharett had a showdown meeting with Lavon and demanded that the defence minister give him swift and accurate reports on every incident and all IDF operations. Lavon made promises but never delivered.

In response to a report he received of what Lavon had said to the General Staff, Sharett ordered an independent inquiry. It concluded that Lavon had lost effective control of the IDF but was too proud and too frightened to say so. Sharett then summoned Dayan. To the chief of staff the prime minister said: "I order you to put an end, once and for all, to this unruly behaviour of crossing the border every Monday and Thursday, without any consideration of the malignant consequences."[26]

Dayan's reply is not known but if the nightmare Sharett noted in his diary was any guide, the chief of staff accused the prime minister of being a traitor. *Sharett had dreamed, he wrote, that he and his wife had been sentenced to death by firing squad on a charge of betraying the state.*[27]

At the time Dayan and his IDF were taking aggressive actions to promote war, Sharett was working with the Eisenhower administration to promote practical co-operation between the Arabs and Israel, essentially for the purpose of preventing an explosion that could endanger U.S. and other Western oil interests in the Middle East.

One of the reasons for hope that there could be progress on promoting practical Arab-Israeli co-operation was that Nasser trusted Sharett and believed him to be a good man who was committed to seeking an accommodation with the Arabs. Also encouraging was that Nasser was developing a working relationship with the U.S., with Kermit Roosevelt, the CIA's chief in the region, in particular.

At the time even Ben-Gurion (the sane half of him) believed that Dayan and the IDF were going too far. When Dayan told the "Old Man" that he wanted a policy that was "more activist" than that of Sharett's government, Ben-Gurion interrupted him with a question.

"What is activism?" Ben-Gurion asked. "What do you want, war?"[28]

Dayan's reply included the following:

"I am against a war initiated by our side (that was a lie, as events would prove), but I am also against making concessions in any sphere, and if the Arabs, as a result, want war—I do not object."[29]

In Israel the stage was now set for the most hawkish of Sharett's opponents (enemies would be a more accurate term) to demonstrate how far they were prepared to go to undermine Nasser and to wreck the prospects for peace on terms that would prevent the creation of Greater Israel.

Through July there were a number of terrorist attacks in Egypt—in Alexandria and Cairo—against British and American interests.

Israelis were conditioned by their government to believe, and the West was invited by Israel to believe, that these attacks were the work of Arab terrorists. They were, in fact, the work of Jewish terrorists, Egyptian Jews controlled by Israel's Directorate of Military Intelligence, which was then headed by Colonel Binyamin Gibli.

The message Israel's hawks were seeking to promote was that Nasser could not be trusted to protect Western interests. Put another way, the purpose in principle was to have Nasser perceived throughout the Western (mainly Gentile) world as the enemy.

The idea for this outrageous and de-stabilising intervention in Egyptian (and also British and American) affairs was born in late May when it seemed certain that Nasser was going to get what he most wanted from the British—a commitment to withdraw from the Suez Canal Zone in 1956.

In Israel the indications that Nasser was about to get his way with Britain were well received by Prime Minister Sharett and his doves. They believed, and they were right to believe, that once Nasser had liberated his country, he could and would proclaim an historic victory that would consolidate his position as undisputed leader and enable him then to proceed with his "Egypt first" policy which, in turn, would make it easier for him to go, if only with caution and gradually, for an accommodation with Israel. (Because they understood the political situation in Egypt, Sharett and the Foreign Ministry's experts on Arab affairs were well aware that the final departure of the British would rob the Muslim Brotherhood of one of its reasons for being, and thus make it easier for Nasser to impose his authority on Egypt).

Israel's hawks, the military planners in particular, chose to present Nasser's impending agreement with Britain as an unmitigated disaster. The line they took was that the withdrawal of British forces from the Suez Canal Zone would remove a barrier between Israel and Egypt. If that was followed, as they assumed it would be, by Western military assistance to Egypt, that would tip the military balance in Egypt's favour and, as a consequence, Nasser, at a moment of his choosing, would go to war to destroy the Jewish state. In cabinet Lavon apparently "went crazy" and suggested that the armistice agreement with Egypt should be torn up and that Israel should capture and keep the Gaza Strip.

Perhaps some of Israel's hawks were by now the victims of their own propaganda and really did believe that Nasser was committed to war with Israel. But for the more strategic thinkers among Israel's warlords, there were other considerations. *A truly independent and stronger Egypt would make it more difficult, more costly, for Israel to impose its will on the Arabs by force. Worse still, if Nasser's Egypt was getting on well with America, there would be greater and probably irresistible pressure (diplomatic and economic) on Israel to make peace on terms that would confine the Zionist state to something like the armistice borders. A peace, in short, that would prevent the creation of a Greater Israel.*

The conclusion of Israel's military planners? Britain's withdrawal from Egypt had to be prevented at any cost and by any means. The assumption made was that Britain would not actually sign an agreement with Nasser—there would be no British withdrawal—if it believed that Nasser was playing the terror card. By the same logic and because American interests were also to be targeted (by Jewish terrorists pretending to be Arab terrorists), the U.S. would most likely conclude that it should not do business with Nasser's Egypt.

In the minds of those Israeli hawks who conceived and directed the Jewish terror campaign in Egypt there was good reason to imagine that Britain and America might well believe that the terrorists were Arabs directed by Nasser.

The fact was that to get Britain to the point at which it was prepared to initial a heads of agreement document for the withdrawal of British forces in 1956, Nasser had applied some violent pressure.

Supported by America, Britain's starting position in the negotiations with Nasser had been that there was absolutely no possibility of it withdrawing from the Canal Zone unless Egypt was prepared to join an anti-Soviet defence alliance. Nasser had said that was not a proposition he could even consider at least until Egypt had won her complete independence by the removal of British forces from its soil. "How can I tell my people", he asked Nutting, "that I am going into a military pact in collaboration with those who are still occupying our soil?" His people, he said to Britain's negotiators, would tell him he was a fraud and they would not buy it. Given that domestic political reality, Nasser said, it would be counterproductive for Britain (and America) to continue to insist that Egypt's agreement to joining a Western military alliance was a condition for Britain's withdrawal. And, anyway, Nasser had added, he did not believe that Egypt was in danger of attack by the Soviet Union. If there was any danger it would come from infiltration and the threat of internal subversion by Communists in Egypt, and that could not be prevented by pacts or alliances. On the contrary, they would only stimulate internal subversion.

U.S. Secretary of State Dulles was an anti-Communist zealot but he had no difficulty in recognising Nasser for what he really was—a fellow-travelling anti-Communist who regarded Communism as an "alien ideology." So it was not surprising that Dulles had taken Nasser's point well. He concluded and said that Egypt could not be expected to join any Western alliance until the British had withdrawn.

The British had taken a different view because they understood better than the Americans at the time that Nasser's objection to Egypt joining a Western defence alliance was driven by more than domestic political considerations of the moment. For Nasser it was a point of principle. The British knew, because Nasser had been honest enough to tell them, that he did not want Egypt or the Arab world to become involved in the Cold War. He wanted Egypt and a united Arab world (the one Arab nation of his dream) to be non-aligned, not owing allegiance and not being subservient to the controlling powers of either the West or the East. In short, when Nasser said he wanted Egypt and all the Arab states to be "truly independent"—he really meant it. In other words, the still imperial British understood only too well that *Nasser was the thing most to be feared—a real Arab nationalist; one who wanted his country (and the Arab nation) to be developed for the best interests of its own people and not those of outside powers.*

Nasser was what Western governments most feared—a real Arab nationalist who wanted his country to be developed for the best interests of its own people, and not those of outside powers.

Simply stated, the real problem for Britain with Nasser was that he understood that the alliance the British wanted (with Iraq, Turkey and Pakistan as well as Egypt) had two purposes—one acknowledged, the other not. The acknowledged purpose was to keep the Soviet Union out of the region and to have the means instantly available to resist Soviet penetration if it happened. The unstated purpose was to have a mechanism for manipulating and to a degree controlling the states which entered into agreements. In other words: for reasons of economic self-interest there were limits to how truly free the British wanted Egypt (or any of its former colonial territories) to be. Nasser for his part was saying "No" to neo-colonialism. So it was not surprising that, effectively, the British told Nasser to go to hell. If he was not willing for Egypt to become a member of a multilateral defence pact which would give them leverage over him, they would not withdraw.

Israel's military (and political) intelligence organisations were, of course, monitoring all of this on the sidelines and they paid great attention to what Nasser did next.

Unable to move the British by diplomacy, he applied some violent pressure. In the year before Nasser's coup, Farouk's last government had initiated what amounted to a war of attrition against the occupying British in the Canal Zone. British installations were sabotaged and British soldiers were shot by commando volunteers known as fedayeen (from the Arabic word for sacrifice). Nasser decided to adopt the same tactic.

For several months the British dug in deeper and took it. And then, as Nutting was subsequently to say, "Whitehall came to realise the sheer absurdity of trying to maintain bases for the protection of the Middle East which were under constant attack from the very territory they were supposed to defend."[30]

In May (1954) Nasser called the fedayeen off. For those who could read the signs it was obvious that he would not have done so if Britain had not said to him, "Okay, we've had enough. Let's talk."

For the monitoring Israelis that was the indication Nasser was going to get what he wanted—Britain's commitment to withdraw in 1956.

And that was when the idea to discredit Nasser with a Jewish terror campaign in Egypt was born in the mind of Israel's Director of Military Intelligence. The logic was simple. Nasser had resorted to violence against the British. On the back of that it ought not to be difficult to persuade them and the Americans that he was now masterminding a new terror campaign against their interests. (Dayan was in America at the time and it subsequently became known that, behind closed doors, he had opposed the activation of Israel's spy ring in Egypt for such a purpose. But the fact that he opposed it meant there had been discussion of the terror campaign at the highest levels of Israel's military establishment).

Unfortunately for Israel's military intelligence chief, one of his agents was caught red-handed.

On 23 July, the second anniversary of the Free Officers' almost bloodless coup, one of Gibli's terrorists set out to plant bombs in a number of cinemas showing British and American films and a post office. The bombs were crude devices and one of them started to emit smoke prematurely—in the pocket of the Israeli agent as he entered the target cinema. He was arrested by the Egyptian authorities and that led to the rounding up of 13 Israeli agents and the public announcement that they were to be put on trial.

The British and American authorities who were supposed to have concluded that the terrorists were Arabs directed by Nasser did not need more than a few hours, if that, to come to the opposite conclusion... that it was a plot hatched by an Israeli intelligence agency beyond the control of Sharett's government.

It was, in fact, only four days after the arrest of the first Israeli agent that Britain's Secretary of State for War, Anthony Head, travelled to Cairo to meet with Nasser and initial a heads of agreement document committing Britain to withdrawal in 1956.

Perhaps to show his disgust at what some Israelis had done, President Eisenhower chose that moment to send a personal letter to President Naguib who, as it happened, was then under palace arrest, very discreetly, because Nasser suspected his puppet was plotting against him with the Muslim Brotherhood. (Earlier that same year Nasser had banned the Brotherhood and jailed many of its leaders including the leader, Hassan el Hodeiby. That was a gamble on Nasser's part because some of his RCC leadership colleagues had been members of the Brotherhood). In his letter Eisenhower stated that Egypt could expect large-scale economic and military assistance once it had resolved its problems with Britain—i.e. when the heads of agreement document had been turned into a full and final agreement and signed.

Nasser's response to the Israeli plot was, it could have been said, unreasonably reasonable. Why so? He was comforted by Eisenhower's promise. And because he was not remotely interested in confrontation with Israel, and because he respected Sharett and regarded him as a good man who would make an accommodation with the Arabs if he could, Nasser was content to believe private assurances that the Israeli conspiracy had had two related purposes—one to discredit himself, the other to destroy Sharett's policy of seeking an accommodation with the Arabs, beginning with Egypt.

It also has to be said that, at the time, Israel was not even a blip on Nasser's radar screen. He was preoccupied with the on-going negotiations with the British (actually with Nutting) for a full and final agreement on Britain's withdrawal, and his campaign to suppress the Muslim Brotherhood was far from over. (The Brothers had gone underground.) Because of those two priorities Nasser had put his secret dialogue with Sharett on hold.

As it happened, it was Sharett who took the initiative to revive it; he did so because of his increasingly difficult domestic political situation, which had been made much worse by the consequence of what Israel's madmen had done. In October the 13 Egyptian Jews, Israel's spies and terrorists, were put on trial before a military tribunal in Cairo and the prosecutor was asking for death sentences.

That was an enormous problem for Sharett because Israelis had been conditioned to believe another big lie—that what had happened in Egypt was the work of Arab terrorists directed by Nasser, and that the Egyptian Jews arrested and now on trial for their life were innocent victims of an "odious" Arab plot, and were facing death as the result of a show trial simply because they were Jews. All of which proved, Israelis were also conditioned to believe, how much Nasser hated Jews and was committed to the destruction of the Jewish state. (If they had not been traumatised by the Nazi holocaust, probably many if not most Israelis would not have bought the lie as easily as they did; but they were traumatised and they did buy it).

Sharett knew better than anybody else that if even one of the Egyptian Jews was sentenced to death, most if not all of his people in the Jewish state and everywhere, would be confirmed in their conviction that Nasser was not an Arab leader with whom any Israeli prime minister should ever attempt to do business.

Israelis had been conditioned to believe another big lie—that the bombing in Egypt was the work of Arab terrorists directed by Nasser, and that Egyptian Jews were being tried for it simply because they were Jews.

At this time Sharret himself did not know who had ordered the Israeli spy ring in Egypt to be activated.

Also at this time Sharett's credibility with Israel's military establishment was close to zero because he had refused to approve any of Dayan's plans for reprisal attacks, which the chief of staff insisted were necessary to stop the Palestinian infiltrations. One of Dayan's proposals had been for a raid on Gaza City at night to blow up a major (Egyptian) government building, the police headquarters or the waterworks. *Sharett wrote in his diary that while he was seeking to present Israel as a "peace-loving nation", Dayan, if his policy was adopted, would only prove to the world that "Israel was bent on aggression and conquest."*[31]

When Sharett revived his dialogue with Nasser, initially through the Divon-Sadeq channel, his priority was to ask Nasser for mercy in the shape of his intervention to prevent the military tribunal passing a death sentence on any of the Egyptian Jews.

Sharett was aware that he needed to pick the best possible moment to seek Nasser's understanding and help, and he thought the best moment had arrived when, on 19 October, Nutting and Nasser signed the full and final agreement for Britain's withdrawal from the Suez Canal Zone. The last British troops were to be out by 18 June 1956. It was reasonable to assume that Nasser, basking in triumph in the days following the signing, would be relaxed, for perhaps the first time since had assumed power.

Unfortunately for Sharett the timing could not have been worse.

To get Britain's signature on the final agreement for its withdrawal from the Suez Canal and thus all of Egypt, Nasser had had to make a concession. He did, in fact, offer it himself. The final agreement included a "reactivation" clause, to the effect that if the region was involved in war with the Soviet Union, the British could return to help protect the canal. Nasser offered this constructive proposal because he thought it would give the British (and the Americans) enough of what they wanted and could reasonably expect, and allow him to claim that he had secured Egypt's independence without providing scope for the Western powers to interfere in Egyptian affairs in the future. (He would not have been able to make the claim if he had caved in to Britain and agreed to Egypt becoming a member of a Western defence alliance or pact while Britain was still in occupation).

But Nasser's concession to the British (and the Americans) was too much for the Muslim Brotherhood. Its leader, Hodeiby, had been released from prison because keeping him locked up might well have sparked a violent confrontation. He denounced Nasser as "a traitor to the national cause" because he had submitted to conditions for Britain's withdrawal. The agreement, Hodeiby declared, should be torn up and the British should be hounded out of Egypt by force and without further delay. In private Nasser told Nutting he believed that Naguib was conspiring with the Brotherhood with a view to getting rid of him, and that if the plot succeeded the agreement with Britain would be torn up.

Nasser could not have been at all surprised when, on 26 October, while he was addressing a public meeting in Alexandria, several shots were fired at him from the audience. He would have been killed if the assassin had been a good shot. The only thing he managed to hit before being dragged down by the police was an electric light bulb on the platform above Nasser's head.

It was showdown time in Egypt between, on the one side, Nasser and those of his RCC colleagues who were loyal to him and, on the other side, the Muslim Brotherhood, Naguib and those members of the RCC loyal to him.

By dawn the following morning the purge was underway. It would see the arrest of more than 500 Brothers. Most were given long terms in prison and death sentences were passed on Nasser's assailant and four of the Brotherhood's leaders including Hodeiby and two "notables" of the Islamic Establishment. (Only Hodeiby's sentence was to be commuted to life imprisonment. The others were hanged).

And that was the background against which Sharett was asking Nasser to interfere with due process to save the lives of Jewish spies and terrorists!

Sharett, poor man, was so desperate for a positive response from Nasser that, in addition to going through his own Divon-Sadeg channel, he used others to plead for him. One of them was Maurice Orbach, a British Labour Party Member of Parliament. Orbach made a number of trips for one-to-one talks with Nasser.

Initially they were confined to the Cairo trial but over a period of weeks they were extended to cover broader aspects of Israeli-Egyptian relations. The topics covered included Egypt's blockade of Israeli shipping in the Suez Canal and the Gulf of Aqaba; Palestinian infiltration—in Egypt's case from the Gaza Strip; avenues for economic co-operation; solutions to the Palestinian refugee problem; and restraints on propaganda—the need for officials on both sides to stop demonising the state and people of the other party.

While these talks continued Israel's hawks were setting new

standards for outrageous behaviour by their state. On 8 December, for example, five Israeli soldiers were captured several miles inside Syrian territory. Under interrogation they confessed that their mission had been to recover telephone-tapping equipment the IDF had installed.

Lavon's response was to order Israeli fighter planes to intercept and force a civilian Syrian airliner to land in Israel. Its crew and passengers were to be used as hostages for the release of the captured Israelis. The IDF's story for the world—a blatant propaganda lie as usual—was that the Syrian airliner had violated Israel's airspace and endangered the security of the Jewish state.

Not surprisingly this act of Israeli air piracy provoked universal condemnation; and the pressure was sufficient to cause the Israelis to release the plane with its crew and passengers. Sharett subsequently let rip with his anger in a letter to Lavon. In it he accused the heads of the military of "short-sightedness" and "stupidity." And he ordered the minister to defence to make clear to all concerned that his government would not tolerate such acts of "independent policy" on the part of the security forces.

In the same letter Sharett complained about the disinformation the IDF was spreading and, in particular, its incitement of Israeli journalists to criticise his government.

Because of the disinformation (called news) the people of Israel did not know there was a link between the mission of the five Israeli soldiers and their capture and the hi-jacking of the Syrian airliner. Israeli public opinion believed, because it was conditioned to believe, that the Syrian airliner had violated Israeli airspace and had represented a security threat. And as for the captured Israelis—they were merely innocent soldiers doing their normal duty and had been kidnapped on Israeli soil and carted across the border to be brutally tortured. To Israelis it was proof of Syrian "barbarity". First Egyptian barbarity. Now Syrian barbarity. What evil monsters these Arabs and their leaders were.

Sharett's only comfort was that his dialogue with Nasser appeared to be making some progress. At a point, through the Divon-Sadeq channel, they had even started to communicate with each other directly, via the device of unsigned private messages on plain paper.

On 21 December, for example, Sharret expressed his "admiration" for the idealism and tenacity shown by Nasser in his struggle to liberate his country from the last vestiges of foreign domination. That was followed by suggestions about what Nasser might do as a first step toward the improvement of relations between their two countries. Sharret concluded by expressing his fervent hope that no death sentences would be passed on any of the defendants in the Cairo trial.

Nasser replied ten days later. He said he was glad that Sharett realised the Egyptian leadership was putting effort into bringing relations between their two countries "to a peaceful solution" for the benefit of both. Nasser added that he would consider the suggestions Sharett had made and that he would convey his detailed responses through Orbach. They included the following:

- That although the defendants at the Cairo trial were mercenaries of a foreign intelligence service, Nasser would use his influence to try to see that the sentences were "not inflammatory".

- That although the Bat Galim would not be allowed to pass through the Suez Canal, the vessel and its crew would be released. (The Israelis had attempted to challenge Egypt's closure of the Suez Canal to Israeli shipping by sending this smallish vessel, flying an Israeli flag, through it. Israel was insisting that Egypt's blockade of the canal to Israeli vessels was a violation of a 1951 Security Council resolution. In fact the situation was not so clear-cut. Egypt was saying that its refusal to allow Israeli vessels a right of passage was in accordance with the "belligerent rights" it had under the Constantinople Convention. Though nobody in power in the Western world wanted to say so out of fear of offending Zionism, Egypt appeared to have legal right on its side).

- That non-Israeli ships would be allowed to carry all cargoes excluding only war materials and oil to and from Israel through the Suez Canal and the Gulf of Aqaba;

- That Egyptian officials would be instructed to refrain from hostile propaganda and political warfare if Israeli officials were similarly instructed;

- That Nasser would make every effort to prevent border incidents if Israel did the same.

- And the best news was still to come. On condition that strict secrecy was observed, *Nasser agreed to high-level talks, preferably in Paris.*

Sharett's nominated representative for the high-level talks was Yigael Yadin who had been the Haganah's chief of staff. At the time he was briefed for his meeting with Nasser's representative, Yadin was studying in London.

That Sharret believed the high-level talks might lead to a breakthrough is indicated by one of the proposals he authorised Yadin to discuss with Nasser's nominated representative. It was to the effect that Israel would agree to give up a sufficient amount of territory in the southern Negev to allow for the creation of a land corridor through the Negev to connect Egypt to Jordan.

In his secret dialogue to this point Sharett had already established that one of Nasser's two cardinal requirements for a formal peace with Israel was its cession of a bit of the southern Negev to Egypt to create a contiguous border between Egypt and Jordan. Through their various channels Nasser and Sharett had already had a spirited discussion about this.

Sharett had insisted that Israel could not give up what Nasser was demanding because all of the Negev had been awarded to the Jewish state by the UN partition plan. Nasser had replied that Sharett's argument was inconsistent (as indeed it was, and as Bernadotte had been the first to say). Israel, Nasser had said, was now claiming all of the territory she had occupied at the time of the armistice in 1949. Yet when the armistice was concluded with Egypt, Israeli forces had not yet occupied the southern Negev. Peace, Nasser had said, had to be based on give and take, and Israel could not expect the Arabs to agree to her having all of the Negev because the UN had awarded it to her and northern Galilee (awarded in the partition plan to the Arab state) because she had conquered it. That was the inconsistency. As Bernadotte had said to Ben-Gurion, Israel could not have it both ways and peace.

The evidence that Sharett agreed with Nasser about the inconsistency and that Israel, if it really wanted peace, had to go at least some way to addressing Nasser's demand, was in the fact that he authorised Yadin to say that Israel would be prepared to give up a bit of the southern Negev to allow for a land corridor between Egypt and Israel. In effect Sharett was saying: "I can't deliver all that you want on this matter but for real peace I can deliver, hopefully, enough to satisfy you." (Sharett was, of course, aware that King Farouk would have made peace with Israel if it had been prepared to give up a part of the southern Negev in his time).

Yadin's brief also included a proposal for the payment of compensation to help with the resettlement of Palestinian refugees in the Gaza Strip.

Nasser was delighted when the CIA offered its services to help guarantee the secrecy of the talks.

The stage for them was well prepared but given the almost impossible situation Sharett was in—caught between the devil of misinformed Israeli public opinion and the deep blue sea of secretly seeking an accommodation with Nasser—something was bound to go wrong; and it did.

On 2 January, two days after his receipt of Nasser's unsigned personal message on plain paper, and after much agonising, Sharett had decided that he needed to know the whole truth about the "mishap"—the agreed euphemism in the highest political and military circles for Israeli state terrorism in Egypt. And he took the gamble of appointing a two-man committee to investigate the facts with speed. The two investigators were Yitzhak Olshan, a high-court judge, and Yaacov Dori, a former chief of staff.

It was a gamble on Sharett's part because Dayan and others in the military establishment did not want an investigation. So... When Sharret insisted there would be one, Dayan, with the assistance of Peres, conspired to rig the committee's findings.

Dayan deemed it necessary to conceal the identity of the real mastermind of the mishap—DMI Glibli. It was perfectly logical to assume that the committee's findings would not remain secret forever, and that considerable damage would be done to Israel's reputation if it was known that its Director of Military Intelligence had taken it upon himself to authorise terrorism in Egypt. Dayan might also have entertained the thought that, if the truth was established, Sharett would leak it to the Americans. For what purpose? Encouraging them to put more pressure on Israel's hawks, which would have the effect of strengthening support for Sharett's policy of seeking an accommodation with the Arabs.

Thus it was that the two investigators were presented with testimony including written evidence that incriminated Lavon. He was to be the fall guy, the minister who had ordered Glibli to do what he did. It was Glibli himself who told the lie to the investigators and his version was supported by Dayan and Peres. To give the lie added credibility, Dayan went out of his way to tell the investigators about Lavon's deficiencies as a minister.

In passing, Dayan was also very candid about his own role in deceiving his prime minister. As he was later to admit, "I did not conceal my passive partnership in the deceiving of Sharett by Lavon."[32] And about his own disagreements with Sharett, Dayan had this to say to the investigators. "I completely disagree with Sharett's political conception and see in his failure to authorise operations from time to time damage to the interests of the state; and I have no reason to help him in that beyond the call of duty."[33]

It was to be five more years, and still behind closed doors, before the truth emerged—that Lavon had not ordered Glibli to do what he did, and that the documents incriminating Lavon were forgeries and the verbal testimony incriminating him was false.

It was therefore to the credit of the original investigators that they did not completely buy the lie. In their report to Sharett they said they had been unable to reach a clear verdict. They could not be sure beyond a reasonable doubt that Glibli had not received from Lavon the order to activate Israel's agents in Egypt; and they were not certain that Lavon did actually give the orders attributed to him. As fudges go, it was a classic. Dayan must have been pleased enough.

In Sharett's own interpretation of events there was no room to doubt that Lavon, even if he had not given Glibli a specific order, bore the political and moral responsibility for what had happened in Egypt because "he constantly preached acts of madness, and taught the army leaders the diabolic lesson of how to set the Middle East on fire, how to cause friction, cause bloody confrontations, sabotage targets and property of the great powers and perform acts of despair and suicide."[34]

What he wrote in his diary on 10 January indicates that Prime Minister Sharett was shocked to the point of being traumatised by the general state of affairs as revealed by the report on the mishap:

> I would never have imagined that we could reach such a

> horrible state of poisoned relations, the unleashing of the basest instincts of hate and revenge and mutual deceit at the top of our most glorious ministry. I wander around like a sleepwalker, horror-stricken and lost, completely helpless... *What shall I do, what shall I do?*[35] [Emphasis added]

Could there be a more eloquent expression of a good man's agony?

The most obvious interpretation of Sharett's "What shall I do?" question is that it was about Lavon. Should Sharett dismiss him and, if he did, would that open the door to Ben-Gurion's return to government as minister of defence? Sharett knew that if it did, it would spell the end, almost by definition, of Sharett's policy of seeking an accommodation with the Arabs, starting with Nasser's Egypt.

My own interpretation is that the "What shall I do?" question was about much more than Lavon. I think it indicated that Sharett was asking himself if he could dare to tell the people of Israel the truth about what had really happened in Egypt and why.

He must have known there was a possibility, even strong one, that at least some of the Egyptian Jews would be sentenced to death. (By this time the Muslim Brotherhood leaders on Cairo's death row had been hanged). Even if Nasser did use his influence as he had promised, it was unlikely that his own difficult circumstances would allow him to be seen to be dictating to the military tribunal to save all the Jewish spies.

That, in Sharett's troubled mind, was (I speculate) on the one hand. On the other was the certainty that even one death sentence would provoke such a degree of anti-Nasser and anti-Egyptian hysteria in Israel that the policy of seeking a non-violent solution to the conflict would be doomed unless... Unless Sharett told his people the truth. If he did, and if then the worst happened in Cairo, he might still have sufficient room for maneuver to continue his search for an accommodation with Nasser.

By the beginning of 1955 Sharett was, in fact, so alarmed at the extent to which Israeli public opinion had been conditioned by IDF disinformation to regard the Arabs as implacable enemies with whom peace would never be possible, that he had decided to take the earliest possible opportunity to do some truth telling. Not a lot but some.

The opportunity came on 17 January when Begin's Herut tabled a motion of no confidence in Sharett and his government. In the course of the Knesset debate, and essentially because he had rejected Dayan's constant demands for military action, Sharett was accused of defeatism, cowardice, appeasement and many other things.

In his reply Sharett went some way to revealing the truth about the mission of the five Israeli soldiers being held in Syria. Unfortunately he did not do it by saying, "I tell you the IDF has been lying," and "here are the facts as I have established them." Instead he read slowly and with emphasis from the report of the UN's Mixed Armistice Commission. It flatly contradicted the IDF's story that the Israelis had been kidnapped; and it told the truth about the forcing down of the Syrian airliner. The problem with revealing the truth in such a way was that it gave those Israelis who wanted it the scope to say: "The UN is prejudiced against us. If our prime minister really believes the lies in the report he read, he's a fool."

When put to the test in public Sharett had, in fact, pulled all of his punches save one. He concluded his Knesset speech with the statement—it was an obvious attack on more than Lavon—*that Israel had to choose between being "a state of law and a state of piracy."*

When the next blow came on 27 January, it was too heavy for Sharett to ride.

On that day the military tribunal in Cairo delivered its verdicts. One of the 13 Israeli agents on trial had previously committed suicide in prison and was presumed by most Israelis to have been tortured to death. Of the other 12, eight were found guilty and two were sentenced to death.

Because Israelis had been conditioned to believe that the Egyptian Jews were all innocent victims of an Arab plot, they were outraged. And Sharett, in a state of blind panic, called off the scheduled high-level talks he had planned and prepared for with Nasser. In his diary entry for that day Sharett wrote, "We will not negotiate in the shadow of the gallows."[36]

There is nothing in the record to suggest what if any influence Nasser had on the military tribunal. It is possible that he had none. And it is possible that his intervention reduced the number of death sentences from eight to two. It is also possible to imagine a conversation in which Nasser's leadership colleagues told him that he would be stretching his credibility too far if he insisted that none of the Israeli agents should be sentenced to death. They might also have pointed out that Sharett's problems with his own people were of Zionism's making, not Egypt's.

Despite the fact that for Nasser himself the high-level secret talks were a high-risk venture, he so much wanted them to take place that he asked the Americans, through the CIA, to use their influence with Sharett. Nasser's own message to him, through the CIA, was that he did not think the two death sentences were a good enough reason not to go ahead with the high-level talks. Nasser was right but he was not dealing with a rational Israel. He also asked the CIA to tell Sharett he wanted him to understand that, with all the goodwill in the world, there was nothing more in the circumstances he could have done.

No doubt with President Eisenhower's blessing, the Americans did two things on their own account. They praised Sharett for the constructive agenda he had proposed for the high-level talks. And they urged him to give the green light for them to go ahead.

But it was too late. *Sharett had effectively thrown in the towel. Because of the extent to which Israeli public opinion had been misinformed about what had happened in Egypt, Dayan and the hawks had won.*

On 10 February Sharett wrote in his diary that "Nasser was either two-faced or unable to keep his word, and either way he was not a serious partner for negotiations."

Was that what Sharett really believed? I think not. The conclusion invited by all that is known today is that he was blaming Nasser in preference to blaming himself for his lack of courage to tell his people the truth.

In retrospect there is a case for saying that, in order to proceed with the high-level talks, Sharett ought to have told his people the truth, at least to the extent that the Egyptian Jews were Israeli agents and terrorists. If he had been prepared to reveal that much, he could have used the truth to expose and isolate the lunatics who, to a considerable extent, had taken over the running of the asylum. And he could then have added what he believed privately—that what passed for democracy in Israel was in danger.

Why did he not do so?

An answer given today by some Israelis who are aware of the opportunity that was missed is that Sharett was too weak in character and personality. I think that is to do him less than justice. I think he realised that, given the way his traumatised people had been conditioned to see the Arabs as implacable enemies with whom there could never be peace, taking on the hawks was a mission impossible; and that if he really did challenge them, Dayan especially, he might provoke a coup. (As we shall see in due course, another Sharett-like Israeli prime minister, Levi Eshkol, was to become more or less paralysed by the same fear in the countdown to the 1967 war).

But there was, I believe, another reason why Sharett opted to blame Nasser and saw no point in telling his people the truth and challenging the hawks. In his brief to Yadin for the high-level talks he had indicated that he *could* deliver what he hoped would be enough of a territorial concession in the Negev to satisfy Nasser. But soundings he took subsequently convinced him that he would not be allowed by the political and military hawks to deliver even that much. (Though Sharett did not know, it, the Negev had a vital role to play in the clandestine development of Israel's atomic bomb. And that's why he would never have been allowed to deliver the concession Nasser needed).

On 10 February, Sharett, if he had been true to himself, could have written in his diary something like the following: "Nasser is not to blame. The problem is that Israel's military and political hawks do not want peace on any terms Nasser can accept, and there's nothing I can do about it."

Things might have been different—I think would have been different—if Israelis had not been lied to, and lied to repeatedly. There were times in the writing of this book, this was one of them, when I wanted to cry out because of the pain of knowing how much the people of Israel have been so completely deceived by most of their leaders most of the time; and I think I can imagine something of the agony Sharett was experiencing.

As it happened, Sharett did not have to make a decision about Lavon. He resigned on 2 February. After that Dayan and others pressed Ben-Gurion to come out of retirement. He did, and rejoined the cabinet as minister of defence on 21 February.

To his most trusted colleagues at the Foreign Ministry Sharett explained that having Ben-Gurion back was the only way to avoid the mother and father of a domestic political crisis. He added: "You understand, my friends, this is the end of my political career."

That was only a slight exaggeration. It was the beginning of the end of Sharett's all too brief period as prime minister, his policy of seeking a nonviolent solution to the Arab-Israeli conflict and his political career.

Things might have been different if the Israelis had not been lied to repeatedly by most of their leaders most of the time to cover their aggression.

Within a week of Ben-Gurion's return, and with war criminal Sharon again the star of the action on the ground, Israel launched a reprisal attack on Gaza.

It was to bring the superpower rivalry of the Cold War to the Middle East.

And this had two consequences.

The first was to give a self-righteous, aggressive, uncompromising Zionist state, hell-bent on taking more Arab land, the opportunity to present itself as the only reliable bastion of anti-communism in the region: and to have Nasser perceived where it mattered most, in Washington, London and Paris, as a communist stooge when he was not—neither a communist nor a Kremlin stooge.

The second was to add strength, great strength, to the Zionist lobby in America. Effectively America's Cold War warriors, some of them privately anti-Semitic, jumped onto Zionism's bandwagon. For America's own hawks Israel could do no wrong and most of the Arabs, Nasser especially, no right.

6

MAKING NASSER THE ENEMY, ACT II

The codename for the Israeli attack on Gaza which went in on the night of 28 February was Black Arrow. It was aimed straight at the heart of the Egyptian army's Gaza headquarters on the outskirts of the city and was a major escalation on Israel's part.

With Ben-Gurion back and threatening to resign immediately if he did not get his way on "defence" matters, and with no means of controlling Dayan, there had been no way for Sharett to influence events on the home front. He was prime minister in name only.

The hawks were out to provoke a confrontation with Nasser and that meant Israeli aggression would have to be presented as self-defence. Sharett knew that meant lying to the world as well as the people of Israel, but there was nothing he could do about it. Except resign. Which he was not yet ready to do. *He was still his country's foreign minister and in that capacity he was hoping that he could, perhaps, prevail upon the big powers to do their bit to require Israel to behave like a normal state.*

Sharett's real crime was that he did not subscribe to gut-Zionism's view that, whatever the Arab opposition, and no matter how much the interests of all other nations might be endangered, Israel had to become big enough to be the insurance policy—the refuge of last resort for Jews everywhere. Put another way, Sharett believed that if an Israeli-provoked catastrophe for the region and possibly the world was to be averted, Israel had to invest some faith in the goodwill of the Gentiles.

From that perspective there is a case for saying that the two big opposites in Israel were not Sharett and Ben-Gurion, but Sharett and Dayan; and that Ben-Gurion was merely the political force that enabled the gut-Zionism which Dayan personified, to prevail.

From the moment of his return to government as minister of defence in Lavon's place, Ben-Gurion made it clear to all that there was no longer any difference between him and Dayan (and also Lavon) on the subject of what to do about Egypt and its leader. Nasser was, Ben-Gurion asserted, an implacable and dangerous enemy who had to be dealt with by military means.

And what of Sharett? How did Ben-Gurion regard him? According to Ze'ev Sharef, the cabinet secretary, Ben-Gurion said the following about the prime minister. "He is raising a generation of cowards. I will not let him... I will not let him. This will be a fighting generation."[1]

The background truth of what happened on the night of 28 February 1955 was that for the previous four months the Gaza–Israel border had been remarkably quiet. Virtually incident free. And that was because Nasser, as he promised Sharett he would, had instructed his security forces—the army and the plain-clothed thugs of Egypt's counter-intelligence services—to do whatever was necessary to stop the infiltrations. Nasser had been desperate to avoid provoking Israel's hawks and anxious to demonstrate to Sharett that he was a man of his word—to the extent that his own difficult circumstances allowed him to be. (As I noted in my book about Arafat and his struggle, there was no way Nasser could have put a complete stop to infiltration unless he had built a sky-high concrete wall around the entire perimeter of the Gaza "concentration camp").

In the days immediately before Sharon attacked Gaza with two platoons of paratroops there had been two infiltration incidents. The first, a quite deep penetration into Israeli territory, had resulted in the theft of some documents. It could have been a Palestinian refugee liberating his property deeds. In the second incident an Israeli cyclist was killed.

When Ben-Gurion and Dayan called on Sharett to get his approval for Operation Black Arrow, they had in their own terms enough of a pretext for an attack, but because it was to be an attack on the Egyptian army, there had to be an Egyptian military link to the infiltrations. *There was no such link, so Ben-Gurion, or Dayan or somebody invented one*. There was evidence, Ben-Gurion and Dayan told Sharett, that Egyptian military intelligence was directing the infiltrations.

Sharett probably thought they were lying to him as usual, but he approved the attack for a number of reasons. The death sentences on the two Egyptian Jews had been carried out and Israelis, still believing that they were the innocent victims of an Arab plot, wanted revenge. Arab blood. For that reason alone Sharett could not have said "No" to Ben-Gurion and Dayan even if he had wanted to. But he was also comforted by the assurances he was given. Dayan told him there would be not more than "about ten" enemy casualties. And Ben-Gurion promised to tighten the reins in order "to avoid excessive bloodshed." In effect Ben-Gurion was saying to Sharett, "We all know that Sharon likes killing Arabs but he will on this occasion act with restraint."

In the event the casualties on both sides were much higher than Dayan had said they would be; and the scale of the destruction of Egyptian and Palestinian property was far greater than Ben-Gurion and Dayan had implied it could be. The number of "enemy" casualties was 39 killed and dozens injured. (I can imagine Sharett saying something like, "Thank God Sharon was restrained!") Eight Israeli paratroopers were killed and nine wounded.

Sharett was stunned and mortified by the scale of the attack and fearful of its consequences for Israel's image in the world and Egyptian-Israeli relations.

It was not until after the attack that Ben-Gurion or Dayan, or both, decided that they needed to tell a bigger lie than they had originally thought would be necessary to justify what Israel had done. The bigger lie was that Israel had acted (out of self-defence, of course) because an IDF patrol was attacked on Israeli territory by an Egyptian army force. When Sharett was told that was going to be the IDF's story for the world, he said to Ben-Gurion, "Nobody will believe it."[2] Ben-Gurion replied with words to the effect of "So what, who cares."

Sharett: Nobody will believe Israel's expanded pretext for the Black Arrow attack on the Egyptian military.
Ben-Gurion: So what.

Nasser was totally humiliated by Israel's Gaza Raid; and there was a very personal element to his humiliation.

Some of the first Egyptian soldiers to be killed were shot in their beds while they were sleeping. And they were sleeping peacefully because Nasser had assured them, personally, that they were not in danger. A few days before the attack Nasser had made a routine inspection of the Gaza garrison. He told his small force there that he was not intending to allow the armistice line to become a battlefront and that he did not believe the Israelis would attack. His men could relax.

Why was Nasser confident enough to give them such assurance?

It was not because he had expectations that his dialogue with Sharett would lead to peace with Israel in the foreseeable future. The gap between their positions was too wide. For a signed, sealed and delivered peace Nasser had to have a territorial concession in the Negev and a solution to the refugee problem which included the return of at least some Palestinians to their homes and land in what was now Israel. Even Sharett was telling him that Israel could not accept the return of any Palestinians because Israelis would be "swamped". But if the prospects for a formal peace with the Jewish state were not too bright for the time being, there was, Nasser had concluded, no reason for war or hostilities of any kind. Why not? He had no interest in confrontation with Israel and if his dialogue with Sharett had achieved nothing else it had, surely, provided sufficient assurance for Israel's prime minister that Egypt had no belligerent intentions. That being so, Israel had no cause to attack Egypt.

The problem with Nasser's logic can be simply stated. It was that of a reasonable man who, despite everything, had the necessary amount of goodwill when his own circumstances allowed, for negotiating peace with an Israel in something like the partition plan borders.

In evidence of that Nutting offered the following insight. The bitterness Nasser felt over the humiliating defeat of the Arab armies in 1948-9 had been directed "more at those rulers who, like Farouk, had sent their soldiers to do battle with defective arms and no coordinated planning, rather than towards the Israelis for whose courage and military skill he had, as a soldier, a very high regard. An Israeli officer, Major Yeruham

Cohen, whom he met and talked to during truces in the Palestine fighting, afterwards wrote that Nasser seemed more inclined to blame the British than the Israelis and that, after their final meeting, they 'parted with the hope that the day would not be far off when we could be friends without barbed wire coming between us.'"[3]

Nasser had failed to take sufficient account of the fact that, with the main exception of Sharett, Israel at leadership level, political and military, was driven by unreasonable men, many of them without any goodwill for Arabs, and for whom peace was not a desired end at least until Greater Israel was a fait accompli and on Israel's take it or leave it terms.

So Nasser's logic and the conclusion to which it had driven him were deeply flawed. And the charge that could be levelled against him by his own people after the Israeli attack was that he was naïve. Not good for any leader's self-esteem or prestige.

Worse still, the army of his new Egypt had been exposed as unbelievably incompetent—unable to defend not only Egypt's own territory, people (including the refugees) and property, but itself.

The nights immediately following Israel's attack were sleepless ones for Nasser and, if he had been keeping a diary, he could have made more or less the same entry as Sharett—"I wander around like a sleepwalker, horror-stricken and lost, completely helpless... What shall I do, what shall I do?"

The first thing Nasser decided to do was to acquire arms from wherever he could get them. *He wanted and needed them not for attacking Israel but to defend Egypt against Israeli attacks and, hopefully, to deter Israel from attacking by making the cost of doing so too great for Israel to bear.*

At the time of Israel's Gaza Raid (and not forgetting that British forces were still occupying the Suez Canal Zone), the regional balance of military power was significantly in Israel's favour in both manpower and equipment terms.

The total strength of the Arab League armies was 205,000, of which 100,000 were Egyptians. Though Israel had a standing army of only some 20,000 or thereabouts, it could mobilise 250,000 men (and women) in 48 hours. In the Israel-Egypt context and in broad terms, Israel could thus mobilise an army two-and-a-half times the size of Egypt's in 48 hours. And that took no account of the fact that the Israelis, *chutzpah* and all, were far superior to the Arabs in terms of military strategy and tactics and the application in action of both.

On the equipment supply side Israel was doing rather well—because the West was seeing to it that the Jewish state had enough for its legitimate defence needs.

Because he did not want to offend the Arabs to the extent of putting America's oil and trade interests in the region at risk, (and for other reasons that will become apparent), President Eisenhower had decided that the U.S. should not be seen as Israel's main arms supplier but... Under the terms of the Tripartite Declaration, and with Britain's consent, he had authorised France to attend to Israel's legitimate defence needs for the time being.

Britain had given its consent in return for Eisenhower's agreement that it, too, could provide Israel with some arms. The British may have kept to their agreement with Eisenhower but the French did not. They had an agenda of their own and were providing Israel with arms in quantities that far exceeded what Eisenhower had approved. In July 1954 France signed an agreement to provide Israel with jet fighters which far outstripped in speed and armament anything possessed by the Arab air forces.

Egypt on the supply side, was doing very badly. It was getting a trickle from Britain only. At the time of Israel's Gaza Raid, Nasser had not more than six serviceable military aircraft and only enough tank ammunition for a one-hour battle. Despite Zionism's propaganda claim that poor little Israel was facing the prospect of annihilation, its intelligence community was aware of Nasser's military situation and that was, of course, why Dayan was supremely confident that he could pick and win a fight with Egypt on any day of any week he fancied.

Nasser's most fervent hope was that Britain and America would be the suppliers of the arms he needed, principally to deter further Israeli attacks in order to prevent himself and his country being further humiliated by Israel's arrogance of power.

As Nutting was subsequently to reveal, Nasser had, in fact, agreed with London and Washington on the need to put the Arab-Israeli issue "into the freezer."[4] That had been Nasser's own way of putting it. At about the time he used his freezer phrase in confidence, January 1955, a month before Israel's attack on Gaza, he wrote the following in an article for the prestigious American quarterly, *Foreign Affairs*:

> War has no place in the constructive policy which we have designed to improve the lot of our people... A war would only cause us to lose, rather than gain, much of what we seek to achieve.[5]

The truth was that those in Britain and America who needed to know did know that Nasser, the real Nasser—i.e. not the Nasser of Zionist and eventually all Western propaganda—had never entertained, and never would entertain, the thought that the Arabs could destroy Israel.

Leaders and other policymakers in Britain and America knew—despite their propaganda to the contrary—that Nasser had never entertained the thought that the Arabs could destroy Israel.

When Nutting returned to London after signing the final agreement for Britain's withdrawal, he had in his pocket a "shopping list" of the arms Nasser wanted. By the time of Israel's Gaza Raid some three months on, Britain had not responded. Never mind. In theory Nasser had reason to be optimistic at least so far as America was concerned because of the personal assurance President Eisenhower had given.

U.S. Secretary of State Dulles then made Eisenhower's promise conditional. Egypt could look forward to the economic assistance Eisenhower had promised, but there was absolutely no prospect of American arms unless and until Egypt agreed to participate in a Western defence alliance.

Nasser, understandably, thought he had overcome that obstacle and had effectively given the Western powers what they wanted by coming up with the reactivation clause for the withdrawal agreement with Britain. It was, in his view, the guarantee that Egypt could be relied upon to play its part in defending the region against Soviet aggression.

So what else, really, were the Americans, at least some Americans, after?

They were, Nasser concluded, no different from the British. The insistence that arms would only be forthcoming if Egypt joined a Western-controlled defence alliance meant that the arms would come with strings attached. The Americans would pull the strings as and when they pleased to influence many aspects of Egyptian policy making and the result would be that Egypt became, effectively, a client state, with its independence seriously compromised. It was the American version of Britain's neo-colonialism and there was no way Nasser, real Arab nationalist that he was, could or would accept that. (Four days before Israel's attack on Gaza, Iraq as a British client state, and Turkey as an American client state, had signed on as members of the Western defence alliance that became known as the Baghdad Pact). What the Americans were demanding of Nasser was in his view against that most precious of all things—the dignity of the people of Egypt. If his revolution was to be given real meaning, Egypt had to be developed for the benefit of its own people in accordance with their priority needs, not for the benefit of outside vested interests.

After Israel's Gaza Raid, Nasser had hoped that the Americans would be more understanding and reconsider their position. Dulles continued to insist that his condition had to be met. It was a "take it or leave it" proposition.

As Nutting put it, Nasser still continued to "hope against hope" that the Americans would change their minds and agree to supply him with the arms he needed; but because of the humiliation he and Egypt had suffered as a consequence of Israel's attack on Gaza, and because of the absolute certainty of more Israeli attacks, he had to explore the possibility of getting arms from the Communist powers. Like it or not, and Nasser did not like it (events were to prove that), the Communist powers were the only practical alternative source of supply.

America's refusal to supply weapons to Nasser to enable him to defend Eygpt against Israeli attacks drove him, with great reluctance, to seek arms from the Soviet Union.

The story of how Nasser found himself obliged to take arms from the Soviet Union via Czechoslovakia, which had helped to guarantee Israel's victory in 1948, is not a complicated one.

A few weeks after Israel's attack on Gaza, Nasser attended the first gathering of 30 newly independent African and Asian states at Bandung in Indonesia. The two main organisers of the conference were India's prime minister, Pandit Nehru, and China's prime minister, Chou En-Lai. The main concern of all of the participating nations was the domination of international affairs by the "quarrel" between the American and Soviet blocs.

Like Nasser, and for the same reason, none of the participating leaders wanted their countries to be involved in the Cold War. They had the wonderful but naïve idea that they could keep their countries out of it by being non-aligned—not being obligated by defence alliances or pacts with either of the two superpowers. They knew that alliances and pacts would require them to spend on buying weapons the money they needed for their absolute first priority—developing their countries. For the leaders of the newly independent nations assembled in Bandung, the war that mattered most was the war against poverty and underdevelopment in their own countries.

What the leaders assembled in Bandung were actually challenging was the Western and mainly American view that there were only two kinds of nations: the "good" ones—America and its friends and allies; and the "evil" ones—the Soviet Union and its friends and allies. The leaders assembled in Bandung did not accept the Western and mainly American view that there could be no such thing as non-alignment; and that the would-be independents had to make up their minds about whose side they were on—that of the "good" powers or that of the "evil" powers.

The non-aligners and would-be independents were, of course, right. The Western and mainly American way of looking at the world was idiotic. But it did have the merit of allowing Western governments to explain to their voters, in as few words as possible, why they were spending so much public money—taxpayers' dollars, pounds, francs etcetera—on defence, meaning the war machine. An explanation could actually be given in a sound bite of 11 words—"We've got to stop the evil ones taking over the world."

At the conference Nasser was asked by Chou En-Lai about the situation in the Middle East. Egypt, Nasser told him, was facing a serious threat of further aggression by Israel and the Western powers were withholding the arms he needed and had requested, in the hope of forcing him to accept their terms. He was not going to accept arms with strings attached. Nasser then asked Chou if China could sell Egypt some arms.

Chou replied that China was too dependent on the Soviet Union to have any to spare but that he was willing, if Nasser wished, to take up the matter with the Russians. Nasser said, "Yes, please." *Chou spoke to the Russians and with something close to the speed of light. They realised they were being presented, on a plate, gift-wrapped, the opportunity to advance their interests in the region by posing as the only true friend of real Arab nationalism.* Soviet strategists were smart enough to realise that the Western powers, by making their promises of arms to the Arabs dependent on agreements with strings attached, were alienating their natural allies.

Nasser was the classic example. As Nutting would later say, the Soviets would have been "insane" not to have seized the moment.

Nasser had been back in Cairo for less than a week when Daniel Solod, the Soviet Ambassador, called to say that his government had "received the Egyptian request from Peking" and was ready to respond. The Soviet Union would be delighted to oblige—no strings attached—"with the supply of any quantity of arms, including modern tanks and aircraft, against deferred payment in Egyptian cotton and rice."[6]

In addition, the Soviet Union was prepared to assist Egypt with industrial projects such as the building of a High Dam at Aswan to increase the storage of water for irrigation and the generation of hydroelectric power. This was Nasser's dream project and the Americans and the British had said they would provide some of the funding for it.

The inference that can be drawn from the way Zionists tell the story is that Nasser danced a jig and said, "Whoopee, (in Arabic, of course) now I can destroy the Jewish state!"

What Nasser actually did was to inform the American and British Ambassadors of the Soviet offer and tell them he did not want to accept it.

With good reason Nasser was more than a little suspicious of the Soviets. He knew that their original and preferred strategy had been to penetrate the Middle East through their most natural allies in the region—the Jews who were to become Israelis. (On the strength of everything that is known today, and as I indicated in Chapter Eleven of Volume One, I think the Soviets were hoping that Truman would not recognise the unilaterally declared Jewish state, and that when he did not, and they did, Israel would throw in its lot with the Soviet Union). Nasser was also aware, of course, of the role the Soviets had played, through Czechoslovakia, in assisting Israel's fighting forces to be resupplied and to go from strength to strength during the first truce of the 1948 war—i.e. when the Arabs, because of the Western embargo on arms to both sides, were not getting so much as a single bullet from the West.

Effectively, the Soviets had been anti-Arab. On that basis alone there was good reason for Nasser to wonder if their new opportunism would make them reliable arms suppliers—if he had to accept their offer.

But there were other reasons why Nasser was still preferring to buy arms from America and Britain if he could do so on acceptable terms. As Nutting put it, Nasser, despite his differences with the West, "was used to dealing with Westerners: he had no experience of the Russians; and the Egyptian army was accustomed to handling Western equipment."[7]

And there were still other considerations which Nasser discussed with his RCC leadership colleagues. Was it sensible to mortgage Egypt's cotton crop to the Soviets? Probably not.

It was true that there would be no formal strings to the Soviet offer—Egypt would not be required to join a Soviet military alliance; but if the Russians became the sole provider of Egypt's arms, would they not have sufficient influence, actually, to put pressure on Egypt, as Britain had done in the past and America clearly wanted to do in the future? No doubt they would try to push their luck, Nasser admitted, but he could and would resist any such pressure, and resisting would be easier because there would be no formal strings.

When he told the American and British Ambassadors that he did not want to accept the Soviet offer, Nasser said he would have no choice if their governments did not change their minds and provide him the arms he required on terms he could accept—terms that would not make Egypt a Western client state of the kind, he regretted, that Iraq had already become.

The American Ambassador, a recent arrival in Cairo, was Henry Byroade. As assistant secretary of state he had exposed himself to a Zionist charge of being anti-Israel. He had publicly called on the Jewish state to "drop the attitude of the conqueror"; and he had accused Israel of having double standards, this on account of its use of German reparations to bolster its economy "while doing nothing towards compensation of Arab refugees."[8] Byroade understood and sympathised with Nasser's position, and he advised Dulles that Egypt's leader was serious, not playing games. Dulles chose to take the view that Nasser was a blackmailer. And so did London. The British said that if Nasser went ahead with the Soviet arms deal he would get nothing more from them.

While America and Britain did nothing, and Nasser continued to hope that they would change their minds, the Soviets concluded that he was playing them off against the Americans. It seemed so but he was not. He simply did not want to accept the Soviet offer.

At the end of June the Soviets decided to test Nasser's seriousness with the suggestion that he should invite Dimitri Shepilov to Cairo. Shepilov was then the editor of *Pravda*, but the Soviet Ambassador briefed Nasser's people to the effect that he played a very important part in shaping Soviet foreign policy and would shortly be succeeding Molotov as foreign minister. It was clear that he would be coming to Cairo to discuss the details of an arms supply agreement. Nasser decided that he could not avoid going that far.

Dimitri duly arrived and within a matter of days had put together a draft agreement. Egypt would buy US$80 million worth of Russian arms including MiG fighters, Ilyushin bombers, Stalin tanks and other equipment, to be paid for with Egyptian cotton. The arms were entirely of Russian manufacture but the deal was to be officially handled by Czechoslovakia—because Nasser believed that would make it seem to be less sinister to the outside world, because it was through Czechoslovakia that Israel had received its military assistance from the Soviets.

Egyptian technicians took off for Prague to look over some of the promised equipment and Nasser was presented with an agreement for signature. That was mid-July.

And still Nasser was hoping for a change of heart by America and Britain. In fact the British had realised that something was not making sense. They and their American allies were saying there was almost nothing more important than keeping the Soviets out of the Middle East yet, by what they were doing or rather not doing, they were more or less obliging Nasser to bring them in. *One possible inference is that the American Military Industrial Complex wanted the Soviets in to guarantee an arms race for the purpose, in America, of creating wealth from the production and sale of weapons.*

Britain had, in fact, signalled a slight change of heart by selling Nasser 32 Centurion tanks and two destroyers. Encouraged by that, Nasser renewed his efforts to persuade Dulles to change his mind.

In due course Nasser summoned his Air Attaché in Washington home for urgent consultations. As the man entered his office, Nasser pointed to the document on his desk and said: "*This is our agreement with the Russians. I should have signed it by now. Please tell the Americans it will remain here on my desk, unsigned, until I have exhausted every possible means of persuading them to supply the weapons we need for defence.*"[9] (emphasis added)

Before the Egyptian Air Attaché returned to Washington, Nasser talked with Ambassador Byroade to ask for his assistance in making sure that Washington was ready to listen.

The best indication of how much Nasser really did *not* want to go ahead with the Soviet arms deal was that he didn't sign the agreement for two more months. Still hoping against hope that the Americans would be his provider.

Then, on 27 September, after two more Israeli attacks on the Gaza Strip, Nasser signed. In a *New York Times* report by Kenneth Love (with whom he enjoyed a good relationship) Nasser said, "Now we will be meeting Mysteres with Migs."

In reality the balance of military power was not changed in favour of the Arabs by the coming on stream of Soviet arms, to Syria as well as Egypt. Zionism's child, David become Goliath, would remain the military superpower of the region, becoming stronger militarily with every passing year—with its arsenal supplemented with nuclear bombs and the missiles to deliver them—and becoming, as a consequence, more and more arrogant and less and less of a normal state with every passing day.

So far as his standoff with Israel was concerned, Nasser's only purpose in acquiring arms was *to be able to respond to its attacks in a way that would cause its leaders and people to understand that attacking Egypt was not a cost-free option.* If he could succeed in delivering that message to Israel, there was at least a chance, Nasser thought, that it would decide to make peace on give-and-take terms the Arabs could accept. There was, he knew, no hope for peace and every prospect of war by default if Israel continued to believe it could impose its will on the Arabs by force.

After Israel's attack on Gaza, Nasser had two main problems and, because of them, he was in a no-win or, one might say, a lose-lose situation. And Israel's hawks, conversely, were in a win-win situation.

One of Nasser's problems, because of his Soviet arms deal, was in the fact that it was much easier for Zionism's incredibly efficient propaganda machine to portray him as the enemy, on the side of the "evil" power and hell bent on annihilating the Jewish state.

Nasser's other problem was the dispossessed Palestinians. What, if anything, could he actually do for them? The truth was that Nasser did not have a plan. The only thing he was sure about was that much would depend on whether or not the organised international community, through the Security Council, had the will to require Israel to honour its obligations as set down in UN resolutions and with reference to the requirements of international law.

Nasser's greatest fear was of a regeneration of Palestinian nationalism because, with right on its side, it would make demands which the Arab states would have to support with words but would be unable to support with deeds. In Nasser's ideal world (and that of all Arab leaders) there would not be a regeneration of Palestinian nationalism. And the time was coming when Nasser would instruct his security forces to make common cause with those of Jordan and Lebanon to liquidate the underground Palestine liberation movement. Though it may come as a surprise to many readers, it was, in fact, Arab regimes, not Israel, which made the first attempt to destroy Arafat's authentic Palestine liberation movement. The irony, perhaps the greatest one of all in the whole story of the making of the Arab–Israeli conflict, is that the regeneration of Palestinian nationalism might not have happened but for Israel's attack on Gaza on 28 February 1955.

Nasser's greatest fear was of a regeneration of Palestinian nationalism which, with right on its side, would make demands which the Arab states would have to support with words but would be unable to support with deeds.

That really did change everything for everybody.

7

NO GO WITH NASSER FOR THE PALESTINIANS

After Israel's military victory in 1948 and the Zionist *fait accompli* as formalised by the Armistice Agreements of 1949, the dispossessed Palestinians were not only completely demoralised. They were without hope.

The best indicator of the depth of their despair is in this fact: Yasser Arafat, the man who was to become the symbol of the indestructibility of regenerated Palestinian nationalism was himself so totally broken in spirit that he applied for an American visa. He said to me: "My relatives suggested that I should complete my studies in America. I was in such total despair that I agreed to go. I made an application for a visa, and I started to prepare my travel plan to America. For several months I was waiting only to hear that I had been granted a visa."[1] (Though his father was from Gaza and his mother from Jerusalem, the family was living in Cairo and Arafat was born there on 24 August 1929. At the time he was studying for an engineering degree at the University of Fuad the First).

What if the system had not taken so long to process his application: would he have settled in America and made a new life there? "No doubt", Arafat told me.

The cause of his despair was not of itself the loss of Palestine or even his knowledge, confirmed by his personal experience of being disarmed by the Egyptians, that his people had been betrayed by their Arab brothers at leadership level. *The cause of his despair was the discovery that there was no money available to fund the organising and arming of a Palestine liberation movement.*

The Palestinian leadership was in the process of learning that the policy of frontline Arab governments was to prevent them from taking action of any kind in order to avoid provoking Israel.

After the signing of the Armistice Agreements, Arafat in Cairo had concluded that the only way the Palestinians could keep their cause alive was by striking at Israel without delay. That was the only way to give his dispossessed people hope that all was not lost for all time. And there were others of his generation in all the frontline Arab states—those who were to become his leadership colleagues—who were thinking the same. *And they, too, were in the process of learning that the policy of the post-war Arab governments was to prevent the Palestinians organising themselves for action of any kind, military or political.*

The task of creating and training even small groups for hit-and-run attacks on Israel was going to be difficult because all the refugee communities were under surveillance by the security services of the host countries. But nothing was possible without funds for organisation and the acquisition of small arms and explosives.

There were, of course, some very wealthy Palestinians but they had taken their leave of Palestine before Israel's unilateral declaration of independence and the war it triggered. They, one might say, had seen the writing on the wall, and their first priority had been to protect their own interests. By the time the Armistice Agreements were signed they were locked into the political and economic establishments of the Arab world and the West, and there was no way they were going to fund a Palestine liberation movement that could only add to instability in the region and put their interests at risk.

So from where was the money coming to fund a Palestine liberation movement?

There was only one possibility—the still existing but discredited leadership of the old Palestinian order led by Haj Amin Husseini, the Mufti of Jerusalem, now resident in Beirut and making occasional trips to other Arab capitals.

Of those Palestinians wanting to organise for struggle with Israel, Arafat was the one with the best connections to Haj Amin. "He was one of my relatives" was all Arafat would tell me. He decided to visit Haj Amin in Beirut, but first he had to raise the money for the trip. According to his eldest sister, Inam, he did it by saving his pocket money, "saving more by eating less." But his sacrifice was in vain. Haj Amin told him there was no prospect of money for a liberation struggle and that he should continue his studies in America. (When other Palestinians including Khalad Hassan in Damascus asked if funds were available, Haj Amin simply did not give them an answer.)

At that moment in time, the end of 1949 or the beginning of 1950, it really did seem, even to Arafat, that the Palestine file had been closed forever. His people had been required to be the sacrifice on the altar of political expediency and there was nothing the Palestinians alone could do about it.

After the coup that brought Nasser to power, Arafat as president of the Union of Palestinian Students led a delegation to meet with President Naguib. The Union presented him with a petition. Dedicated to the memory of all Egyptians and Palestinians who had fought and died in Palestine, its message to the new regime was "Do not forget Palestine." It was written in blood.

Arafat was entertaining the hope that a new Arab Order led by revolutionary Egypt would welcome the creation of an independent Palestine liberation movement and would support it. But his more cautious student leadership colleagues were not so sure. Many years later one of them, Abu Adeeb, said to me: "We admired Arafat's dedication and his obvious leadership qualities, but not all of us took him so seriously when he talked about an independent Palestine liberation movement. I do not mean to say that any of us were opposed to that idea—far from it. The point was that some of us did not think it would be possible for the Palestinians to shape their own destiny. And we thought in this way because the conspiracy against us, by the Arab regimes as well as the big powers, was so great."

If he shared those doubts Arafat did not say so. And his own optimism was reinforced when Nasser, to put pressure on the British during the negotiations for their withdrawal, took a leaf out of the old regime's book and unleashed the *fedayeen* against the British. Arafat and those he had trained in his university facility joined in that action. And then came the first indication that his more cautious colleagues might be right.

When the British signalled they were willing to talk seriously about withdrawal, Nasser not only called off the *fedayeen* attacks, he ordered the closure of Arafat's training facility. As Arafat put it to me, the clear message from Nasser's security people was, "We want no trouble from you Palestinians and we don't intend to give you any freedom to organise in our country."

Arafat was saved from a return to despair by a report he had received about the activities of a young Palestinian in Gaza, one Khalil Wazir. He had already created a small underground organisation which had carried out a number of operations—mainly planting mines in the path of Israeli border patrols. (These operations were in the one or two per cent of infiltrations that Israel's hawks could claim with some justification to be threats to the Jewish state's security). Nasser was preoccupied with his negotiations for Britain's withdrawal and Arafat decided to go to Gaza to meet with Wazir. Arafat had to be extremely careful because he was under surveillance in Cairo and Wazir had been arrested, tortured and jailed by Egyptian security people in the Gaza Strip. Arafat's cover story was that he was visiting relatives.

After they had reviewed the situation, Wazir told Arafat they had to be realistic. Like Palestinians everywhere they had hoped that new Arab leaders, Nasser especially, would be seriously dedicated to the liberation of Palestine. But it was not going to happen. As a matter of fact, Wazir said, the new regimes in Egypt and Jordan were treating those Palestinians who wanted to continue the struggle with brutality and inhumanity. So there was, Arafat and Wazir concluded, only one strategy available.

Whatever the difficulties, they had to create their own liberation movement, to make hit-and-run attacks on Israel, to provoke bigger and bigger Israeli reprisals on the frontline Arab states. *Their underlying assumption—with hindsight a tragic but inevitable miscalculation—was that if only the Arabs could be forced to fight Israel, and fight seriously, they were bound to win.*

At the time Wazir and Arafat had absolutely no understanding of how overwhelming Israel's military superiority already was. They also knew nothing worth knowing about what passed for politics in Israel. So they also had no idea that, by adopting such a strategy, they would be playing into the hands of Israel's hawks.

Were Arafat and Wazir stupid? No. As well as being embittered by the terrible injustice that had been done to their people, they were young and inexperienced. Wazir was barely out of his teens, and Arafat was only seven years older. Their learning experience, the one that mattered, was still ahead of them.

And things were about to get more difficult than even they could have imagined.

Shortly after Arafat returned to Cairo, the Muslim Brotherhood made its attempt to assassinate Nasser. And Nasser's crackdown on the Brotherhood had consequences for both Wazir and Arafat.

Wazir had been relying for his mines and explosives on a Brotherhood source. That supply line was cut and no doubt the Brothers involved were terminated. And Wazir's operations came to a stop. (Which was a particular reason why Egypt's Gaza Strip border with Israel was unusually quiet in the four months prior to Israel's attack).

Arafat was arrested and charged with being a member of the Muslim Brotherhood and complicity in the plot to kill Nasser. In reality, and unlike a number of Nasser's RCC leadership colleagues, Arafat was not then, and never had been, a member of the Brotherhood: but he had fought with it in Palestine, and after the war he had used it for his own ends—to guarantee his election as president of the General Union of Palestinian Students. And he had recently visited Wazir in Gaza. It was not the first and would not be the last time Arafat was incarcerated and tortured in an Arab prison. He said, "They wanted me to give them all the information I had about the Brothers—names, places where I made contact with them, and so on. But they did not succeed in breaking me."

The day came when Arafat had had enough and turned the tables on his torturers. He said to them: "Look, if you really want the truth, if you really want proof that I am not a member of the Muslim Brotherhood, then go and ask Abdel Hakim Amer, go and ask Kemal Hussein." (Both were senior members of the RCC who had helped Nasser to plan and execute the coup, and Hakim Amer was Nasser's choice as Commander-in-Chief of the Egyptian army). In the end it was Kemal Hussein himself who came to release Arafat.

As 1954 drew to its close Arafat and Wazir were physically free but, as both of them agreed many years later, the attitude of the various Egyptian authorities was "negative to hostile"; and it could have been said that prospects for bringing about a regeneration of Palestinian nationalism were close to zero.

And then came Israel's attack on Gaza.

When he was recalling how he and Arafat had exploited the opportunity Israel's hawks had given them, Abu Jihad (Wazir) said: "It was the first of not a few times when we had reason to be thankful for Israel's iron fist policy." Through the smile he added: "*To tell you the truth, the Israelis probably saved us from extinction with that attack!*"

The way in which Wazir and Arafat exploited Sharon's handiwork contributed greatly to Nasser's humiliation, not only in Egypt but throughout the Arab world. Abu Jihad explained:

> After the attack I gathered the students and we dipped our handkerchiefs in the blood of those who had been killed—they were mainly Palestinians. And when the morning light came we began to make our demonstrations. We had two slogans which were our message to Nasser. 'If you want to save us, train us. If you want to save us, arm us.' It was the biggest demonstration I had seen in Gaza in my life. All the people joined in. Then, because of the feeling of the people, we had clashes with the Egyptian authorities. We burned their offices. It was a very great shock for Nasser. But we had more activities planned.

While Arafat in Cairo waited for his cue, Wazir despatched eyewitnesses from Gaza to a number of Arab countries, including Jordan, Syria and Lebanon. Their mission was to tell the story of the Israeli attack and the Egyptian army's defeat. Up to this point Arab newspapers had been banned from giving space to the Palestinian point of view. But as Wazir and Arafat had correctly calculated, Arab editors, most of them unwilling lackeys of their governments, were unable to resist firsthand accounts of the most serious clash between Israel and Egypt since the signing of the Armistice Agreements. Abu Jihad said: "For the first time since our tragedy, our voice, the voice of the Palestinian people, was heard everywhere in the Arab world. And the story we had to tell made a very big scandal for Nasser. He was humiliated."

Though even Wazir himself did not then appreciate the full significance of his public relations success, he had made the first breach in the wall of official Arab silence about what the dispossessed Palestinians were thinking and wanting. Arab governments would continue to see to it that their media institutions did not promote the cause of Palestinian nationalism, but as a result of the reporting of Israel's attack on Gaza, and Wazir's exploitation of it, *the Arab masses were aware that there was in the background a ticking time-bomb of unfinished Palestine business.*

While Arab governments saw to it that Arab media did not support the cause of Palestinian nationalism, the mere reporting of Israel's attack on Gaza served that purpose among the Arab masses.

On cue, Arafat staged a demonstration at the Arab League's headquarters in Cairo. He demanded that Nasser receive him and a student delegation to consider the situation in Gaza. Nasser was extremely sensitive to the mood of Egypt's student community, and now he was anxious to placate them, the Palestinians especially. He agreed to the meeting. According to Arafat's memory: "Nasser said not less than 40 times that he was greatly shocked, and that he had learned many things for the first time, including how much the Palestinian people were suffering."

To buy time while he considered his options, Nasser agreed to let Arafat and his delegation visit Gaza to study the situation and make a report.

"Arafat came officially to Gaza for three days", Abu Jihad said. "We stayed together the whole time and he made a very big impression on our people, not just the students but all of the people. We felt and we knew that he was living our emotions." And that, simply stated, was to be the key to Arafat's hold on his refugee people including, without exception, his internal critics and opponents. Abu Jihad added: "When any of our people were killed, Arafat gave us the impression that a small part of him had died, too."

On his return to Cairo, Arafat submitted a report to Nasser. It said the main problem was that Egypt and the other Arab states had left the Palestinians without arms to defend themselves. The dispossessed Palestinians had to be armed for self-defence because the armies of the host Arab states were incapable of protecting them from Israeli attacks. Arafat was hoping that Nasser would agree to the establishment of a Palestinian defence force, which he himself would command with Wazir as his number two, and which, in due course, they would transform into the strike force of a Palestine liberation movement.

The dispossessed Palestinians had to be armed for self-defence because the armies of the host Arab states were incapable of protecting them from Israeli attacks.

Nasser had no intention of allowing the Palestinians to have more than a token voice and role in determining the future, whatever it was to be. He was determined—he hoped he could do it without being seen as a traitor—to prevent the regeneration of active Palestinian nationalism if he could, and if he failed, to contain it, *prevent it becoming the tail that wagged the Arab dog*. If it did there would be war at some point. Nasser knew that (as did all other Arab leaders). He also knew it would be a war the Arabs could not win. But in the face of Israel's attacks, he had to do something to appease the Palestinians Wazir and Arafat had so successfully stirred up. He also had an urgent need to demonstrate to his soldiers, his general public and the Arab world that he would not take Israel's attacks lying down.

But what to do? His room for maneuver was too small to be measured.

His own army was in no shape to demonstrate anything but its inability to stand up to the IDF. Nasser then was still hoping that the British and the Americans would supply him with the arms he needed for defence, and the offer from the Soviets was in the future. But because of Israel's aggression he had to seen to be doing something. It was not just a matter of face for Nasser. It was about the politics of staying on top in Egypt.

As Nasser saw it, his least bad but still dangerous option was to make short-term, tactical use of the Palestinians. He decided that some, a few to be described only as *fedayeen*, should be trained and armed and let loose against Israel. That, he knew, would play into the hands of Israel's hawks; but he hoped that his way of handling the situation would limit the loss of goodwill for him and Egypt in the West, goodwill that was needed in the first instance for pressure on Israel to stop its attacks. *The key to Nasser's game plan was to have the ability to blame the Palestinians while using them.* At his insistence the training and arming of a small number of them, and the selection of targets, would be controlled by Egyptian army intelligence officers who would not officially exist. Most important of all, because he would be in control of events on his own side, was that he could call off the *fedayeen* attacks when they had served his purpose—won him some respect in Egypt and the Arab world. And that, he hoped, would be before Israel's hawks heaped further humiliation upon him.

Young and inexperienced though they were, Arafat and Wazir were not fooled. They understood Nasser was signalling that he had no use for them; that he would not support the creation of an independent Palestine liberation movement (Abu Adeeb had been right); and that Egypt would not tolerate its existence if such a thing came into being.

Within two years Wazir would leave Gaza for employment in Saudi Arabia. And Arafat would make a hurried exit from Cairo for Kuwait. He went, he told me, certain that he was within a day or two, perhaps less, of being arrested and liquidated by Nasser's security people.

As it happened, tiny Kuwait, little more than an extended, oil-rich city state, was the only Arab country prepared to give Arafat and those who were to become his leadership colleagues the sanctuary they needed to plan and prepare for struggle.

But one of two things was needed if there was to be a regeneration of Palestinian nationalism—a miracle or a continuing and escalating demonstration of Israel's arrogance of power.

8

GOODBYE, MR. SHARETT —VICTORY FOR "SATAN"

Apart from those who were killed, the first casualty of Israel's attack on Gaza was Sharett's dialogue with Nasser. Their two front men, Divon and Sadeq, had been scheduled to have a follow-up meeting in early March—within days of Israel's attack, if it had not happened. Sadeq's codename was Albert. He sent Divon what must be the shortest telegram in history. "No. Albert."[1] Nasser had told his emissary that he had lost his faith in the idea that Israel could be prevailed upon to reach a peaceful accommodation with the Arabs.

On the Israeli side Prime Minister Sharett was virtually alone in wanting to recognise the truth of what had happened—*that Israel's attack on Gaza was the cause of, and not the pretext for, Nasser's decision to turn to the Soviets for arms.* Sharett was also virtually alone in wanting to recognise another truth as events developed—*that Nasser had resorted to the tactic of using the* fedayeen *as a response to Israeli aggression, and it was therefore Israel which was responsible for the subsequent escalation.*

On behalf of the hawks Dayan's stated view was that Nasser's decision to unleash the *fedayeen* was not, as Sharett contended, a reversal of a previous policy of restraint brought about by Israeli aggression. It was a continuation with escalation of Nasser's policy, the policy of all the regimes of the frontline Arab states, of approving and assisting Palestinian infiltration as a substitute for war until the Arabs were well enough armed to make war on their own account.

That was pure fiction but it was not the interpretation of a deluded man. If he had ever put into words what he really thought, Dayan the moody and magnificent master of Zionist deception would have said something like this: "If we are to justify to the world the aggression necessary to create the Greater Israel of our Zionist dream, and if we are to carry our own people with us—we must have enemies."

On 25 March Chief of Staff Dayan was summoned by Defence Minister Ben-Gurion. Without consulting Prime and Foreign Minister Sharett or any cabinet colleague, Ben-Gurion told Dayan to prepare a plan for expelling the Egyptians from the Gaza Strip and for Israel to capture for keeping that chunk of Egyptian territory. There had been a *fedayeen* attack on a house in an Israeli settlement in the Negev. It was a new Jewish settlement being developed by immigrants from Iran. At the time of the attack with automatic fire and grenades, a wedding was taking place in the house. One of the settlers, a young woman, had been killed and 20 were wounded.

Dayan was astonished by Ben-Gurion's request because, up to this moment, the "Old Man" had shared his view that the very last thing Israel wanted was possession of a hellhole containing 300,000 Palestinian refugees who, down to the last man, woman and child, were united in their hatred of the Jewish state. Ben-Gurion said that what he wanted Dayan to do was "the only way" to prevent attacks on settlers from the Gaza Strip: and that if they failed to stop them, the settlers already in place might panic and leave and, as word spread, the flow of immigrants to Israel might be greatly reduced, might even stop.

Ben-Gurion was not moved by Dayan's repeated opposition to the idea, and Dayan, as instructed, prepared a detailed military plan which Ben-Gurion then presented to the cabinet. Sharett was frightened by what it told him about how far the hawks were prepared to go. In opposing the plan, he said he still had a preference for making peace with their Arab neighbours on the basis of Israel's existing borders. The policy he wanted to pursue, he said, was reducing tension on the borders, strengthening Israel's relations with the Western powers and cultivating international sympathy. If they adopted Ben-Gurion's proposal, Israel would be seen as the aggressor and they might very well provoke war with Egypt. Which was, of course, what Dayan wanted.

At some point somebody at the cabinet table must have intimated that when the Gaza Strip was captured by the IDF and it became part of Israel, they would need to resort to more ethnic cleansing—because if they did not, the incorporation into the Jewish state of 300,000 embittered Palestinian refugees would present an unmanageable security problem. Sharett said that if even half the refugees living in the Gaza Strip "fled or were made to flee to the Hebron Hills", that would not solve any security problem because "their hatred for Israel would only be inflamed, breeding more and more frequent acts of vengeance and despair."[2]

Sharett secured a cabinet majority of 9 to 4 to defeat that Ben-Gurion proposal, but his relief was short-lived.

Three days later Ben-Gurion presented the cabinet with another and much more explosive proposal. *The essence of it was that Israel should abrogate its armistice agreement with Egypt.* In presenting his case Ben-Gurion demonstrated that he had anticipated Sharett's counter-argument that Israel could not possibly do such a thing because it would expose the Jewish state as being the party not interested in peace, and would bring upon it the condemnation of the world.

At his disingenuous best Ben-Gurion told the cabinet that he was not asking for Israel to unilaterally abrogate the armistice agreement. That, he agreed, would be a most unwise and even foolish thing to do because it would invite condemnation by the world. No, the way to do it was by blaming Egypt. How so? Egypt, Israel could say, had in practise already destroyed the armistice agreement by, among other things, ignoring the Security Council's decision concerning the freedom of shipping through international waterways. On that basis Israel could say that it did not regard itself as being bound by the armistice agreement. For good measure, and to add to the impression that Israel was the sinned-against party, Israel could then say to the world that it was ready to conduct negotiations with Egypt, and that if Egypt refused (Ben-Gurion knew that Nasser could not then enter into public negotiations which he, Ben-Gurion, did not want, anyway) Israel would regard itself as being free to act as it thought fit; and the world should understand—Nazi holocaust, Arab threat to Israel's existence, etcetera, etcetera. By playing the game that way, Israel could blame Egypt for whatever happened.

Sharett understood what Ben-Gurion was really after—cabinet backing for a clearing of the decks to enable him and Dayan to have the war with Egypt they wanted—when they wanted it and how they wanted it. In what might have been his finest hour as prime minister, Sharett opposed Ben-Gurion's proposal with all the intellectual force and nervous energy at his command. As Shlaim noted, Sharett managed to surprise even himself by "the extreme lengths to which he could go in his moderation."[3]

In the first place, Sharett said, Ben-Gurion was ignoring the fact that it would be difficult and perhaps impossible for Israel to prove that Egypt's denial of maritime rights constituted a violation of the armistice agreement. It was true that the pan-Arab ban on Israeli shipping through the Suez Canal and the Gulf of Aqaba was in defiance of a Security Council resolution, but it did not violate the armistice agreement. It was also the case that Egypt might have good grounds for banning Israeli shipping with a claim to belligerent rights under the Constantinople Convention (a claim Egypt had actually made). But even if the Egyptian ban on Israeli shipping could be shown to be a violation of the armistice agreement, Israel would then have the difficulty of explaining why it had waited four years to declare Egypt to be in breach of it. The point? In all the circumstances as they were, the outside world could see the claim that Ben-Gurion would have Israel make for what it was—*nothing more than a pretext for the Jewish state to free itself from the restrictions imposed on it by the armistice agreement "in order to embark on a campaign of territorial expansion."*[4]

And then there was the little matter of the Jewish state's legitimacy. Whatever else it may or may not have done, the armistice agreement had conferred *de facto* legitimacy on one of Israel's borders. Abrogating the armistice agreement would be to abrogate that legitimacy.

All said and done, what Ben-Gurion was proposing was dangerous nonsense, a continuation but with escalation of a policy that was itself the prime cause of the worsening security situation on Israel's borders. *The time had come, Prime Minister Sharett said, for Israel to make a clear decision about its basic objective—either to consolidate its existence within its borders as they were by making peace with the Arabs and, if that was not yet possible, by ceasing to provoke Arab hostility: or to seek a new resolution of the conflict by war, to expand Israel's borders (to create the Greater Israel of Zionism's mad dream)*.

In effect Sharett was saying to his cabinet colleagues: "Ben-Gurion, Dayan and his IDF want war. You must support me as prime minister in opposing them."

The votes were six in favour of Ben-Gurion's proposal for renunciation (in his devious way) of the armistice agreement and six against, with a number of abstentions. If just one of those who abstained had voted for the proposal, it would have become government policy and Sharett would have been finished. After his comprehensive rubbishing of the proposal and its sponsor, he would have had no choice but to resign.

But from here on Sharett's relationship with Ben-Gurion went from bad to worse.

Prevented for the time being from launching military operations against Egypt which he hoped would provoke a full-scale war on that front, *Dayan went to work on the detailed planning for his own pet project—an invasion of Lebanon for the purpose of annexing the south of that country and turning the rest of it into a Christian (Maronite) Israeli client state.* At the time his intelligence people were telling him that the British were in the process of encouraging Iraq (now a member of Britain's anti-Soviet Baghdad Pact) to invade Syria for the purpose of annexing it, to prevent Syria becoming a Soviet client state. On the basis of that information Dayan might have said to his associates: "If the British are prepared to have one of their client states behave in such a way, they'll have no cause for complaint if we make some territorial adjustments in the name of improving our security."

Dayan then persuaded Ben-Gurion to arrange a meeting for the two of them with Sharett. The only difference between the two hawks was that Dayan wanted to invade Lebanon immediately while Ben-Gurion wanted to wait for Iraq's invasion of Syria as the pretext.

Sharett reminded them that he had turned down the idea when Ben-Gurion had first floated it and now, he said, there was no purpose in embarking on a detailed discussion of what was a "fantastic and adventurist plan", which was "surprising in its crudeness and divorce from reality"[5] Sharett went on to say—I think they were intended to be his last dismissive words on the subject and to which he expected no response—that the Maronite Christians were internally divided, had no daring leaders (of the kind Dayan's plan called for) and would prove to be unreliable allies.

Dayan was stung by Sharett's putdown of his plan and was determined to tell his prime minister that he was badly underestimating Israel's ability to get what it wanted in Lebanon. Implementing his plan would be a piece of cake. Why so? Dayan explained:

> All that is required is to find an officer, even a captain would do, to win his heart or buy him with money to get him to agree to declare himself the saviour of the Maronite

> population. Then the Israeli army will enter Lebanon, occupying the necessary territory, and create a Christian regime that will ally itself with Israel. The territory from the Litani (River) southward will be totally annexed to Israel and everything will fall into place.[6]

Having a Maronite Christian officer seduced by a beautiful Israeli agent or bribed into calling for the IDF's intervention was the key. In public relations terms it would give Israel a fig leaf of justification for its action. In Dayan's scenario that would enable Israel, when it was before the court of international opinion on a charge of the most naked aggression and the most monstrous interference in the affairs of another state, to defend itself along something like the following lines: "In making these utterly false and outrageous charges the world is doing the Jewish state a terrible injustice. Israel is a democratic and peace-loving nation, a fragile, vulnerable vessel afloat in sea of hatred. Israel is not an aggressor. Israeli forces are in Lebanon and assisting its endangered Christians because the government of Israel decided to answer their call for help." Whatever its actual wording, an Israeli statement of justification would also have included (par for the course) the accusation that the charges against the Jewish state were motivated by anti-Semitism.

On the day he said "No" to Dayan and Ben-Gurion, Sharett made an entry in his diary that demonstrated he was capable of seeing the future [emphasis added]: *"I saw clearly how those who saved the state so heroically and courageously in the War of Independence would be capable of bringing a catastrophe upon it if they are given the chance in normal times."*[7] (When Dayan's plan for re-making Lebanon was implemented a quarter of a century later—by Sharon as the defence minister in Begin's second-term coalition government—it did have disastrous consequences, and not just for Israel).

Sharett was also shocked by what Ben-Gurion's support for Dayan's plan revealed to him about the double standards of the man who deserved more than any other to be regarded as Israel's founding father. As Shlaim put it: "The same man (Ben-Gurion) who was so touchy about Israel's independence and territorial integrity, and so quick to react to the slightest manifestation of foreign interference in its affairs, also showed complete disregard for the rights of other sovereign states."[8]

As Sharett knew well, the plan for invading and dismembering Lebanon was all the more reprehensible because it was not prompted by any provocation on Lebanon's part. The usual argument about responding to force with force could not be invoked in this context, for the simple reason that Lebanon had scrupulously abided by all the provisions of the armistice agreement it had concluded with Israel.

By rejecting the plan for invading and dismembering Lebanon, Prime Minister Sharett stopped Israel's hawks in their tank tracks. For the time being.

Ben-Gurion was now at one with Dayan in asserting that Israel's top priority was getting rid of Nasser.

The day after Sharett said "No" to an invasion of Lebanon, Ben-Gurion was ranting and raving behind closed doors about Nasser's "crimes." According to Sharett's diary account, Ben-Gurion's diatribe against Nasser included this: "It is definitely possible to topple him, and it is even a *mitzvah* (a sacred obligation) to do so." And then: "Who is he, anyway, this Nasser Shmasser?"[9]

The refocusing on Egypt was triggered by the explosion of a landmine that injured four Israeli soldiers. Unfortunately this relatively minor incident—probably the handiwork of Nasser's *fedayeen*—happened when a critical new factor started to have influence on the Israeli decision-making process.

Sharett's party was Mapai. It was the biggest faction in the Knesset and therefore the ruling party—the one with the most seats in the coalition government. The majority of Mapai's ministers were in favour of a military response to the landmine incident. It no longer mattered to most of them that a reprisal attack on Egypt would put a further strain on Israel's relations with the Western powers and increase the depth of Arab hatred at street level and, by so doing, make it less likely that Nasser or any Arab leader could be seen to be adopting a positive position on Israel. There just had to be an Israeli reprisal attack on Egypt. Why?

Israeli policy was now to be determined by domestic political considerations—the need to win votes—not by genuine security considerations or real longer-term interests. And the key to winning votes was to take a hard line against the Arabs.

An election was approaching and most Mapai ministers feared that they and their party would suffer at the polls if they and it were not seen to be hammering the Arabs to teach them lessons. *Policy was now to be determined by domestic political considerations—the need to win votes—not by genuine security considerations or what under any heading was best for Israel's real and longer-term interests. And not for the first time, and by no means the last time, what passed for democracy in Israel was about to be hijacked.*

If the cabinet of the coalition government had taken the decision, there would not have been a reprisal attack on Egypt in response to the injuring of the four Israeli soldiers. In cabinet, with the support of his own doves and those of his coalition partners, Prime Minister Sharett could and would have secured a majority in favour of saying "No" to Ben-Gurion again. The "Old Man" was aware of that. His solution to the problem was therefore to ignore the cabinet. Incredibly, at Ben-Gurion's insistence, the decision to retaliate was taken in a party forum—by a cabal of Mapai ministers and party managers.

When he realised that he and the cabinet were being excluded from the decision-making process, Sharett, for the third time in a month, considered resigning. The case for leaving the running of the asylum to the lunatics was a strong one. *Because of the extent to which Israeli public opinion had been conditioned to believe that Nasser and his fellow Arab leaders were intent on destroying the Jewish state and that peace would never be possible except, perhaps, on Israel's terms over the barrel of a gun, there simply was not an environment for rational public debate about real choices and options. Israel was a basket case, ungovernable by rational men and women.*

Behind closed doors Sharett had previously summoned up the courage to tell his cabinet colleagues, all of them, that they had to decide what Israel's basic objective was. But given the uninformed and inflamed state of Israeli public opinion, it was not a proposition that could be taken to the country. In all other so-called democratic nations you could best guarantee to win votes, or not to lose them, by promising to cut taxes or some such. *In Israel you had to promise that you would knock the hell out of the Arabs.*

Probably the main reason why Sharett did not resign then was that Israel had just received an offer from the Eisenhower administration—American assistance to help the Jewish state finance the construction and fuelling of a small nuclear reactor for research into the peaceful uses of atomic energy. The reactor was to be located at Nahal Soreq to the south of Tel Aviv.

Sharett knew better than anybody else that Israel was under intense pressure from the Eisenhower administration, driven by the President himself, to abandon its policy of massively disproportionate and predictably counterproductive reprisal attacks. (In reality the attacks were only counterproductive in the eyes of those who wanted peace. For Dayan and Israel's warlords they were the opposite, extremely productive—the means by which Israel could provoke the Arabs into responding to give Israel the pretext for war to take more Arab land).

In Sharett's analysis there was a possibility that if Israel continued to reject calls for an end to its belligerency, the U.S. would withdraw the offer of assistance for the development of atomic energy. He believed that he had to hang on to use whatever was left of his influence to try to restrain the hawks in order to prevent the loss of Eisenhower's goodwill.

An agreement between the U.S. and Israel for the Nahal Soreq project did get signed; but it did not achieve its intended purpose so far as the Eisenhower administration was concerned.

In the light of all that is known today, it is clear that that the Eisenhower administration saw co-operation with Israel on the use of atomic energy for peaceful uses as the means (hopefully) of preventing it from developing nuclear weapons. How so?

When Israel put its signature to the agreement with the U.S., it guaranteed that nuclear materials would not be diverted to weapons research. On its own the guarantee was not enough of an assurance and Israel was required to accept, which it did by signing the agreement, that the U.S. would have inspection rights—access whenever they wanted it for American inspectors to verify that Israel was not cheating.

Nobody will ever know what misgivings Eisenhower may have entertained when he agreed that an arrogant and aggressive Israel should be one of the countries invited to participate in his Atoms for Peace programme. He should have known that Israel had a brilliant scientist (Bergmann) who, probably, would be capable of developing nuclear weapons. He may also have known that Ben-Gurion was bragging to selected and very wealthy Jewish American visitors that Israel would develop its own atom bomb. My guess is that Eisenhower said to himself and perhaps his advisers something like the following: "If Israel ever possesses the bomb, it will never feel the need to make peace on terms the Arabs can accept and will create mayhem in the region, and there would be nothing we could do to prevent a catastrophe that may take us all to Kingdom Come." In any event, I think it is reasonable to assume Eisenhower hoped that having the Jewish state committed by written agreement to inspection and verification would prevent it from developing its own ultimate weapon of mass destruction.

As it happened, the agreement was of no consequence because Israel had already embarked on its own super secret nuclear weapons development programme. The guarantee it had given, and the inspection procedures to which it had agreed, only had meaning in the context of co-operation with the U.S. on the Nahal Soreq project. And the real beauty of it from Israel's point of view was that American inspection at Nahal Soreq would reduce the chances of American snooping elsewhere.

Deception was as ever the name of Zionism's game; and the people of Israel were among those deceived.

In 1953 they were informed in a radio broadcast that Israel had an Atomic Energy Commission. It had actually been created the previous year with Bergmann its chairman. The story for the public was that the work of the Commission was research for the development of the peaceful uses of nuclear energy and for the particular purpose, by generating cheap electricity and the production of desalinated water, of making the Negev desert bloom. *What the people of Israel were not told was that their Atomic Energy Commission was under the direct jurisdiction of the Ministry of Defence, with Director General Peres running its show for the prime purpose of developing an atomic bomb.* That was the secret of four men in Israel—Ben-Gurion, Peres, Dayan and Bergmann—and a small number of extremely wealthy Jews of the world (citizens of America and a number of European nations) whose money was needed to make it happen.

Israel had its own weapon of mass destruction by the late 1960s due to secret collaboration at Dimona with the French during the period when both were conspiring to destroy Nasser by conventional means.

That it did happen—Israel had its own weapon of mass destruction by the late 1960s—was due to secret collaboration, at Dimona in the Negev, with the French; a joint venture Peres arranged when France and Britain and Israel were conspiring to destroy Nasser by conventional means.

In retrospect it can be seen that there might well have been a link between the exciting discovery which triggered the idea that Israel could make its own atomic bomb and Ben-Gurion's refusal to consider Sharett's proposition that, in order to give prospects for peace with Nasser's Egypt their best chance, Israel should make a territorial concession in the Negev desert. How so?

As Seymour Hersh revealed in *The Samson Option*, it was in the Negev that Bergmann made an exciting discovery. *Its large phosphate fields contained meagre but recoverable traces of natural uranium.* That was in 1947, prior to Israel's unilateral declaration of independence. By 1953 Bergmann's researchers had devised an efficient means of extracting the uranium. They had also pioneered by then a new process for creating the heavy water needed to modulate a nuclear chain reaction. As Hersh put it with a touch of the class one expects from America's top investigative journalist, "Nuclear power [for peaceful purposes] was not Ben-Gurion's first priority: the desert would glow before it bloomed."[10]

In my analysis the question of why Ben-Gurion insisted that Israel should and would have its own nuclear strike capability does not have the easy and simple answer that some might suppose. The easy and simple answer is in a single word—deterrence. *But who or what was to be deterred by Israel's possession of nuclear weapons?* I offer my own answer in a moment.

An indication that President Eisenhower did fear that Israel would seek to develop its own nuclear bomb is in the fact that his administration offered the Jewish state an American security guarantee. It was in the form of a proposed mutual defence pact. Though not stated, this was clearly Eisenhower's way of saying to Israel's leaders, in effect: "You have no need to develop nuclear weapons because America will guarantee your security and you can rely on us."

An American offer to guarantee Israel's security was not taken up because it was conditional on Israel abandoning its policy of reprisal attacks on Arab states and not expanding its borders by force.

The problem for Israel's hawks was that the proposed guarantee had two conditions. *One was that Israel would abandon its policy of reprisal attacks against the neighbouring Arab states.* (At the time one of Washington's hopes was that an American-Israel defence agreement would induce the Arabs to make peace with the Jewish state.) *The other condition was that Israel would undertake not to expand its borders by force.*

It was Dayan for Ben-Gurion who led the campaign behind closed doors to reject the offer of an American security guarantee.

There was, it seems, never a moment when Israel ever said "No thanks" to the American offer. It was considered and considered over months, and Israel never said "Yes".

My answer to the question of why Ben-Gurion (and Dayan) insisted on Israel having its own atomic bomb is this.

It was much less to do with the need for Israel to have the ultimate deterrent vis-à-vis the Arabs. It was much more to do with the perception that a day might come when the leaders of an expanded Zionist state might have to say to the leaders of the Gentile world: "Be careful. Don't press us to make concessions which you think we should make to protect your vested interests but which we believe will threaten the security and possibly even the survival of our state." In other words, and crudely stated, *Israel's independent nuclear capability was to be the ultimate deterrent for stopping the Gentile world from obliging an expanded Zionist state, the Greater Israel of Zionism's mad dream, to make territorial concessions it was unwilling to make.* "Don't push us too far or we'll use these things." Such a threat—implicit, it never had to be stated—was bound to mean that, when Israel did have its own independent nuclear capability, there would be limits to what the Gentile world would do to require Zionism to play its part in righting the wrong it had done to the Arabs.

Why else, for example, would Ben-Gurion have told his leadership colleagues with such confidence that, apart from moral pressure, Israel need not fear being pressed too far? In retrospect I think it can be seen that the awesome political power of the Zionist lobby in the Gentile world, and America especially, was only one factor in Israel's ability to put two fingers up to the whole world and get away with it.

During the internal debate about whether or not to accept an American security guarantee, Dayan let slip a comment that gave rare insight into how, really, his mind worked and also, in my view, why the Zionist state is what it is. In an informal talk with Israel's ambassadors to Washington, London and Paris, Dayan explained why he was totally opposed—whatever the pressure from the West in general and America in particular—to the idea that Israel should abandon its policy of reprisal attacks. They were, he said, "a life drug."[11]

The Israeli reprisal attacks were a "life drug" (Dayan) because they fostered the belief that the Jewish state was in constant danger, without which, many reservists might lose their motivation to respond when called upon.

What he meant, he explained, was that reprisal attacks enabled the Israeli government "to maintain a high degree of tension in the country and the army."[12] What, really, did that mean?

Israel's standing or full-time army was relatively small, not more than about 23,000 souls in all. The other quarter of a million fighting men and women who could be mobilised in 48 hours were reservists from every walk of Israel's civil society. The real point? Without Israeli reprisal attacks and all they implied—that the Jewish state was in constant danger of being annihilated (when actually it was not)—there was the possibility that some and perhaps many of the reservists would not be motivated enough to respond to the call of duty.

Among those present when Dayan made his remarks to Israel's three most important ambassadors to the West was the Foreign Ministry's Gideon Rafael. After he had reported Dayan's remarks to Sharett, he said [emphasis added]: "*This is how fascism began in Italy and Germany!*"[13]

Was he suggesting, by implication, that a day might come when some would say this was how neo-fascism began in the Zionist state?

The real tragedy was that Dayan's life drug would not have been needed if the people of Israel had been told the truth by their leaders.

The real significance of Israel's general election on 20 July 1955 was that it ushered in the end of Sharett as prime minister, but not because the expressed will of the people amounted to a demand for him to stand down.

When the votes had been counted it was clear that Mapai would continue to be the ruling party and that its leader would have the responsibility of cobbling together the next coalition government; but Mapai had lost five of its 45 seats in the 120-member Knesset. The most gains were made by the so-called "activist" or more extreme parties. Begin's Herut, for example, nearly doubled the number of its Knesset seats from eight to 15. That was enough for Ben-Gurion's Mapai supporters to say the election had proved that the country wanted the government to hit the Arabs harder than Sharett had allowed it to do. And they launched an internal campaign to have him replaced as party leader and prime minister by Ben-Gurion.

To his supporters Ben-Gurion said: "I will not participate in any government that goes against my views on defence policy, and if such a government is formed—I shall fight it."[14] What he meant, they knew, was: "Of course I intend to form the next government, and I will not stand any nonsense from Sharett if he chooses to serve again as foreign minister. Make that clear to all concerned."

Ben-Gurion himself could not have made that more clear when he addressed Mapai's Central Committee on 8 August. The subject for discussion was foreign policy.

At his vituperative best Ben-Gurion attacked Sharett and all he represented. As prime minister and foreign minister until the formation of the new coalition government, Sharett was in the audience. Ben-Gurion did not need to name him as the target of his attack on the enemy within. The verbal onslaught was directed at those whose sole concern was with "what Gentiles will say."[15] The Foreign Ministry was charged with arrogating the authority to determine defence policy. If that continued it would spell disaster for Israel's security. The Foreign Ministry should serve the Ministry of Defence and not the other way round. The latter's role was to make defence policy and the former's role was to explain it to the world. (My guess is that one of Ben-Gurion's main reasons for wanting to be in complete control again despite his advancing years was that he believed, with good reason, that

Sharett could not be relied upon to continue the research and development programme for the production of Israel's own atomic bomb—if and when he got to know about it).

It would take Ben-Gurion more than two months to put together a new coalition government (a length of time that, because of Israel's crazy system of proportional representation, would become par for the course of the haggling for cabinet posts that follows every general election). But it was to be less than two weeks before his determination to take no more nonsense from Sharett was put to its first test.

At about the time Ben-Gurion was rubbishing Sharett at the Mapai Central Committee meeting, Nasser was having serious second thoughts about the wisdom of his tactical use of the *fedayeen*. He still believed he had had no choice but to make use of them because of his desperate need to demonstrate to his own people, and the Arab world, that he would not take Israel's attacks lying down. But the strategy had become counter-productive because it was giving those Israelis who wanted it the pretext to escalate their violence. What then to do? *Nasser decided to explore again the possibility of reaching some kind of understanding with Israel.* His emissary for this secret mission was a prominent American Quaker, Elmore Jackson.

Nasser briefed him on his secret diplomacy to date and how, as it progressed, he had developed great confidence in Sharett. Nasser also explained that it was Sharett who had called off scheduled high level talks in Paris after two of Israel's spies were sentenced to death, and that he himself had had no choice but to respond to Israel's escalation of violence with tactical use of the *fedayeen*. The thing Nasser needed to know now, he told Jackson, was whether or not he should have any confidence in either Sharett or Ben-Gurion as peacemakers. The message Nasser wanted Jackson to give them was in two parts. The first was that he favoured a resumption of secret talks for the purpose of moving towards a political settlement. The second, the priority so far as Nasser was concerned, was the need for a *modus vivendi* between Egypt and Israel to prevent any further escalation of violence. (That, of course, was the last thing Dayan and Ben-Gurion wanted to hear).

To indicate how much he really did want a *modus vivendi* with Israel, Nasser told Jackson of an initiative he had taken to reduce and hopefully prevent clashes between Egyptian and Israeli forces.

- He had proposed to General Burns, the head of the United Nations Truce Supervision Organisation (UNTSO), that each side should pull its forces back one kilometre from the demarcation (armistice) line. Burns was fully aware of the reason for Nasser's proposal. After Sharon's first attack on Gaza the Israelis had resorted to provoking the Egyptians.

As Nutting was subsequently to put it: "Israeli tanks or armoured cars would drive headlong at an Egyptian border post, their crews shouting insults at the defenders. Inevitably the Egyptians would open fire and, as the first attacking wave receded, Israeli forces would pour in and wipe out the post."[16] And that was before Nasser resorted to the tactic of using the *fedayeen* to score points for him. (I think it is reasonable to assume that Sharett and probably even Ben-Gurion had no idea of what Dayan was doing to provoke confrontation).

- General Burns thought the Egyptian leader's proposal was a good one and asked the Israelis to consider it. They rejected it on the grounds that such a withdrawal (one kilometre to reduce the prospect of clashes) would involve for them "an unacceptable renunciation of sovereignty."[17] Amazing. But not surprising. A prudent Nasser ordered his troops to make a unilateral pullback.

Nasser then explained to Jackson how, when Israel's first attack on the Gaza Strip was followed by others, his position became so impossible that, at the end of his wits, he resorted to the tactic of telling his people that the Egyptian army was successfully driving out the Israeli invaders with counterattacks which never actually took place! *It really was a most absurd interlude. Israel's hawks were lying to their people to have them believe that Nasser was the aggressor hell bent on destroying the Jewish state. And Nasser was lying to his people to cover up the fact that there was nothing he could do to prevent Dayan's IDF attacking Egypt at will.*

Just before Jackson met with Sharett and Ben-Gurion, seven Israelis were killed and an IDF radio mast was damaged by a *fedayeen* operation. (Was it possible that Nasser himself had determined the timing of the operation in order to underline the need of both sides for a *modus vivendi*? Perhaps, but in my view Nasser would not have been hands-on to that extent. I think the timing of the *fedayeen* attack was more likely a case of Sod's Law).

The two Israeli leaders informed the American emissary of the *fedayeen* operation and said that a reprisal attack on Khan Yunis, a Gaza Strip gateway to the Sinai, had already been authorised. Jackson said that in his judgment hope for an accommodation with Nasser was still alive but would probably be killed by the Israeli reprisal. The American would later say he had had the impression that Sharett was in agreement with him while Ben-Gurion was non-committal.

Jackson's impression was correct. Sharett did believe that restarting a dialogue with Nasser was indescribably more important than a reprisal attack in any event, and all the more so given that a demonstration of Israeli military superiority now might very well destroy the prospect of dialogue with Nasser for many years to come. The problem was that if Sharett took the time to argue the point with Ben-Gurion, it might be too late to stop the reprisal attack on Khan Yunis. So Sharett waited for the "Old Man" to leave his office and then gave the order to cancel the attack.

And then the proverbial excrement hit the fan.

In "Yes, prime minister" mode Dayan recalled the units that had already crossed the border. He then sat down to write his letter of resignation. In it he said that current defence policy made it impossible for him to continue to discharge his responsibilities as chief of staff. Then he drove to Jerusalem to submit his resignation personally to Ben-Gurion. It was a tactic designed to challenge the "Old Man" to put his money where his mouth had been when he addressed Mapai's Central Committee.

Ben-Gurion responded by convening an emergency meeting of Mapai's ministers in the caretaker coalition government. They had to choose, he told them—the Sharett line or the Ben-Gurion line. If they favoured the Sharett line he, too, would quit. To give the impression that he meant what he said, he stormed out of the room and, the next day, absented himself from the Defence Ministry.

Under pressure Sharett buckled. He convened a cabinet meeting and, on his recommendation, it approved the cancelled reprisal attack on Khan Yunis. Dayan withdrew his resignation and Ben-Gurion returned to his office at the Ministry of Defence.

The Israeli attack took the lives of 39 Egyptians and Palestinians. *And still Nasser waited another month before putting his signature on the agreement for Soviet arms.*

Shortly after their attack on Khan Yunis at the end of August. Israeli forces, in open breach of the Israel-Egypt armistice agreement, occupied the demilitarised zone of El-Auja on the Negev border. It contained a key road junction of vital importance to a would-be aggressor from either side. Israeli control of it was a critical element in Dayan's future plans. As the occupation of El-Auja was happening Nasser was powerless (as was General Burns) to prevent it.

After Nasser signed and made public his agreement with the Soviet Union for arms via Czechoslovakia, and while a sick but apparently mentally alert Ben-Gurion was putting the finishing touches to the new coalition government he would lead, Sharett was still of the opinion (with reality on his side) that Israel's survival was not on the line. But he knew that Ben-Gurion and Dayan were intent on promoting the opposite view to justify further Israeli escalation and war.

In his remaining days as Prime Minister Sharett was presented with a demand for a reprisal attack after each and every border incident. Aware that Dayan and his IDF were to some degree beyond control, Sharett told Ben-Gurion that reprisal attacks could lead to war and therefore should not be launched without an explicit decision by the cabinet.

Sharett was then shocked by the news that even the most dovish of his Foreign Ministry officials and soul mates had become hawkish and were in favour of a "preventive war" with Egypt. The news came to him in a long telegram from Eban in America.

It informed Sharett that Israeli diplomats in Washington had received indications from the Eisenhower administration that the Jewish state could not count on American arms to "balance" those about to be supplied by the Soviet Union. That being so, and after consultations with various Foreign Ministry officials, Eban and they were advising that Israel should prepare for the possibility of a preventive war to break the backbone of Nasser's army—before it became stronger with the assistance of Soviet weapons.

That, Sharett reasoned, was truly the logic of the mad house. Suppose Israel did go to war and destroyed Egypt's armed forces—weapons and manpower, what would happen next? The Soviets would re-supply and Nasser would re-build, and, at a point, Israel would have to fight another preventive war. And another. And another. It was while he was considering where the idea of preventive war might take the Jewish state that, in his diary, Sharett asked the question that told of his total despair: "*What is our vision on this earth—war to the end of all generations and life by the sword?*"[18]

But there was another reason why Sharett was totally opposed to preventive war. He believed (and he was right to believe) that there was nothing to prevent—in the sense that Nasser, with or without Soviet arms, had no intention of fighting Israel to liberate Palestine or, depending on how you looked at it, destroy the Jewish state.

In reality all that would be changed by Soviet arms for Egypt (and Syria) was that they would make it more costly in terms of IDF casualties for the Jewish state to continue with its policy of seeking to impose its will on the Arabs by force. With Soviet arms Nasser would not have to take Israeli attacks lying down, he would be able to offer real resistance.

It may even have occurred to Sharett that Soviet arms for Egypt just might assist the peace-making—if analysis in Israel was driven by men prepared to come to judgment on the basis of the facts and the known realities of the time. The problem was that they had to be men for whom the creation of the Greater Israel of Zionism's mad dream was not a sensible proposition in practise even if it was desirable in theory. By definition such men had to be as rational as Sharett.

As Sharett must have realised, President Eisenhower did not regard Nasser's arms deal with the Soviets as a threat to Israel's security. His reason for signalling that the U.S. would not necessarily provide Israel with "balancing" arms was not difficult to fathom. It was the president's way of saying to Israel, "The U.S. won't supply you with arms if you don't abandon your policy of reprisals."

As it happened, Sharett did have one important ally. Glibli had been removed from his post of Director of Military intelligence (presumably at Sharett's insistence), and his place had been taken by his deputy, Harkabi, who had previously rubbished Dayan's assertion that the frontline Arab states were not doing their best to prevent infiltrations and border incidents. DMI Harkabi was among those who read and studied Eban's long telegram and its advice that Israel should prepare for a preventive war with Egypt. *In a memorandum of his own, Harkabi said he did not agree with the conclusion that preventive war was necessary.*

But there was another memorandum, one written by Isser Harel, the head of Mossad. It was a vigorous endorsement of the need for preventive war with Egypt.

Sharett was more comforted by Harkabi's memorandum than he was disturbed by Harel's. That was logical because Israel's Director of Military Intelligence was best placed to make the most informed judgment about the balance of military power, actual and projected, and the implications arising for the Jewish state. So... Before handing the premiership back to Ben-Gurion, Sharett decided to undertake a major diplomatic mission of his own, to try to prevent the hawks getting their way. He took off for Paris and Geneva.

Ben-Gurion at the time, prime minister-in-waiting, was confined to his sickbed in the President Hotel in Jerusalem.

In Paris Sharett talked with the French Prime Minister, Edgar Faure. In Geneva he talked with the American and British (and Soviet) foreign ministers—Dulles for America and Selwyn Lloyd for Britain. (Lloyd's predecessor as Britain's foreign minister, Sir Anthony Eden, had succeeded Churchill as prime minister in April). If it had been possible for Sharett to come clean about what was happening in the Jewish state and why he needed assistance, he would have said to his British, American and French listeners something like the following:

"Before I ask for your assistance I want you to be aware of the difficulties I will face if I stay on as foreign minister in the new coalition government Ben-Gurion will shortly be leading. He lives in a fantasy world with few if any connections to reality, and sometimes gives cause for doubts about his sanity. Dayan is hell bent on provoking war. If he can't be stopped, the IDF will gobble up the Sinai and the strategic locations that control the Straits of Tiran, the West Bank of Jordan, Lebanon up to the Litani River and probably a bit of Syria, too. And, of course, he'll take the Old City of Jerusalem when the best opportunity presents itself. And my dear, dear people will cheer it all because they've been conditioned to believe the Arabs want to destroy us and that peace with them is impossible... Yes, gentlemen, it's a terrible, terrifying mess, largely of our own making if one forgets our history of persecution and the Nazi contribution to it. If you say to me that I've come to you from a lunatic asylum, I will not object. All that you may know, but here's something you may not know... When he becomes prime minister again, Ben-Gurion will not get the majority support he needs in cabinet to make war on the Arabs for the purpose of creating Greater Israel if those of us who oppose such foolish adventurism receive the necessary assistance from the outside. The assistance those of us who represent the voice of sanity in my country will need is of two kinds. First the big powers, Britain and America especially, must become actively involved in promoting a resolution of the conflict through dialogue and negotiations. That means making constructive proposals and putting real pressure on Israel as well as the Arabs to take them seriously. Second, and if I am to take the lead as foreign minister in stopping the madness, I must be able to tell to my colleagues that I have secured a promise of certain arms from the West to balance those Nasser is about to receive from the Soviets."

Sharett had gone to Paris and Geneva briefed by Harkabi. The briefing was to the effect that while the arms Nasser was about to receive from the Soviets via Czechoslovakia would not alter the balance of military power in Egypt's favour, there would come a point when Israel's military superiority would need to be topped up by the acquisition of the latest jet fighters, to guarantee that the Israeli air force would have no problems at all if it had to take on Soviet-supplied Illyshin bombers and MiG-I5s. In other words, Harkabi had said to Sharett something like the following: "If you are to stay on as foreign minister, and if you are to have the credibility to face down our hawks, you'll need a promise from the Western powers that they will do the topping up as necessary."

Sharett could not, of course, talk to America, Britain and France in the way I suggested he would like to have done. His challenge was to find a way to say what had to be said without washing too much of his country's dirty political linen in front of his listeners. Subsequent events indicate that he succeeded to some extent.

Meanwhile, back in the asylum, a conversation of a very different kind was taking place.

Ben-Gurion and Dayan were discussing and apparently agreeing on what Israel's "defence" policy would be when, in a few days time, the new coalition government came into being with the "Old Man" back in complete control as prime minister and defence minister. Dayan had returned to Israel as Sharett was leaving for Paris and Geneva. The chief of staff had been recalled from his "holiday" in France for urgent business with the prime minister-in-waiting.

The policy discussion took place at the President Hotel with Ben-Gurion still resting in his sickbed there. Neither of them took notes but a decade later (in his book *Diary of the Sinai Campaign*) Dayan was to give his sanitized, summary version of what took place. "At the end of the talk, he, as minister of defence, instructed me, among other things, to be prepared to capture the Straits of Tiran—Sharm el-Sheikh, Ras Nastrani and the islands of Tiran and Sanapir—in order to ensure freedom of shipping through the Gulf of Aqaba and the Red Sea."[19]

Dayan was never to give in public a hint of the "other things" he had been instructed to do, but three days later he convened a special meeting of the General Staff to brief it on what, he said, were the basic guidelines as agreed with Ben-Gurion for the IDF's work in the coming months.

Lieutenant Colonel Mordechai Bar-On, Dayan's chief of bureau at the time, subsequently provided an insider's account of that meeting. In *Challenge and Quarrel, The Road to the Sinai Campaign*,[20] Bar-On said that Dayan's points included the following [emphasis added]:

- "*The basic solution to Israel's worsening security problem is the overthrow of Nasser's regime in Egypt.* Various means can alleviate the situation, but no solution, barring the absolute removal of Nasser from power, will remove the root cause of the danger threatening Israel.

- In order to topple Nasser's regime, it is necessary to arrive at a decisive confrontation with the Egyptians at the earliest possible date, before the absorption of the Soviet arms in Egypt makes the operation too difficult (he meant costly) or perhaps impossible.

- Supreme efforts must be made to acquire more arms and ammunition until the date of the clash, but one thing must not be made dependent on the other. (Dayan was obviously confident that the IDF could defeat Nasser's forces with available weapons and stockpiles of ammunition).

The assumption was that Nasser would not survive the defeat of his army.

How was the "decisive confrontation"—Dayan's euphemism for war—to be "arrived at"? By provoking the Egyptians with escalating Israeli reprisal attacks.

That was the reality Ben-Gurion did not want the outside world to be aware of, and which Dayan did not want his most senior officers to think too much about.

Ben-Gurion had previously said he was against "an initiated war"—a war initiated by Israel. What he meant was that Israel could not afford to be seen as the party that started war. It was vital to maintain the fiction that Israeli aggression was self-defence.

It was vital to maintain the fiction that Israeli aggression was self-defence. But even as Israel was proclaiming itself to be a peace-loving state, the IDF's best brains were being asked not to defend Israel, but to *provoke war.*

My reading of Dayan's address to the General Staff suggests that in advance of making it he was acutely aware that, unless he pre-empted them in argument, some of his most thoughtful senior officers might ask awkward questions—about the contradiction between declared and actual policy and perhaps even the morality of what they were being asked to do. *Israel was proclaiming itself to be a peace-loving state which was leaving no stone unturned in its efforts to make peace with the Arabs, yet here they were, the IDF's best brains, being asked to provoke war.* I think Dayan's use of the term "decisive confrontation" as a euphemism for war was an indication of how sensitive he judged the matter to be.

He described the concept he was outlining as one that "fundamentally rejects the idea of a preventive war." How so? "A preventive war means an aggressive war initiated by Israel... Israel cannot afford to stand against the entire world and be denounced as the aggressor." (So for starters they were not going to use terminology which could undermine the claim that Nasser was to blame).

More to the point, the General Staff officers should not see themselves as provoking war. Israel's reprisal attacks were a response to Egyptian provocations. If the armistice lines were opened by the Arab regimes to attackers, they would not be closed to the IDF's defenders. Israel therefore "does not need to resort to provocation." The reality was, of course, more or less the opposite, but the IDF's General Staff officers were not to acknowledge it.

Dayan ended his briefing with this: "Israel can make do with the method of detonation—that is to say, to stand on its rights stubbornly and uncompromisingly and to react sharply to every Egyptian aggression. Such a policy will in the end bring about an explosion."

Effectively Dayan was conditioning his own senior officers, a necessary thing for him to do because the arguments on which the policy was based were disingenuous in the extreme, open not only to challenge but complete demolition by anybody who was aware of all the facts.

The line Ben-Gurion was intending to take was "We seek peace but not suicide." In support of it Dayan said that in the first nine months of 1955, there had been 153 Israeli casualties, killed and wounded, as a result of enemy "forays" from the Gaza Strip alone. What the statistic out of its context did not say was that there would have been very few Israeli casualties but for Israel's policy of massively disproportionate reprisal attacks in addition to the IDF's own blatant provocations at Egyptian border posts.

Subsequently Dayan's most explicit repudiation of Sharett's policy of seeking an accommodation with the Arabs through negotiation was this:

> The alternative to the use of force—settling controversial problems by negotiation—was denied to Israel because the Arabs refused to negotiate. This refusal was not accidental. It sprang from their opposition to the recognition of Israel and the establishment of peaceful relations with her. For the Arabs the question was not one of finding a solution to this or that problem; the question for them was the very existence of Israel. Their aim was to annihilate Israel, and this cannot be done at the conference table.[21]

As President Carter would later say in another context, that was "BS"—bullshit. But it was the essence of Zionism's propaganda. Dayan wrote the words quoted in the last paragraph above in 1966 and their purpose then was not only to justify Israel's past actions, but to prepare the ground for justifying the big war he was within a year of initiating as minister of defence. *The reality was that Israel's hawks were not interested in negotiations that carried with them the danger of peace on terms that would prevent the creation of Greater Israel.*

Sharett did not return from Paris and Geneva as empty-handed as was supposed at the time.

Dulles had said he would talk to President Eisenhower about the possibility of American arms for Israel—to give Sharett the political support he needed in order to have a good prospect of keeping Israel's hawks in check if he stayed on as foreign minister in Ben-Gurion's new government. As briefed by Harkabi, Sharett had suggested that his hand would be greatly strengthened if Eisenhower would agree, for starters, to supply Israel with 50 jet fighters with tanks to follow in due course. In Geneva Dulles was not in a position to make any promises because he knew that Eisenhower was completely aware of military reality in the Middle East and, as a consequence, did not buy the myth of poor little Israel exposed to the danger of annihilation. (I do not myself think that any of Eisenhower's successors or other Western leaders ever believed this to be the case. It was just convenient for them to pretend that they did). So it is reasonable to suppose that Dulles promised Sharett only that he would do his best with Eisenhower.

At that time Secretary of State Dulles had no disagreement with Eisenhower about how the U.S. should seek to manage the Middle East in general and a belligerent Jewish state in particular. *Apart from the fact that there was no pressing military need for Israel's arsenal to be supplemented, they believed that the U.S. could not then risk further alienating the Arab world by being seen as Israel's arms supplier.* Fundamentally, and as Forrestal had said from the beginning, it was all about OIL—maintaining the flow of cheap Arab oil to fuel the development, at the lowest possible cost, of the Western economies, of which the American economy was the engine. If the U.S. armed Israel then, it might provoke a degree of Arab hostility that could threaten the flow of oil.

Eisenhower, Dulles and Sharett agreed: The only guarantee for Israel's survival was not weapons but peace with the Arabs, and for that, territorial concessions and the return of some refugees were necessary.

On what had to happen to guarantee Israel's survival, Dulles was then at one with Eisenhower and Sharett. The only guarantee was not weapons but peace with the Arabs. And if Israel really wanted that, Dulles said to Sharett, it would have to make territorial concessions and take back some Palestinian refugees.

When Sharett handed back the premiership to Ben-Gurion on 2 November, he had thought long and hard about whether or not there was any point in staying on as foreign minister (to lead the fight in cabinet against the warmongers). He decided to stay for two reasons. The first was the British promise, given to him in Geneva, that in a forthcoming Guildhall speech Prime Minister Eden would signal Britain's determination to work seriously for peace in the Middle East. The second, because of what Dulles had said, was in the prospect of arms from America. In Sharett's view they would give him a strong argument against war—because they would signal the beginning of a good relationship with the U.S. that would end Israel's isolation as something of a pariah state. Sharett was fully aware that, at leadership level in the Gentile world, including and especially in the Eisenhower White House, Israel was regarded as something of a pariah state (Lovett's "pig-in-a-poke") because of its contempt for UN resolutions, its belligerency, its refusal to make even the smallest concession for peace and, all up, its refusal to behave like any normal and reasonably civilised state.

Sharett was looking forward to visiting Washington for what he believed would be successful follow-up talks with Dulles, talks which Sharett was reasonably confident would give him what he needed to get the better of Prime Minister Ben-Gurion in cabinet, in order to prevent Dayan's IDF being given the green light to provoke confrontation all the way to war. But if Sharett could have known how Ben-Gurion would use his visit as part of a strategy to destroy him, he would not have gone to America and, probably, would have quit politics when he stepped down as prime minister.

In his first address to the Knesset as (once more) prime minister and defence minister, Ben-Gurion resorted to his old trick of telling the world that he was ready to meet with any Arab leader to discuss a settlement. (If he had believed there was any prospect of an Arab leader wanting to meet with him, he would not have said it). But his main message was to the Arabs—a promise that Israel would defend its rights "in the most effective manner" if those rights were assailed on land or sea or in the air. "We seek peace but not suicide!" he thundered. That same night, in part to demonstrate that this promise was not an empty one, Israeli forces attacked and destroyed Egyptian positions at al-Sabha in the Sinai. (The Israeli attack was launched from El-Auja, the vital road junction in the demilitarised zone that Dayan had previously ordered the IDF to occupy and hold in open defiance of the armistice agreement. The Egyptian fortifications at al-Sabha were destroyed and 70 Egyptian soldiers were killed. It was another of the occasions when Nasser, to save his face and protect his back, had to resort to lying—telling his people that the valiant Egyptian army had successfully driven out the Israeli aggressors with a counterattack that never actually happened). A week later Eden delivered his Guildhall speech. It was an attempt to give Project Alpha the kiss of life.[22]

"We seek peace but not suicide!" Ben-Gurion thundered, and that same night, Israeli forces attacked and destroyed Egyptian positions in the Sinai.

Project Alpha revolved around a secret Anglo-American understanding of what the essential ingredients for a political solution to the Palestine problem had to be. Britain and America had agreed to do their best to press the parties—Israel and Nasser's Egypt especially—to look upon the Alpha ingredients as the recipe for peace. The essential ingredients were:

- Linking Egypt to Jordan by ceding to them two triangles in the

Negev without cutting Israel's link to Eilat (this required Israel to make two small territorial concessions in the Negev).

- Ceding to Jordan certain "problematic" areas Israel had occupied beyond the partition plan borders.
- Dividing the DMZ's between Israel and her Arab neighbours.
- Repatriation of a limited number of Palestinian refugees and compensation for the rest.
- An agreement on the distribution of the Jordan waters.
- Termination of the Arab economic boycott of Israel.
- Western guarantees for the new frontiers.

Leaving aside the fact that it ignored the right of the Palestinians to self-determination, Project Alpha offered a settlement that was clearly in the best interests of Israel and the Arab states. The Israel to be recognised by all the Arab states in such a settlement would be bigger than that of the vitiated partition plan. And it would be the real winner. The real losers would be the Palestinians. (In retrospect it can be said that the Arab states would also have been real winners—because their leaders could have got on with the business of developing their countries and they would not have lost more land and suffered further and unending humiliation).

The ingredients of the Alpha solution had been the subject of discussions between British and American diplomats over many months. *And they were in large part a recognition by Britain and America of the fact that Nasser was serious about wanting an accommodation with Israel.*

In April, without any mention of Alpha as such, or the Anglo-American understanding behind it, Eden had made a speech calling for a settlement of the Palestine problem by negotiation, in which he presented the essence of the Alpha ingredients as proposals for all parties to consider. In August Dulles had made a similar speech. *It included an expression of sympathy for "the tragic plight of 900,000 refugees" whose grievances, he said, were every bit as important to any ultimate settlement as the question of frontiers.*

Eden's Guildhall speech in November was far more explicit about what Israel had to do for peace than any statement previously made by any Western leader.

The Arabs were insisting on an Israeli withdrawal to the partition plan borders. London and Washington knew there was no way Israel would agree to that. What then was the answer to the question of frontiers? There had to be, Eden said, a compromise between the borders of the partition plan and the borders Israel had established by war and conquest.

Eden also made it clear that, to give negotiations for peace their best possible chance, Britain and America wanted Israel to make concessions in the Negev to enable Jordan and Egypt to establish a "land bridge"—to enable Arabs to travel by land from one Arab country to another without having to pass through Israeli territory. This, as London and Washington knew, was the concession Nasser had to have if Egypt was to play its leadership role in moving the frontline Arab states, and so the whole Arab world, along the road to peace with the Jewish state. At this moment, when reason was prevailing in London and Washington, Britain and America understood that with such a concession, Nasser could claim that the territorial integrity of the "Arab nation" had not been violated by the coming into being of the Jewish state. In effect what Nasser had been saying to the British and the Americans was something like this: "Given the humiliation we Arabs have suffered, it is necessary if we are to make peace that we have a way of saving our faces. The land-bridge in the Negev will do the trick." With his Guildhall speech Eden was saying to Nasser, "We British and we Americans hear you." (As Prime Minister Sharett had).

It was another of those moments in history—perhaps the best of the early ones—when peace was there for the taking by negotiation: a peace that would have seen a Jewish state bigger than the one of the vitiated partition plan recognised by the whole Arab world. And with nothing the dispossessed Palestinians could do about it.

After Eden's Guildhall speech everything depended on the responses to it. Eden had indicated that if they were positive, he was prepared to offer his services as the mediator.

Nasser's response was very positive. He welcomed Eden's speech as marking the first occasion on which a major Western leader had taken a constructive line on what had to be done to resolve the Palestine problem; and he accepted Eden's mediation.

From Israel there was a very different response. Ben-Gurion firmly rejected Eden's offer to mediate. "His proposal to truncate the territory of Israel for the benefit of its neighbours has no legal, moral or logical basis", Ben-Gurion told the Knesset on 15 November. Many if not most Israelis were confirmed in their view that Britain was the same old enemy. And there was hardly an Israeli leader who did not declare that there were no circumstances in which Israel would yield one inch of its territory.

If there was one moment above all others when it would have been in the best longer-term interests of all concerned for the international community to have read the riot act to Zionism's child, this (November 1955) was it. The message that ought to have been delivered to Israel was something like this: "What's done is done and there's no point in arguing about how and why it was done. Israel exists but from here on the international community is going to insist that it lives in accordance with the rules of international law and the norms of behaviour for civilised states. Israel, if you are not willing to negotiate for peace on terms acceptable to the Arabs, the international community, through the Security Council, will take whatever enforcement action is necessary to compel you to do so. There cannot be two sets of rules—one for all other nations and one for Israel. While it is prepared to guarantee the security of the Jewish state inside agreed and recognised borders, the international community is not prepared to stand idly by and allow the Jewish state to create mayhem in the region with predictable and catastrophic consequences for the whole world."

That or something like it was, in fact, the approach Ben-Gurion feared the international community as led by Prime Minister Eden and President Eisenhower might take.

In Ben-Gurion's fevered imagination Britain wanted Israel to make concessions to Jordan and Egypt in the Negev for a military purpose of its own—i.e. one that was concerned with more than keeping the Soviets at bay. Hawk-like in every way, the "Old Man" had been monitoring the twists and turns in Britain's efforts to get more Arab states locked into defence (and actually all-purpose agreements) under the umbrella of the Baghdad Pact. He would have been aware that King Hussein and General Glubb had indicated to Britain that Jordan might join the Baghdad Pact if Britain provided the Hashemite kingdom with more arms. Ben-Gurion might also have known that Britain's ambition was to have Jordan in the Baghdad Pact and then linked to Iraq to create, effectively, one vast Arab client entity.

But what, Ben-Gurion asked himself, was the even bigger picture of Britain's real intentions? What was the hidden agenda? The answer seemed to him to be obvious. Britain was seeking to create defence pacts with Arab states not simply to have a shield against Soviet penetration, and not simply to have the means of controlling the Arabs to determine the terms of trade and so forth, but to have in place what was needed to move and move quickly to compel Israel, by force if necessary, to make peace on terms the Arab states could just about accept.

It was Ben-Gurion's fear of how Britain might respond that caused him to have a temporary loss of enthusiasm for what he had instructed Dayan to do when they talked in the Hotel President.

Dayan's instant, gut-reaction to Eden's Guildhall speech was that Britain should be told to go to hell with deeds as well as words. He wanted Ben-Gurion to authorise Operation Omer without delay. This was Dayan's plan to capture the Straits of Tiran. An Israeli vessel would approach the straits and, when the Egyptians opened fire, an Israeli mechanised force would sweep down the eastern shore of the Sinai Peninsula to capture and keep the straits. Support would be provided by naval and air power and paratroops. Dayan knew the operation could trigger a general war with Egypt—he hoped it would—so a special task force was to be assembled under the command of Colonel Chaim Bar-Lev. It could be ready for action, full-scale war if necessary, by the end of December.

Because he thought it was possible that British forces still stationed in the Suez Canal Zone might be ordered to intervene against Israel, Ben-Gurion's initial response to Dayan's request for authorisation was that Operation Omer should be postponed until the end of January. There was a prospect, the prime minister told his chief of staff, of weapons from America. If they provoked Eisenhower's displeasure now he might say "No" again. (It would later become clear that Ben-Gurion's stated concern was not genuine.) Dayan replied that he would rather fight immediately without American weapons than later with them.

I think it is reasonable to assume that when Ben-Gurion raised the prospect of British forces intervening, Dayan replied, "They won't" or "So what if they do, we'll fight them, too."

Over some days Dayan subjected Ben-Gurion to intense pressure. He might have told his mentor that he had gone soft and was in danger of becoming a Sharett.

Ben-Gurion was the first to blink and he agreed to authorise Operation Omer subject to the cabinet's approval. It was not forthcoming. Sharett was down but not yet out. He secured a majority for postponing Operation Omer on the grounds that the moment was "not propitious"—because he was about to visit Washington and was confident that he could bring American arms on stream.

Dayan was furious. He was certain that postponement meant cancellation.

According to the received wisdom of history—even that as revised by Shlaim—Ben-Gurion's position was "rather ambiguous". The prime minister "submitted the plan to the cabinet but did not put all of his weight behind it. Nor did he fight back when a majority of the ministers, including the moderates in his own party, voted against it."[23]

My own interpretation (which I think is fully supported by what happened next) is different. Ben-Gurion was as furious as Dayan but, for once, he did not show his anger. *Instead, and without giving anybody around the cabinet table a clue about what he was really thinking, he decided that his priority now was to get rid of Sharett by creating a situation that would force him to resign.* In the "Old Man's" view the foreign minister was not merely a coward and Zionism's own Neville Chamberlain, he was the cancer destroying the backbones of others.

On the night of 11 December (a date to keep in mind), Israeli forces launched from land and sea a three-pronged attack on extremely well dug-in and heavily fortified Syrian gun positions on the north eastern shore of the Sea of Galilee (Lake Kinneret to Israelis). Operation Olive Leaves was the most fiercely fought and brilliantly executed Israeli offensive since the 1948 war. The main attack force was a paratroop brigade led by Sharon, now promoted to Lieutenant Colonel.

The Israelis killed 56 Syrians, took 30 prisoners and reduced the Syrian fortifications to rubble. Israel casualties were 6 dead and 10 wounded.

As ever Israel's justification was self-defence. Operation Olive Leaves, the world and the people of Israel were told, was a reprisal in response to an attack on the forces of the Jewish state by the Syrians.

The truth was that Sharon had been training and rehearsing his paratroops for weeks. All they had been waiting for was a pretext. And when the Syrians did not oblige by firing so much as a single shot into Israel, the Israelis created one. On 10 December an Israeli police patrol boat was sent close to the shore for the purpose of provoking Syrian fire. A Syrian soldier did then fire a few shots. They scraped some paint of the boat's bottom but no Israeli was hit. And that was it. "Go" for Operation Olive Leaves. Israeli aggression pure and simple; its nakedness covered only by a propaganda lie.

When the Syrians did not oblige by creating a pretext—not so much as firing a single shot into Israel—an Israeli police patrol boat was sent close to the shore for the purpose of provoking fire. A few shots were fired, but no Israeli was hit. This was the pretext for Operation Olive Leaves.

Exciting stuff but the real drama was in the untold story of why operation Olive Leaves was authorised.

At the time of the attack Sharett was in Washington waiting for confirmation that his efforts to secure an American commitment to provide Israel with arms had been successful. In his absence Ben-Gurion was acting foreign minister in addition to his other posts.

Apart from his anger and frustration on account of the cabinet's refusal to authorise Operation Omer, Dayan had his own reasons, three, for the attack on Syria.

First was that the Syrian army had not been smashed in 1948 and had reason to feel confident that it could acquit itself well in any engagement with the Israelis. By inflicting a token but crushing defeat on it, Dayan was hoping to break or seriously dent that confidence. His message to the Syrians on that December night was, "We can take you any time we like." (This from the man most responsible for having Jews everywhere believe that poor little Israel was in danger of annihilation!)

Second was the need to test Nasser's reaction. The previous month he had concluded a defence agreement with Syria. Dayan wanted to find out if Nasser would respond to give the Syrians proof that they could count on him when they were attacked. (The reality was that Egypt's armed forces were incapable of responding with a military solidarity gesture even if Nasser had wanted them to do so. Which he did not.) If Nasser did respond, Dayan would have, he hoped, the pretext for developing the full-scale war he wanted.

Third was the need to test in the heat of battle how efficient and how well coordinated or not the IDF was. There were limits to how much the flaws in men and equipment, communications and tactics, could be exposed by rehearsals. Only the real thing would confirm that the fighting Jews had come of age. *And that they could cope with the real challenge ahead— not protecting existing borders but expanding them to create Greater Israel.*

The key to understanding why Ben-Gurion authorised Operation Olive Leaves, and why he did not consult his cabinet, is a telephone message he received from Washington on 27 November. (The truth is so incredible that if a writer of fiction had put it into a novel, his editor might have said: "Take it out. Nobody's going to believe that.")

The caller was Sharett. He had three points and a plea to make. The points were that his negotiations with the Americans had gone well; that he was confident his mission would succeed—America would agree to provide Israel with some arms; and that he had been promised a definite answer by 12 December. Sharett's plea was that no reprisal attack be authorised before then—because it would test Eisenhower's patience with Israel to its limits and destroy the otherwise excellent prospects for bringing American arms on stream.

After they had said their goodbyes on the telephone it occurred to Ben-Gurion that 12 December was some way off and that Sharett might come home, perhaps to return to Washington only a day or so before the announcement. On reflection, Ben-Gurion called Sharett to tell him to stay in Washington until he had received the answer from Dulles on 12 December.

When Sharett's diaries were published in 1980, they indicated that he was aware on 10 December 1955 that there would be a reprisal attack—i.e. in response to the alleged Syrian attack on Israeli forces. On that day he wrote, "*My world became black, the matter of arms (from America) was murdered.*"[24]

If he had been in Israel he would have been able to mobilise the cabinet to cause the IDF's attack to be aborted. Of that there can be no doubt whatsoever. Cabinet ministers were dumbfounded when they were told about the attack by their morning newspapers. One minister said the IDF was out of control and pursuing its own agenda. For this minister and no doubt others the only other explanation was too incredible to be true. It was obvious that the nature and scale of Israel's attack was bound to destroy the apparently good prospect of arms from America. Unless he was totally bonkers, the "Old Man" would not have wanted that to happen. The idea of him authorising an attack to cause the Eisenhower administration to say "No" to Sharett was preposterous. Unthinkable. But not for Sharett.

His first response to news of the attack was an angry cable of protest to Ben-Gurion. In it he questioned how many governments Israel had and if the policy of one of them was to sabotage his efforts and to foil his objectives.

It was Eban in Washington who took the call from the State Department that confirmed Sharett's fears of the damage that had been done. A decision on Israel's request for arms had been postponed, because of the latest act of Israeli aggression (and Israel's continuing refusal to consider concessions of any kind to make negotiations with the Arabs possible).

Though Ben-Gurion would subsequently pretend he did not believe it, the truth on the eve of the Israeli attack was that Eisenhower had agreed that Dulles could give Sharret a qualified "Yes." If Operation Olive Leaves had not happened, Dulles would have told Sharett on 12 December that the U.S. was ready immediately to sell Israel some weapons for defensive purposes but not yet tanks and planes. And Dulles would have gone on to say that tanks and planes would follow in stages over the course of the coming year.

There were two related reasons for this change in America's policy (change in its way of handling Israel, that is).

The first was that Eisenhower understood and accepted what Sharret had said in Geneva—that, in the aftermath of Nasser's arms deal with the Soviets, Sharett had to be seen to be delivering something from the U.S. if he was to have a chance of stopping Israel's hawks from having their way and launching a preventive war.

The second was that not supplying Israel with arms, as a means of pressing it to abandon its policy of reprisal attacks and be serious about peace, had not worked. The new hope was that supplying arms would give the U.S. the leverage to bring Israel to heel. (If they had talked on 12 December, it might have been that Dulles, with a wink, would have said to Sharett, "Between ourselves, the tanks and planes will be dependent on your country's good behaviour.")

Before he left Washington empty-handed for home, Sharett told Eban he had no doubt that Ben-Gurion had authorised the attack on Syria to deny him a personal victory in his quest for American arms.

Sharett was, of course, right. Ben-Gurion did authorise Operation Olive Leaves to sabotage Sharett's mission. It was the start of Ben-Gurion's campaign to get rid of Sharett by leaving him with no choice but to resign. Nearly a quarter of a century after the events Major General Uzi Narkis, one of Israel's most illustrious and respected military commanders, was prepared to go on record in conversation with Avi Shlaim. On page 151 of *The Iron Wall* he quoted Narkis as saying: "I maintain that there was coordinated action on the part of Ben-Gurion and Dayan to hurt Sharett. The scope of the operation (Olive Leaves) was widened in order to deliver a body blow to Sharett. Between Dayan and Sharett there were no relations to speak of. Dayan was contemptuous of Sharett. Between the minister of defence and the chief of staff there was apparently a pact to cause Sharett to fail and to remove him from power. This was the first shot in the campaign against Sharett."

As we shall see in the next chapter, there were good reasons why Ben-Gurion was not bothered by the fact that attacking Syria to damage Sharett would result in another Eisenhower "No" to Israel's request for American arms. *Ben-Gurion's strategy took account of the fact that 1956 was election year in America*. That meant the time was approaching when he could mobilise the Zionist lobby for maximum impact. President Eisenhower was his own man and above pork-barrel politics, but many others seeking election or re-election were not. Ben-Gurion was also secure in the knowledge that if he failed to get arms from America on President Eisenhower's watch, there was a prostitute waiting to offer more of her services. Her name was France.

Why did Sharett have to go? The reality Ben-Gurion could no

longer tolerate, not least because he was coming under greater and greater pressure from Dayan, was that as long as Sharett remained a member of the cabinet he could command a majority against the military escalation Dayan's IDF wanted. (I think it is not impossible that Ben-Gurion entertained the fear that Dayan might inspire if not actually lead a military coup if Sharett remained a member of the government).

When Sharett arrived back in Israel he was met at the airport by Ben-Gurion's military secretary, Colonel Nehemia Argov. To him Sharett said, "*You stabbed me in the back!*"[25]

Sharett's description of the decision-making process that authorised the attack on Syria was this: "Ben-Gurion the defence minister consulted Ben-Gurion the foreign minister and received the green light from Ben-Gurion the prime minister."[26]

The real fireworks were reserved for the meeting of Mapai's Political Committee on 27 December, at which Sharret was to report on his mission to America.

In advance of the meeting he received a report of what Dayan had said to the General Staff. "This government will not declare war but the army can bring it about through border clashes."[27]

That prompted Sharett to open his counterattack with a statement of the reasons why he was opposed to preventive war. But his main purpose was to condemn Ben-Gurion for causing him to fail in his mission to secure arms from America and all they would have symbolized—the end of Israel's isolation as a pariah state so far as the Eisenhower administration, and the President himself in particular, was concerned.

Ben-Gurion had declined an invitation to take his normal place at the head of the table and was sitting at the side of the room.

Having described the disastrous consequences of the attack on Syria, Sharett delivered his judgment of Ben-Gurion in nine words. And his real message was in the first of them.

"*Satan himself could not have chosen a worse timing!*"[28]

On 19 January 1956, the Security Council issued its strongest ever condemnation of Israel. The resolution of that day condemned the attack on Syria, recalled Israel's earlier violations of the armistice agreements, called on Israel to respect those agreements and threatened sanctions if it did not.

In the end it was Ben-Gurion's decision to back Dayan's policy of developing the French connection that brought about Sharett's resignation.

That connection had to be Israel's best kept secret partly because the French were willing to defy Eisenhower and supply the Israelis with whatever weapons they wanted and could afford; but also because of the contributions French scientists were already making to the development of Israel's atom bomb, in a deal which would include Israel's willingness to go to war with Egypt to topple Nasser.

To keep the French connection as secret as possible, Ben-Gurion transferred control over the acquisition of arms from Sharett's foreign ministry to his own defence ministry. Then, on 10 June, Ben-Gurion authorised Dayan to go ahead with secret negotiations with France on far-reaching cooperation, which was eventually to include joint preparations for war with Egypt.

Sharett resigned on 18 June (to be replaced by Golda Meir). Before resigning he tried to make one last stand for sanity by telling Ben-Gurion that he wanted a debate in a responsible party forum. What he wanted behind Mapai's closed doors, he said, was a discussion about the contending approaches that had led to Ben-Gurion's decision to transfer responsibility for arms purchases from the foreign ministry to the defence ministry. But that, as they both knew, was another way of asking the ruling party to choose—Ben-Gurion's way or Sharett's way. The implication is that Sharett said to Ben-Gurion something like the following: "If you will agree to such a debate, and if the party wants to go your way when it knows all the facts, I will, of course resign."

There was no way Ben-Gurion could agree to such a debate because there was no guarantee he would win it. He probably would have lost it. So Ben-Gurion said "No" to debate and that he would be the one to resign if Sharett insisted on discussion.

And that was the end of Sharett. *His exit from the stage marked the end of his policy of seeking an accommodation with the Arabs through negotiation.*

From here on Israel's future would be determined by three men—Dayan, Dayan and Dayan. To keep up the pretence that the Jewish state was a well functioning democracy, Ben-Gurion would continue to take decisions as prime minister and defence minister: and Peres would make critical inputs, but Zionism's one-eyed, charismatic warlord was in the driving seat. Back or front made no difference to him.

And he was only four months away from getting the war he wanted, with the assistance of France and Britain and a coalition of anti-Nasser American interests, a coalition that did not include President Eisenhower.

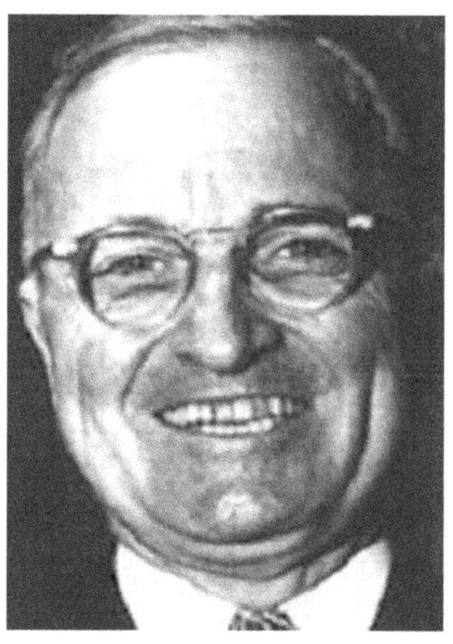

President Harry S. Truman
American Godfather of,modern Israel

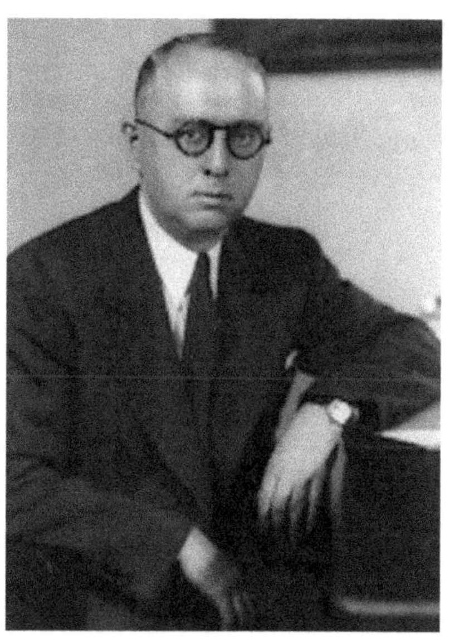

David K. Niles
Zionism's Top Man in Truman's White House

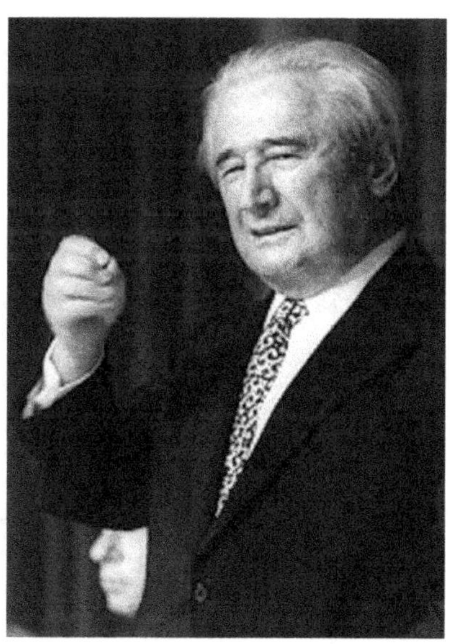

Nahum Goldmann
Zionist leader who did not believe war with the Arabs was necessary and who eventually urged President Carter to"break the back" of the Zionist lobby

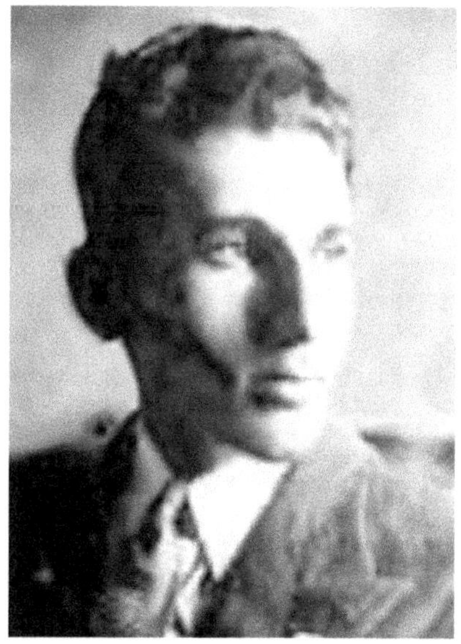

Avraham Stern
Zionist terrorist leader who wantedto collaborate with the Nazis

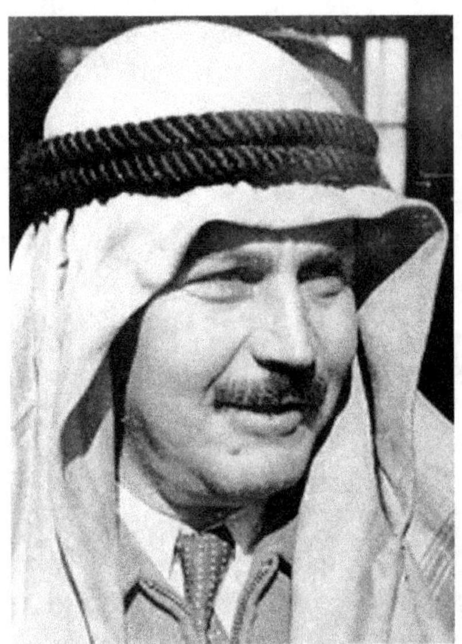

Abdul Khader Husseini
First authentic Palestinian resistance leader

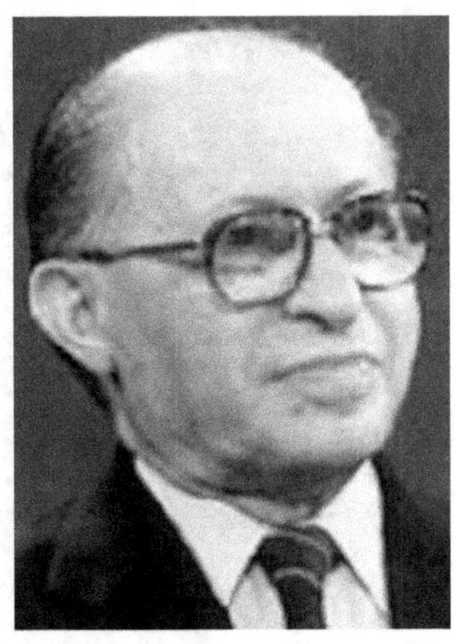

Menachem Begin
Zionist terrorist leader who became Israel's prime minister

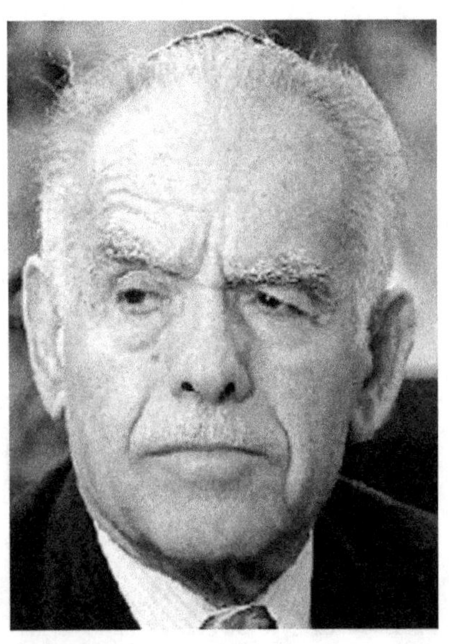

Yitzhak Shamir
Zionist terrorist leader who became Israel's Prime Minister (after Begin)

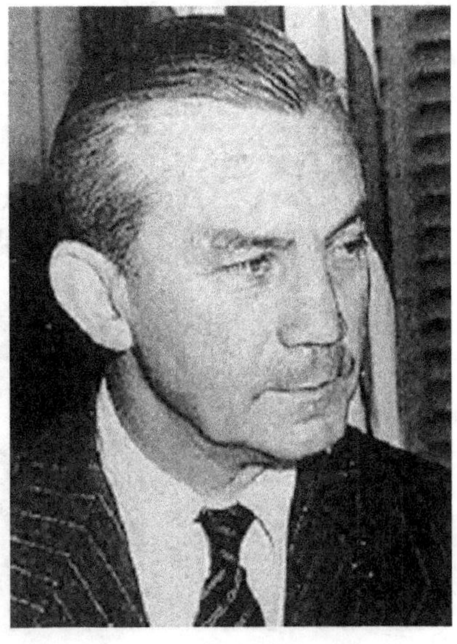

James Vincent Forrestal
Defence Secretary who tried to take the Palestine problem out of the pork-barrel of US politics. What brought about his suicide?

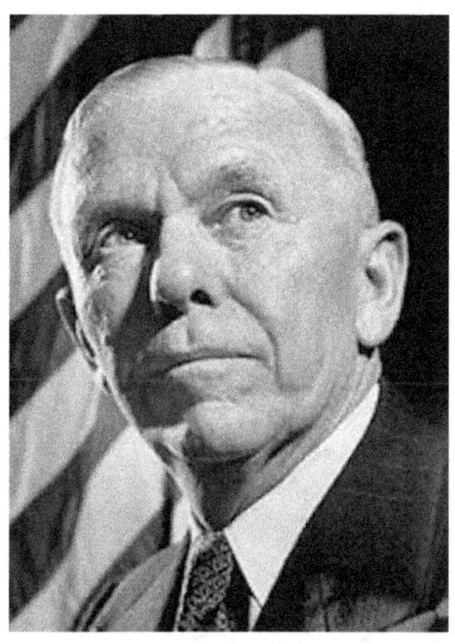

General George C. Marshall
Secretary of State who wanted to put US interests before Zionism's

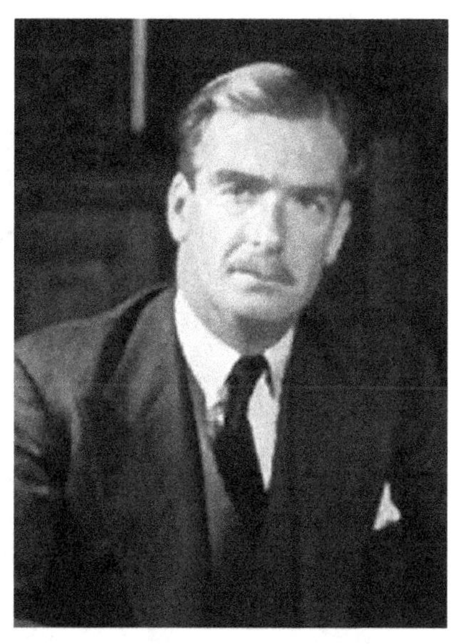

Sir Anthony Eden
British Prime Minister who, with France, sent Israel to war in 1956 to destroy Nasser

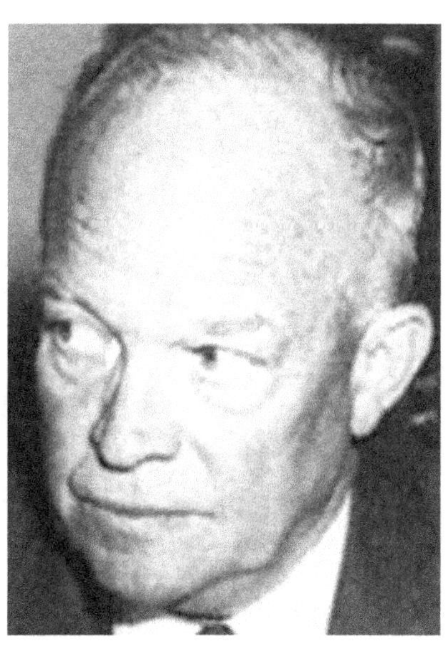

President Eisenhower
Contained Zionism on his watch

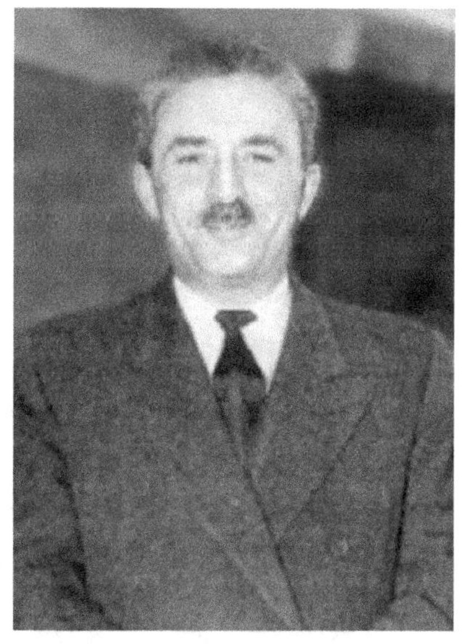

Moshe Sharett
Voice of reason who wanted Israel to be a "normal" state

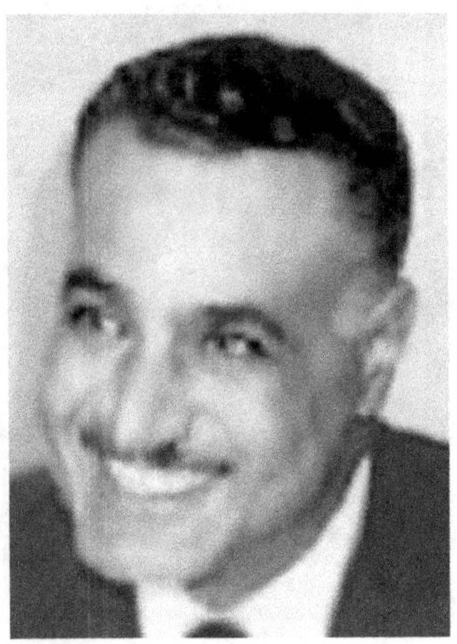

Gamel Abdul Nasser
Egypt's President who wanted peace but got war

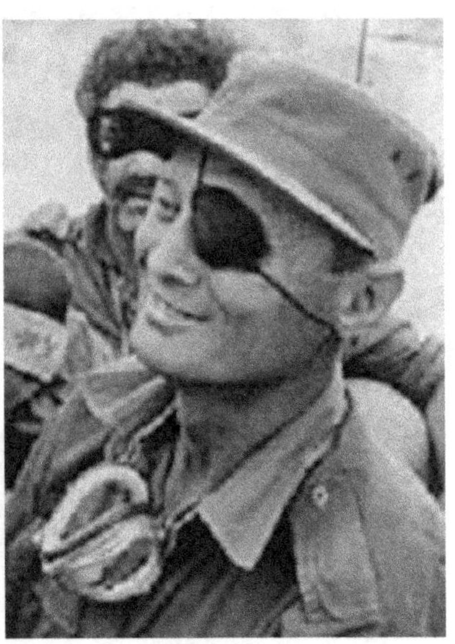

General Moshe Dayan
The creator of Greater Israel

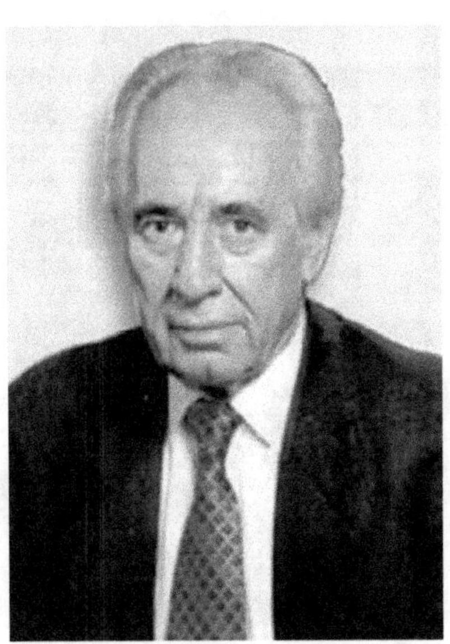

Shimon Peres
Atom bomb and olive branch

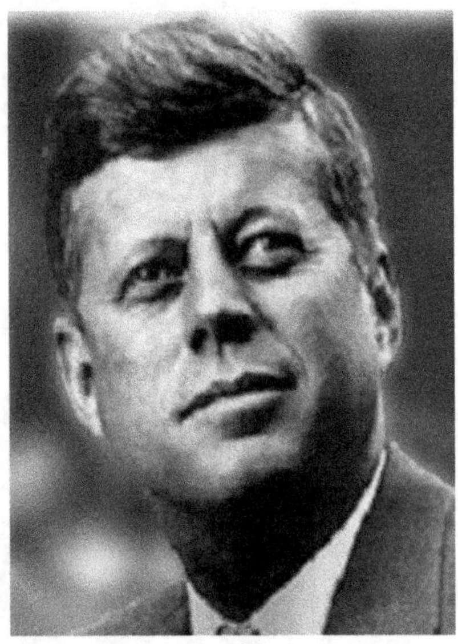

President John F. Kennedy
Intended to contain Zionism

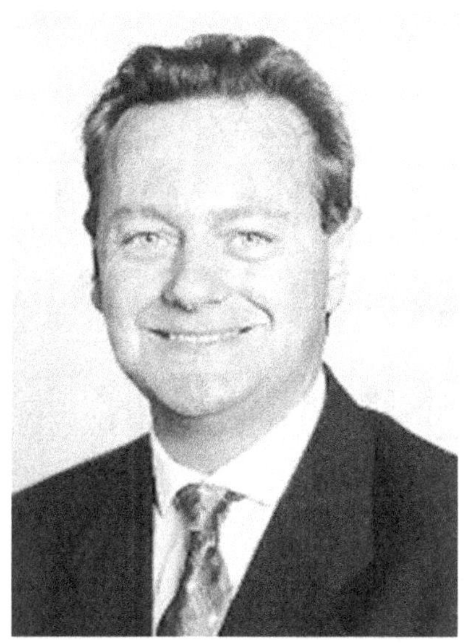

Philip L. Graham
Publisher who helped to impose pro-Zionist Johnson on Kennedy

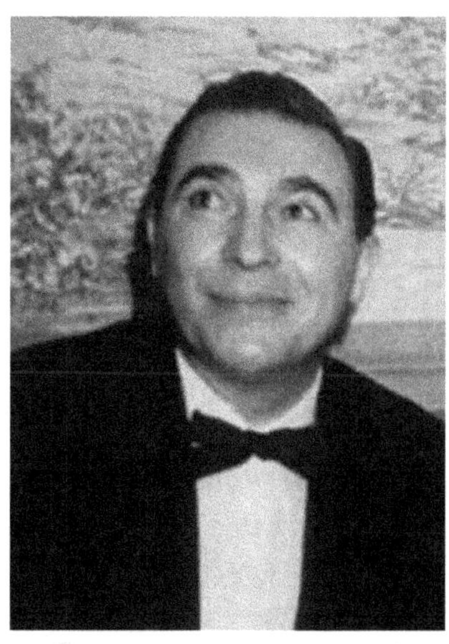

Abraham Feinburg
Key to Zionist influence outside Kennedy White House

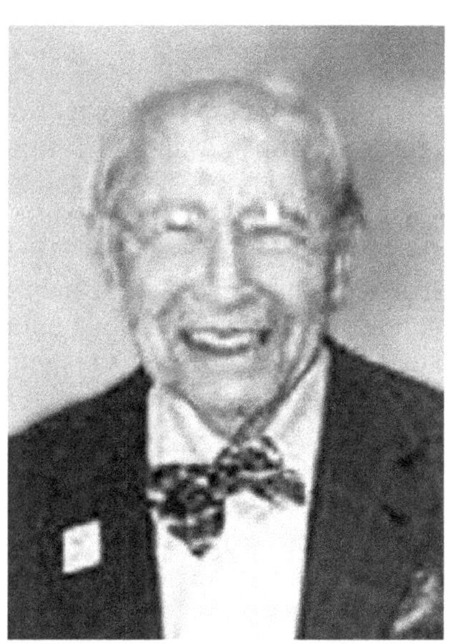

Meyer Feldman
Key to ZIonist influence inside Johnson White House

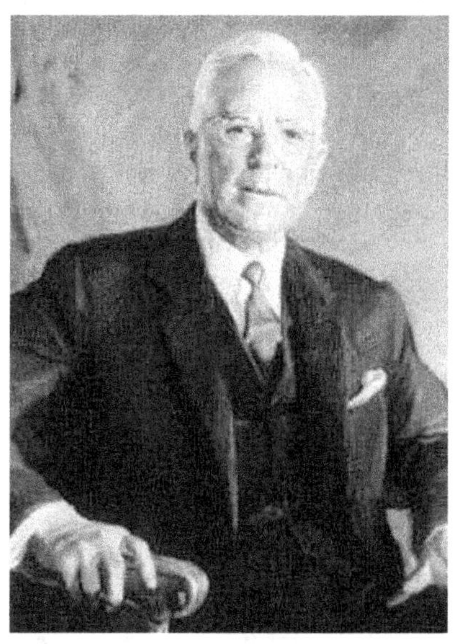

John McCone
Kennedy's CIA director who tried to stop Israel's atomic bomb

9

WAR WITH NASSER, ACT I AND CONFRONTATION WITH EISENHOWER

Today there are no serious historians or writers of any kind who dispute the essence of what happened in October 1956. Israel went to war with Nasser's Egypt in a conspiracy with France and Britain. There is also no dispute about how this short, sharp war ended. President Eisenhower read the riot act to the conspirators, and then confronted Zionism by insisting that Israel withdraw unconditionally from the Egyptian territory it had occupied and from which it had not been intending to withdraw. But there are still questions which need answers about who did what and why.

The extent to which leaders of the anti-Nasser coalition of American vested interests were a party to the conspiracy from the beginning is still a matter for speculation, but... They kept what they knew from President Eisenhower and it was a decision taken by Secretary of State Dulles that triggered the explosion.

According to the authorised British, French and Israeli versions of events, it started with Nasser's nationalisation of the Suez Canal on 26 July. (The last British forces had withdrawn on 13 June, a week before Sharett's resignation). But this gesture of defiance was Nasser's response to the announcement Secretary of State Dulles made on 19 July that he was pulling the plug on funding of the High Dam at Aswan.

This was the project Nasser regarded as the key to Egypt's development. The priority need of his rapidly expanding population was water for irrigation, with due attention to conservation and storage to guarantee that parched lands could be irrigated even in unusually dry years. And nor was it just a question of water for sustaining daily life. There was need to guarantee the future of the cotton crop that was Egypt's biggest foreign exchange earner.

For Nasser nothing was more important than the High Dam project. He might not have said to his RCC leadership colleagues "War with Israel—forget about it", but that was his view. Almost the first thing he did on coming to power was to approach the West German government for funding and technical assistance to conduct a feasibility study of the High Dam project and then to come up with the design. His winning argument to the West Germans was something like: "You're paying a lot of money to Israel in the form of reparations on account of what the Nazis did to the Jews, this is your opportunity to do some balancing."

The estimated cost of constructing the High Dam was enormous—close to US$1 billion. Nasser also approached the World Bank, America and Britain for funding. After it became known that the Russians had said they were ready to finance the High Dam project as well as provide arms for Egypt, Eden panicked. He told Nutting and others that he wanted to "keep the Russian bear out of the Nile Valley" at all costs. Britain was ready, desperate, to put up some of the money for Nasser's dream project. Dulles did not share Eden's fears. Dulles believed that when push came to shove the Russians would not be able to put their money where their mouth was. But Dulles did want (as all budding American imperialists wanted) a way of making Egypt dependent on, and therefore to some extent subservient to, Uncle Sam, all the more so because of Nasser's refusal to join a Western defence pact. The way was funding the High Dam project. Eventually it was agreed that the World Bank would put up half the funding, conditional upon America and Britain providing the balance.

When Dulles pulled the plug on America's contribution he brought the whole house down. The following day Eden announced that Britain would not be providing any funding and the World Bank (its president was disgusted by the politics of what was happening) had no say in the matter. Its offer automatically lapsed when American and Britain reneged on their commitments.

To the few insiders on both sides of the Atlantic who could read the signals, Dulles was effectively saying: "There must be regime change in Egypt. Nasser has got to go." America's Secretary of State had, in fact, come to that conclusion some months previously.

Any attempt to get at the whole truth has to begin, I think, with appreciation of the real significance of a letter Ben-Gurion wrote to Eisenhower on 14 February 1956.

In this letter Ben-Gurion depicted Nasser as a threat to Western interests in the Middle East as well as Israel's survival. And that was the Israeli leader's preface to a protest against America's denial of arms to the Jewish state.

Ben-Gurion knew very well that Eisenhower himself would not buy such nonsense. So why did he write the letter?

The short answer is that he knew there were other very influential Americans (the Cold War warriors) who would buy his "Nasser is the threat" line, and who were ready to make common cause with Zionism's most reliable stooges in Congress. And with the auction for campaign funds and votes about to get underway again in America, the time for the Zionist lobby to go to work had arrived. Effectively the letter to Eisenhower was Ben-Gurion's way of calling the Zionist lobby in all of its manifestations to action and giving it a powerful message.

The message was that President Eisenhower was not assisting poor little Israel in its struggle to survive. (In Israel many people had been conditioned to regard Eisenhower as at best "unfriendly" to the Jewish state and at worst "hostile"). So on one level Ben-Gurion was looking to the Zionist lobby to make use of his letter to generate pressure on Eisenhower not only to supply arms to Israel, but also to supply them without conditions—without, for example, the insistence that Israel commit itself to not extending its borders by force. A condition Sharett had accepted. But that was only a part of Ben-Gurion's big picture strategy.

In his view the time had come for American Zionists to begin the implementation of phase two of the grand plan. Phase one had climaxed with the subversion of the UN and the bending of President Truman to Zionism's will. Phase two was the propaganda campaign necessary to have the Jewish state perceived by most if not quite all Americans as the only true and reliable friend and ally the U.S. had in the region.

Phase Two of Ben-Gurion's plan was a propaganda campaign to have the Jewish state perceived by most Americans as the only reliable friend and ally the U.S. had in the region.

The key to success would be assisting Americans to understand the natural affinity they had with the people of Israel in terms of a shared culture and values. The Israel of Zionism's propaganda was an open, democratic, freedom-loving, peace-seeking and progressive state, committed to the thing called capitalism and by definition an anti-Communist bastion. Might almost be the 51st state of the American union. The Arab world? It was composed of closed, undemocratic, backward even primitive states, and the most barbaric of them were opening their doors to the evil empire—the Soviet Union, America's enemy—for the purpose of having the means to destroy Israel. Americans were among the most under-informed, naïve and gullible people on earth with a predilection for dividing the world into "good guys" and "bad guys". With effort it would not be difficult to have most if not all Americans understanding that the best way to protect U.S. interests in the region was to assist the Jewish state to keep the forces of evil at bay.

When Ben-Gurion wrote his letter to Eisenhower, he was aware that CIA director Allen Dulles was already of a mind to regard Israel as America's only reliable ally in the region. This Dulles understood that while it was possible to buy Arab leaders—Nasser excluded—"loyalty" obtained on that basis could not be counted upon in all circumstances, especially when it became clear to the Arab masses, as no doubt it would one day, that their leaders were more or less American puppets. Ben-Gurion knew how the mind of Allen Dulles was working because of the developing and very special personal relationship between the CIA's director and his Mossad counterpart, Isser Harel.

The point? When Ben-Gurion wrote to Eisenhower on 14 February, he knew there were some very powerful Americans who, for reasons of

American self-interest (their perception of it) were about ready to see things Israel's way. Eisenhower himself would never be a supporter of Israel right or wrong, but after four more years of him there would be a return to pork-barrel politics from the top down. And then the Zionist lobby could really do its stuff.

The moment when Secretary of State John Foster Dulles turned against Nasser and agreed with his CIA director brother Allen that Nasser should be toppled was identified by one of Britain's key players of the time, the minister of state at the Foreign Office—Nutting. *The moment came at the end of March with the failure of a secret Eisenhower peace initiative.*

Codenamed Operation Gamma, its purpose was to explore the possibility of an understanding between Nasser and Ben-Gurion which, Eisenhower hoped, would form the basis of negotiations for a final settlement of the Palestine problem. In the President's own ideal scenario Nasser and Ben-Gurion would agree to a face-to-face meeting at some point. The man given the responsibility by Eisenhower for making it all happen was his friend, Robert Anderson, a former deputy secretary of defence, a Texas oil millionaire and a future Secretary of the Treasury.

As it happened, the first of three rounds of super secret talks Anderson had over four months—December to March—could not have taken place at a worse time for Nasser. Israel's attack on Syria had just taken place and because the Arabs had been humiliated once more, Nasser was so frightened of news of the Anderson mission leaking that he told only two of his leadership colleagues about it. (He was under pressure from his army to hit back at the Israelis, not to talk peace). Nasser's fear of a leak was, in fact, so great that he and the two had their meetings with Anderson late at night in a private flat.

Ben-Gurion for his part was not remotely interested in the Anderson mission, but because it was an Eisenhower initiative he had to go through the motions of taking it seriously. He played his hand brilliantly. Because he knew there was not the slightest prospect of Nasser meeting with him, he told Anderson that he attached the greatest possible importance to such a meeting! If only he and Nasser could meet face-to-face, Ben-Gurion said, peace might be reached "in two or three days." *From the beginning, Israel's prime minister and defence minister had only one purpose—to put the blame for failure of the mission on Nasser.*

Nasser explained to Anderson why there was no way he could meet with Ben-Gurion even if he wanted to. His army, his people and the Arab world would not allow it. He would be assassinated. In his report to Eisenhower when he knew his mission had failed, Anderson said that on at least four occasions Nasser had made reference to the assassination of King Abdullah.

But the Egyptian leader was prepared to negotiate. His position was not that an accommodation with Israel was out of the question. If it was understood that the problem was not just between Israel and Egypt and that all the Arabs had to be involved, *Nasser was willing to negotiate through America as the mediator.*

On matters of substance Nasser told Anderson he had to have what Eden had called for in his Guildhall speech—an Israeli concession in the Negev. He also said he wanted the Palestinians to have a choice between repatriation and compensation.

Ben-Gurion's way of getting around the problem of having to negotiate about anything was to tell Anderson that while Israel was prepared in principle to discuss "minor territorial adjustments" and "a contribution" to compensation for Palestinian refugees, such discussions could only take place in the framework of direct negotiations for peace. Nasser could take it or leave it on that basis. If Ben-Gurion had been at all interested in exploring the prospects for a settlement on terms other than those dictated by Israeli military might, he could have said to Anderson something like: "Okay. Let's try to make a serious start by using the good offices of the President of the United States of America for mediation."

Eisenhower's stated response to Anderson's report on the failure of his mission was even-handed. *He blamed both leaders, Nasser and Ben-Gurion.* Secretary of State Dulles chose to put all the blame for the failure of Operation Gamma on Nasser—a judgment that was clearly not justified. But it enabled this Dulles to support his brother's view that Nasser had to be toppled. As Nutting put it: "From now on Dulles was nevertheless at one with his British and French allies in resolving that Nasser was a net liability to the West and should be eliminated at the earliest possible opportunity."[1]

At the time, and as Nutting revealed, CIA agents were "busily discussing" with their counterparts in Britain's Secret Intelligence Service (SIS) the possibilities of organising a coup in Egypt. It was to be along the lines of the one the CIA had organised to topple Iran's Mossadeq three years previously and restore the young Shah to power.

A brief explanation of why Eden had turned against Nasser and wanted him toppled (i.e. months before the Egyptian leader nationalised the Suez Canal) is now in order.

Through the British Ambassador in Cairo, Sir Humphrey Trevelyan, Eden had been lying to Nasser. Britain, Trevelyan had assured Nasser, was no longer seeking to draw Jordan into the Baghdad Pact. Nasser took the assurance at face value and called off his war of words against continuing British imperialism in general and its principal Arab client state, Iraq, in particular.

Perfidious Eden responded by re-doubling Britain's efforts to bribe and bully Jordan into joining the Baghdad Pact. In Britain's grand design Jordan and Iraq were to become one under the umbrella of the defence agreement. This, the British were intending to argue when they had pulled it off, was for the sake of having the strongest possible shield against Soviet penetration. That was largely nonsense. Britain's real objective was to have Iraq and Jordan as one large client state. And the defence pact was to be the mechanism though which Britain controlled it, essentially for dictating the terms of trade and keeping their American rivals out.

At the point when it seemed to the British that Jordan was about to join the Baghdad Pact, there was serious rioting in Amman and towns throughout Jordan. It was evident that very many of King Hussein's subjects shared Nasser's view of the real purpose of the defence alliances Britain wanted—they were the means of having Arab governments do Britain's will.

The real purpose of Britain's defence alliances with Arab states was not to shield against Soviet influence but to turn them into British clients—a reality the Arab masses understood.

The young king responded with a very dramatic gesture. He dismissed General Glubb from his post of Commander of the Arab Legion and required him—after two decades of service—to leave Jordan forever within 24 hours.

Hussein insisted that the decision was his and his alone. And his explanation could not have been more explicit. As long as Glubb remained in command in Jordan, every Jordanian government when faced with the need to make any important political decision would have to continue the practise of consulting with him or the British Embassy before it talked to its own sovereign.

Eden's hopes of having Jordan and Iraq as one vast puppet state were in ruins. Among those who were convinced that Hussein had told the truth—that the decision to dismiss Glubb had been his and his alone—was Sir Alexander Kirkbride, Britain's long-serving ambassador in Jordan. But Eden, incandescent with rage to an extent that shook even those used to his vile temper, chose to blame Nasser. Glubb had been the victim of Egyptian intrigues. That was, as Nutting put it, a false premise, but on the basis of it Eden "decided that Nasser was the incarnation of all evils in Arabia who would destroy every British interest in the Middle East, unless he himself was destroyed."[2]

And that was why Eden authorised Britain's SIS to work with America's CIA to get rid of Nasser.

From the perspective of the vested interests represented in Britain by Eden and in America by the Dulles brothers, Nasser really was the enemy, because, as previously noted, he was a true Arab nationalist who wanted Egypt to be truly independent, in the sense of being free to develop in accordance with the priority needs of its own people. Put another way, Nasser wanted to prevent the big powers from having sufficient influence to exploit his country for their own ends, at the expense of its own people. And what he wanted for Egypt, he wanted for all Arab states—the one Arab nation of the Arab imagination. In other words Nasser was the most potent symbol of the real enemy—real Arab nationalism. And that was the real enemy not because it was pro the Soviet Union—it absolutely was not; but because it was anti being dominated and ripped off by the major Western powers.

The reality of the time was that those in Britain who wanted to get rid of Nasser were seeking to keep British imperialism alive; and those in America who wanted to get rid of Nasser were seeing him as the main obstacle in the region to the rise of American imperialism. It would never be called that at the time—America's image of itself then would never permit such labeling—but from the perspective of the beginning of the 21st century it can be seen and is readily admitted for what it was and is. The Cold War was the cover for the emergence of American imperialism. Once the Soviets had been seen off, the world would be America's to rule. (At the dawn of the 21st century President "Dubya" Bush actually said—if not quite in so many words—"We Americans now run the world." In the wake of the dissolution of the Soviet Union, his father had said, "What we say, goes."

Ben-Gurion, perhaps because he walked the line between madness and genius, was the first to understand that just as Britain had used Zionism to further its imperial ambitions in 1917, there were now, in the mid 1950s, Americans who were seeing merit in the idea of using Zionism to serve America's unstated but nonetheless real imperial ambitions.

Ben-Gurion understood that anything the British had done, the Americans could do bigger and better. From this perspective Eisenhower was the enemy. His view of how the world ought to be and how it ought to be managed was not that different from Woodrow Wilson's. Eisenhower could never have contemplated an alliance with Zionism. Ben-Gurion knew that too; and that was why priority had to be given to getting arms from France while Eisenhower was in power.

When Secretary of State Dulles pulled the plug on American, British and World Bank funding for the High Dam at Aswan, there was only one difference between him and the others who were to make common cause to get rid of Nasser—the French, the Israelis and the British. Dulles did not believe it was necessary for anybody to resort to war to topple Nasser. Dulles had calculated that the Soviet Union could not provide alternative funding and that, as a consequence, Nasser would have no hope of fulfilling his dream. In due course there would be huge disappointment in Egypt. The disillusioned Egyptian masses would take their discontent to the streets and that could be exploited by the CIA. That was the way to topple Nasser and have him replaced by somebody, preferably another military man who was not that fussed about democracy and who would do America's bidding. (American leaders talked a lot about their commitment to democracy in all the "over theres" of the developing world, but a cursory glance at the record shows a clear preference for having dictators and repressive regimes in place to do America's bidding. Of course there was a reason for that. Only dictators and repressive regimes did not quibble about spending a disproportionate amount of their country's money on buying weapons in the name of keeping Communism at bay).

At the time Dulles signalled his wish to have Nasser destroyed by means of a coup, Eden was at one with him. War with Egypt was not yet on the British prime minister's agenda. At this moment the war party was being led by Dayan, and his task now was to get the French whore to see things his way.

Israel's secret French connection was institutionalised at a three-day conference (24 to 26 June) that took place in a chateau at Vermars to the south of Paris. It was a meeting of top military and intelligence people from both sides.

Before Dayan left for Paris, Ben-Gurion said to him: "France will give us the arms only if we give it serious help in the Algerian matter. Serious help means killing Egyptians, nothing less."[3] (What was the Algerian matter? France was seeking to prevent the sun from setting on all of its empire in North Africa. Tunisia and Morocco were due to get their independence but France did not want to let go of Algeria. There an escalating and bloody struggle for independence was underway which would eventually claim 250,000 lives and come close to destroying France. And Nasser was being a very naughty nationalist, *très méchant*. He was backing his Algerian Arab brothers against the French imperialists).

Dayan was the star of the Vermars conference and the first to speak. In the picture he painted for his distinguished French audience Nasser was the danger; a threat not merely to stability in the Middle East and North Africa, but a threat to the whole of the "Free World". Nasser's purpose was to eliminate all European influence in the region and turn Egypt into a "forward base" for the Soviet Union.[4] Israel had no general quarrel with the Arab world, only a particular quarrel with Nasser; and Israel's main aim was to overthrow him. And the Jewish state would be doing the "Free World" a favour—because preventing the establishment of a Soviet forward base in Egypt was in the best interests of the whole of the "Free World", not just Israel's.

It is interesting to note that a few weeks before Dayan was soliciting French assistance by playing up the Soviet menace, the Soviet leader, Nikita Khrushchev, made a remarkable public statement in London. *At the end of talks with Eden he told a press conference that the Soviet Union would be prepared to take part in a United Nations embargo on the delivery of arms to such trouble spots as the Middle East.* Khrushchev made the statement because he had been frightened by what Eden had said to him in private—that Britain would fight to preserve her oil interests in the Middle East. (Despite what all Western leaders said to their publics, they knew that the Soviet military presence in the Middle East did not constitute a real threat to Western interests in the region).

Dayan's first purpose at the Vermars conference was to persuade the French to ignore their undertaking not to supply Israel with weapons except as agreed with America and Britain. The undertaking was the one France had given when it signed the Tripartite Declaration on regulating the supply of arms to the Middle East and which was still in force. *In short, Dayan was asking the French to take a major step on the road to deceiving her American and British allies.*

To get what he wanted Dayan knew he had to indicate that Israel was prepared to assist the French to deal with the matter of greatest concern to them—Algeria and Nasser's support for its violent, ruthless and increasingly effective liberation movement, the Front de Liberation Nationale

(FLN). It was on its way to becoming to the French in Algeria what the Irgun and the Stern Gang were to the British in Palestine—except that the FLN was composed almost entirely of indigenous Algerians fighting a genuine war of national liberation, and the Irgun and Stern Gang were composed almost entirely of Jews who were aliens in Palestine.

Dayan's pitch to the French was this. The stronger Nasser got, the more he would step up his activities "on other fronts"—meaning Algeria. In return for the latest (most modern) weapons the French had, tanks and aircraft especially, *Israel would assist France in its struggle to prevent the triumph of Egyptian-backed Arab nationalism in Algeria in the following ways*:

- By hitting Nasser's Egypt with more and more reprisal attacks. (After Sharett's resignation the IDF could act without restraint).

- By passing to the French every scrap of intelligence Israeli agents could glean about the FLN, including information about its future operations as gathered by Israeli agents on the ground in Algeria. (Israel's breathtaking success in the business of intelligence gathering was due in no small part to the fact that some of its best agents were Jews of North African origin. Their ability to pass as Arabs was such they managed to penetrate Arab terrorist organisations as well as the intelligence establishments of Arab governments. And this, in turn, was the reason why the CIA came to rely so much on Mossad. Israeli agents could reach the Arab parts that no American agent ever could. In 2003 this was one of the reasons why American intelligence on what was happening in Iraq was so at odds with reality. They were relying too much on Mossad feeds—effectively disinformation tooled to suit Zionism's agenda).

The CIA had to rely on Mossad intelligence because its agents could reach the Arab sectors inaccessible to the U.S. But Mossad intelligence feeds were tooled to suit Zionism's agenda.

- By Israeli agents collaborating with French agents to sabotage radio stations and other communication facilities Nasser's propaganda people were using to encourage Algeria's revolutionaries.

That was precisely what the French needed to hear. They wanted Israel to distract Nasser—to give him so much to think about that support for the FLN would cease to be an important item on his agenda.

Their assumption was that if Nasser could be prevented from escalating his support for the FLN and if, better still, his support actually declined, French occupation forces in Algeria could and would defeat the Arab liberation movement there. The French had clearly learned nothing from their humiliating defeat in Vietnam. (Subsequent events would prove that the Americans learned nothing from it either).

In return for the Israeli services to be rendered (and which needed Ben-Gurion's approval), the French at Vermars agreed to sell the Jewish state 72 Mystere planes and 240 AMX tanks.

With that under his belt Dayan asked the French if they were prepared to collaborate with Israel, directly or indirectly, in overthrowing Nasser. They were a bit embarrassed. "We are military men", they replied. "Overthrowing Nasser is a political matter. We have no authority to commit our government to such a course of action."[5] Joint action to foil Nasser was as far as they could go.

The problem then was keeping the deal secret. If word leaked out America and Britain would block it, and there was no telling how much damage would be done by the fall-out from the political explosion. President Eisenhower especially would be furious. He would have been the first to understand that Israel's acquisition of the latest military hardware in defiance of the Tripartite Declaration would probably destroy any remaining prospect for pressing Israel to negotiate for peace on terms the Arabs could accept. Dayan hoped it would be one of those occasions when Ben-Gurion would see the sense of not telling any of his cabinet colleagues. Democracy had its uses but it was not the military's best friend.

Ben-Gurion told Dayan that he had to consult with two of his cabinet colleagues—Levi Eshkol the finance minister and Golda Meir, Sharett's successor as foreign minister. He had to get Eshkol's approval because of the cost of the French planes and tanks—more than US$100 million—was an astronomical sum in those days. And he had to consult with Golda because she would have to clean up the diplomatic mess that would be created if the secret could not be kept until delivery was taking place. She would undoubtedly do her duty even if it meant lying to her American and British counterparts, but she would not take kindly to being dropped in it without warning.

The money would be forthcoming. Funds for the purchase of weapons and the development of Israel's own atom bomb could always be found. (The only thing for which money was not available was compensation for Palestinian refugees. The Israelis were in the process of extracting an initial $300 million from the government of West Germany on account of what Hitler had done to Jews, but compensation for the Palestinians on account of what Zionism had done to them—forget it).

It was the Arab world's enthusiastic response to Nasser's announcement that Egypt had nationalised the Suez Canal that served as the invitation for France and Britain to join Dayan's war party.

In part Nasser's decision was a grand "Screw you, too" gesture to America, Britain and France. It was also the most dramatic way of demonstrating to his people and the Arab world that he was not going to be dominated by the arrogant West. But he also had an economic motivation. The Suez Canal, or rather the fees paid by the ships of the world which passed through it, was an important revenue source.

Prior to nationalisation Egypt was receiving only seven percent of the gross profits of the operating Canal Company. The majority and controlling shareholders, Britain and France, were taking the rest. Only five of the company's 30 directors were Egyptian. That was Nasser's inheritance. Soon after he came to power he had put Britain and France on notice, courteously, that he wished to negotiate a fairer deal for Egypt and a bigger say in managing the Canal. The British and the French had replied that they might be prepared to consider a better deal for Egypt but on one condition. It was that Nasser would commit himself to extending the Canal Company's concession when it came up for renewal in 1968. What they had wanted, in short, was a guarantee that Nasser would not nationalise the Canal.

Prior to nationalization of the Suez Canal, Egypt was receiving only seven percent of the gross profits; the British and French were taking the rest.

Nasser's early venom was directed at Dulles. The reason he had given for pulling the plug on the High Dam funding was Egypt's "unsound economy". The implication was that Nasser's Egypt did not have the management talent to run a hamburger establishment. Nasser, by now the President, demonstrated his hurt and his anger in a speech that included this: "When Washington broadcasts the lie that Egypt's economy is unsound... then I look them in the face and say—drop dead of your fury for you will never be able to dictate to Egypt."[6]

As I have indicated, Secretary of State Dulles did what he did on account of his own conviction that Nasser had to go because he was an obstacle to America's unstated and unstatable imperial ambitions in the Middle East. But it was not just a matter of his own conviction. Because it was election year and another high time for pork-barrel politics, there were domestic political considerations Dulles had to take account of.

- The Zionist lobby was campaigning for any action that would damage Nasser.

- American farmers did not want the High Dam project to go ahead because of the increased competition they would face from Egypt's cotton growers.

- America's ultra conservatives, the less than rational armchair Cold War warriors, were seeing Nasser as the agent of the evil empire. They were, in short, in knee-jerk agreement with the Zionists. Funding the High Dam would help Nasser to secure his position, make him stronger. "No, Mr. Secretary of State." The ultra conservatives had been incensed by Nasser's arms agreement with the Soviet Union and the very last straw for them had been Egypt's recognition of Communist "Red" China.

In America this was also the high time of Senator McCarthy's infamous anti-Communist crusade.

When Secretary of State Dulles took account of those domestic political considerations he might well have concluded that even if he put his own conviction to one side, he would not get a request for the High Dam Funding through Congress—either at all or without a big, bruising fight with, among others, the supporters of Zionism right or wrong. My point is that if even Dulles had had doubts about the wisdom of pulling the plug on the High Dam funding, they would have cancelled by domestic political considerations.

In passing it's worth noting that Nasser had not wanted to recognise China because he knew it would cause America's ultra conservatives to foam at the mouth. He did so on 16 May only because of what Khrushchev had said in London the previous month—that the Soviet Union would be prepared to participate in a UN embargo on arms to the Middle East. That confirmed to Nasser what he had all along suspected—there were or could be limits to how far the Russians would go to antagonise the West on its own patch and as a consequence, they could not be looked upon as reliable arms suppliers. His decision to recognise China and exchange ambassadors was thus born of the need for an insurance policy in the event of the Russians letting him down under pressure from the West. *In reality Nasser was not so much playing the West against the East but doing what he could to prevent himself being screwed by both superpowers.* He had also noted that when Israel recognised the government in Peking in 1950, it had not provoked any wrath in America. But that, of course, was in the days when Zionism was calling the shots on President Truman's watch.

From an Arab world perspective it was not possible to exaggerate the significance of Nasser's nationalisation of the Suez Canal. His arms deal with the Soviet Union was seen by many as a well-merited rebuff to Western attempts to impose what Nutting called "servilities" on Egypt as the price of arms from the West. But there had been a downside. Arab conservatives everywhere, in Saudi Arabia especially, regarded the Soviet Union as an abomination and were quietly and deeply troubled by what Nasser had done. But there were no downsides to his nationalisation of the Suez Canal. From Morocco to Muscat peoples and leaders were filled with a pride they had never known. Here at last was an Arab leader with the will and the courage to say to the imperial powers—the old established and the Americans preparing to replace them, "The days of your dominating us are gone forever."

With one dramatic gesture—albeit one that had been forced upon him—Nasser had become the unrivalled champion of real Arab nationalism.

In retrospect I think it can be said that this was a great hinge moment in the history of the modern world. I mean that events could have gone either way—the way they did or, if reason had prevailed in Israel (and Paris and London), in a wonderfully different way.

Though it's water under history's bridge, let us for a moment reflect on what that wonderfully different way could have been and why.

In the immediate aftermath of his nationalisation of the Suez Canal, Nasser's standing in the Arab world was such that, politically, he could have done anything including, if he had had an Israeli partner, some peacemaking.

If Ben-Gurion and Dayan had been interested in peace, and if they had been men of real vision, this was the moment they could have seized to make the best of all dreams come true. If they had offered the hand of friendship to Nasser then, he and they could have gone on to create a new order in the Middle East, one in which Jews could have played a joint leadership and management role out of all proportion to their numbers, not least because of their expertise in so many things and the financial resources on which they could call.

The Israel of the peace that could have been made would have remained small in terms of territory; but there would not have been the need for the Greater Israel of Zionism's mad dream—because the Jews would have had security of the best kind, the security of peace and partnership with their biblical blood brothers.

In reality such a future was not possible because it required Israel's leaders to see their state as an integrated part of its region—i.e. instead of a colonial outpost of British and French imperialism or a forward base for the new American imperialism in-the-making. The only Israeli leader with the vision to see an Israeli future worth having was Sharett and he was gone. Destroyed.

The sad truth is that gut-Zionism was congenitally incapable of thinking in such a way—seeing its state as an integrated part of the region. For two reasons.

The first was that political Zionism *WAS an outside or alien force*. The Zionist project was conceived by European Jews for implementation by European Jews. And the thing they had in common with almost all Europeans of the time was an imperial mindset and all the baggage that came with it, including the belief that Europeans were superior to "wogs" of all kinds. The Arabs were lighter skinned than the black "wogs" and the dark brown "wogs", but they were still "wogs". Inferior people to be dominated.

The insuperable problem was that Israel was congenitally incapable of seeing itself as an integrated part of the region.

The second was that political Zionism *WAS a creature of imperialism* because its leaders had got their show on the road by saying to the imperial powers "Use us".

But in 1956 it was not only the Zionists who decided that reason and wisdom would not be allowed to prevail. The biggest criminals—state terrorists some might say—were Eden and his French collaborators. *The name of their game was using Zionism's child for their own ends.*

Ben-Gurion had some initial reservations but Zionism was more than content to be used. Again.

When Nasser nationalised the Canal he was inclined to the view, on balance, that Britain and France would not resort to military action; but he did put a question mark over Eden's intentions. He did think Britain's prime minister might not be averse to war if world public opinion was with him, and if risks to British oil supplies could be avoided. But Nasser was also convinced that world public opinion would not be with Eden if he chose the war option. Why? Nasser had done nothing illegal. He had acted in Egypt's best interests and he had said that British and French shareholders would be fairly compensated.

While the British and French used Israel for their own ends, Israel consented, even offered, to be used for its own ends.

The one thing Nasser ruled out as being totally unthinkable—not worthy of serious discussion with his army commanders—was the possibility that Eden, if he took the war option, would allow the Israelis to be involved. Nasser simply refused to believe that Eden would be mad enough to make war on Egypt with Israel. If he did, Britain could kiss goodbye to its position as the dominant player in the Arab world.

Amazing though it is in the light of what happened, Eden's starting position was that Israel should not be involved. Before he went bonkers, Eden did understand that collaboration with Israel would be the kiss of death for Britain's position as the dominant player in the Middle East. The story of how and why he changed his mind, and who changed it, is at the heart of the conspiracy that took Israel, Britain and France to war with Nasser on 29 October.

Discussions between Britain and France on the need for a military confrontation with Nasser began within hours of the announcement of his nationalisation of the Canal. The difference between the two Western allies (who were still rivals as they always had been) was the timing of military action. France wanted them to strike with the minimum of delay. Eden wanted to give diplomacy a chance and was under pressure from President Eisenhower to do so.

It was the French who set the pace in the propaganda war. Nasser, they insisted, was "the Hitler on the Nile". On the other side of the English Channel British politicians were quick to jump onto this bandwagon, including the big boys of the Opposition Labour Party led by Hugh Gaitskell. In parliament the British were not going to allow the French to beat them in the game of demonising Nasser.

Eden's publicly stated case for action against Nasser was, as Nutting would later describe it, "thoroughly disingenuous."[7] Britain was the biggest single user of the canal and oil was the most vital cargo her ships transported through it. The essence of Eden's case was this: "If Colonel Nasser were to succeed (in keeping control of the Canal) each one of us would be at the mercy of one man for the supplies on which we live."[8] The clear implication was that Nasser would use the Canal as a weapon and close it at will. For anybody in Britain who stopped to think about it, that was nonsense. Nasser had nationalised the Canal to make more money for Egypt. What his economy desperately needed was more ships through the Canal not fewer.

At an early point in their discussions with the British, the French suggested they should supply Israel with weapons. (The ones they had already agreed to provide behind the backs of their British and American allies in defiance of the Tripartite Declaration). Eden hit the roof. It would be madness to supply Israel with weapons. More to the point, Eden insisted, Israel was not to be informed that Britain and France were even considering the possibility of military action against Egypt.

Did the French tell Eden they were already plotting with the Israelis? Probably not.

The day after Nasser nationalised the Canal, Maurice Bourges-Maunoury, the French minister of defence, summoned two Israelis to an urgent meeting in his office. The Israelis were Shimon Peres, director general of Ben-Gurion's Defence ministry and the man with the executive responsibility for the management of Israel's secret French connection, and Yosef Nachmias, the ministry's representative in Paris. Both had attended the Vermars conference.

When the two Israelis entered the French minister's office they were surprised to find him, flanked by several generals, crouched over maps. He had two questions for his visitors.

The first was: "How long would it take the IDF to fight its way across the Sinai and reach the Canal?"[9]

"Two weeks or less," Peres replied.

Second question. "Would Israel be prepared to take part in a tripartite military operation in which Israel's specific role would be to cross the Sinai?"[10]

Peres said he presumed the answer would be "Yes" in certain circumstances.

The French defence minister then briefed the two Israelis on Operation Musketeer, a joint Anglo-French plan to capture the Suez Canal. It was obviously a contingency plan the British and the French had agreed in principle, probably with little or no thought about actual implementation, before the British withdrew from Canal Zone and all of Egypt six weeks previously. In other words, it was not a response to the actual situation, it was only the bone on which flesh had to be put.

When the two Israelis were leaving the French minister's office, Nachmias said to Peres that he deserved to be hanged for speaking on a matter of such gravity without prior authorisation. In *Battling For Peace*, Peres would subsequently quote himself as replying that he would rather risk his neck than risk missing a unique opportunity.

Ben-Gurion's own first response to the news of Egypt's nationalisation of the Suez Canal had been to ask Mossad director Harel to speak with CIA director Dulles about the possibility of joint action to topple Nasser. Dulles was in a difficult position. His agents were working up a coup plot. Britain's SIS and he knew that Eden was terrified by the prospect of any Israeli involvement. So his reply to Harel was, apparently, non-committal. In his diary for 29 July (Peres had not yet reported on the conversation with Bourges-Maunoury) a dejected Ben-Gurion wrote: "The Western powers are furious... but I am afraid that they will do nothing. France will not dare to act alone; Eden is not a man of action; Washington will avoid any reaction."[11]

But Dayan was not a man to be despondent. The idea of letting any opportunity for military action pass was unthinkable. With the French and the British saying they saw Nasser as "the Hitler on the Nile", there could not be a better time for Israel to strike. The French and the British might even say thanks.

Dayan then presented Ben-Gurion with three options for military action:[12]

- The capture for keeping of the whole of the Sinai Peninsula right up to the Suez Canal.
- The capture for keeping of the Straits of Tiran.
- The capture for keeping of the Gaza Strip.

Ben-Gurion turned down all three options on the grounds that the West would oppose any such Israeli initiatives out of fear that the Soviet Union would be provoked into action to support Nasser. But Dayan continued to press Ben-Gurion and by 10 August he had refined his thinking. The starting point of his new analysis was that force had to be used. President Eisenhower was insisting that the dispute be settled by negotiation. Negotiations would end with victory for Nasser. As Ben-Gurion now saw it, the West was in the process of appeasing the Egyptian leader just as it had appeased Hitler. And what would happen when Nasser had been appeased? Ben-Gurion committed his answer to his diary:

> The growth in Nasser's prestige is bound to make him want to destroy Israel—not by a direct attack but first by a 'peace offensive' and an attempt to reduce our territory, especially in the Negev, and when we refuse—he will attack us.[13]

The problem was that Israel could not afford to act alone. On this occasion the assertion of need to make a pre-emptive strike in the name of ensuring the Jewish state's survival would not be sufficient to protect it from universal condemnation. What to do? A way had to be found to involve another party. What about the French whore? Would she help? The answer from Peres was "Yes".

On 18 September Peres flew to Paris for another meeting with the French defence minister, ostensibly to expedite the delivery of the Mystere planes and the AMX tanks. But what Peres wanted most of all was a frank talk with Bourges-Maunoury about the possibility of a "common policy" for the Middle East. Common policy was the euphemism for France joining with Israel in a war to topple Nasser.

Peres must have struggled to suppress his delight at what he heard. The French were exasperated by Eden's indecisiveness. There were, Bourges-Maunoury told Peres, three different time scales. France wanted immediate military action. Eden under pressure from Eisenhower wanted to give diplomacy at least two more months. Perhaps, when push came to shove, Eden would not have the balls for war. And the CIA was opposed to war and wanted much more time to undermine Nasser.

Encouraged by what he heard Peres suggested that the secret contact between their two states should be extended to take in the political dimension.

The French responded positively and swiftly with a proposal for a secret meeting of political as well as military people from both sides. It was to be a two-day conference in St. Germain starting on 30 September. In the event Israel's heavyweight political representatives were Foreign Minister Golda Meir and Transport Minister Moshe Carmel.

And then... On 14 October, two weeks after the conference, the French presented Eden, at a secret meeting at Chequers (the Prime Minister's official country residence) with a plan, *the Challe Plan, for British and French military intervention using an Israeli attack on Egypt as the pretext for intervention.*

To this day there is still something of a mystery about what really happened and why in the first two weeks of October. The question at the heart of the mystery is this: Eden changed his mind about involving the Israelis but did the French change their mind about involving the British?

In what I will call scenario "A" they did. In scenario "B" they did not.

In scenario "A" the French wanted all the glory, were intending to go to war against Egypt with Israel but without Britain, and were obliged by their inability to provide Ben-Gurion with insurance cover to invite the British to join the conspiracy.

Scenario "B" assumes that the French never contemplated going to war without the British and saw France as only the matchmaker, with the task of first persuading the Israelis to play their assigned role as in the Challe Plan, and then persuading Eden to agree to let them play it.

Giving some credence, perhaps, to the supposition that the French preference was for glory without Britain's involvement is this fact. Through September the new French Prime Minister, Guy Mollet, had a number of secret encounters with Dayan (and other Israelis). *According to Nutting, Mollet gave Dayan a pledge. If Israeli forces invaded the Sinai and drove the Egyptians back across the Canal, French forces would join in to seize the waterway, leaving the Israelis free to take whatever territory they wanted to put an end to Egypt's blockade of the Straits of Tiran and finish off the* fedayeen.

As it happened France could not have gone to war without Britain even if it had wanted to—because Ben-Gurion insisted on some insurance cover the French could not provide.

Nasser was taking delivery of his Russian arms. Ben-Gurion said he feared that while his forces were advancing in the Sinai, Nasser's Ilyushin bombers might raze Tel Aviv and other Israeli cities to the ground. Dayan did not believe that was a possibility and said so. The military intelligence assessment was that very few of Nasser's Ilyushins were operational and that Egyptian pilots were not yet trained enough to fly them. (Dayan might also have known that the Soviets had no intention of allowing Nasser to use their weapons for offensive purposes). Ben-Gurion still wanted the risk covered. The only way it could be covered was by having the French air force take out Egypt's air force before the Israelis attacked. That presented the French with two problems. The first was that they would be seen as the ones who started the war. The second was that France did not have bomber bases close enough to Egypt to do what Ben-Gurion wanted. Only the British did. When Ben-Gurion dug his heals in, Mollet suggested that Eden should be invited to join the conspiracy. Ben-Gurion agreed that the French should approach Eden but he did not like the way things were now going, mainly because he did not trust the British in general and their prime minister in particular.

Eden's French visitors on 14 October were Albert Gazier, the acting foreign minister, and Maurice Challe, an air force general and the deputy chief of staff of the French armed forces. Though it still needed some detailed work, Eden liked Challe's plan. Nutting was present and later wrote that the British prime minister "could scarcely control his glee."[14] And why is not difficult to understand.

Despite what Eden had been saying in public to whip up anti-Nasser hysteria, he knew that Nasser had not acted illegally and was perfectly within his rights when he nationalised the Canal. It followed that if Britain and France went to war without some other justification, they would be branded as aggressors by the international community and by President Eisenhower in particular. *In short, Britain and France could not actually go to war unless Israel was prepared to give them the pretext by playing the role of aggressor.*

The essence of the Challe Plan: Israel (the bad guy) would attack Egypt, and Britain and France (the good guys) would stop the fighting. A ceasefire would be called, Israel would accept it, Nasser would reject it, and Britain and France would then seize the Canal and topple Nasser.

The essence of the Challe Plan was that Israel (the bad guy) would attack Egypt, and Britain and France (the good guys) would intervene to stop the fighting... Britain and France would call on both sides to agree to a ceasefire... When Israel accepted the call and Egypt rejected it, Britain and France would issue an ultimatum to Egypt... When Egypt rejected it, Britain and

France would launch their own full-scale war on Egypt to take back the Canal and bring about Nasser's downfall.

Question. How could Britain, France and Israel be absolutely certain that Nasser would reject the call for a ceasefire and by so doing trigger the ultimatum?

Answer. There was no way Nasser could accept its terms. The Egyptians and the Israelis were going to be required to withdraw their forces ten miles either side of the Canal. *That meant Egypt, the victim of Israeli aggression, would be required to accept a ceasefire on the basis of a withdrawal from between 65 to 135 miles of its own territory; and Israel, the aggressor, would be accepting a ceasefire having gained between 55 and 125 miles of Egyptian territory!* The words Nutting subsequently used to describe the terms of the intended and actual ultimatum were "fantastic" and "grotesque".[15] I think diabolical—as in its real meaning devilish—is a more appropriate term.

The ceasefire terms: Egypt, the victim of Israeli aggression, would be required to withdraw from its own territory, while Israel would gain between 55-125 miles of Egyptian territory.

Eden told his French visitors he was interested enough to want follow-up discussions between himself and Selwyn Lloyd and Mollet and his foreign minister, Christian Pineau. He would make the arrangements after he had discussed the matter with Lloyd when he returned from America, where he was involved in the politics of seeking a peaceful resolution of the Canal crisis.

On the day (16 October) Eden briefed Lloyd, and before they took off for Paris, Israel carried out the third and most ferocious of a series of reprisal attacks on Jordan. The target this time was the village of Qalqilya and more than 100 Arabs were killed.

That attack prompted Eden, probably at Lloyd's suggestion, to add two conditions to Britain's approval of the French plan to involve Israel. The conditions were that Israel should cease attacks on Jordan immediately and give an assurance that when it went to war with Egypt it would not take advantage of the situation to grab the West Bank. *The British Foreign Office was well aware that Dayan was itching to do just that. And King Hussein was in despair.*

When the French conveyed Eden's conditions to Israel, Ben-Gurion was seized by the idea that Britain was setting a trap for him. In the event of war Britain was committed by treaty to go to Egypt's defence... What was there to say, he worried, that when Israel attacked Egypt, Britain would not go to its aid and attack Israel—for the purpose of liberating the chunk of the Negev that Nasser wanted, and perhaps even to get the Jewish state back to something like the partition plan boundaries?

Ben-Gurion told the French to tell the British that he had a condition of his own. He wanted a letter from Eden stating that in the event of war between Egypt and Israel, "His Majesty's government will not come to the assistance of Egypt."[16]

Eden was hugely embarrassed. He tried to get away with a verbal assurance to that effect via the French which, for the purpose of history, he could deny he ever gave. Ben-Gurion said, in effect, "Go to hell, I want it in writing." When Eden dithered the French said to him something like, "If you want war, you must give Ben-Gurion the letter he wants." Eventually Eden did because his obsession with knocking Nasser off his perch was now so great that it outweighed considerations of how perfidious he would look in history if it became known that he had given Ben-Gurion such an undertaking.

The Eden-Mollet handshake that confirmed Britain's acceptance of the Challe Plan took place at the Palais Matignon, the official residence of the French prime minister. The only witnesses were Lloyd and Pineau. It was a very black day for democracy. Neither the peoples nor even the governments of the two once great but fading imperial powers had any idea of the commitment that had been made in their names. *It was secret and dangerously deluded diplomacy of the kind that President Wilson had hoped would be made impossible by the coming into being of the new world order of his wonderful but naïve vision.* If President Eisenhower had had any knowledge of what Britain, France and Israel were up to, he would have stopped them in their tracks.

But it was not yet a done deal. When word of the Anglo-French ministerial meeting in Paris reached him, Ben-Gurion sent a message to Nachmias. It instructed him to contact the French to ask whether the discussions could be made tripartite. Nachmias was to tell the French that "Israeli representatives are ready to come immediately in the utmost secrecy. Their rank will be equal to the ranks of the British and French representatives."[17]

Ben-Gurion's dearest wish was for a partnership of equals with explicit coordination of military plans. And what he wanted most of all was a face-to-face meeting with Eden.

There was, of course, no way Eden could take the risk of being seen to be associated with any Israeli. Mollet argued that unless the Israelis were invited to Paris, Ben-Gurion would do a Dulles and pull the plug on the whole thing. And, anyway, the Israelis had to be involved in the final military planning. Eden said, in effect, "Okay, invite them, but for God's sake wait until I am back in London." Before Eden made his exit, he told Mollet that if he could not button the thing up without the presence of a senior British political figure, he would instruct Lloyd to attend.

So it was that Mollet invited Ben-Gurion to Paris to participate in the final planning. That was to be the business of a top-secret conference to take place in a private villa in Sevres on the outskirts of Paris, scheduled to begin on 22 October. Mollet's invitation to Ben-Gurion said that a member of the British Government would also be invited "if the need arose."

The initial Israeli response to the French invitation was an angry rejection. Effectively "No Eden, no Ben-Gurion."

In the end it was Dayan who persuaded a reluctant Ben-Gurion to get on the plane for Paris. According to Israeli accounts the chief of staff's argument to his prime minister was this: Britain and France did not need any help from Israel to defeat Egypt and the only thing the Jewish state could provide was the pretext for their intervention. That, and that alone, was the price of Israel's entry ticket.[18]

The reality (as Dayan knew) was that Britain and France could not go to war unless Israel was prepared to play the role of aggressor. In fact Ben-Gurion's bargaining position was far stronger than Dayan's argument implied it to be. But that was not the point. Dayan feared that if Ben-Gurion continued to insist on a meeting with Eden, the British prime minister might well say something like: "Bugger this. I'd prefer to live with Nasser rather than Ben-Gurion calling the shots."

What Dayan was actually saying to Ben-Gurion was something like this: "We should not give a damn about being seen as the aggressor on this occasion. The opportunity to do what we intend to do at some point but to do it now with the blessing of Britain and France is too great to pass up."

It was about to become clear that Ben-Gurion decided to lead Israel's delegation to the Sevres conference less for the purpose of making his necessary contribution to the implementation of the Challe Plan, and more in the hope that he could persuade France and Britain to junk it in favour of his own fantastic scheme for reorganising the Middle East!

Britain's foreign secretary had not arrived when the first session of the Sevres conference was due to get underway, so Mollet decided that it was a good time to give Ben-Gurion the floor. (I imagine the French prime minister thought it would not be possible to get down to the real business of the meeting until the "Old Man" had let off steam).

Ben-Gurion cheerfully admitted that his audience would regard the comprehensive plan he was about to unveil was "fantastic", but it was, he said, *one that would serve the interests of all the Western powers as well as those of Israel by destroying Nasser and the movement of Arab nationalism he had unleashed.*

The main elements of Ben-Gurion's Zionist strategy for reorganising the Middle East—a strategy he wanted the French and the British to consider seriously before rushing into a military campaign against Egypt—were the following:

- Jordan was not viable as an independent state and should be carved up. The East Bank should be given to Iraq (Britain's puppet state) in return for a promise to settle the Palestinian refugees there and make peace with Israel. The West Bank should be attached to Israel on the understanding that its inhabitants would have a degree of autonomy.
- Lebanon "suffered" from having a large Muslim population, which was concentrated in the south. The "problem" (the predictable emergence of a Muslim majority in Lebanon) could be solved by Israel's expansion up to the Litani river, thus

helping to turn Lebanon into a Christian state that would make peace with Israel. (What was to happen to the Muslims in the south if they did not roll over and accept Israeli occupation? The obvious implication was that they would have to be put down, somehow).

- The Suez Canal should be given international status and the Straits of Tiran in the Gulf of Aqaba should come under Israeli control to ensure all nations including Israel freedom of navigation.

The short to mid-term benefits for Britain and France were obvious, Ben-Gurion said. Britain would restore its hegemony in Iraq and Jordan and secure its access to Iraq's oil; France would consolidate its (waning) influence in the region through Lebanon and Israel; and the French problem in Algeria would be solved by Nasser's removal.

What Ben-Gurion was actually making by obvious implication was the case for British and French acquiescence in the creation of Greater Israel. As a consequence of its creation in the way Ben-Gurion outlined, the threat posed by real Arab nationalism to Western domination of the region would be removed. Thereafter the expanded Jewish state would exist to serve the interests of the West as well as its own. Ben-Gurion was so convinced of the benefits for the West in what he was proposing that he offered his opinion that "even America" might be persuaded to support his plan because, he said, "it would promote stable, pro-Western Arab regimes and help to check Soviet advances in the region."

By Israeli participation in the Suez conspiracy, Ben-Gurion sought to achieve British and French acquiescence in the creation of Greater Israel. Having removed the threat of Arab nationalism, he contended, the Israeli presence would promote "stable, pro-Western Arab regimes".

The French prime minister said Ben-Gurion's strategy was not fantastic but that right now they had a unique opportunity to strike at their common enemy and any delay might be fatal. Why? Eden himself was now determined to fight, the French explained, but he was facing growing opposition in the country and within his own cabinet. It was not a secret in their small, closed circle that even his foreign secretary, due at any moment, was not enthusiastic about resolving the Canal dispute by war.

When Lloyd arrived they got down to discussing the practical priorities of the moment, and it soon became clear that Ben-Gurion was prepared to veto the whole thing if his conditions were not met. The first, not new, was his insistence on an insurance policy. He wanted an undertaking that the Royal Air Force would eliminate the Egyptian air force on the ground before Israeli troops moved. The other thing he wanted was an agreement that British, French and Israeli ground forces would strike at the same time.

When push came to shove he was not prepared for Israel to be seen as the aggressor while Britain and France posed as the peace-makers.

Lloyd was not a man to be intimidated except by his own prime minister. He flatly rejected Ben-Gurion's demands and said the position was clear. All that Britain had agreed to was the French proposal that if Israel attacked Egypt, Britain and France would intervene to protect the Canal.

When it was obvious that Ben-Gurion was not going to back down, Lloyd tried to mollify him by saying that Britain did want to see Nasser's regime destroyed. He defined the aim of any allied military operations as "the conquest of the Canal Zone and the destruction of Nasser."

But it was still no go as far as Ben-Gurion was concerned. And it seemed that the Challe Plan was dead. The "Old Man" was not prepared to give Britain and France the pretext they needed.

Dayan then made a suggestion to break the deadlock—cause Ben-Gurion to change his mind—and clear the path to war.

Dayan addressed the practical problem. It was this: They had estimated it could take Israeli forces up to 72 hours to fight their way through Egypt's Sinai defences and get to the east bank of the Canal. Until the Israelis were at least within sight of the waterway, Britain and France could not issue their ultimatum calling on the warring parties to cease fire and withdraw 10 miles from either side of it, Israeli forces from the east side, Egyptian forces from the west side. That meant Israel would be alone for the first 72 hours of the fighting with her cities not best protected if Nasser deployed his Ilyushin bombers.

Dayan's solution? Israel would start its offensive with a paratroop drop in the Mitla Pass, 30 miles from the Canal. That would greatly reduce the time needed for Britain and France to issue their ultimatum and begin an aerial bombardment of Egyptian airfields following Nasser's anticipated rejection of it. Dayan's proposed amendment to the Challe Plan satisfied both the British and French need for "a real act of war" to justify their intervention and gave Ben-Gurion what Dayan knew he really wanted—an escape route in the event of the British and French intervention failing to materialise. In such an event Israel could present its assault on Egyptian forces in the Mitla pass as just another reprisal attack, not the overture to war.

That was still not enough to cause Ben-Gurion to change his mind. So, prompted perhaps by Dayan, the French offered him a further inducement. They were prepared to station two squadrons of Mystere fighter-bombers in Israel and to have two of their warships put into Israel ports to protect the Jewish state's skies for the first two days of the fighting.

That, apparently, was enough to cause Ben-Gurion to change his mind. The conspirators were "Go" for war. Israel would launch a large-scale attack on the evening of 29 October. Or so Ben-Gurion said.

Lloyd was a reluctant conspirator and very soon after Ben-Gurion's apparent "Yes", he put distance between himself and the Israelis, and returned to London. Any tidying up that needed a British input was to be done by Patrick Dean, deputy undersecretary of state at the Foreign Office and Donald Logan, Lloyd's private secretary.

As it happened there was at least one more sting in Ben-Gurion's tail. He insisted that a formal protocol of what had been agreed be drawn up and signed by all three parties. More insurance. The Jew who trusted Gentiles was an idiot. The British and the French had to be denied any scope for misrepresenting at some future date who had agreed what.

The Protocol of Sevres was drafted by Israeli and French officials. Article six of seven required all three governments to keep the provisions of the accord strictly secret. When the draft of the damning document was presented to the two British officials for approval it had been initialled by Ben-Gurion for Israel and Pineau for France. Dean and Logan were more than surprised. Nobody had told them there was to be anything in writing and they assumed, correctly, that it was the very last thing Eden wanted. But they had no choice. The draft document was an accurate record of what had been agreed. Dean initialled the draft and made clear that when he put his signature to the final document alongside those of Ben-Gurion and Pineau it would be *ad referendum*—subject to the approval of his government. Ben-Gurion did not give a damn. He would have what he wanted. Something the British and the French could never deny.

Eden had the British copy destroyed. The Israeli copy would be kept under lock and key in the Ben-Gurion Archive in Sede-Boker for 40 years. The French copy was said to have been "lost". But a copy surfaced 40 years later, almost to the day, in a BBC documentary on the Suez crisis. (Somebody had a motive for belated truth-telling.)

However... The full truth of what happened in the French villa on the outskirts of Paris is not to be found in the Protocol of Sevres.

Before Ben-Gurion put his full signature to the final version of that document, the French, prodded masterfully by Peres, did a side deal with him. *This was in the form of an agreement that France would provide the Jewish state with a small nuclear reactor to be located at Dimona in the Negev and the natural uranium to fuel it.*

It was a great personal triumph for Peres, the conclusion to many months of negotiations with the French. Initially they had been divided about whether or not to go so far in assisting Israel to develop its own nuclear weapons. Defence Minister Bourges-Maunoury had said "Oui". Foreign Minister Pineau had said "Non". And Prime Minister Mollet had been undecided. Then, a month before the conspirators gathered at Sevres, Peres secured the agreement of the French military establishment to provide Israel with a small nuclear reactor and the natural uranium to fuel it. Alone with Mollet and Bourges-Maunoury at Sevres, Peres seized the moment to secure the agreement of the French political establishment. A year later, when Bourges-Maunoury was prime minister, France delivered to Israel a nuclear reactor with twice the capacity of the one promised at Sevres.

In *Battling for Peace* published in 1995, Peres confirmed that he had done the nuclear deal with the French at Sevres. Seven years later I heard him say in a BBC radio interview that "in perhaps a hundred years" more of the truth could be told about how Israel had obtained and developed its nuclear arsenal.

Question. Why, then and there, in Sevres, did the French agree to give the Zionist state what it needed to become a nuclear Goliath? I think there is only one possible answer.

The French prime minister of the moment feared, and probably was encouraged by Peres to fear, that Ben-Gurion, upon reflection, either might not put his final signature to the Protocol of Sevres or, if he did, might change his mind when he was back in Israel, in the five days remaining before the IDF was supposed to launch the offensive needed to give France and Britain the pretext for war. *In short the French calculation was that Ben-Gurion with the nuclear agreement in his pocket could not say "No" to Israel playing the role of aggressor.*

Put another way, there were absolutely no limits to what the French whore would do to bring about Nasser's downfall.

In retrospect there are two intriguing questions without answers:

One: If Eden had known about the French nuclear side deal with Israel, and if he had believed it was necessary to guarantee that Ben-Gurion's "Yes" would not become a "No" when final push came to final shove, would he have approved it?

Two: Had Ben-Gurion been obdurate on his own account and, therefore, did Peres progress the nuclear side deal because he believed it was necessary in order to have his prime minister irrevocably committed to doing what the French and the British wanted; *or, did Ben-Gurion, Dayan and Peres go to Sevres with a prior agreement on how they would play their cards to get the nuclear deal they wanted?* In other words, did they conspire against their fellow conspirators? (Is this the more of the truth that Peres said might be for the telling in perhaps another hundred years?")

On the afternoon of 29 October 1956—five days after Russian tanks rolled into Budapest to crush the Hungarian uprising, a timely and wonderful distraction of world attention so far as the Israelis, the British and the French were concerned, and a week before the American elections—the IDF launched its four-pronged offensive against Egypt. Two thrusts including the paratroop drop into the Mitla Pass were aimed at the Canal. The other objectives were the capture for keeping of Sharm el-Sheik at the southernmost tip of the Sinai Peninsula—the gateway to the Gulf of Aqaba, and the occupation of the Gaza Strip.

The following morning, putting on a good show of being shocked and surprised by this most regrettable and menacing turn of events in the Middle East, Mollet and Pineau rushed to Downing Street for urgent discussion with Eden. At 4.15 p.m. the Foreign Office duly delivered the pre-arranged ultimatums on behalf of the two governments to the Egyptian Ambassador and the Israeli Charge d'Affaires.

Because the terms were so outrageous, Nasser's first response was to assume the ultimatum was hoax, an Israeli ruse to cause him to withdraw his forces from their defensive positions in the Sinai, to make the IDF's task of conquering it easier. Two months previously he had withdrawn forces from the Sinai and re-deployed them, a precautionary move, to resist a possible British and French invasion of Egypt west of the Canal. Now he ordered the withdrawn forces to return to the Sinai to resist the advancing Israelis.

While Nasser remained calm the British and French ultimatum caused panic at the very top of Egypt's armed forces. The Commander-in-Chief, Amer, said the army was in a hopeless position and could not possibly resist an invasion by two imperial powers. The only way for Egypt to be saved from catastrophe, he declared, was for President Nasser to go at once to the British embassy and offer immediate surrender to the British and French demand. Nasser said Egypt would not submit without a fight to the indignities of the ultimatum. But he had to secure a cabinet majority for rejecting it and taking the consequences. He did and then made arrangements for every member of the cabinet to be provided with a lethal dose of potassium cyanide tablets.

Amer was right about the state of Egypt's armed forces. They were in no position to fight a war or even to offer serious main force resistance to the coming British and French invasion. Only 50 of 200 Soviet tanks, only 30 of 100 MiG fighters and only 10 of the 30 Ilyushin bombers were operational; and that was only on paper. Most of the Egyptian tank crews and pilots who were to man the new weapons were still learning how to handle them in training schools in the Soviet Union!

For Nasser what mattered above all was Arab dignity. How was it to be preserved? He asked his leadership colleagues to place their faith in the idea that if the army and the people could resist the coming British and French invasion for long enough, the force of world public opinion could be mobilised to oblige the aggressors to withdraw.

Still calm, Nasser went to army headquarters to tell Amer to cancel all previous orders and instruct all units in Sinai to conduct a fighting withdrawal back to the Canal. His main purpose was to save the lives of his men. (Some would fight bravely but they were no match for the Israelis).

That done Nasser ordered plans for guerrilla resistance to be put in effect immediately.

Following Egypt's anticipated rejection of the ultimatum, the British and French aerial bombardment of its airfields was supposed to have commenced at dawn on 31 October. When it did not Ben-Gurion became anxious and then angry. When the delay continued he threatened to call off Israel's attack. It was not until that evening that Nasser's airfields and the sitting duck Soviet planes on them were hit for the first time. And then the bombardment was relentless. The destruction of the Egyptian air force was quickly achieved. Was the delay caused by Eden having second thoughts about the wisdom of going to war? No. The truth was that those planning and implementing Britain's military activities were in an uncoordinated, bugger's muddle. *Because of the need for secrecy on account of the collusion with Israel, Eden had not given his military people sufficient notice of what was required.*

While Nasser was getting his mind around the destruction of his air force he received a message from Khrushchev. *It told him, bluntly, that the Soviet Union would not risk getting involved in a third world war for the sake of the Suez Canal.* If there was to be such a war, the Soviets would choose a more appropriate place and time. Khrushchev's advice? Britain and France's superior strength made further resistance futile, so Egypt should make peace with them as soon as possible. The Soviet Union would continue to give its "moral support" but could supply no further assistance at this stage.

Nasser was not surprised by the substance of the message, it merely confirmed his private expectation of the use the Soviets would be in a time of crisis—i.e. in a region in which they would not seriously challenge Western dominance; but he was astonished by Khrushchev's brutal candour. (Nasser put Khrushchev's message into his private safe. He would make good use of it four years later when the Syrians were pressing for an attack on Israel. Nasser told them to forget about it because the West would oppose such action. Not to worry, the Syrians said, the Soviets would fight for the Arabs. Nasser then produced Khrushchev's message from his safe and showed it to his Syrian brothers. His unspoken message to them was, in effect, "Grow up.")

By 5 November Israel had got everything it wanted from the war in terms of Egyptian territory. Israeli forces were then in occupation of the whole of the Sinai Peninsula. The Gaza Strip had been taken on 2 November.

Israel's official explanation was that it went to war because of the threat Nasser represented to the Jewish state's existence. Dayan was not fussed about whether or not the outside world believed the IDF's propaganda lie. More important to him was that his own people did. His entire strategy depended on Israelis believing that their survival was at stake. *If they stopped believing that, it would be difficult and perhaps impossible to provoke the further military confrontations that would be necessary for the creation of an even greater Israel.*

So Israel had performed as promised. It was now up to the British and French to get rid of Nasser by pressing on with their invasion.

Prior to the entry of British and French ground forces, Port Said and Ismalia had been heavily bombed. Large parts of the cities had been destroyed and hundreds of Egyptians had been killed. Amazingly in the circumstances, Nasser called upon his people not to harm Western nationals. But in one respect the British and French invasion had already been counter-productive in a quite spectacular way.

Eden had gone to war, allegedly, to guarantee that the flow of oil through the Canal would not be interrupted. As of 1 November the Canal was closed for business. Nasser had given the order to halt the passage of all vessels through it by sinking "blockships" at both ends. Nutting described it as a "Samson-like gesture." It was also the only gesture of defiance Nasser could make. If Eden believed it would not happen, he was, by 29 October, a complete idiot.

Just how far Eden and Mollet might have gone to get rid of Nasser if they had not been stopped remains a matter for speculation. Would they actually have been prepared, if necessary, to impose martial law on Egypt and hunt Nasser down? Their hope was that the people of Egypt would, at a point, do the job for them by taking to the streets and demanding Nasser's resignation.

The British propaganda campaign to incite the people of Egypt to rise up and overthrow their leader was launched on 2 November. The day before one of Nasser's leadership colleagues said they would be in big trouble if the British bombed Cairo Radio and "The Voice of the Arabs" off the air. Without those transmission facilities there would be no way of maintaining contact with the people. Nasser replied that in such an event he would tour Cairo in an open car and call upon the people to resist by loudspeaker.

The following morning British Canberra bombers took out the two radio stations. Within minutes the vacant air waves were filled with British propaganda from a transmitter in Cyprus, calling on the Egyptian people to rise against Nasser who had "gone mad ... rejected a fair solution (to the Canal problem)... exposed you to Israeli attacks... betrayed Egypt... adopted dictatorship." By any standards of psychological warfare it was, as Nutting observed, "a pathetic effort at subversion."[19]

Ignoring the anxiety of his bodyguards and some of his leadership colleagues. Nasser then did what he promised. He toured the streets of Cairo in an open car to demonstrate to his people that he was still among them. Leading from the front. (He could not have known but no doubt would have assumed that real life British 007's had orders to assassinate him). Nasser knew he was secure in the affection of his people. The only British politician who understood what was really happening in Egypt was Nutting, now on the point of resigning in protest at Eden's folly. He was later to write: "There can be no doubt that Nasser's leadership at this critical juncture established him finally and completely as the *rais*, the captain of the Egyptian ship of state, whose word henceforth was law for every member of the crew."[20]

When British propaganda incited Egyptians to rise up and overthrow their leader, Nasser took to the streets in an open car to call upon his people to resist. The response to his leadership from the front greatly strengthened his position as head of the Egyptian state.

And now it was time for President Eisenhower to demonstrate that he was the *rais* of the Western ship. This great and good man of advancing years who was not in the best of health—he had had a heart attack the previous year and was still recovering from an operation for ileitis—was furious, probably more furious than he had ever been in his life to date. He believed the madness of what was happening spoke for itself. But worst of all was the real message of the conspiracy that had taken Britain and France to war in collusion with

Israel. His British and French allies, so-called, had betrayed him. (He might also have entertained the thought that some of his own people had kept their knowledge of conspiracy from him).

The public manifestation of Eisenhower's fury was the presentation to the Security Council, by American Ambassador Cabot Lodge, of a resolution calling on Israel to withdraw and all other UN members to refrain from using or threatening force in the area of the conflict.

By this time, and just as Nasser had hoped, there was virtually universal condemnation of the Israeli, British and French aggression. Even most of Britain's Commonwealth partners (including Canada, India, Pakistan and Ceylon) had condemned it.

But Britain and France had no fear of the Security Council. They had the power of veto and they used it (both of them for the first time in the UN's short and troubled history). Lodge was then instructed to support a Yugoslav proposal to summon a special emergency session of the General Assembly. The purpose was to create moral pressure by giving all the member states the opportunity to express their disgust and to approve a resolution calling for an immediate ceasefire and the withdrawal of the Israeli army from Egyptian territory.

The private manifestation of Eisenhower's fury was his reading of the riot act to the British and the Israelis.

Eisenhower's private message to the British was, in effect: "Stop it and get the hell out of Egypt!" *If they did not, the message said, and taking account of the fact that the Canal was blocked, the United States would not help to save the now tottering British pound or finance alternative sources of supplies of oil for Britain while the Canal remained blocked.*[21]

Eden had no choice but to do as he was told; and tell Mollet that the French, too, had to stop and get out. And thus it was, at two o'clock in the morning local time on 7 November, just after the capture of Port Said, that the Anglo-French invasion came to an abrupt and humiliating end. It was also the beginning of the end for Eden.

Eden was subsequently to tell some of his friends that he had been screwed by Dulles. In this version of events Eden told Dulles that he was considering a military operation and asked if Eisenhower would object, and Dulles had said the President would not object but would prefer not to know. According to this conspiracy within a conspiracy, Dulles wanted to get his own back on Eden because, as foreign secretary, he had used his influence to stop Dulles getting his way when he wanted the U.S. to drop an atom bomb on North Korea. If Dulles did give Eden a green light, I think it would not have been for the reason Eden said. I think it would have been because Dulles saw the future—that British military action would finish Britain as the Western power with the most influence in the region and give America, on a plate, the opportunity to take over—become the new Western imperialist of the region, not by occupying land but through defence and trade agreements and buying Arab regimes.

At the time Eisenhower was reading the riot act to Britain, Dulles was out of action, in hospital undergoing an operation on his cancer. In private conversation with Selwyn Lloyd he would later make comments that astonished the British foreign secretary. Dulles said that if he had not been removed by illness from the conduct of American policy, Britain would not have had to endure the weight of censure which Eisenhower and his deputies, Herbert Hoover Junior and Cabot Lodge, had heaped upon her.

But Britain and France, having embarked on their venture, should have seen it through instead of stopping short of bringing about Nasser's downfall.

That statement cannot be taken at face value because the implication of it is that Dulles thought Eden could and should have told Eisenhower to go to hell. Dulles knew that was not an option for Eden, so why did he say such a thing to Lloyd? My speculation is that Dulles wanted the British to draw something like the following conclusion: "Since you didn't have the balls to go the whole way once you had started, you'll have no cause for complaint when we Americans are the dominating power in the region."

On the same day as Eden and Mollet aborted their invasion of Egypt, 7 November, Ben-Gurion delivered an arrogant victory speech in the Knesset. The armistice agreement with Egypt was dead. With that triumphant declaration there was a broad hint that Israel planned to annex the entire Sinai Peninsula as well as the Straits of Tiran. What about the calls for Israel to withdraw? "We will not humble ourselves before the world powers when they are not right."[22]

Ben-Gurion's main target was Eisenhower. The speech was a warning shot across his bow, the implied message being, "You can dictate to Eden and Mollet but not to the prime minister of Israel." The President lost no time in returning the fire. It was in the form of a letter to Ben-Gurion which included the following [emphasis added]:

> Statements attributed to your government to the effect that Israel does not intend to withdraw from Egyptian territory, as requested by the United Nations, have been drawn to my attention. *I must say frankly, Mr. Prime Minister, that the United States views these reports, if true, with deep concern. Any such decision by the government of Israel would seriously undermine the urgent efforts being made by the United Nations to restore peace in the Middle East, and could not but bring about the condemnation of Israel as a violator of the principles as well as the directives of the United Nations.*
>
> It is our belief that as a matter of the highest priority peace should be restored and foreign troops, except for United Nations forces, be withdrawn from Egypt, after which new and energetic steps should be undertaken within the framework of the United Nations to solve the basic

> problems which have given rise to the present difficulty...
>
> I need not assure you of the deep interest which the United States has in your country, nor recall the various elements of our policy of support for Israel in so many ways. It is in this context that I urge you to comply with the resolutions of the United Nations General Assembly dealing with the current crisis and to make your decision known immediately. *It would be a matter of the greatest regret to all of my countrymen if Israeli policy on a matter of such grave concern to the world should in any way impair the friendly co-operation between our two countries.*[23]

It was a veiled threat. But of what precisely? In a few more hours Ben-Gurion would know.

To this moment Eisenhower had not dared to offend Zionism by indicating what he might do to oblige Israel to withdraw. Why not? This dramatic day in the Middle East was also election day in America.

On his own account as the Republican Party's presidential standard-bearer Eisenhower had not needed to have the slightest concern about offending Zionism. Everybody knew that his personal prestige and popularity were still such that he was on a landslide course for a second term in the White House. There was no way his re-election prospects were going to be damaged by the smear campaign some Zionists were running. Its most public form had been in the shape of election pamphlets proclaiming that "A vote for Ike is a vote for Nasser". Hundreds of thousands of these pamphlets were distributed in constituencies where the Jewish vote was critical. The purpose of the smear campaign was to influence the outcome of the pork-barrel contest for seats in the House of Representatives and, more critically, the Senate. On Eisenhower's first watch the Democrats had controlled both houses of Congress. Zionism obviously wanted and needed Eisenhower's hands to be tied in the same way in his second term. It was obvious that the contest for Senate seats was going to be a very close one, but there was some reason for Eisenhower to entertain the hope that Republicans might gain control of the Senate. If they did, the task of taking on Zionism to require Israel to withdraw might not be one that would keep him awake seven nights a week.

"Everybody" in the paragraph above included American Zionist leaders. As related by Stephen Green in *Taking Sides*, Eisenhower received Rabbi Silver in the White House in April and told him that he would not be swayed by "domestic political considerations"; even in an election year. Silver replied: "You can be re-elected without a single Jewish vote."

Reality check. Though he did not need to be concerned on his own account about offending Zionism, Eisenhower could not say anything, even in private, that would assist the Zionists in their campaigns against targeted candidates running in the Senate race. And that was why he had to wait until the votes were cast to put the flesh on the bone of the veiled threat in his letter to Ben-Gurion.

Eban was the recipient of Eisenhower's private follow-up message. It could not have been more stark or dramatic. If Israel did not make an unconditional withdrawal from Egyptian territory, all official aid from the U.S. government and private aid from American Jewry would be cut off, and the United States would not oppose Israel's expulsion from the UN.

Israel's most eloquent and brilliant diplomat knew that Eisenhower was not bluffing and told Ben-Gurion so.

On 8 November, after a long and agonised debate, the Israeli cabinet decided not to decide. Its only decision was to leave everything to Ben-Gurion. He and he alone should make the decision about whether or not Israel would do what Eisenhower was demanding. There were, probably, some around the cabinet table who thought, even if they did not say it, "You got us into this mess, now you get us out of it."

Eisenhower: If Israel does not withdraw unconditionally from Egyptian territory, all official aid from the U.S. government and private aid from American Jewry will be cut off, and the U.S. would not oppose Israel's expulsion from the UN.

For Ben-Gurion quite a lot had been riding on the outcome of the elections in America. The Democrats won control, again, of the Senate as well as the House of Representatives. Question. How much scope did that give Ben-Gurion to play games with Eisenhower? Outright rejection of his demand was not a good idea. But perhaps there was scope for Ben-Gurion to say that Israel would withdraw while it worked with Zionism's stooges in Congress to have Eisenhower change his position. From that perspective control of Congress by the Democrats was good news. But there was bad news too.

Within hours of the final confirmation of the election results Eisenhower had summoned Congressional leaders to demand bi-partisan support for his Middle East policy. (He might well have said to himself "Forrestal my friend, this one's for you.") And Eisenhower's defeated Democratic opponent in the contest for White House, Adlai Stevenson, had pledged his support. *Message: this President was going to do his best to prevent Zionism determining his agenda.*

Ben-Gurion was on the point of announcing Israel's immediate and unconditional withdrawal when Eban proposed a way of salvaging something from the wreckage of what Israel called its Sinai Campaign. Eban's idea was that Israel should make its withdrawal conditional on satisfactory arrangements being made for UN peacekeeping forces to act as a buffer between Israel and Egypt at potential flashpoints. In the normal course of events, and pushed by Dayan, Ben-Gurion would have dismissed such an idea—reliance on Gentiles—with contempt; but in the circumstances as they were he could see merit and lots of political mileage in it. Agreements with the UN would have to be negotiated. Negotiations could be dragged out. Israel was not without bargaining power. Eisenhower might not have things all his own way.

Thus it was, half an hour after the striking of the midnight clocks in Israel on 9 November, that Ben-Gurion addressed his people by radio. The IDF, he told them, would be withdrawing from Egyptian territory upon the conclusion of satisfactory arrangements with the UN for the introduction of an international force.

At this moment in time the Zionist state was totally isolated, perceived by the international community as a rogue state. And this was not a consequence of anti-Semitism but of Israel's arrogance of power to date. Its latest military adventure in collusion with France and Britain was an aggression too far.

It was an appropriate moment for Israel's leaders to do some soul searching about the nature of their state and where they were taking it. But with Sharett gone they were incapable of introspection. The isolation the Zionist state had brought upon itself only confirmed Israel's political and military hawks in the rightness of their conviction—that it was "us" against "them", the them being not only the Arabs but the whole non-Jewish world.

The stage was now set for a battle of wills between Ben-Gurion and Eisenhower, with Nasser on the sidelines effectively doing what he was advised to do by UN Secretary General Dag Hammarskold. And it was to be four months before Eisenhower got his way. Or so it seemed at the time.

At UN headquarters in New York, Eban demonstrated that he had no equal as a diplomatic fixer. He was not less than brilliant in negotiating the agreements that would lead to the withdrawal of Israeli forces and the replacement of them at strategic flashpoints by the blue-bereted peacekeepers of the United Nations Emergency Force (UNEF).

But Eban's task was to be complicated by Ben-Gurion's insistence that unless and until Egypt made peace with the Jewish state, Israeli forces would never withdraw from Sharm el-Sheik at the southern tip of the Sinai peninsula. In the absence of a signed, sealed peace with Egypt, on Israel's terms of course, the presence of UNEF forces in Sharm el-Sheik was not sufficient, Ben-Gurion insisted, to guarantee freedom of passage for Israeli vessels through the Straits of Tiran.

What was about to happen is the key to understanding how a greater Israel was created in the 1967 war.

What follows is the amazing story of how, in the process of negotiating its withdrawal, Israel was encouraged to believe that it had been given a *casus belli* and, more than that, the actual green light for its next war. It is also the story of how the French whore, locked into her nuclear embrace with Israel, played the leading role in assisting the Jewish state to make nonsense of Eisenhower's best intentions.

The French knew the British were finished in terms of being the dominating influence in the Middle East and that the U.S. would replace Britain as the leading imperial power in the Arab world. France was intending to cling on to Israel at any cost, as a means of maintaining its influence in the region. It may even have been that the French were hoping that the developing confrontation between Eisenhower and Ben-Gurion would lead to the U.S. and Israel becoming estranged—to enable France to remain the Jewish state's main arms supplier. The notion that everything happening in the Middle East had to do with oil was not quite correct. It had to do with oil *and weapons*. Buying the former as cheaply as possible and selling the latter as expensively as possible. Because of its commitment to nuclear energy on the home front, France was in the process of becoming less dependent than her Western allies on oil, and that meant, for France, that selling its nuclear technology (for war as well as peace) would become more important than buying oil.

On 4 February 1957, Eisenhower wrote to Ben-Gurion putting him on notice, again, that nothing less than Israel's unconditional withdrawal would do. His letter included the following:

> You know how greatly our people value close ties of friendship with your people, and how interested we are in continuing the friendly co-operation that has contributed to Israel's national development. I therefore make the strongest possible plea to Israel that she cease ignoring the United Nations resolutions which, taken as a whole, can help, I believe, to bring tranquillity and justice to your country and her neighbours. *Continued disregard for international opinion, as expressed in the UN resolutions, will almost certainly lead to further UN action which will seriously damage relations between Israel and UN members, including the United States.*[24] [Emphasis added]

Ben-Gurion's letter of reply included this: "We stand ready to withdraw our forces from Sharm el-Sheik if there is a guarantee of passage through the Straits of Tiran."[25]

For reasons he would spell out in due course there was no way Eisenhower could agree to Israel the aggressor laying down conditions for its withdrawal.

My interpretation of events is that Eisenhower had had enough of Ben-Gurion's intransigence and wanted to get really tough with Israel in line with the warning given to Eban, *but was prevented from doing so because he could not get enough support in Congress—because the Zionist lobby had activated its stooges there.*

Ben-Gurion wrote the following after quoting the full text of his letter to Eisenhower:

> The great work of our Embassy in Washington and our

> delegation to the UN General Assembly headed by Golda Meir and Abba Eban left its mark on American public opinion. The press, Congressional circles and intellectuals showed greater understanding of Israel's position and the justice of its cause. *The pressure of public opinion led to a change in (U.S.) policy...* [26] [Emphasis added]

Ben-Gurion: "The press, Congressional circles and intellectuals showed greater understanding of Israel's position... The pressure of public opinion led to a change in [U.S.] policy."

In the light of what did not happen, that could be translated to mean, "Our Zionist lobby went to work to get Eisenhower to put out of his mind thoughts about cutting off aid to Israel."

The crisis—President Eisenhower v Zionism—was real. And big.

10

THE SHOWDOWN THAT NEVER WAS

On 11 February, 1957 Secretary of State Dulles sought to defuse the crisis by putting an *aide-memoire* into play. He hoped it would give Ben-Gurion enough of a guarantee to cause him to back down and agree that Israel had to be seen to be making an unconditional withdrawal from Sharm el-Sheik.

The Dulles memorandum addressed Ben-Gurion's demand for a guarantee in this way. It said that if after Israel's unconditional withdrawal Egypt ever again denied Israeli vessels their right of passage through the Straits of Tiran, *the U.S. would be prepared to work with other nations to restore Israel's freedom of passage*. But there was a sting in the tail of the Dulles memorandum. "It is of course clear that the enjoyment of a right of free and innocent passage by Israel would depend on its prior withdrawal accordance with the United Nations resolutions."[1]

Ben-Gurion still had no intention of backing down and his first response to the Dulles memorandum was to summon Eban to Israel for consultations. Then, on 18 February, Ben-Gurion wrote to Dulles. It was a dramatic and emotional letter. The unspecified threat it contained was in these words:

> At this last moment, before the clock strikes twelve, I turn to you personally in an attempt to prevent a fateful misunderstanding between our two peoples.[2]

"Last moment" was a reference to the fact that there was about to be a General Assembly debate, which everybody knew would end with a resolution demanding Israel's immediate and unconditional withdrawal from Sharm el-Sheik (and Gaza). In his letter Ben-Gurion asked Dulles to arrange for a temporary postponement of the General Assembly debate, and the appointment of a committee of disinterested states to facilitate an agreed settlement of the outstanding problems with regard to Sharm el-Sheik (and Gaza)—i.e. problems which, in Ben-Gurion's view, had to be solved before Israel would withdraw.

Question. What could Ben-Gurion have meant when he said to Dulles that he was seeking his intervention to prevent "a fateful misunderstanding between our two peoples"? Use of the word "fateful" implied very serious consequences for the relationship between Israel and the U.S. One possible implication is that Ben-Gurion was threatening to break with America and look to France as its most reliable ally and main arms supplier.

It was Eisenhower himself who replied to Ben-Gurion's letter to Dulles. (I can imagine the President saying to his Secretary of State something like, "Writing to you, especially in the terms he did, was his roundabout way of telling me to get stuffed.") The only purpose of this Eisenhower letter, on 20 February, was to inform Ben-Gurion that later in that American day he would be making a radio and television address on the subject of the Middle East.

Eisenhower, no doubt more than angry because the influence of the Zionist lobby in Congress was preventing him from dealing with Israel in the way he believed to be necessary, had concluded that it was time for him to tell the people of America—over the heads of the Zionist lobby and its stooges in Congress—why they and the international community could not afford to reward aggression by allowing Israel to set conditions for its withdrawal.

The following were some of the key points the President made in his address to the nation.[3]

- "Military force to solve international disputes cannot be reconciled with the principles and purposes of the United Nations."

- "Israeli forces have been withdrawn from much of the territory of Egypt that they occupied. They remain at the mouth of the Gulf of Aqaba, which is about a hundred miles from the nearest Israeli territory. Israeli forces still remain outside the Armistice lines and they are in the Gaza Strip which, under the Armistice Agreement, was to be occupied by Egypt. These facts create the present crisis. A fateful moment approaches when either we must recognise that the United Nations in unable to restore peace in this area or the United Nations must renew with increased vigour its efforts to bring about an Israeli withdrawal."

- "Peace and justice are two sides of the same coin. Perhaps the world community has been at fault in not having paid enough attention to this basic truth. The United States for its part will vigorously seek solutions of the problems in the area in accordance with justice and international law."

- "The United Nations has no choice but to exert pressure on Israel to comply with the withdrawal resolutions."

As indicated in the note above, the quotations are from Ben-Gurion's detailed account of Eisenhower's address (in *Israel, A Personal History*). Readers of Ben-Gurion's account could be forgiven for thinking that it was a summary of all the President's main points. It was not. In Ben-Gurion's account for the record there was no mention of Eisenhower's main point, which, as noted by Lilienthal, was this:

> Israel insists on firm guarantees as a condition to withdrawing its forces of invasion. *If we agree that armed attack can properly achieve the purposes of the assailant, then I fear we will have turned back the clock of international order.* We will have countenanced the use of force as a means of settling international differences and gaining national advantage... *If the UN once admits that international disputes can be settled using force, then we will have destroyed the very foundation of the organisation and our best hope for establishing a real world order.* [Emphasis added]

In his closing remarks Eisenhower sought to defuse his crisis with Zionism, and cause Ben-Gurion to back down, by putting the full weight of his presidential authority behind the guarantee for Israel implicit in the Dulles memorandum. If at any time after Israel's withdrawal from Sharm el-Sheik Egypt denied Israeli vessels access to the Gulf of Aqaba, "this should be dealt with firmly by the society of nations."[4] This most important American commitment to Israel had its context in what had been agreed informally by the members of the Security Council about what would happen when Israel withdrew. The plan was for UNEF peacekeeping forces—i.e. not Egyptian troops—to be stationed in Sharm el-Sheik. This to prevent Egypt denying Israeli vessels access to the Gulf of Aqaba after the IDF had withdrawn.

In principle Nasser had had a profound objection to the stationing of foreign forces on Egypt's soil, but he had bowed to the inevitable after receiving assurances from the UN's Secretary General that Egypt's sovereignty was not being compromised. UNEF forces would be in Sharm el-Sheik and other potential flashpoints only with Egypt's blessing. *That meant Egypt was free to ask them to leave.* (Israel for its part had refused to have UNEF forces stationed on its soil because, its leaders said, their presence would be a violation of the Jewish state's territorial integrity. In other words, Nasser was flexible on that matter of stationing UNEF troops on Egyptian soil, and Israel was totally inflexible about stationing UNEF forces on its soil). When Nasser accepted the stationing of a UNEF force in Sharm el-Sheik, he knew, of course, that it was the end of his ability to deny Israeli vessels access to the Gulf of Aqaba.

In the context sketched above Eisenhower was saying, by obvious implication, that if in the future Egypt asked UNEF forces to withdraw and denied Israeli vessels access to the Gulf of Aqaba, that would *NOT* constitute a *casus belli* for Israel—because of the American commitment to work with "the society of nations" to have Israel's freedom of passage restored.

When he broadcast to the nation, Eisenhower's domestic political purpose was to cause Jewish Americans to ask themselves a question—were they Americans first or Zionists first? *Were they with their President or Ben-Gurion?* (President Roosevelt had once dared to say in public that Jewish Americans could not have "dual loyalty"—i.e. to America and Israel).

There were two answers.

Some Jewish American Zionists met with Dulles and told him in no uncertain terms—"firmly" as Ben-Gurion subsequently put it—that the President was wrong. Israel was "completely justified in demanding safeguards before leaving the conquered areas."[5]

Eisenhower's domestic political purpose was to cause Jewish Americans to ask themselves a question—were they Americans first or Zionists first? There were two answers...

But other influential Jewish Americans—those who had never doubted that their first loyalty was to the country of which they were citizens and to its President—had a different message. They told Eisenhower they were deeply troubled by Israel's attitudes and policies in general and, in particular, Ben-Gurion's apparent wish for confrontation with the President and his administration. They also promised they would use their influence with Ben-Gurion.

They did and to good effect. Or so it seemed.

Eban returned to Israel for urgent consultations. He was intending to tell Ben-Gurion to climb down—because President Eisenhower was determined to confront him and Israel if he did not.

I can imagine Ben-Gurion saying to Eban something like, "But Congress won't let him." And I can imagine Eban replying: "Perhaps, but don't count on it. Eisenhower has appealed to the people of America over the heads of Congress and he is serious."

When Eban returned to America it was with the instruction to tell the Eisenhower administration that Israel did now see "eye to eye" with it on the matter of how to guarantee Israel's freedom of navigation in the Gulf of Aqaba. The climb-down. Or so it seemed. Israel would now withdraw without conditions because it was satisfied with the assurances that first Dulles and then Eisenhower himself had given. If ever Nasser asked UNEF to leave Sharm el-Sheik and then put Egyptian forces there to close the Straits of Tiran to Israeli shipping, the "society of nations", led by America, would act to restore Israel's freedom of navigation. Israel was, apparently, content to rely on that commitment.

The crisis with Eisenhower and his administration was over. Troubled Jewish American leaders could uncross their fingers. Golda would travel to New York and, on 1 March, she would tell the General Assembly that Israel had agreed to complete its unconditional withdrawal from the Sinai Peninsula and the Gaza Strip. And then...

Something happened to cause Ben-Gurion to cable Eban with additional instructions. One of them, in Ben-Gurion's own words, was that Eban should tell the American government that Israel required it to "publicly acknowledge" that if Egypt interfered with Israeli shipping after Israel's withdrawal, "Israel would have the right in self-defence to adopt all forceful measures necessary to secure freedom passage."[6] Israel's withdrawal had not merely become conditional again. *Ben-Gurion was demanding that the U.S. should acknowledge that Israel would have the right to go to war if ever again Egypt closed the Straits of Tiran to Israeli vessels.*

The something that happened was an intervention by Dayan. He told Ben-Gurion that so far as the IDF was concerned, any further interference with Israel's freedom of navigation (after the IDF had withdrawn, if it withdrew) would be regarded as Egyptian aggression and therefore a *casus belli* for Israel. Effectively Dayan was saying to Ben-Gurion something like: "If Egypt interferes with our freedom of passage again, it will be the military not the politicians who determine Israel's response."

There were two considerations in Dayan's mind. One was the need for an insurance policy. If Egypt asked UNEF forces to leave and closed the Gulf of Aqaba to Israeli vessels, and if then the international community was unwilling or unable to oblige Egypt to restore Israel's freedom of passage by diplomatic or other means, Israel would be free, without hassle from or sanction by the international community to do the job itself by military means. But there was much more to it.

Israel's brilliant but deeply flawed warlord had learned a lesson. *It was that Israel could not afford to be seen as the aggressor the next time it went to war.* In other words, Israel could not go to war again unless it was apparent to the international community from the evidence of its own eyes that Nasser was intending to attack the Jewish state. *That meant the Israelis who wanted war would have to set a trap for Nasser and draw him into it.* (As we shall see in due course, Sharm el-Sheik was to be the spring of the trap. In February 1957 Dayan was already planning in his mind Israel's next war—the war to create Greater Israel).

In the Knesset on 25 February, Ben-Gurion went public with Israel's new condition for withdrawal from Sharm el-Sheik. "If we got the recognition of the UN and of the Great Powers for our right to use force to defend our shipping in the Straits and the Red Sea ... we would see in this the safest guarantee for freedom of navigation, at least for a fairly long period."[7]

It was back to full-blown crisis. The question waiting for an answer was quite simply this: *Who finally was going to make U.S. policy—President Eisenhower or Zionism?*

President Eisenhower was determined to take Zionism on; and this, I believe, was the moment when he wanted Congress to back him so that he could start to deliver on his threat, as conveyed to Eban, to cut off official U.S. government aid to Israel and private aid from American Jewry, and, if necessary, have Israel expelled from the UN.

Eisenhower knew how high the stakes were.

If Israel the aggressor was allowed to get away with laying down conditions for its withdrawal, neither this president nor any of his successors would be able to contain Zionism or rather, the territorial ambitions of its self-righteous and aggressive child. And a mighty and most dangerous precedent would be set. One that made nonsense of what the UN stood for by turning the obligations of membership in the world body as set down in its Charter into a pick and mix menu. And as a consequence of that the Security Council and the U.S. would be forever accused of operating a double standard. One set of rules for Israel and one for all other nations. And that, in turn, would make the task of stopping conflicts anywhere in the world all the more difficult, if not impossible.

If on the other hand Israel could now be held accountable to the rule of law and the norms of international behaviour by civilised states, there would be real hope for peace, and not only in the Middle East.

So the stage was set for the showdown. The one that Defence Secretary Forrestal had deemed to be necessary for the best protection of America's security and other interests, and the one that President Truman had walked away from.

But it did not happen. Why not?

The short answer is that The System closed ranks—I think conspired is not too strong a term—to prevent it happening. The System came up with an amazing diplomatic fudge, which gave Eisenhower the appearance of what he wanted and Dayan for Zionism the appearance of what he and it wanted.

Eisenhower had no choice but to accept it because the fudge was arranged behind his back and because, anyway, the pork-barrel Congress of the United States of America was not going to give him the support he needed to get really tough with Israel. The nature of the fudge and how it was put together emerges with clarity from the events as they happened.

On 28 February Eban met with Secretary of State Dulles to find out if the U.S. was prepared to make the statement Israel wanted (that if Egypt denied Israeli vessels freedom of passage in the Gulf of Aqaba after Israel's withdrawal, Israel would have the right, in self-defence, to go to war).

That morning, Dulles told Eban, he and the President had had a meeting with French Prime Minister Mollet and Foreign Minister Pineau. The French had made a proposal which the four of them thought might lead to a solution. According to Ben-Gurion's subsequent account, Dulles then told Eban that he and the President supported the French proposal "but that he was not permitted to divulge its nature."[8] *The truth, demonstrated by subsequent developments, was that Dulles could not divulge what the French had proposed because Eisenhower had not supported their plan.*

So Eban took himself off to the French Embassy to find out from the mouths of the horses what had been proposed. It amounted to another French conspiracy, this one with Dulles a party to it. The main purpose of the French proposal was, behind Eisenhower's back and without consulting the UN General Assembly, to give Dayan enough of what he wanted. The General Assembly could not be consulted, the French said, because the necessary two-thirds majority for what they were proposing would not be forthcoming. (Eban would not have needed to be told that).

Dulles was going along with the French proposal because it was, he believed, the only way of preventing the showdown between Eisenhower and Zionism, a confrontation that Dulles believed the President could not win. (Was Dulles right about that? What if President Eisenhower had said something like, "I am prepared to address the people of America again and ask them to bring their pork-barrel Congress to heel"?)

The essence of the French proposal, which Eisenhower had allegedly approved, was this:

Israel should make an *assumption* that America and France recognised that Egyptian interference with Israel's freedom of navigation after Israel's withdrawal would be an act of aggression "to which Israel would be entitled to respond with force in the name of self-defence in accordance with Article 51 of the UN Charter."[9]

When Israeli Foreign Minister Golda Meir addressed the General Assembly, she would say that it was solely on the basis of *this assumption*, which she would spell out, that she was announcing Israel's withdrawal from Sharm el-Sheik.

In the speeches they made to welcome Golda's withdrawal announcement, the representatives of the U.S. and France, and those of a few other nations who could be relied upon to do as they were told, would say that their governments recognised that in the event of Egyptian interference with Israel's freedom of navigation, Israel would have, as her Foreign Minister had *assumed*, the right to self-defence in accordance with Article 5l of the UN Charter.

Ben-Gurion subsequently wrote that Israel had agreed to the French proposal because "it was obviously impossible to mobilise two-thirds of the UN members for this purpose."

According to Ben-Gurion's version of the story, Eban and Golda then worked on the speech she was going to make to the General Assembly "with the concurrence of the delegates of the United States and France."[10]

Initially things went according to the French plan. On the afternoon of 1 March Golda announced to the General Assembly that Israel would be withdrawing from Sharm el-Sheik, to make way for UNEF forces whose main function would be "the prevention of belligerent acts" and to guarantee "freedom of navigation for Israeli and international shipping." She added: "Interference by armed force with ships of Israeli flag exercising free and innocent passage in the Gulf of Aqaba and through the Straits of Tiran will be regarded by Israel as an attack entitling it to exercise its inherent right of self-defence under Article 51 of the Charter."[11]

Golda then waited with apprehension for the French and the American representatives to confirm the view of their governments that

Israel would indeed have the right it claimed in the circumstances to which she had referred.

The French Ambassador, Georges Picot, did his stuff to Israel's expectation and satisfaction. *The American Ambassador, Cabot Lodge did not. He made no mention of the possibility of future Egyptian action giving Israel a right to respond by military means which would be justified as self-defence in accordance with Article 51 of the UN Charter.* The assumption has to be that Eisenhower insisted on Lodge sticking to the Presidential script—that future problems arising from Israel's withdrawal would be solved by the "society of nations" and not by Israel resorting to military means.

Eban was then instructed to meet with Dulles again to seek an explanation for what Ben-Gurion subsequently described as "the discrepancies between Lodge's speech and the agreement arrived at previously", and to say that "these discrepancies had perplexed the Israel government and its people."[12] What he meant was, "It would appear that Eisenhower has screwed us. Find out precisely what happened." (More than a decade later Golda told me that making the withdrawal speech had been a mistake which she regretted. She was still very bitter).

Dulles said he could not give Eban an explanation until he did some consulting to find out for himself what had happened.

It would seem that Lodge had received two instructions. The first, from Dulles authorising him to make the speech as agreed with the French. The other from Eisenhower saying, in effect, "Don't you dare say that!"

Eventually Dulles told Eban that the President, as they were speaking, was writing to Ben-Gurion. The letter would say, among other things, that Israel's assumptions as voiced by Golda in her speech were acceptable to the U.S.

In fact, Eisenhower's letter said no such thing. It was a short letter of only three paragraphs and was cabled to Ben-Gurion within minutes.

The President's main point was this: "I venture to express the hope that the carrying out of the withdrawals will go forward with the utmost speed."[13]

Eisenhower made no reference whatsoever to Israel's assumption that, in the event of an Egyptian attempt to deny Israeli vessels the freedom of navigation, Israel would have a right, endorsed by America, to resort to military action in the name of self-defence in accordance with Article 51 of the UN Charter.

This President was not going to give Israel's hawks what he knew they wanted—advance American approval for their next war.

President Truman had surrendered to Zionism. President Eisenhower had done his best to contain it. What would happen in June 1967 would be the most dramatic proof of how completely Eisenhower's even-handed policy had been reversed—as it happened by President Johnson following President Kennedy's assassination.

As we shall see in due course when the time came for America to give substance to Eisenhower's commitment, it did not do so because

President Johnson and America's hawks (Zionists and others) were in favour of Israel going to war with Egypt and getting rid of Nasser.

In the light of the material in the next chapter, readers who believe that history is often best explained by conspiracy rather than cock-up theories may wonder if I am seeking to imply that there was a causal link between Kennedy's assassination and the switching of American policy to support for Israel right or wrong.

No! No! No! I am not. But...

I do believe that an understanding of why the Middle East (and the world) is in the mess it is today requires an explanation of the fundamental difference between Eisenhower (and also Kennedy) and Johnson who was more or less Zionism's man.

Over the course of his two terms as President, Eisenhower came to his own conclusion about who or rather what the most menacing power on Planet Earth was. It was not Soviet or Chinese Communism. It was the power he dared to name in his farewell speech to his nation as President—*the Military-Industrial Complex (MIC).*

The MIC did not actually exist as an entity in any institutional sense. It didn't have, for example, a corporate headquarters building or a board of directors. The term was coined by Eisenhower to describe powerful vested interests with a common purpose. *It was job-creation and wealth-generation by the production and selling of weapons, with the built-in need for never-ending research and development to produce and sell ever more sophisticated, expensive and deadly weapons.*

The principal vested interests which made (and make) up the MIC were the large-scale, technology-based industries which manufactured and sold weapons; the banks which loaned them money; and the highest-ranking military people who were, so to speak, the end-users. Associate members of the MIC included leading figures in the intelligence community and those politicians who did the MIC's bidding, the latter by lobbying government for taxpayers' money to fund the MIC's research and development programmes.

All the major powers had (and have) their own MIC. And in all the major capitalist countries (America, Britain and France especially) the MIC had (and has) a bigger influence on government policy making than any other vested interest because of the great contribution the business of manufacturing and marketing weapons makes to job and wealth creation. In that context the Cold War was at least to some extent a game being played, in accordance with rules more or less agreed by the rival superpowers, to enable them to do the necessary job creating and wealth generating by producing and selling weapons. *The rival superpowers and their respective allies needed enemies to justify to their peoples why so much of their money was being spent on producing and developing weapons.* (Someday,

The rival superpowers needed enemies to justify to their peoples why so much of their money was spent on producing and developing weapons.

perhaps, somebody will calculate whether or not the number of jobs created and the amount of wealth generated by the MIC could have been matched or even bettered by investment in more humanly useful and less pernicious development projects).

In his second term President Eisenhower had viewed with growing alarm the way in which the military-industrial vested interests were developing their ability to influence decision-making in Congress and so ultimately the White House. The way was ensuring that most of the 50 states of the Union had a military-industrial facility of one kind or another—everything from design through production to testing. That meant, for example, that if the President wanted to cut back the amount of taxpayers' money which went into feeding the war machine, the military-industrial vested interests could mobilise targeted Congressmen (and women) to say to the President: "You can't do it. It will cost the people jobs and us our seats in Congress at the next election."

I think there were two reasons why President Eisenhower named the MIC and warned his people to be on their guard against it. First was his fear that unless it was held properly and fully to account, the MIC would demand and would receive a vastly disproportionate amount of taxpayers' money to fund its research and development programmes. *Second was his fear that if Zionism could not be contained, the MIC would end up calling the policy shots with Zionism as its ally.*

The fundamental difference between President Eisenhower and President Johnson came down to this: Eisenhower (the most distinguished and respected military gentleman of modern times and not a pork-barrel politician) was *for containing the MIC and Zionism*. Johnson (a shrewd, crude political fixer and the master of pork-barrel politics) was, at least initially, *in favour of giving the MIC its head in association with Zionism*.

When Kennedy entered the White House it was his intention to continue Eisenhower's policy of seeking to contain both Zionism and the MIC. If he had been allowed to live there would not have been a shift of U.S. policy in favour of Israel right or wrong; in all probability the 1967 war would not have happened—a greater Israel would not have been created; and the Zionist state would not have been allowed to develop nuclear weapons.

Really?

That, on balance, is my conclusion and why the next chapter is titled "Turning Point—The Assassination of President Kennedy".

But readers can judge for themselves.

11

TURNING POINT— THE ASSASSINATION OF PRESIDENT KENNEDY

Rather like President Wilson, President Kennedy not only wanted to change the world for the better, he believed that changing it was possible—provided the peoples of nations, starting with his own, could be inspired to play their necessary part.

When he was assassinated in Dallas, Texas on 22 November 1963, there were millions around the world who, without prompting, could recall and recite the two key sentences from his inaugural address on 21 January 1961. "And so, my fellow Americans: ask not what your country can do for you—ask what you can do for your country. My fellow citizens of the world: ask not what America will do for you, but what together we can do for the freedom of man." Prior to that he had said that the task of the new generation he represented was "to bear the burden of a long twilight struggle... against the common enemies of man—tyranny, poverty, disease and war itself". And that, too, inspired many around the world to believe that President Kennedy really would change the world for the better.

In a world shocked and horrified by the assassination it was Britain's Prime Minister, Harold Macmillan, who asked and best answered the question of the dreadful moment. "Why this feeling—this sorrow—at once so universal and so individual? Was it not because he seemed, in his own person, to embody all the hopes and aspirations of this new world that is struggling to emerge—to rise, phoenix-like, from the ashes of the old?"

A similar but more explicit comment was the highlight of the treatment of Kennedy's assassination by the BBC's satirical programme, *That Was The Week That Was.* Satire was in shocked suspension. President Kennedy was described as "the first Western politician to make politics a respectable profession for 30 years—to make it once again the highest of the professions, and not just a fabric of fraud and sham."

I take Kennedy's description of "war itself" as one of the common enemies of man to mean that he shared Eisenhower's views about the need to contain the MIC.

We will never know how different and better a place the world might have been today if President Kennedy had been allowed to serve two terms in the White House. But we can be certain that the policy of containing Zionism would have continued and that the prospects for peace in the Middle East would have been much improved if he had lived.

On the matter of policy for the Middle East, the story of Kennedy's time in the White House is the story of a President trying to free himself from Zionism's grip on policy making; a grip that, in Kennedy's case, was all the more firm because he would not have beaten Republican candidate Richard Nixon to become president without Jewish campaign funds and organised Jewish votes.

The truth is that Kennedy did not want to become what he himself described as a "political whore", but because of the pork-barrel nature of American politics—which he tried unsuccessfully to change in his first year as President—he had no choice.

This is an appropriate place to repeat some paragraphs already quoted in the first volume of this book which explain with some precision the mechanics behind the pork-barrel nature of American politics. They are from the monumental work Alfred M. Lilienthal, the man who was, in my opinion, the most informed and courageous Jewish American of his day. (As we shall see, he received a "Dear Alfred" letter from candidate Kennedy at a critical moment in JFK'S campaign for the White House). In his epic work *The Zionist Connection II*, Lilienthal opened his chapter headed "Whose Congress; Thwarting the National Interest" as follows:

> The reason for the remarkable political success achieved by the Jewish connection and the Zionist connectors lies deep in the American political system. Our system of representative government has been profoundly affected by the growing influence and affluence of minority pressure groups, whose strengths invariably increases as presidential elections approach, making it virtually impossible to formulate foreign policy in the American national interest. And the Electoral College system has greatly fortified the position of the national lobbies established by ethnic, religious and other pressure groups, the Jewish-Zionist Israel lobby in particular.
>
> An added tower of strength to the Jewish connection has been the Jewish location: 76 percent of American Jewry is concentrated in 16 cities of six states—New York, California, Pennsylvania, Illinois, Ohio and Florida—with 181 electoral votes. It takes only 270 electoral votes to elect the next President of the U.S. Our Chief Executive is chosen by a plurality of the Electoral College votes, not of the popular vote. Under this system the votes of a state go as a unit to the candidate winning a plurality of voters, which

endows a well-organised lobby with a powerful bargaining position. For example, in the presidential election of 1884, in the State of New York, Democratic candidate Grover Cleveland received 563,015 popular votes while his Republican rival, James G. Blaine received 562,011 votes. With a bare 1,004 plurality Cleveland received all of New York's electoral votes, resulting in his election. A change of 503 votes would have shifted the election to Blaine. This explains why the politicians have been mesmerised by fear of the 'Jewish vote' and by those who claim they can deliver the 'swing vote' in a hotly contested state.

The will of the majority has often been frustrated. Three Presidents—John Quincy Adams in 1824, Rutherford B. Hayes in 1876 and Benjamin Harrison in 1888—were elected with fewer popular votes than their leading opponents. [In a note Lilienthal added that, in all, 12 Presidents had been elected with an actual minority of the popular votes. The last edition of his book was published in 1982. In an up-to-date edition he might well have noted that at least one President, George W. Bush, secured the White House only because the Florida vote, if not others, was rigged.] But it is the Cleveland 1884 election that is the classic example, under the prevailing system, of how a minority group such as the Zionists possesses a potent bargaining strength by pandering the votes of a block.

The inordinate Israelist influence over the White House, the Congress and other elected officials, stems principally from the ability to pander to the alleged 'Jewish vote' as well as fill the campaign coffers of both parties with timely contributions on a national as well as a local level, while taking full advantage of the anachronistic system by which American Presidents are elected.

None of the many powerful political lobbies in Washington is better entrenched than the meticulously organised brokers of the 'Jewish vote'. The individual Jew, who might not go along with the Zionist ideology or Jewish nationalism, is too cowardly to speak up and take the usurpers of his voice to task, and so the peddling of his vote goes forward. Hence the happy alliance dating back to World War I, between the supine American politicians and the Zionists, who have controlled the Congress in its near 100 percent pro-Israel stance.

From the Zionist perspective Eisenhower was the enemy and the end of the Eisenhower era could not come quickly enough. Everybody knew that the 1960 race for the White House was going to be a close run thing. Nobody took it for granted that any Democratic candidate would beat the Republican Richard Nixon, Eisenhower's Vice-President. In the event it was the most closely contested election of the century. Kennedy for the Democrats won 303 electoral college votes to Nixon's 219 but, in the popular vote of more than 68,000,000, Kennedy's margin was only 118,000. According to Arthur M. Schlesinger in *A Thousand Days, John F. Kennedy in The White House*, there were some in the Kennedy campaign management team who thought that Nixon would have won if the campaigning had gone on for three more days.

The predictable closeness of the 1960 election meant that Jewish campaign funds and votes—in large part the gift of the Zionist lobby—were going to be critical. Probably decisive. It could be taken as read that most of the Jewish vote would go to the Democratic Party and the presidential candidate nominated by its convention in Los Angeles in July. But who would it be and, more to the point, *who did the Zionists want?*

The closeness of the 1960 election meant that Jewish campaign funds and votes, largely the gift of the Zionist lobby, would be crucial—and the Zionists wanted Johnson.

There were three main frontrunners for the primaries: Senators Hubert Humphrey from Minnesota; Lyndon Baines Johnson (LBJ) from Texas; and John Fitzgerald Kennedy (JFK) from Massachusetts. And brooding in the background was the party's elder statesmen—Adlai Stevenson, the Governor of Illinois. Stevenson did not want to put himself forward because he had been a two-time loser to Eisenhower, but he was, some believed and hoped, available for drafting if the convention was deadlocked. Stevenson was much more than a twice-failed presidential candidate. He had transformed the Democratic Party by appealing to idealism. JFK's brother Edward would later say that because of Stevenson "a whole new generation was drawn to take an interest in public affairs."[2] (Some of the best and the brightest of this new generation—they included Schlesinger himself—were looking upon JFK as "the heir and executor of the Stevenson revolution.")[3]

The man Zionism wanted in the White House was Johnson. And only Johnson. Why? He was pro-Israel. As president, they assumed, he would not have to be coerced into doing Zionism's bidding. (As we shall see, the Zionists and their powerful media friends had a strategy which they believed would guarantee Johnson's victory at the nominating convention in Los Angeles). Johnson's ties to Israel were strong and had been well tested in the heat of political battle in Congress. The fundraising for his successful campaign for a Senate seat in 1948 was masterminded by Abraham Feinberg. Who was he? The financial godfather of Israel's atomic bomb. (Feinberg also assisted the revival of President Truman's re-election prospects in the same year—after he had recognised the unilaterally declared Jewish state).

But there was more to it than Jewish campaign money and votes. Johnson was pro-Israel in his gut; and that was because he had visited the Nazi concentration camp at Dachau only two days after its liberation on 30 April 1945. Then a member of the House of Representatives, Johnson was on a congressional fact-finding mission. Years after his own death, his wife, Lady Bird, said that he had returned "Just shaken, bursting with overpowering revulsion and incredulous horror at what he had seen. Hearing about it is one thing, being there is another."[4]

As the leader of the Democratic majority in the Senate, Johnson in 1957 had played the starring role in the successful campaign to stop the Republican President Eisenhower imposing sanctions on Israel when Ben-Gurion was refusing to withdraw from Sharm el-Sheik.

According to the story to be found in the official Congressional Record and pieced together with additional research by Lilienthal, Senator Johnson, when he was made aware that Eisenhower was serious about imposing sanctions on the Jewish state, summoned his driver. "Where to, Senator?" "The White House, pdq or quicker!" There "a heated session ensued". Johnson's blunt message to Eisenhower was that the Senate would "never" approve punitive sanctions against Israel. Johnson also read the riot act to Secretary of State Dulles. He was told that Eisenhower's threats were "unwise, unfair and one-sided."[5]

Johnson's blunt message to Eisenhower was that the Senate would "never" approve punitive sanctions against Israel.

Apart from wanting Johnson in the White House, *Zionists were anti-Kennedy*. The explanation for this antipathy was "sins of the father". Joseph P. Kennedy, wealthy and dominating, had made good and bad history. The good, was his appointment in 1937—reward for his contributions to the financial health of the Democratic Party—as U.S. ambassador to Great Britain. For an Irish-American, and a Roman Catholic to boot, that was quite something. In due course he became convinced—the bad part—that Britain was doomed to Nazi conquest, and he said that America's only hope lay in isolationism. That was sufficient for Zionism to brand him as a Nazi sympathiser and to assert that he was full of the "poison" of anti-Semitism. (In fact, and as President Truman said to Forrestal on the day he asked him to be America's first Secretary of Defence, the Nazis very probably could have occupied Britain if Hitler had had the nerve to give the order).

So the father's alleged support for the Nazis became the stick for Zionists—Jewish Americans and Israelis—to beat the son with.

At an early point in his election campaign candidate Kennedy gave the Zionists cause for offence on his own account. *He dared to say that he would be even-handed with regard to policy for the Middle East*. He pledged that he would be an "activist" on the matter of resolving the basic issues "dividing Arab and Jew", and that he would seek to involve the United States "with both sides at once".

Worse still, his personal feeling of deep sympathy for the Palestinian refugees was a matter of record. In 1956 he had travelled to Southeast Asia and, on the way back, he had visited a number of Palestinian refugee camps. *On his return to America he expressed on television his deep sympathy for the "displaced" Palestinian people.* By 1958 Kennedy had developed his thinking. In February of that year he said in a speech to a Jewish group that the refugee problem "must be resolved through negotiations, resettlement and outside international assistance."[6] Some in his audience objected to even the mention of the Palestinian refugee problem. And some implied that a call for Palestinian refugees to be allowed to return to their homeland was tantamount to a call for the Jewish state's destruction. Kennedy responded by saying that to recognise the refugee problem was "quite different from saying that the problem is insoluble short of the destruction of Israel... or must be solved by Israel alone."[7]

Kennedy: To recognize that there is a Palestinian refugee problem is "quite different from saying that the problem is insoluble short of the destruction of Israel... or must be solved by Israel alone."

One of the most unusual features of the 1960 American election campaign was the Israeli intrusion, viciously anti-Kennedy.

For example: *Herut*, the organ of Begin's zealots, asserted that Senator Kennedy's father "never loved the Jews and therefore there is a question about whether the father did not inject some poisonous drops of anti-Semitism in the minds of his children, including his son John's."[8]

This was followed by the allegation that two of Kennedy's closest advisers—Governor Stevenson and Senator Fulbright—were Nasser's stooges. Said Herut: "How can the future of Israel be entrusted to these men who might come to power thanks to Jewish votes, strange and paradoxical as this may seem?"[9]

Leaflets containing these and other poisonous attacks on candidate Kennedy were distributed to the Jewish-American community. In 1948 Begin's American network had funded Zionist terrorism in Palestine and marshalled political support for it across the Land of the Free. Now that network was mobilised to stop Kennedy winning. Rabbi Silver (remember him?) was among those who took public pride in endorsing the Nixon ticket because it was an anti-Kennedy ticket.

For one Jewish American the Israeli intrusions were too much to stomach. Writing in the *Jewish Newsletter* on 28 November, William Zukerman said they revealed "the curious dogmatic mentality of the Israelis, who seriously looked upon American Jews as their colonial subjects to whom they can give orders in an important election."[10]

As it happened, candidate Kennedy got to the convention in Los Angeles with a chance of winning the nomination without having taken a cent of organised Jewish (Zionist lobby) funding; and the stage seemed to be set for a straight fight for delegates between him and Johnson. To this point Kennedy had not been offered Jewish campaign funding and he would not have taken it. Why not had been explained by Kennedy himself in a private conversation. In it he had been talking about Stevenson and he said the following:

> One reason I admire him is that *he is not a political whore like most of the others*. Too many politicians will say anything when they think it will bring them votes or money. I remember in 1956 when Adlai met with Judge Dewey Stone and some other big contributors in Boston after Suez. *They wanted him to endorse the Israeli attack on Egypt. If he had said the things they wanted, he could have got a lot of money out of that room; but he refused. I admired that. You have to stick to what you believe.*"[11] [Emphasis added]

Translated, that meant Kennedy admired Stevenson because he had been one of the few at leadership level who had not allowed the Zionist lobby to buy him.

That Kennedy comment was reported by Schlesinger on page 27 of his epic book. And it was to Schlesinger, his wife Marian and Kenneth Galbraith (the celebrated economist) that Kennedy said it. The conversation took place about a month before the nominating convention in Los Angeles. The Schlesingers and Galbraith were discussing campaign strategy with JFK at Hyannis Port, the Kennedy family home.

At this point some brief background about Schlesinger and his extraordinary book is essential.

There is a reason why *A Thousand Days: John F. Kennedy in the White House* is such a gold mine of information. Schlesinger was not merely one of the leading historians of his time, he was a Kennedy insider and soul mate. His book is informed above all by the fact that he was a Special Assistant to President Kennedy. The book, described by one reviewer as "A work of matchless interest", is wonderfully readable but it's also remarkable, in my view astonishingly so, *for what it does not include*. In its 872 pages there is hardly a mention of Kennedy and the Middle East and no reference at all to Zionism and its lobby. On page 493, where he mentions in passing Kennedy's correspondence with Nasser, Schlesinger wrote: "I had little to do with the Middle East, except as it occasionally impinged on the UN." He went on to say he hoped that some day others "who watched this troubled region for the President" would provide their own accounts.

That is strange not least because Schlesinger drew off interviews with all the key players—i.e. when he did not have sufficient inside knowledge of policy matters with which he himself was not intimately familiar, he talked to those who did have the knowledge. And with the main exception of JFK's brother Robert, who masterminded the election strategy,

Schlesinger's personal relationship with the President was such that he, Schlesinger, would have been one of the very few insiders to whom the President let off steam when he was really angry.

There is, I think, only one possible explanation for Schlesinger's refusal to come to grips with Kennedy and his Middle East policy in general, and his battle with Zionism in particular. It was too dangerous. (In his book, Seymour Hersh quoted an American defence analyst who asked and answered a rhetorical question: "*What is the lesson the United States draws from the Suez Crisis? It is terribly dangerous to stop Israel from doing what it thinks is essential to its national security.*"[12]) The truth about what happened during the election campaign and on President Kennedy's watch was the most dramatic proof of Zionism's influence as a maker, and when necessary breaker, of American policy for the Middle East. I think it is obvious that Schlesinger could not bear to be the teller of this truth because he knew that it could bring down the wrath of the Zionist lobby upon himself, the Democratic Party and the surviving Kennedys, at least one of whom, Robert, was intending to run for the presidency, and was only stopped from completing his run by an assassin's bullets on 5 June 1968. I think it is also possible that Schlesinger was fully aware that fear of offending the Zionist lobby might cause all mainstream publishers to refuse to take on his book if it washed dirty Zionist and American political linen in public.

In the context outlined briefly above, I think it is remarkable that Schlesinger, on page 27, quoted the Kennedy comment about political whores and his determination, at that moment in time, not to be one of them. As I write I find myself wondering if that was Schlesinger's way of saying to readers something like: "Here is a clue. I can't tell you more. The rest you must work out for yourselves."

Schlesinger wrote that he approached the Democratic convention in Los Angeles with a "distinct foreboding."[13] There were two interrelated reasons for that.

The first had to do with the looming possibility of a crisis of conscience—for himself. He was "vigorously" for Kennedy. He had proved that by being, with Galbraith, the moving spirit of an appeal to the party's new generation of liberals. It was in the form of a letter that was finally made public on 17 June, about a month before the Los Angeles convention. It began: "The purpose of this letter is to urge, now that Senator Humphrey has withdrawn from the race and Mr. Stevenson continues to stand aside, that the liberals of America turn to Senator Kennedy for President."[14]

For the Zionists committed to getting Johnson nominated it was a potentially damaging blow and they hit back immediately by trying to discredit and intimidate Schlesinger and Galbraith. Schlesinger in particular received a flood of abusive letters and telegrams (from fellow Democrats!) Though he did not say so himself, it had all the hallmarks of a campaign organised by the Zionist lobby, which was effectively Johnson's clandestine public relations firm.

That, however, was not what troubled Schlesinger. Not too much.

The looming crisis of conscience he saw was in this fact. As the convention approached, there were signs that a bandwagon for Stevenson was beginning to roll. As Schlesinger put it, Stevenson "evidently against his conscious will, was emerging as the candidate of a growing and impassioned movement."[15] The problem for Schlesinger was that he deeply admired Stevenson and had retained very strong personal ties with him. If Stevenson did allow himself to be drafted at the convention, could he, Schlesinger, continue to support Kennedy?

When Schlesinger arrived in Los Angeles, Galbraith warned him to be on his guard against "old friends" from earlier Stevenson campaigns. To make the point Galbraith recounted what had happened when he attended a party given by Mrs. Eugene Myer, the wife of the owner of the *Washington Post*. One of "the Stevenson women" had hissed at him that in coming out for Kennedy, he and Schlesinger had committed "the worst personal betrayal in American history."[16]

There were also remarks at the party about Joseph Kennedy's alleged sympathy for the Nazis and the son who had been poisoned by the father's (alleged) anti-Semitism. Zionists and their supporters took great delight in spreading this smear. With the utmost circumspection and discretion, of course.

The second and related reason for Schlesinger's "distinct foreboding" was the knowledge he had of Zionism's strategy for getting Johnson nominated and how, actually, the strategy was unfolding as they gathered in Los Angeles for the convention. The strategy had been outlined in a talk given in December 1959 by Philip L. Graham, the publisher of the *Washington Post*. (As we shall see, Graham behind closed doors was by far the most influential figure at the convention and was to perform an incredible service for Zionism, something of a miracle in political terms.) Schlesinger wrote:

> Philip L. Graham, the publisher of the *Washington Post* and a close friend of Johnson's, outlined the strategy. He predicted that Kennedy and Johnson would be the only candidates to come into the convention with sizeable blocs of delegates—about 500 for Kennedy, perhaps 300 for Johnson. But Kennedy would not quite make it (would not secure enough delegates for a first ballot victory), and after one or two ballots Stevenson would emerge as the northern candidate. Then the convention would settle down to a struggle between Johnson and Stevenson. In this fight, the northern pros—Truman, Daley, Lawrence, De Sapio—would go for Johnson partly because, Graham said, they disliked Stevenson and partly because they did not believe he could be elected."[17] [Former President Truman had already played one Zionist card by coming out against Kennedy on the grounds that he was too young and inexperienced for the job. JFK was 42].

In that light it seemed obvious that the bandwagon for Stevenson was by no means entirely spontaneous. It was being propelled, at least to an extent, by some who were Zionists first and Democrats second. The purpose was to get enough delegates who would vote for Kennedy in a straightforward Kennedy v Johnson contest to declare for Stevenson—even though he was not a candidate, thus denying Kennedy the first ballot victory he needed. If he did not win on the first ballot he was out of the contest.

On the day of the first ballot it was campaign director Robert Kennedy who halted and then reversed the Stevenson bandwagon. Before he went into battle he said to his troops: "We can't miss a trick in the next 12 hours. If we don't win tonight, we're dead."[18]

Robert Kennedy succeeded because of a categorical promise he made to the most liberal elements. *If JFK secured the nomination, there was no way, absolutely no way, he would have Johnson as his vice-presidential running mate.*

If Robert Kennedy had not made that promise, his brother would not have won the nomination.

At the time the promise was made, it was not an empty one. *Candidate Kennedy was determined that Johnson would not be his running mate.* The differences between the two men—not least because of Johnson's avowed support for Israel—were too great for them to have a tolerable working relationship. Johnson, by his own admission a "compromiser and a maneuverer", was the master of pork-barrel politics. Kennedy was hoping to be a President who would not be a prisoner of powerful vested interests, the two most powerful being Zionism and the emerging MIC (which Eisenhower had not yet named and which was a manifestation of American imperialism in-the-making).

When candidate Kennedy talked about Johnson in his own closed circle it was with "mingled admiration and despair". According to Schlesinger, candidate Kennedy called Johnson the "riverboat gambler" and evoked a picture of "the tall Texan in ruffles and a long black coat, a pistol by his side and aces up his sleeve, moving menacingly through the saloon of a Mississippi steamer."[19]

In a private conversation with Stevenson, candidate Kennedy said there was only one way to deal with Johnson—"to beat him."[20]

Johnson for his part said he "could not stand being pushed around by a 42 year-old kid."[21] At a point, and in order to discredit Kennedy at the convention, Johnson seriously considered taking the advice of his campaign managers and using Zionism's "Don't forget that Kennedy is the son of a pro-Nazi" line. Graham told Johnson that would be "a bit harsh and personal" and that he should not say anything he might regret later.[22]

Kennedy's own first choice for the vice-presidential slot on the Democratic ticket was Senator Humphrey, and if he was not ready and willing "another Midwestern liberal."

Kennedy's victory on the first ballot was a huge blow for the Zionists and those non-Jewish American Democrats who were pro-Israel right or wrong. The short story of what happened after Kennedy won the nomination on the first ballot could be told in one sentence.

Kennedy was forced by Israel's supporters to take Johnson as his vice-presidential running mate.

Schlesinger's detailed and fascinating account of the behind-closed-doors politics of this coup includes his own statement that the confusion on the Thursday afternoon of the decision—Kennedy's final decision to accept Johnson—was such that it "defies historical reconstruction."[23]

In my analysis, which has the benefit of hindsight—i.e. takes account of what actually happened in the days, weeks, months and years that followed—Schlesinger's statement was accurate only because, for whatever reason, *he chose to exclude the Zionist factor from the equation. When that factor is included, what happened does not defy historical reconstruction.*

At the Democratic convention the man with the best and actually unique access to all of the key figures was Graham, the publisher of the *Washington Post.* On Monday, two days before the first ballot, this most perceptive man realised that the strategy he had outlined more than six months previously was not going to succeed. All of his instincts told him that Kennedy was going to win on the first ballot. Graham then discussed tactics with Joseph Alsop, one of America's most influential newspaper columnists, pro-Israel and also a long-time Johnson admirer. (Probably one thing led to the other). Alsop said that Kennedy had got to be persuaded to take Johnson as his running mate. Graham knew, because Robert Kennedy had told him, that his brother would not consider Johnson. Graham and Alsop then went to Kennedy's suite in the Biltmore Hotel. On arrival they sent in a message requesting five minutes of Kennedy's time.

When he received them it was Alsop who opened the conversation. In Schlesinger's account, Alsop "made a brief argument for Johnson, adding that Senator Herman Talmade of Georgia thought that Johnson would accept. Then he fell into unwonted silence and whispered to Graham, 'You do the talking.' Graham developed the case for Johnson."[24]

What was it?

The election was going to be a very close run thing. If the Democrats did not have the benefit of the organised Jewish vote, Nixon and the Republicans would win. The active Jewish-American community not only wanted Johnson to be the Democrats' presidential candidate, it was suspicious of, and in some quarters hostile to, Kennedy. *Unless he had Johnson as his running mate, Kennedy and the Democrats could kiss goodbye to the White House.*

Kennedy gave Graham and Alsop the impression that he would do as they advised but, as subsequent developments were to prove, he did so only because he was convinced in his own mind that Johnson would say "No".

Graham came away from the meeting troubled by the speed and

the ease with which Kennedy had apparently accepted the proposition that had been put to him. The next thing the publisher of the *Washington Post* did was to instruct his most influential newspaper to run a story that "the word in Los Angeles is that Kennedy will offer the vice-presidency to Lyndon Johnson."[25] With that instruction there was an injunction forbidding the newspaper to be more explicit—because Graham did not want Kennedy to think the worst of him.

The story was planted to put pressure on Kennedy and give Graham the opening to go to work on Johnson. Graham knew he was going to have a tough time persuading his Texan friend to accept the indignity of being Kennedy's running mate, but it was a battle of wills he, Graham, had to win—*if the Democratic Party and Israel were to win.*

At 8.45 on the morning after the evening of his first ballot victory, Kennedy called Johnson's suite to ask if he could come down for a chat. Johnson was still sleeping and Lady Bird answered. She woke him and conveyed the request. He nodded his assent. As she put the phone down she said: "Honey, I know he's going to offer the vice-presidency, and I hope you won't take it."[26]

Lady Bird could not have known but exactly the same hope was in Kennedy's mind when he closed his end of the line. He was thus in for a very big surprise when, a little more than an hour later, he was sitting with the "riverboat gambler."

Schlesinger wrote: "To Kennedy's astonishment, Johnson showed every interest in the project." Schlesinger then quoted Kennedy as later telling a friend: "I didn't offer the vice-presidency to him, I just held it out (at this point Kennedy simulated taking an object out of his pocket and holding it close to his body) and he grabbed at it."[27]

Johnson told Kennedy he needed time to think about it and to consult, but he had, in fact, already decided to take Graham's advice and be JFK's running mate when the offer was formally made. Kennedy returned to his own suite in a state of "considerable bafflement". He said, "You just won't believe it... He wants it!" [28]

Kennedy then had a crisis discussion with brother Robert. He, Robert, was fiercely opposed to having Johnson on the ticket, not least because of his promise to the liberals and the black American constituency—the promise that had stopped the Stevenson bandwagon and secured the nomination for his brother.

There were, JFK said, two good reasons for having Johnson on the ticket. The first was that he would probably deliver states that Kennedy might not otherwise carry—Texas and possibly other states in the south. The second was that a Kennedy administration might have a greater prospect of success with Johnson as a collaborator in the executive branch instead of as a "competitor" in Congress. That had particular meaning in the context of Middle East policy making. If Johnson remained the leader of the Democrats in the Senate, and all the more so if the Democrats had the majority there, he could do on Kennedy's watch what he had done on

Eisenhower's watch—block Congressional approval for sanctions against Israel if they were needed to oblige the Jewish state to comply with UN resolutions and U.S. policy preferences.

But there were, the Kennedy brothers agreed, downsides to having Johnson on the ticket. The liberal wing of the party and the black American constituency would be outraged. From that perspective the gains from having the Texan as running mate might be matched or even outweighed by the losses.

JFK was also seriously concerned about whether he and Johnson could work together, and not just on the Middle East.

There can be no doubt that Robert Kennedy believed he had his brother's green light to see to it that Johnson would not be the running mate. Subsequently Robert became convinced that if Johnson's nomination went forward for approval by the convention, the liberals and the black American delegates would revolt. At a point Robert met with Johnson. He said he was speaking on behalf of his brother to report that an ugly floor fight was in prospect and that it might divide the party and cast a shadow over the whole election campaign. If Johnson did not want to subject himself to this unpleasantness, his brother would understand. His brother continued to hope that Johnson would play a major role in the election, but should Johnson prefer to withdraw his interest in the vice-presidential slot, his brother would wish to make him chairman of the Democratic National Convention. The implication was that Johnson, through his control of the party machinery, could lay a basis for his own national future.

Johnson was now thoroughly confused. Graham had told him that JFK did want him as his running mate and he was working on his nomination speech. Johnson said "Shit!" and summoned Graham.[29]

My interpretation is that JFK was still somewhat divided in his own mind, but was coming to terms with the fact that he had got to have Johnson in order to give the Zionists what they needed to deliver the organised Jewish vote.

Not in doubt is that it was Graham who orchestrated the final moves to secure Johnson's nomination as the vice-presidential candidate. He called presidential candidate Kennedy from Johnson's suite. He reported what Robert had said about wanting Johnson to withdraw and asked what exactly it was that JFK wanted Johnson to do.

JFK said, "I want him to make a statement (accepting the nomination) right away."[30]

Graham said, "You'd better speak to Lyndon."[31]

Johnson, sprawled across the bed, took the phone. He said: "Yes.... yes... yes," and finally, "OK, here's Phil."[32]

Graham then said to JFK, "You had better speak to Bobby."[33]

They continued to chat while Robert Kennedy was located and brought to the phone at Graham's end of the line. He came in white-faced and exhausted. Then he listened to his brother saying that party leaders felt the delay was disastrous, and that he had to *"go through with Johnson or blow the whole business."*[34]

My guess is that it was Graham who told JFK that the whole business would be blown if he did not take Johnson.

The convention in Los Angeles was the beginning of a learning process for JFK. He had accepted Johnson as his running mate to secure the organised Jewish vote. *The next lesson was about the importance of Jewish campaign funding.* He did not want to become a "political whore". The question was—did he really have a choice given the pork-barrel nature of American politics and, more to the point, the Democratic Party's dependence on Zionism's largesse?

As he was soon to discover for himself, the answer in the short term was "No".

The truth was that the Democratic Party could not fight and win an election campaign without Jewish funding. The man who took presidential candidate Kennedy to the source of it was the Governor of Connecticut, Abraham Ribicoff. He had been the Kennedys' floor manager at the Los Angeles convention and was subsequently to say: "I was the only Jew for him. I realised that Jews were for anybody but Jack Kennedy. I told him I was going to get in touch with Abe Feinberg, who I thought was the key Jew."[35]

The Democratic Party could not fight and win an election campaign without Jewish funding—and the Jews (according to Ribicoff) were for anybody but Kennedy. A major issue was his father's alleged anti-Semitism.

Ribicoff arranged for a meeting in Feinberg's apartment at the Hotel Pierre in New York—the place where the funding for the top-secret development of Israel's atomic bomb was discussed and agreed. (Feinberg had made his fortune in the hosiery and clothing business). Ribicoff said that "all the leading Jews were invited". On the day set for the meeting with Kennedy, about 20 of the most prominent Jewish American businessmen and financiers showed up.

Except for Ribicoff as his chaperone Kennedy went to the meeting alone. According to various accounts it was a rough session for the Democratic presidential candidate. Because of the initial hostility, he could have been forgiven for wondering if he was before some kind of kangaroo court.

The initial hostile tone was set by the prominent Bostonian, Dewey D. Stone. He said: "Jack, everybody knows the reputation of your father concerning the Jews and Hitler. And everybody knows that the apple doesn't fall far from the tree."[36]

Kennedy kept his cool and replied, "You know, my mother was part of that tree, too."[37]

Ribicoff, probably ashamed and embarrassed by what Stone had said, interjected. "The sins of the father shouldn't fall on the son."[38]

After some discussion—most of its substance was taken by men to their graves—Kennedy was asked to go with Ribicoff to an upstairs room to await the judgment.

It was that the group would provide an initial contribution of US$500,000 to the Kennedy campaign, with more to come. The obvious implication—it was not said because it did not have to be said—was that *the more would depend on candidate Kennedy speaking in support of Israel.*

In Feinberg's version of what happened, he called Kennedy to give him the news right away. "His voice broke," Feinberg would later say. "He got emotional" with, Feinberg intimated, "gratitude."[39]

It might have been that Kennedy's voice did break and that there was emotion in it, but it was not the emotion of gratitude.

The following morning in northwest Washington, Kennedy drove himself to the house of an old and trusted friend, the newspaper columnist Charles L. Bartlett. Kennedy needed somebody to talk to about his meeting with Feinberg and his funders. On arrival Kennedy prevailed upon his friend to take a walk with him. (Was it the fresh air Kennedy wanted or did he assume that his friend's house was bugged?)

According to Bartlett's subsequent account of their conversation on the move, Kennedy said: "As an American citizen I am outraged to have a Zionist group come to me and say—'We know your campaign is in trouble. We're willing to pay your bills if you'll let us have control of your Middle East policy.'"[40] Bartlett also recalled Kennedy saying that, as a presidential candidate, he resented the crudity with which he had been approached. "They wanted control!" he quoted Kennedy as saying with great anger in his voice.[41]

Immediately after his meeting with Feinberg and his funders, Kennedy made a promise to himself. And he told Bartlett what it was. "If I get to be President, I am going to do something about it."[42] The "it" was a candidate's perennial need for money and resulting vulnerability to the demands of those who contributed.

Once elected, Kennedy tried to pursue election reforms to reduce dependence on special interest groups and the wealthy—but he did not succeed.

President Kennedy did, in fact, try to honour his promise to himself.

- In the October of his first year in office he appointed a bipartisan commission to recommend ways "to broaden the financial base of our presidential campaigns." The commission recommended, among other things, the use of federal tax credits to encourage political donations by individuals—to reduce dependence on special interest groups and the wealthy.

- In 1962, President Kennedy submitted five draft bills to Congress for reform of presidential campaign funding. All were rejected.

- The following year he tried again, this time with two bills. Both were rejected.

For all of his genuine outrage as expressed to Bartlett, and because he had an election to win, it was not long before candidate Kennedy was reading from Zionism's script in public.

In August he returned to New York City to address the Zionist Organisation of America (ZOA) convention. New York State's 45 Electoral College votes were critical and could well be decisive.

On the matter of greatest concern to Israel—getting rid of the Palestinian refugees as a problem outstanding—Zionism had already been allowed to determine the Democrat's election platform. It talked in vague terms of giving encouragement "to the resettlement of Arab refugees in lands where there is room and opportunity to them." *This verbal abomination implied, no, stated, that the Palestinian refugees would have to be settled outside Israel.* It was thus a two-fingered gesture to UN Resolution 194 that required the refugees to be given the choice of repatriation to the homeland from which they had been expelled or compensation.

Because of Zionist influence, the Democratic platform advocated "the resettlement of Arab refugees in lands where there is room and opportunity to them", i.e. outside Israel—despite UN Resolution 194.

In his address to the Zionists, Kennedy noted that "the ideals of Zionism have been endorsed by both parties."[43] He then proceeded to place the complete blame for continued unrest in the Middle East on the Arabs, depicting "little Israel" as the most sinned-against party.

Senator Kennedy knew that was, to say the very least, a grotesque misrepresentation of reality and truth. Candidate Kennedy said it because it had to be said if he was to defeat Nixon.

It was not only what Kennedy said that amazed and troubled those Jewish Americans who were opposed to Zionism, it was how he said it. Lilienthal, then on his way to becoming the most perceptive and best informed of all Jewish American critics of Zionism, was subsequently to write the following about that Kennedy performance. "It was almost inconceivable that the Democratic candidate, a student as well as a writer of history, could have prepared, no less presented, so partisan an account of the tensions besetting the area. The familiarity he displayed in this address with Zionist phraseology and dogma, dating from Herzl to the present day, clearly indicated that a battery of Zionist-oriented writers must have worked closely with him in preparing this talk."[44]

The man mainly responsible for Kennedy's apparent familiarity with Zionist phraseology and dogma for speeches was Myer Feldman. A member of Kennedy's office team, he was the string the Zionists attached to Jewish funding for the Kennedy campaign. As the funds came on stream Feldman took his place as Kennedy's personal adviser—for which read 'minder'—on the Middle East. As we shall see, Feldman was on his way to becoming Zionism's top man in the Kennedy and then the Johnson White House, where his influence on Zionism's behalf, as Lilienthal put it, "Far eclipsed in importance that of David Niles on Truman's watch and Maxwell Rabb on Eisenhower's."[45] (Rabb was secretary to the Eisenhower cabinet).

Lilienthal was so disturbed by Kennedy's pro-Zionist campaign rhetoric that, on 30 September, he wrote to him to say so. It was a chiding letter of the kind one friend can send to another.

Kennedy's "Dear Alfred" reply, which Lilienthal did not make public until 1978, included this [emphasis added]: "*I wholly agree with you that American partisanship in the Arab-Israeli conflict is dangerous both to the United States and the Free World.*" Forrestal could not have put it better. Kennedy added: "Your sobering analysis of my speeches is provocative of additional thought."[46]

I imagine Lilienthal was comforted by the indication, implicit but obvious, that, if he made it to the White House, Kennedy would do his best to prevent Zionism from determining his agenda for the Middle East.

As the election campaign gathered momentum, it seemed to some neutral observers that there were times when both Kennedy and Nixon were conducting themselves more as candidates for the presidency of Israel than the U.S.

In private President Kennedy was the first to acknowledge that he owed his victory over Nixon to "the votes of American Jews."

As President, Kennedy was seriously committed to nuclear non-proliferation and, a priority, *to stopping Israel developing its own atomic bomb*. And that meant he was on a course for confrontation with Israel's hawks, and the Zionist lobby funder Feinberg especially, from the moment he set foot in the White House.

The confrontation would take place behind closed doors, with little of its substance recorded for de-classification at some future date. As with most matters to do with high politics and Zionism, the truth was considered not to be in the public interest. But there was a public indication that confrontation was inevitable.

It was a story on the front page of the *New York Times* on 19 December, when President-elect Kennedy was a month away from taking office. Reporter John W. Finney did not have to dig for his scoop. It was handed to him on a plate. *The story was that Israel had been lying to the Eisenhower administration and, in secret collusion with France, was building at Dimona in the Negev a nuclear reactor to produce plutonium. Message—Israel was seeking to produce its own nuclear bomb.*

Prior to the publication of Finney's story, knowledge of what the Israelis were up to in Dimona was the Eisenhower administration's best kept secret. The number of its people who knew all there was to know from photographic intelligence gathered by America's U-2 spy planes could be counted on two hands—fingers minus thumbs. They were: the President himself; the Dulles brothers—CIA Director Allen, and Secretary of State John Foster, (when the latter died of cancer in May 1959, his place was taken by

Christian A. Herter); the two CIA officials responsible for directing the U-2 missions and interpreting the intelligence gathered—Arthur C. Lundahl and Dino A. Brugioni; and Lewis L. Strauss, chairman of the U.S. Atomic Energy Commission (AEC). Total number of American government people in the know—eight. The number of wealthy Jews who were aware of what was happening in Dimona was nearly four times greater. To fund Israel's nuclear weapons development programme, Ben-Gurion and Peres had established the Committee of Thirty. Its distinguished members included Abe Feinberg in America and Baron Edmund de Rothschild in France.

During the early U-2 watch on Israel's Dimona activities, Lundahl's standing orders required him to provide the intelligence gathered only to President Eisenhower himself, in person, and then, unless otherwise directed, to pass it to AEC Commissioner Strauss. When Lundahl briefed Eisenhower at the White House, both the Dulles brothers were usually present.

Lundahl and Brugioni were quickly aware that Israel was building a nuclear reactor. The question was—what for? Was it for peaceful purposes or were the Israelis already embarked on a nuclear weapons programme?

The problem for Eisenhower initially was that he had to rely for that judgment call on Strauss at the AEC, formerly the top man in America's own nuclear establishment. And Strauss—even close associates regarded him aloof, arrogant and calculating—was compromised by his knowledge and private approval of Israel's nuclear weapons development programme. So he did not tell Eisenhower what he could have told him with reference to the photographic evidence Lundahl and Brugioni were gathering.

Lewis Strauss was a classic case of a Jewish American with dual loyalty. On the matter of Israel he could not be an American first. But he was not a Zionist. In 1933, in Weizmann's presence, he had fervently opposed the creation of a Jewish state in Palestine. But after the Nazi holocaust, Strauss, like not a few other wealthy and influential Jewish Americans, was ravaged by guilt because, he believed, he had not done enough "to alleviate the tragedies". (It might have been that the guilt he and others felt was on account of their failure to back Truman's visa initiative, which could have enabled 400,000 Jewish refugees to make a new life in the USA.) When Israel came into being, Strauss assumed that the Arabs had both the ability and the intention to destroy it. His conclusion—Israel had to be a nuclear-armed state, dependent on no outside power for its survival.

In July 1958, very quietly, Eisenhower required Strauss to stand down as chairman of the AEC. His successor, John McCone, was a very wealthy Republican businessman from California and a devout Roman Catholic. He was totally committed to nuclear non-proliferation and sworn to doing his best to prevent Israel getting away with anything. And he was the source of Finney's story.

The key to understanding what most probably happened in the transition from Eisenhower's administration to Kennedy's, and thus why McCone leaked the story to the *New York Times*, is that *Eisenhower,*

McCone and Kennedy were as one in believing that America would not have the necessary credibility to lead a global campaign for nuclear non-proliferation if it could not prevent Israel from developing nuclear weapons.

When McCone took over as chairman, the AEC's cupboard was bare. There was no documentation of any kind—not one classified memorandum—to indicate that Strauss had been on the receiving end of the intelligence information obtained by the U-2 watch on Israel. And the out-going Strauss said nothing to brief the in-coming McCone.

By the beginning of 1960 at the latest, Lundahl, Brugioni and McCone were convinced that Israel was going nuclear for weapons, but they could not prove it. The proof—the chemical reprocessing plant for turning uranium into plutonium—was underground.

As the months passed McCone became more and more alarmed by the Eisenhower administration's refusal to insist that Israel open Dimona to inspection by the International Atomic Energy Authority (IAEA). And it was almost certainly his fuss-making that led, at the beginning of December, to what Hersh described as "a co-ordinated effort at the top levels of the government to make Israel acknowledge what it was doing at Dimona."[47]

One manifestation of this effort was that Secretary of State Herter became hands-on. He caused the French to be asked some straightforward questions. The first French lie was told by France's ambassador in Washington. He insisted that Dimona was "merely a research reactor." That proposition was considered and dismissed as nonsense by the NSC (National Security Council). Eisenhower then instructed Herter to make a formal diplomatic protest—"We know you're lying"—to the French. The second French lie was told by Foreign Minister Couve de Murville on a visit to Washington. He assured the State Department that the Israeli reactor was "benign" and that any plutonium generated in its operation would be returned to France for "safekeeping." (President de Gaulle would later claim that he ordered his people to stop their work on the development of Israel's nuclear bomb. If he did give such an order, it was ignored).

On 9 December, about a week before McCone leaked to Finney what the Eisenhower administration knew, Herter summoned the Israeli Ambassador, Avraham Harman. At the time Armin H. Meyer was a senior State Department officer, soon to be posted as an ambassador to the Arab world. Recalling the moment when Herter summoned the Israeli, Meyer said the following to Hersh: "I remember being amazed that he felt he could take on the Israelis. It was the only time I really saw him burn. Something must have happened in the nuclear field that gave him the safety to raise the issue."[48]

"The safety" meant Herter was so alarmed that, for once, an American Secretary of State was not going to refrain from challenging Israel out of fear of provoking the wrath of the Zionist lobby.

Herter asked Harman to confirm or deny that Israel was working on the production of a nuclear bomb. The Israeli denied it.

The next thing Harman did was to warn Peres that he had better go to work on some cover stories. For Peres this was a crisis situation. He was awaiting delivery from Norway of 20 tons of heavy water to fuel the reactor. Without it Israel could not go nuclear. Peres had lied to the Norwegians. He had assured them the heavy water was wanted to fuel an experimental power station. Peaceful purposes only. Peres was terrified that further publicity now might bring the nuclear weapons program to a halt, perhaps forever.

The "something" that had happened to cause Herter to summon Israeli Ambassador Harman was that Couve de Murville had inadvertently let a bit of the Israeli nuclear cat out of the bag. He had inferred that plutonium could be produced at Dimona. That being so there could no longer be any doubt—Israel *was* going nuclear for weapons.

By this time there was something close to panic behind a few of Washington's closed doors. House and Senate members of the Joint Committee on Atomic Energy were summoned urgently from Christmas recess to a secret briefing on Dimona by CIA Director Allen Dulles.

When McCone received reporter Finney, his first words were: "They lied to us."[49]

"Who's they?" Finney asked.[50]

McCone replied: "The Israelis. They told us it was a textile plant."[51]

The chairman of the AEC then proceeded to tell Finney more or less everything the Eisenhower administration knew about what the Israelis were doing at Dimona.

That turned out to be McCone's parting shot as chairman of the AEC. He resigned the day before Finney's story was published. Zionism's immediate response was to condemn McCone as an anti-Semite. *It was a charge completely without foundation, made for the purpose of trying to shift the focus of debate away from the real issue—whether or not the U.S. should compel Israel to open Dimona to IAEA inspection.*

One of the men who admired McCone for his commitment to nuclear non-proliferation, and his willingness to expose Israel, was President-elect Kennedy. Less than a year later CIA Director Allen Dulles resigned in the wake of the "Bay of Pigs" fiasco (the CIA's bungled and never-likely-to succeed attempt to overthrow Cuba's Fidel Castro). Who did President Kennedy appoint to succeed Dulles? John McCone.

It was an appointment opposed even by many Kennedy loyalists, including Schlesinger, and came, most of them thought, out of the blue. It did not.

At the time McCone was leaking to Finney, President-elect Kennedy was in the process of being briefed about critical issues by key people in the outgoing Eisenhower administration and agencies including the CIA and the AEC. Allen Dulles, for example, made arrangements for the in-coming President to be told everything there was to know about what the Israelis were doing at Dimona. I think it was then, probably, that Kennedy took his first measure of McCone. Hersh wrote that President Kennedy found in McCone a "soul mate". (Schlesinger's brief account of Kennedy's reasons for subsequently putting McCone in charge at the CIA included this: "The President thought it politically prudent to have a CIA chief conservative enough to give the Agency a margin of protection in Congress."[52] That could be interpreted to mean that Kennedy saw in McCone a man who could be relied upon to do his best to see to it that America's interests in the Middle East did not take second place to those of Zionism and its child).

On the basis of my own research conversations I think it is inconceivable that the decision to leak to the *New York Times* was McCone's alone. The issue was simply too big and too politically sensitive for him to have presumed that he alone had either the authority or the responsibility for blowing the whistle. So who authorised him to leak?

There is only one answer that makes sense to me—outgoing President Eisenhower with the blessing, and perhaps at the suggestion of, incoming President Kennedy.

The truth, I think, is that Eisenhower was politically paralysed by his knowledge that he could not take on Israel and win—because of the Zionist lobby's controlling grip on Congress, the Senate especially. Taking on Israel meant demanding that Dimona be opened to inspection by the IAEA. If Israel was telling the truth when it categorically and repeatedly said it had no intention of going nuclear for weapons, it had no grounds for rejecting IAEA inspection. But it was rejecting inspection. Though they have never been released, Eisenhower did write letters to Ben-Gurion asking for Israel to submit to IAEA inspection. And the answer was always "No".

In other words, Eisenhower knew that he himself could not initiate action to compel Israel to submit to inspection. In theory he could go public with a demand, but there was no point in doing so unless he could back a demand with sanctions when Israel publicly said "No". The Zionists and their stooges in Congress (led by Senate majority leader Johnson) had prevented him from imposing sanctions on Israel in1956. They would do so again if he attempted to press Israel on the Dimona business.

So Eisenhower had reason to want the truth about Dimona leaked. What would President Kennedy have gained from having it in the public domain? It would give him some leverage, and some protection, when the Zionists and their stooges in Congress moved to block his efforts to require Israel to open Dimona to inspection. With the truth in the open President Kennedy could say something like the following to his Zionist fundraisers: "Gentlemen, I have no choice. Israel's nuclear development programme is now a matter of global political and public concern. I've got to insist that Israel opens Dimona to IAEA inspection."

The day after Finney's story appeared in the *New York Times*, Ben-Gurion addressed a packed Knesset. It was the first time any members of Israel's parliament were told officially that a nuclear reactor was being constructed (it actually had been constructed) at Dimona. Ben-Gurion insisted that it was "dedicated entirely to peaceful purposes." When asked about the reports published in the U.S. and Europe, he said, casually, that they were "either a deliberate or unconscious untruth."[53]

Nobody in the Knesset or the Israeli media dared to ask the obvious questions. If the Dimona reactor was for peaceful purposes only, to provide cheap electricity and water and to make the Negev desert bloom, why all the secrecy? Why until this point had the Knesset and thus the nation been told nothing?

While Ben-Gurion was lying to Israel's parliament, Peres was urging Feinberg and his associates to turn the maximum heat on the out-going Eisenhower administration—to cause it to play down the significance of the *New York Times* story and, more importantly, to publicly acknowledge that it accepted Israel's assurance that the Dimona reactor was coming on stream for peaceful purposes only. The Norwegians had promised delivery of the heavy water by the end of December, and Peres was terrified they might conclude that they had been lied to, if talk about Israel going nuclear for weapons could not be shut down. No heavy water, no nuclear bomb.

Feinberg and his associates gave their orders and the Eisenhower administration obeyed them. It issued a statement, apparently approved by the President, accepting Israel's cover story at face value. "The government of Israel has given assurances that its new reactor...is dedicated solely for research to develop scientific knowledge and thus to serve the needs of industry, agriculture, health and science... It is gratifying to note that as made public the Israel atomic energy programme does not represent cause for special concern."[54]

But that was not all. On 22 December what Hersh described as "a private State Department circular" was sent to all American embassies around the world. Hersh got his hands on the cable (a copy) by insisting on his right of access to it under the Freedom of Information Act. The following is Hersh's account.

The circular, written in cable-ese, "noted that the government 'believes Israel atomic energy program as made public does not represent cause for special concern.' Officials of the department, who had been involved in the initial decision earlier in the month to pressure Israel, were now said, according to the circular, to be 'considerably disturbed by the large amount of info re USG (United States Government) interest in Israel's atomic program which has leaked into American and world press. Effort has been made to create more excitement than facts as revealed by Israelis warrant. Department will do what it can in Washington and hopes addressee posts can assist in stilling atmosphere.'"[55]

Assuming it was Secretary of State Herter who authorised the sending of that message, why did he do it when he knew the Israelis had been lying and that there was every reason to assume—even though it could not yet be proved—that they were going nuclear for weapons?

The most likely explanation is that it was pure appeasement—to get Zionism to call off the insufferable pressure it was applying to his department and the whole institution of government including the White House. Only those who have been on the receiving end of an organised Zionist campaign of harassment and intimidation can know how intolerable the pressure is.

For those of my readers who may wish to know more about this particular matter, I recommend a book—*They Dare To Speak Out.*[56] It was written by Paul Findley, a U.S. Congressman who represented Illinois for 22 years. At the time of his election defeat in 1980, for which the Zionist lobby claimed the credit in public, Representative Findley was the senior member of the House Middle East Committee. His book is the detailed, inside story of how, on policy matters concerning Israel, the Zionist lobby manipulated and effectively controlled the Congress of the United States and its Presidents and, with the connivance of the pork-barrel politicians, restricted debate and subverted democracy in the Land of the Free. The evidence in Findley's book is irrefutable and it includes open, public boasts made by Zionist lobby leaders about how they fixed Congressmen and women—had them politically eliminated—when they dared to criticise Israel or would not do Zionism's bidding 100 per cent of the time.

From my own conversations with American politicians over the years I know that many of them hate themselves for being "political whores", but in the pork-barrel system as it is, they regard themselves as having no choice. *The best thing any American President could do for peace in the Middle East is to restore democracy to his own land.*

The last thing known about Secretary of State Herter is that he was still deeply alarmed by what was happening at Dimona when he gave his farewell briefing to the Senate Foreign Relations Committee on 6 January 1961. Herter spoke of Dimona as the "disturbing new element" in the Middle East.[57] At that point he was interrupted by Senator Bourke B. Hickenlooper, the conservative Republican from Iowa. He was also the chairman of the Joint Committee on Atomic Energy. Hickenlooper was very angry because they were having to discuss the matter in "closed" session. He said:

> I think the Israelis have just lied to us like horse thieves in the night. They have completely distorted, misrepresented and falsified facts in the past. I think it is very serious... to have them perform in this manner in connection with this very definite production reactor facility, and which they have consistently, and with a completely straight face, denied to us they were building.[58]

The question waiting for an answer when Eisenhower handed over to Kennedy was (as Senator Hickenlooper might have put it) something like this: Would JFK have the balls to take on Zionism and its lobby by insisting that Dimona be opened to international inspection before it was too late—before there was no stopping the Zionist state from having a finger on a nuclear trigger?

On only his second day as President, when countless millions around the world were still uplifted by the vision of his inauguration speech,

Kennedy took the decision that effectively tied one of his hands behind his back. The string was his appointment of Myer (Mike) Feldman as his special adviser on the Middle East. It was a political debt that had to be paid. Feldman's appointment was one of the conditions of the campaign funding provided by Feinberg and his associates.

Everybody in the White House including Feldman knew that Kennedy did not need a special adviser. The new President, as any President, had the whole apparatus of government to advise him on matters to do with the Middle East—the State Department, the Defence Department, the NSC and the CIA in particular. But as everybody also knew, Feldman was not really there to advise. *He was in the White House to monitor developments and to call the Zionist lobby to action to block policy initiatives not to Israel's liking.*

By all accounts, except most notably Schlesinger's, Feldman's presence created a certain amount of bureaucratic chaos and disharmony. President Kennedy's senior advisers (the official ones) tried their best to cut Feldman out of the flow of Middle East paperwork. McGeorge Bundy was Kennedy's national security adviser. Many years later a Jewish American member of his staff, Robert W. Kommer, told Hersh: "Mac Bundy had a standing rule. He sent nothing to Feldman because he was getting involved in issues in which he had no business. It was hard to tell the difference between what Feldman said and what the Israeli ambassador said."[59]

When he was relaxing with trusted friends, President Kennedy never sought to pretend that Feldman was anything other than Zionism's eyes and ears in the White House. Bartlett was a quite regular visitor to Hyannis Port and had an amusing story about a JFK contribution when the friends were chatting there one Saturday morning. Saturday is, of course, the Jewish Sabbath, the traditional time for synagogue services. Somebody wondered where Feldman was. The President said, "*I imagine Mike's having a meeting of the Zionists in the cabinet room.*"[60]

Feldman also had an appropriate sense of humour. On one of his last visits to Ben-Gurion (who died in 1974) he was accompanied by Teddy Kollek, the mayor of Jerusalem. The two men stood watching as Ben-Gurion scribbled away, turning his diary notes into a book. Feldman was later to recall both the question he asked Kollek and the answer. "What's he doing?" Kollek replied with a smile, "Oh, he's falsifying history!"[61]

In Kennedy's Presidential papers released in 1988 there was reference to a comment by Robert Kennedy on the subject of his brother and Feldman. His brother, he said, had valued Feldman's work but Feldman's major interest "was Israel rather than the United States."[62]

Feldman for his part was not bothered by the atmosphere in which he worked. He knew he was regarded by the President as a necessary evil. But so what? Feldman was in the White House to do a job for Zionism and its child. And doing that job to the best of his ability was all that mattered.

President Kennedy wasted no time in getting off a first letter to Ben-Gurion. The text of it and Ben-Gurion's reply have never been made public. But the State Department official who produced the first draft of the

President's letter, William R. Crawford, the director of Israeli affairs, did some remembering many years later.

The President's letter emphasised his concern that America's world leadership position on nuclear non-proliferation "would be compromised if a state regarded as being dependent on us, as Israel is, pursues an independent course."[63] There was also a demand for Dimona to be opened to IAEA inspection. To deny Ben-Gurion grounds for making the spurious argument that Israel could not agree to inspection because it would compromise the Jewish state's "sovereignty", the President's letter pointed out that Israel had already agreed in principle to permit the IAEA to replace the U.S. in the twice-a-year inspection of the small research reactor at Nahal Soreq.

Kennedy to Ben-Gurion: America's leadership position on nuclear non-proliferation "would be compromised if a state regarded as being dependent on us, as Israel is, pursues an independent course." Dimona must be opened to IAEA inspection.

Ben-Gurion's eventual reply was long, rambling and evasive. Effectively it was "No" to inspection of Dimona. And it was the beginning of a bad relationship that could only get worse. With Feldman in the White House and Feinberg on the outside squeezing the President's political balls, Ben-Gurion felt that he could treat Kennedy with some contempt.

The two men met only once, in private at the Waldorf-Astoria Hotel in New York in May. Ben-Gurion had wanted to make a state visit to America. His ego needed the boost that such a visit would provide but, far more important, was the political gain for Israel. The main message of a state visit to America by Israel's prime minister would be to the Arabs—the Jewish state was America's best and special friend in the region. It was precisely because President Kennedy did not want the Arabs to get such a message that he resisted the Feldman-Feinberg pressure for a Ben-Gurion state visit. The compromise was the private meeting in the Waldorf-Astoria arranged by Feinberg.

At the time President Kennedy was seeking to honour his early campaign pledge to deal even-handedly with Israel and the Arabs. He had written letters to all the Arab leaders who mattered asking for their views on how the U.S. could best involve itself in helping to resolve their dispute with Israel. *He was encouraged by the response he received from Nasser, so much so that he decided to invite him to Washington "when political conditions permitted"* (Schlesinger's words).[64] Kennedy's strategic hope was that he could get Nasser and Ben-Gurion together in Washington at the same time. The conditions were never right—the Zionist lobby and its stooges in Congress did not want a Nasser visit, but Kennedy and Nasser did continue to exchange letters and the correspondence was ongoing when Kennedy was assassinated.

Partly and perhaps mainly because of his own dialogue with Nasser, Kennedy was convinced that the Arab-Israeli conflict could be ended by negotiations. And he had a major policy difference with America's Cold War warriors. *He did not share their enthusiasm for pacts and regional defence alliances as the means of keeping the Soviet Union at bay. And why not had two explanations.*

The first was that Kennedy recognised an underlying truth that America's Cold War warriors (like Israel's hawks) were either too blind to see or did not want to see. As I have previously mentioned, this underlying truth was:

(a) that the Arabs, regimes and peoples, were not pro-Communism—many, including Nasser himself, were actually anti-Communist; and

(b) that Egypt, followed by Syria, had turned to the Soviet Union for arms *only because they had to have the means of defence in the face of Israeli attacks designed to impose Zionism's will on them by brute force.*

The second and related reason for President Kennedy's lack of enthusiasm for defence pacts and alliances was his belief—he was absolutely right—that an end to the Arab-Israeli conflict, peace, would of itself halt Soviet penetration of the region. Kennedy understood that the Soviet Union would not have gotten even a toehold in the region if America had been willing to arm Egypt for defence against Israeli attacks.

There is nothing from the Kennedy side to indicate how the private meeting in the Waldorf-Astoria went and what was said; but Feinberg and Ben-Gurion did subsequently provide some fragments of insight, mainly about the atmosphere.

According to Feinberg, Kennedy asked him to sit in. Feinberg declined the invitation. He said he would introduce Ben-Gurion to the President and then leave them to it. Feinberg was worried that Ben-Gurion, because "he could be vicious" and because "he had such hatred for the old man" (Kennedy's father), would insult the President. Feinberg did not want to take the risk of being a party to insult. He was later to say, "There's no way of describing the relationship between Jack Kennedy and Ben-Gurion because there's no way BG was dealing with JFK as an equal." Ben-Gurion, Feinberg continued, "had the typical attitude of an old-fashioned Jew toward the young. He disrespected him as a youth."[65]

In Ben-Gurion's own account, Kennedy "looked to me like a 25 year-old boy. I asked myself—How can a man so young be elected President? At first I did not take him seriously."[66]

Their last exchange was an intriguing one. According to Ben-Gurion's account, they had said their goodbyes and the President was on his way out of the room. He stopped, turned around and walked back to Ben-Gurion to tell him "something important."[67] What was it?

Kennedy said: "I know that I was elected by the votes of American Jews. I owe them my victory. Tell me, is there something I ought to do?"[68]

Ben-Gurion replied: "You must do whatever is good for the Free World."[69]

That, I suspect, was not an exchange that can be taken at face value. I think President Kennedy, on a whim, was setting Ben-Gurion up to provoke him into naming a price for Jewish votes and, by so doing, demonstrating that he was a prize blackmailer. Ben-Gurion's reply suggests that he was smart enough not to rise to the bait.

It can be taken as read that Kennedy asked Ben-Gurion to open Dimona to inspection; and subsequent developments confirm that his answer was once again "No".

When they parted both men knew they could never be friends or even allies. There was coming a moment when Kennedy would tell other Israeli leaders (as we shall see, Golda Meir was the messenger) that if they wanted their state to have an agreeable relationship with the U.S., they would have to find themselves another prime minister.

Two months after the standoff in the Waldorf-Astoria, Israel tested its first rocket in the Negev. As Hersh put it, the American intelligence community as well as Israel's Arab neighbours got the message. "It was only a matter of time and money before Israel developed a missile system capable of delivering nuclear warheads."[70]

There is some evidence to suggest that Ben-Gurion might have been tormented by doubts about the wisdom of Israel developing its own nuclear bomb in defiance of American policy. When Crawford was recalling Ben-Gurion's long, rambling and evasive first letter to President Kennedy, he said the Israeli leader may have made an allusion to being under America's nuclear umbrella and had used language including "were we able to rely on the United States."[71] One implication is that the rational part of Ben-Gurion understood and even accepted that, for a whole load of reasons, Israel's interests would best be served by co-operating with the U.S. and accepting an American guarantee of Israel's survival—*a guarantee that, as we have seen, had already been offered by President Eisenhower but not taken up.*

But in the final analysis Ben-Gurion's gut-Zionism, like Dayan's, would not allow him to rely on Gentiles. The Zionist doctrine of *ein brera*—"no alternative"—would not be modified while Ben-Gurion remained in charge. Because of the Nazi holocaust the doctrine of *ein brera* was the first article of faith for many Israelis and the Feinbergs and the Strausses of the Jewish world. A nuclear-armed Israel might not prevent another holocaust, but never again would Jews go like lambs to the slaughter. If there was a next time, the Jews would take others with them to hell.

Enter John McCone, now as CIA director.

I think there can be no doubt that Kennedy's determination to stop Israel developing its own nuclear bomb was the prime factor in his decision to appoint McCone. The President regarded the former whistle-blowing chairman of the AEC as not merely a soul mate on the matter of nuclear non-proliferation in general, but a necessary ally in his struggle to oblige Ben-Gurion to open Dimona to inspection. As we shall see in a moment, the Zionist lobby's combination of Feldman in the White House and Feinberg on the outside was beginning to exert enormous pressure on the President to stop pushing Ben-Gurion over Dimona.

McCone's first suggestion was that the President himself should write Ben-Gurion a very stiff letter demanding inspection. "Mention the

United States' international obligations, and our suspicions of the French. Lay it on the line."[72] Kennedy acted on that advice and Ben-Gurion's reply was equally stiff, even "rude", the President thought. Walt Elder was McCone's executive assistant. In later years he would say that Ben-Gurion's reply amounted to, "Bug off, this is none of your business."[73] Ben-Gurion believed he could treat Kennedy with contempt because of the control he thought Feinberg had over him.

On the subject of President Kennedy's correspondence with Ben-Gurion, Hersh offered this footnote: "The Kennedy exchanges with Ben-Gurion also have not been released to U.S. government officials with full clearance. 'The culminate result' of such rigid security', one former American official lamented, 'is a very poorly informed bureaucracy—even if there are people willing to buck the system and ask taboo questions.'" [74]

With the bureaucracy poorly informed and public opinion almost completely ignorant, is it really any wonder that Zionism was frequently beyond serious challenge in pork barrel America?

One indication of President Kennedy's determination to bring Ben-Gurion to heel was that he gave McCone the authority to step-up covert activities to prove that Israel was developing a nuclear bomb. McCone commissioned a new round of U-2 missions and then set about organising an attempt to get an agent, a spy, into Dimona. The proof they needed was underground—the reprocessing chamber. According to what Eddy told Hersh: "It was one hell of an operation." Even the CIA station chiefs in Israel and throughout the Middle East did not know of it. "We ran it right out of McCone's office."[75]

The reason for running it out of McCone's office was that the CIA under Dulles had been compromised by its relationship with Mossad, a relationship that was developed in part because of the CIA's dependency, to a great extent, on information obtained by Israeli penetration of Arab institutions and groups. If Mossad was not to be tipped off, there was almost nobody McCone could afford to trust.

There is nothing in the available record of the Kennedy administration to so much as hint at the confrontation that took place between, on the one side, President Kennedy himself and some of his most trusted people and, on the other side, Feinberg and Feldman for Ben-Gurion and Peres. But the record of all that happened as researched by Hersh gives us, in Feinberg's words, an indication of how intense the confrontation was.

Feinberg: "*I fought the strongest battle of my career to keep them from full inspection; I violently intervened not once but half a dozen times.*"[76]

The man himself, Feinberg, never discussed the matter directly with the President. It was Feldman who kept Feinberg informed about Kennedy's pressure on Ben-Gurion, and it was mainly through Feldman that Feinberg relayed his complaints and his threat to Kennedy—*that continued pressure on Ben-Gurion to agree to full inspection of Dimona would result in no support for his 1964 presidential re-election campaign.*

In his talkative moments when, probably, he did not think his words would ever find their way into Gentile print, Feinberg explained his secret.

"My path to power was cooperation in terms of what they needed—campaign money."[77]

On at least one occasion Feinberg did go into battle himself. He said he met with Robert S. McNamara, Kennedy's Secretary of Defence, and Paul H. Nitze, then a senior McNamara aide. His purpose was to give them the same message that he was giving the President through Feldman about Dimona. "*I said to them, you've got to keep your nose out of it* ."[78]

Feinberg: "My path to power was cooperation in terms of what they needed —campaign money."

In a subsequent interview with Hersh, Nitze did not recall such a meeting, but... he did remember a one-on-one confrontation with Feinberg over Dimona. The Israelis wanted to purchase advanced U.S. fighter aircraft. Nitze recalled: "I said no—unless they came clean about Dimona. Then suddenly this fellow Feinberg comes into my office and says right out, 'You can't do that to us'. I said, 'I've already done it!' Feinberg said, '*I'll see to it that you get overruled*'. I remember throwing him out of my office... Three days later I got a call from McNamara. He said he'd been instructed to tell me to change my mind and release the planes. And I did... Feinberg had the power and he brought it to bear. I was surprised McNamara did this."

When McNamara was asked about the incident he would only say cryptically: "I can understand why Israel wanted a nuclear bomb. There is a basic problem there. The existence of Israel has been a question mark in history—and that's the essential issue."[79]

At a point when the confrontation between Kennedy and the Zionists was becoming too hot for both sides to handle with safety, somebody (it might have been McNamara) had suggested a way of enticing Ben-Gurion to agree to open up Dimona for inspection.

When they talked privately in the Waldorf-Astoria, Ben-Gurion had asked Kennedy to do what Eisenhower had refused to do—sell Israel Hawk surface-to-air missiles. They were, as Ben-Gurion stressed, for genuine defence needs—the implication being that if Kennedy had any real concern for Israel's security, he ought to have no problem in approving the sale, especially since everybody knew that Egyptian pilots were now capable of flying their Soviet supplied MiG fighters. Kennedy told Ben-Gurion he would look into the matter.

On his watch Eisenhower had refused to approve the sale because he did not believe Nasser had any intention of attacking Israel and, also, because he was convinced that Israel could handle any Arab attack with the weapons it already had. Kennedy's private assessment was the same as Eisenhower's, but in the summer of 1962, with the Zionist lobby and its stooges in Congress preventing him from applying effective pressure on Ben-Gurion, and with the failure of McCone's secret agent to get below the ground at Dimona, Kennedy decided to try bargaining with Ben-Gurion—the Hawk missiles as the *quid pro quo* for Israel's agreement to open Dimona to inspection.

In August Kennedy sent Feldman to Israel to sound out Ben-Gurion on the possibility of doing business on that basis. Feldman was not a poacher turned gamekeeper and his only purpose, with Feinberg's blessing, was to assist the Israelis to give Kennedy the appearance of what he was demanding while actually deceiving him. What Feinberg would later describe as the "scam job" they did on the Americans was breathtaking even by Zionism's standards. *Chutzpah* taken to a new level.

Feldman's first report to the President was to the effect that a deal was possible. Ben-Gurion was prepared to compromise if Kennedy would match him. Israel would not agree to inspection by the IAEA (because that would compromise Israel's sovereignty), but it would agree to *American inspection*.

McCone told the President that they could not afford to trust the Israelis on anything to do with Dimona, but Kennedy compromised. They had an agreement.

Then, predictably, the Israelis watered it down with further conditions. The American inspectors would have to schedule their visits well in advance and the Israelis would have the right to say when an American inspection was or was not convenient. Israel would not permit spot checks.

By this time President Kennedy must have known the Israelis were playing a game, but it was the only one in town and he went along with it.

The Dimona inspection scam would probably still be a secret today but for Hersh's research. His account:

> The Israeli scheme, based on plans supplied by the French, was simple: a false control room was constructed at Dimona, complete with false control panels and computer-driven measuring devices that seemed to be gauging the thermal output of a 24-megawatt reactor (as Israel claimed Dimona to be) in full operation. There were extensive practice sessions in the fake control room, as Israeli technicians sought to avoid any slips when the Americans arrived. The goal was to convince the Americans that no chemical reprocessing plant existed or was possible. One big fear was that the Americans would seek to inspect the reactor core physically, and presumably discover that Dimona was utilising large amounts of heavy water—much of it illicitly obtained from France and Norway—and obviously operating the reactor at far greater output than the acknowledged 24 megawatts. It was agreed that the inspection team would not be permitted to enter the core for safety reasons.[80]

The American inspectors were led by Floyd D. Culler, Junior, a leading expert on the science of nuclear reprocessing and, at the time, deputy director of the Chemical Technology Division at the Oak Ridge

National Laboratory in Tennessee, where the first uranium for American nuclear weapons had been enriched.

Best of all from the Israeli point of view was that none of the American inspectors spoke a word of Hebrew. That gave the Israeli interpreter the opportunity to prevent any Israeli technician inadvertently saying too much in response to questions from the American inspectors. On the condition that he was not named, one interpreter told Hersh that when an Israeli technician did say too much in Hebrew, he would say to him, in seemingly casual conversation, "Listen you mother-fucker, don't answer that question."[81] And the Americans thought he was translating.

To what extent, if at all, were the American inspectors fooled? There has not been a satisfactory answer to that question. The only thing not in doubt is that President Kennedy was not deceived by the Dimona scam. He continued to press Ben-Gurion to agree to IAEA inspection.

At Hyannis Port the President angrily told his friend Bartlett that "*the Israeli sons of bitches lie to me constantly about their nuclear capability!*"[82]

Despite the pork-barrel constraints on his freedom of action, Kennedy, unlike some of his top people (I mean the loyalists), was not reconciled to the idea that nothing could be done to stop Israel developing its own nuclear bomb. *As the end of 1962 approached, he was turning over in his mind, assisted perhaps by brother Robert and McCone, a strategy for regime change in Israel.*

The idea beginning to take shape in Kennedy's mind was inspired by developments in Israel.

A group calling itself the Committee for the De-Nuclearisation of the Middle East had gone public. It was founded by prominent Israeli scholars and scientists. Because of all the secrecy, they had assumed their prime minister was lying when, the day after Finney's story hit the front page of the *New York Times*, he assured the Knesset and the nation that Israel had no intention of producing nuclear weapons. The group's publicly stated agenda could not have been more explicit. It was to end the secrecy surrounding Dimona and to stop the work on the bomb. The group proclaimed that the development of nuclear weapons constituted "a danger to Israel and to peace in the Middle East." And it called for UN intervention "to prevent military nuclear production."[83]

The group's existence was obviously important in its own right, but it was also the evidence that, at last, the thing called democracy was struggling to assert itself in Ben-Gurion and Dayan's Israel. *From here on those who believed that Israel was doomed to live by the sword might not be the main arbiters of the Jewish state's destiny. Perhaps.*

Israel's anti-nuclear community was not without influence on, and even in, Ben-Gurion's government. Of those cabinet ministers who knew by this time that Israel was hell-bent on producing nuclear weapons, some were troubled, confused and ambivalent to a degree. And the main cause of their growing concern was the disproportionate cost for little Israel of going nuclear. It was not just a matter of money; the nuclear project was draining resources of all kinds including brainpower which, in a sensible order of priorities, would have been assigned to all other aspects of the country's development. But raising the money to pay for the development of the doomsday weapon was becoming a problem.

Out of a mixture of guilt and misplaced fear for Israel's survival prospects, the 30 millionaires had assisted Ben-Gurion and Peres to get going with the research and early development of their doomsday weapon. They had contributed tens of millions of U.S dollars and possibly much more; but by the time President Kennedy entered the White House, Israel's nuclear weapons development programme was costing hundreds of millions a year. And the budgets of almost all government departments and agencies were being cut. In some cases slashed. At a point, officials of the ministry of commerce and industry went public with criticism of the reduced level of industrial research in the nation. Industry was increasingly lagging behind science. Israeli Jews, the intellectual elite of the Western world in so many fields, were still coming up with innovations, but there were, for example, few engineering companies capable of turning their ideas into products and processes for the market place. A Dimona official would later say: "We raided every place in the country. We depleted Israel's industrial system!"[84] At the height of the Dimona development programme some 1,500 Israeli scientists, many with doctorates, were giving their all to the production of the bomb and the missiles to deliver it.

I imagine that only the Nazi holocaust could have inspired such madness. As I write, I can't help wondering, again, how different it all might have been if Israel had taken Sharett's road to the future.

Among those who caused surprise by his opposition to the bomb was Lavon. The former defence minister wanted the money spent on it to go into housing and assistance for the new arrivals. At a point he said to a Dimona official, "We're taking five hundred million dollars away from settling the Galilee and instead we build a bomb."[85]

By no means were all the military in favour of the bomb. Those who, to say the least, were not enthusiastic about it included Rabin, then the army chief of operations and shortly to become chief of staff, and Sharon. They belonged to what was sometimes called the "old fashioned" school of military thought. It believed that Israel's essential advantage over the Arabs was the quality and training of its personnel, and that such an advantage would be lost if there was a nuclear arms race. If Israel possessed nuclear weapons, it would be impossible (the argument went) to deny them to Egypt or other

Nuclear weapons development was costing hundreds of millions a year. Not all the military were in favor of it. If Israel possessed nuclear weapons, the argument went, it would be impossible to deny them to other nations in the Middle East.

nations in the Middle East. In that event nuclear weapons would be nothing more than a great "equaliser". An Egypt with the bomb would be far more dangerous to Israel than an Egypt limited to conventional weapons.

At the heart of Ben-Gurion's government those who were ambivalent about the leader's nuclear weapons policy included his most likely successor, Levi Eshkol, the Finance Minister. In the privacy of his own mind Eshkol's ambition was not only to be prime minister, but to pursue a Sharett-like policy of seriously seeking peace with the Arabs. In other words, Eshkol was not a man who believed that the Arabs should be further humiliated or that Israel should gobble up more Arab land. I think he was, probably, opposed to Ben-Gurion's nuclear weapons project but, to protect his back, he had to go through the motions, when the crisis came, of pretending that the approach he favoured was delaying production of the bomb, for the purpose, he said, of having more money and resources of all kinds to develop the state in all ways.

The cabinet colleague Eshkol most admired and respected was Foreign Minister Golda Meir. Mother Israel. She had what Eshkol knew he himself lacked—the courage to stand up to Ben-Gurion.

When President Kennedy surveyed the scene from afar he concluded that he had, or ought to have, allies in Israel at the very heart of government. If he could find a way to mobilise them, it was possible that he could get the better of Ben-Gurion without confronting the Israeli leader's protectors in Washington, and therefore without putting at risk their necessary contributions to campaign funds for his re-election bid in 1964. The idea of screwing the Zionist lobby instead of being screwed by it would doubtless have brought the most radiant of smiles to JFK's handsome face.

On 27 December, two days after what was to be his last Christmas, President Kennedy had a very private conversation with Golda Meir in Florida. The only record of their conversation was an eight-page summary memorandum marked SECRET. Some parts of it were declassified in 1979 but, on grounds of "national security", other parts were deleted and remain suppressed to this day. It can be assumed that the missing bits are those which would enable any reasonably well-informed reader to work out what President Kennedy's real purpose was and the true nature of the understanding he reached with Golda.

The eight-page memorandum was written by Philips Talbot, Assistant Secretary of State for Near Eastern Affairs. He was a career officer in whose presence Kennedy felt comfortable enough to talk frankly about the differences between what an American government ought to do to make peace in the Middle East and what an American government could do because of the Zionist lobby's influence on policy-making and implementation. In the first days of the Kennedy administration Talbot had been comforted and cheered by a message from the White House, via a senior Kennedy aide but obviously from the President himself. The message was to the effect that just because Kennedy had secured nearly 90 percent of the Jewish vote, "it does not mean that he is in their pocket."[86]

The conversation between JFK and Golda took place on the veranda of his Palm Beach holiday home. He was relaxed and very informal. He was, as Golda subsequently put it, "vacationing". Her own memory of the occasion did not fade with the years. After her retirement from public life she would write: "I can still see him, in his rocking chair, without a tie, sleeves rolled up, listening very attentively as I tried to explain why we so desperately needed arms from the United States. He looked so handsome and still so boyish that it was hard for me to remember that I was talking to the President of the United States—lthough I suppose he didn't think I looked much like a foreign minister either!"[87]

There was a particular reason why Israel was now desperate to purchase weapons from America and for the U.S. to become its main supplier. The French whore required payment in cash. In addition to the money being lavished on the nuclear weapons development programme, arms purchases for hard currency were now becoming a huge and growing burden on the Jewish state's economy. It was possible to see a time when Israel would not have the cash to go on buying weapons of the type needed and in the quantity required to stay on top of the Arabs. The hope of Israel's leaders was that arms from the U.S. would be financed by American loans on soft terms—long payback and concessionary rates of interest.

Golda's eventual account of her Florida discussion with JFK was concerned almost exclusively with what she said to him. Basically she gave the President a little lecture on Jewish history and the dangers of another holocaust. Her only mention of what he said to her was this: "When I finished, Kennedy leaned over to me. He took my hand, looked into my eyes and said very solemnly: 'I understand, Mrs Meir. Don't worry. Nothing will happen to Israel'. And I think he did truly understand."[88]

There was also something Golda truly understood—the essence of the President's message to her.

It was to the effect that he was ready, willing and able to give Israel an irrevocable commitment that America would guarantee Israel's security and survival, but that the giving of such a commitment was conditional. *The U.S. could not and would not give it to a nuclear-armed Jewish state.* Israel had to agree to IAEA inspection of Dimona and if that proved, as he suspected it would, that Israel was in the process of producing a nuclear bomb of its own, work on the project would have to be stopped. Terminated. And... *If that meant Golda and her colleagues getting rid of Ben-Gurion, they should do it.*

That was not, of course, how President Kennedy would have put it. No American President could have spoken in such terms, even in private on the secluded veranda of his holiday home. But it was the message Golda could extract from what he did say to her; and he knew she was more than smart enough to do the extracting.

The known record of what JFK said to Golda indicates that he started out by defining what he called *the "limitations" of America's relationship with Israel.* [89] It was the case, he said, that "the United States has a special relationship with Israel in the Middle East really comparable to that which it has with Britain over a wide range of world affairs. *But for us to play properly the role we are called upon to play, we cannot afford the luxury of identifying Israel as our exclusive friend.*"

The best way for the United States to effectively serve Israel's national security interests, he went on, was "to maintain and develop America's relations with other nations in the region. Our influence could then be brought to bear, as needed in particular disputes, to ensure that Israel's essential interests are not compromised. If we pulled out of the Arab Middle East and maintained our ties only with Israel this would not be in Israel's interests."

The idea of America "pulling out" of the Arab Middle East was not on anybody's public agenda, so why did President Kennedy feel the need to talk about it? The implication is that he was under mounting pressure from the Zionist lobby and its stooges in Congress to abandon Eisenhower's policy of even-handedness, and to look upon Israel as America's only true friend and reliable ally in the region.

On the subject of America's relations with the Arabs, the President said this: "Israel's actions and policies are making it difficult for the United States to maintain good relations with the Arabs and support Israel." The examples he cited were the diversion of the Jordan River waters, reprisal attacks and cross-border raids, and the continuing refusal to address the Palestinian refugee problem. Those matters, together with the U.S. sale to Israel of advanced Hawk missiles, were "putting severe strain on American relations with Arab countries."

Though she would not have liked hearing it, Kennedy was also frank about what he regarded as an essential element of Israel's security. *It was Israel's behaviour towards the Arabs.*

Of course there would be differences about how to handle certain matters, Kennedy said. He believed, for example, that greater use should be made of the UN in dealing with border problems. (They both knew that Ben-Gurion and Dayan and their fans had nothing but contempt for the UN).

Then, with a firmness no doubt masked to some extent by his charm, the President told Golda that the United States required Israel to recognise that American and Israeli security interests were not always one and the same. He said:

> We know that Israel faces enormous security problems but we do, too. We came almost to direct confrontation with the Soviet Union last spring and again recently in Cuba. Because we have taken on wide security responsibilities we always have the potential of becoming involved in a major crisis not of our own making.

And that was why:

> [W]e have got to concern ourselves with the whole Middle

> East. We would like Israel's recognition that this partnership we have with it produces strains for the United States in the Middle East... when Israel takes such action as it did last spring, whether right or wrong, those actions involve not just Israel but also the United States.

The particular action to which Kennedy was referring was the massive Israeli reprisal attack on Syria that had embarrassed the Soviet Union and for which Israel was condemned by the Security Council.

President Kennedy's bottom line was that Israel had to consider the interests of the United States. He said: "*What we want from Israel arises because our relationship is a two-way street.*"

Never before had an American President dared to speak so frankly to an Israeli leader. The tragedy was—because of the ability of Jewish Americans and other supporters of Israel right or wrong to promote Zionist interests through the pork-barrel American political process—that it had to be said in private.

As he indicated to Golda, Kennedy's real fear was that *Israel's policy of seeking to impose its will on the Arabs by force could provoke a superpower confrontation*. He knew that Soviet leaders did not want a military confrontation with the U.S. over the Middle East and that they were every bit as frightened as he was by the prospect of it happening; but he was wise enough to know that they might have to respond if Israel went on humiliating the Arabs with demonstrations of military superiority. If it did, there was a possibility of Soviet leaders going for confrontation in order to save their own faces as well as those of their Egyptian and Syrian customers. That was what Kennedy really meant when he told Golda of the dangers he saw of the U.S becoming involved in a major crisis "not of our own making."

President Kennedy was so concerned about the possibility of a superpower confrontation being provoked by Israel's arrogance of power that he saw merit in the idea of the Jewish state being "neutral", meaning non-aligned. We know that from an off-the-record interview he gave to Amos Elon, Washington correspondent of *Ha'aretz*, Israel's daily newspaper for seriously thoughtful people. The interview took place in August 1961 (when Zionist lobby pressure on Kennedy was intense), but it was not published until two days after Kennedy's assassination. According to Elon, the President said he would be pleased to see a neutral Israel if that would lead to improved relations between the United States and the Soviet Union and, as a consequence, to improved relations between Israel and the Arab world.[90]

That was explosive political stuff. In my analysis there is no better or more dramatic illustration of the great gulf that existed between President Kennedy and the vested military-industrial interests named by President Eisenhower. The MIC would have regarded Kennedy's concept of a neutral Israel as heresy. How so? The MIC in America had wanted the Soviet Union to be drawn into the Middle East, in order to have a much bigger board on which to play the Cold War Game. (Could that have been one of the reasons why Dulles refused to provide Nasser with arms for defence?) Though there were moments of great tension and extreme crisis—the Cuban missile crisis, for example—when one of the two superpowers did not play by the rules, the Cold War really was more a game than not, played for the purpose of creating jobs and generating wealth by the production and selling of weapons. What Kennedy really wanted (and what Gorbachev would come to want for the Soviet Union before it fell apart) was an end to that nonsense, and for the vast resources of all kinds that went in waging the Cold War to be diverted to the long twilight struggle of his inaugural speech—the struggle "against the common enemies of man" including "poverty and disease and war itself."

Golda left her meeting with President Kennedy believing that if Ben-Gurion continued to defy him on Dimona, Israel would be on a confrontation course with him for the remainder of his first term and all of his second; and that, she knew, would be disastrous for the Jewish state and no doubt Jews everywhere. If Ben-Gurion could not be persuaded to change his mind and agree to IAEA inspection of Dimona, he would have to go.

That was the message Kennedy wanted Mother Israel to get. She got it. And the question now was—would she, could she, put it to good use?

The next important Israeli with whom President Kennedy had a conversation was Peres, Ben-Gurion's "Mr. Bomb."

Four months after Golda's meeting, in April (1963), Peres travelled to Washington, apparently to chase-up the still-pending Hawk sale. It was also the opportunity for him to have a one-on-one tactical discussion with Feinberg. Given the growing influence of the anti-nuclear community in Israel, it might also have been that Peres was desperate for more money to speed up the development of the nuclear weapons programme.

For his part Kennedy took advantage of the Peres visit to ask him personally what was really happening at Dimona. The President looked Peres in the eye and said: "*An Israeli nuclear bomb would create a very perilous situation. That's why we've been diligent about keeping an eye on your effort in the atomic field. What can you tell me about that?*"[91] [Emphasis added]

Peres looked the President in the eye and replied: "*I can tell you forthrightly that we will not introduce atomic weapons into the region. We certainly won't be the first to do so. We have no interest in that. On the contrary, our interest is in de-escalating the armament tension, even in total disarmament.*"[92] [Emphasis added]

I can imagine the President telling himself that his "sons of bitches" comment to Bartlett had been much too polite.

Peres had been encouraged to lie to the President by Senator Stuart Symington, a Kennedy supporter and a senior member of the Senate Armed Services Committee. As Peres would later reveal to his biographer,

Symington said to him two days before his meeting with the president: "Don't be a bunch of fools. Don't stop making atomic bombs. And don't listen to the administration. Do whatever you think best."[93]

The truth was—President Kennedy knew it as well as anybody else—that pork-barrel politics had resulted in many senior members of Congress becoming supporters of the concept of a nuclear-armed Israel.

Despite that, Kennedy continued to press Ben-Gurion hard for assurances that Israel was not developing nuclear weapons and to agree to IAEA inspection of Dimona; but it was obvious that unless something dramatic happened in the Jewish state, the President's hopes of preventing it from going nuclear were doomed.

With the probable exceptions of President Kennedy and Golda, everybody in their two countries and much of the world was taken completely by surprise when, on 16 June, Ben-Gurion resigned.

There were a number of reasons for the revolt against him, not the least of them his undemocratic and sometimes tyrannical ways; but the main one was *Golda's promotion of the idea that Israel had to take account of America's interests as articulated by President Kennedy (the "two-way street"), and that pushing the development of Israel's nuclear bomb to the point of confrontation with Kennedy would have disastrous consequences for Israel's future.*

Eshkol's contribution to the revolt was a statement that the nuclear weapons project could not be funded for much longer out of the state budget unless they were prepared to have the economy collapse in ruins around the bomb.

Partly because his speciality was economic affairs, and partly because he was a man of consensus and compromise, Eshkol was everybody's first choice as Ben-Gurion's successor. With few exceptions the ruling politicians really had had enough of Ben-Gurion. He was 76, exhausted and, some said, beginning to have his own doubts about his sanity.

Back in the White House, President Kennedy was delighted by the regime change in Israel and lost no time in sending the new prime minister a message. It urged nuclear restraint and reiterated the need for international inspection of Dimona; but there was not yet to be pressure on Eshkol. Having made his point it was more prudent, Kennedy thought, to give him time.

There were several reasons for the President's view that time was now on his side:

- Israel, it seemed, was still some way off from actually producing a nuclear bomb.
- Eshkol was a man he was sure he could do the business with, provided he, Eshkol, was not put under too much pressure too quickly.

- Most important of all, the U.S., the Soviet Union and Britain were on course to sign an historic nuclear test-ban treaty in Moscow. It would stop all testing of nuclear weapons in the atmosphere, in outer space and under water, thus permitting only underground tests, which did not contaminate the atmosphere. It would be the first giant step on the road to nuclear non-proliferation. Congress, it was reasonable to assume, would ratify the treaty by, say, the fall; and there would then be widespread public appreciation of the President's progress on making the world a safer place. In such an environment the Zionist lobby could perhaps be wrong-footed, and be less well-placed to obstruct JFK's insistence that Israel agree to international inspection of Dimona. (The test-ban treaty was signed in Moscow on 5 August; the Senate did ratify it in the fall; and within months more than 100 other nations had signed—Israel being one of the few which did not).

By the late summer of 1963, and because of the dramatically improving international situation, President Kennedy was looking upon the regime change in Israel as the opportunity to do much more in the Middle East than stopping the Jewish state from going nuclear. He was preparing to be hands-on with a major peace initiative that included solving the Palestinian refugee problem in accordance with UN resolutions.

Kennedy was preparing to be hands-on with a major peace initiative that included solving the Palestinian refugee problem in accordance with UN resolutions.

From his briefing papers President Kennedy would have known that Israel's new prime minister was in principle the man most likely, after Sharett, to make peace on terms the Arabs could accept. Simply stated Levi Eshkol was not an expansionist, not a proponent of the Greater Israel of gut-Zionism's mad dream. That would have been obvious to Kennedy as he read the file on Ben-Gurion's successor.

Eshkol was born in the Ukraine in 1895 as Levi Shkolnik. In that homeland he became a member of a moderate Jewish political party, Hapoel Hatzair (the Young Worker). Then, in 1914, at the age of 19, he emigrated to Palestine with other members of the party. From the beginning Eshkol and his group had believed in the possibility of Jewish-Arab co-existence. In Palestine he worked as a humble farm labourer, a watchman and an operator of a water pumping station; and he became a trade union leader. He was also one of the founding members of a kibbutz and the founder of the Mekorot water company. He was not an ideologue and was best described as an unassuming son of the soil who was happiest when he could dirty his hands with the practical work of building a new homeland. His attitude towards the Arabs was one of live and let live. He was not, so to speak, a Zionist oppressor of the kind condemned and reviled by Ahad Ha-am.

The key to understanding the hope Eshkol represented when he succeeded Ben-Gurion was neatly summarised by Shlaim. "Like Moshe Sharett, he saw the Arabs not just as an enemy but as a people. Like Sharett, he did not think that Israel was doomed forever to live by the sword. And like Sharett, he saw the value of dialogue and patient diplomacy in pursuit of the long-term goal of peaceful coexistence between Israel and its neighbours."[94]

The main point was that although Eshkol had not explicitly identified himself with Sharett's line in Ben-Gurion's time—because to have done so would have invited political crucifixion—his own preferred way was Sharett's way. More or less.

I think it is reasonable to imagine that when President Kennedy read Eshkol's file, he might well have said to himself something like the following: "We did not give Sharett the support he needed to emerge as the peacemaker on his side. We must not let the opportunity Eshkol represents slip through our fingers—because it might be the last."

Though President Kennedy was not allowed to live long enough to know it, there was to be early proof that Prime Minister Eshkol would not be a willing party to the realisation of Zionism's Greater Israel. On 1 January 1964, Eshkol promoted Rabin to chief of staff. Though he had played his part in forcing the Palestinians to flee their homeland—to that extent he was an ethnic cleanser—Rabin, like Eshkol, was not an expansionist. At the time of his appointment as chief of staff, he was the IDF's most experienced field commander and an excellent staff officer who combined military professionalism with sound political judgment; judgment that was very much in evidence in the five-year plan he prepared with Eshkol for the IDF's work. The political idea around which the military strategy was constructed was explicitly stated. "Israel can realise fully its national goals within the borders of the armistice agreements."[95]

Eshkol and Rabin prepared a five-year military plan constructed around the political idea that "Israel can realise fully its national goals within the borders of the armistice agreements."

There were three clear implications.

1. *Israel did not require more territory than it already possessed.*

2. *Israel would go to war only if it was attacked (by definition an Israeli-initiated war to take more territory was ruled out).*

3. *Israel was prepared to make peace with the frontline Arab states on the basis of the borders created by the Armistice Agreements.*

It was, so to speak, a Sharett plan—i.e. not a Ben-Gurion or a Dayan plan; not a gut-Zionist plan. (The next chapter tells how Dayan, on behalf of gut-Zionism, initiated the 1967 war then hi-jacked it to create a greater Israel that Eshkol and Rabin had effectively ruled out).

Though the proof of Eshkol's intent was not available to President Kennedy in the late summer of 1963, he did know enough by then to regard Ben-Gurion's Sharett-like successor as a man who would respond positively to a determined American push for peace.

What of Nasser, the other key player in the region?

One of President Kennedy's disappointments was that his running fight with Ben-Gurion and the Zionist lobby over Dimona had distracted and prevented him from developing a relationship with Nasser in the way he had intended. But there was still quite a lot to go on. There was the secret record of America's own dialogue with the Egyptian leader over a decade. It included a number of assurances from Nasser that he was serious about wanting an accommodation with Israel. There was the secret record of Sharett's dialogue with Nasser. And there was Kennedy's own ongoing correspondence with the Egyptian leader.

All up President Kennedy knew enough by the late summer of 1963 to have faith in the idea that, probably, he could get Nasser into a real peace process if he could satisfy the Egyptian leader on two matters.

The first was friendship. There was, actually, nothing Nasser wanted more than for Egypt to be regarded as a friend of America on an equal footing with Israel. Nasser's only condition for that friendship was that the U.S. would respect Egypt's independence. That was fine by President Kennedy because his vision of how the world ought to be was similar to that President Wilson had articulated.

The other matter on which President Kennedy needed to satisfy Nasser was the fate of the Palestinian refugees. Nasser needed evidence that the U.S. was seriously committed to resolving that problem.

In what turned out to be the last month of his life, President Kennedy did demonstrate that his administration was serious about wanting a solution to the refugee problem.

The Kennedy administration's first attempt to resolve the Palestinian refugee problem had been abandoned after Ben-Gurion protested and the Zionist lobby went to work for him.

That first attempt was kick-started by the message Philip Talbot at the State Department received from the White House very soon after the Kennedys took the place over. (This was the message that said just because 90 per cent of the Jewish vote had gone for Kennedy; it didn't mean that he was in their pocket). President Kennedy himself had followed up by asking Talbot for "innovative ideas."

The State Department's suggestion, approved by the President, was that they should make another attempt to resolve the Palestinian refugee problem. The formula was already on the table—UN Resolution 194, which gave the refugees the choice of returning to their homes if they wished so to do, or being compensated if they did not.

In the hope of making Resolution 194 more palatable to Israel, the State Department came up with a number of ideas such as spreading the repatriation of those refugees who wanted to return over a period of 10 years, and giving the Israelis a veto over every returning Palestinian in order to minimise the security risk. *Eventually President Kennedy authorised a highly secret State Department effort to implement a new variant of Resolution 194*. After many months of diplomacy a workable compromise was accepted by the Arab states and endorsed by the President. Initially Ben-Gurion did not believe it was necessary for him to oppose the American plan and seek to have the Zionist lobby block it. He was convinced it would wither on the vine of Arab rejection. The Arab states, he assumed, would not agree to negotiate implementation directly with Israel because to do so would be to recognise the Jewish state. He was wrong. When the Arab states said they were ready to negotiate a solution to the Palestinian refugee problem directly with Israel, Ben-Gurion hit the panic button and the Zionist lobby subjected the White House to immense pressure. The President was already in confrontation with Ben-Gurion and Feinberg over Dimona and backed down. And the Kennedy administration's first effort to resolve the Palestinian refugee problem was terminated.

The State Department officials who had put so much effort into securing the acquiescence of the Arab states were bitterly disappointed. The assurance that the President was not in Zionism's pocket had been taken in good faith, but he could not deliver. Many years later Talbot recalled a comment JFK had made to him: "*Phil, that was a great plan with only one flaw—you've never had to run for election*."[96] [Emphasis added]

Talbot's assistant at the time was Armin Meyer. He would go on to serve as America's ambassador to Jordan, Iran and Japan before retiring in 1972, by which time the Palestinians had turned to terror to get the world's attention. In retirement Meyer said: "I *think we could have been spared all this terrorism business and other miseries if we had gone ahead with that project at that time*."[97] [Emphasis added]

The new (November 1963) initiative was nothing less than Presidential authorisation of U.S sponsorship of a resolution in the General Assembly that demanded action on resolving the Palestinian refugee problem.

Kennedy's November 1963 initiative was nothing less than Presidential authorisation of U.S. sponsorship of a General Assembly resolution that demanded action on resolving the Palestinian refugee problem. He advised Arab leaders this would be done "on the basis of the principle of repatriation and compensation."

When President Kennedy authorised U.S. sponsorship of the resolution, he wrote a letter to Arab leaders. It said: "We are willing to agree to help resolve the tragic Palestine refugee problem on the basis of the principle of repatriation and compensation." [98]

In my analysis it is inconceivable that President Kennedy would have taken the bull of the Palestinian refugee problem by the horns, in public, if he had not been determined to take advantage of the regime change in

Israel to launch a major diplomatic offensive for a comprehensive peace early in 1964. Apart from the fact that he believed it was the right thing to do, what better way to launch his campaign for re-election? If he could get the Arab states to agree (again) on something very like the 194 resolution to the refugee problem, and if he could pull Eshkol and Nasser into discussions as a first step to negotiations, he would have momentum enough, perhaps, to prevent the Zionist lobby putting the brake on him.

On 12 November, President Kennedy convened his first campaign strategy meeting for the 1964 election. The notable absentee was Vice President Johnson. Curious. Schlesinger wrote: "One saw much less of him around the White House than in 1961 and 1962. He seemed to have faded astonishingly into the background and appeared almost a spectral presence at meetings in the Cabinet room."[99] The truth was that the pro-Zionist Johnson had many policy differences with Kennedy and did not find it easy to refrain from expressing his angry opposition in crude, cowboy language. The better option was not being around so much.

Johnson's absence from that campaign strategy meeting led to media speculation that Kennedy was intending to dump him as his running mate for the 1964 race. Schlesinger asserted that these stories were "wholly fanciful." My speculation is that President Kennedy did not want Johnson to be in attendance because he, Kennedy, wanted to talk freely about the implications of going for broke with a major Middle East peace initiative.

Ten days later, on Friday 22 November in Forth Worth, Texas, President Kennedy started his day by reading a most extraordinary attack on him in the *Dallas Morning News*. The day before, the paper's sports columnist had suggested that in order to avoid trouble for himself in Dallas, the President should talk about "sailing". If he confined his speech to that topic he would be warmly welcomed and admired. But... If the speech "is about Cuba, civil rights, taxes or Vietnam, there will sure as shootin' by some who heave to and let go with a broadside of grapeshot in the Presidential rigging."

The Friday edition of the paper, the one he was reading, contained a full-page advertisement headed: WELCOME MR. (not President) KENNEDY TO DALLAS. It was a vicious, sick, ultra-rightwing attack on him, designed to suggest that he was a traitor. How could that possibly be? President Kennedy was, an assortment of his most rabid rightwing enemies asserted, letting the communists in through the front door—i.e. because of his support for the civil rights movement, and through the back door because of his position on Vietnam. (In principle President Kennedy had taken the decision to pull U.S. forces out of the Vietnam War before they got bogged down and defeated. It was a decision that signalled his intention to deny the MIC the ten-year war it wanted in Vietnam).

Kennedy's first engagement of the day was a breakfast address to the Fort Worth Chamber of Commerce. What happened when the President had done his thing was described by Schlesinger.

"At the conclusion the chairman of the meeting presented him with a cowboy hat. The President, who never put on funny hats, looked at it with suspicion and finally said, 'I'll put it on at the White House and you can photograph it there'. Back in the Texas Hotel he chatted with Kenneth O'Donnell, his Appointments Secretary, about the role of the Secret Service. All they could do, he said, was to protect a President from unruly or overexcited crowds. *But if someone really wanted to kill a President, it was not too difficult.* Put a man on a high building with a telescopic rifle, and there was nothing anybody could do to defend a President's life. O'Donnell said afterwards that Kennedy regarded assassination as 'a risk inherent in a democracy.' It didn't disturb him at all."[100]

The journey by plane from Fort Worth to Dallas was a very short one. When the President arrived at Love Field, Congressman Henry Gonzalez said jokingly: "Well, I'm taking risks. I haven't got my steel vest yet."[101]

The shots were fired just after the presidential motorcade turned into Elm Street and started down the little slope past the Texas School Book Depository. There was a quizzical look on the President's face just before he pitched over. As she cradled his blasted head in her arms Jacqueline was crying: "Oh, no, no... Oh, my God, they have shot my husband." [102]

A conclusion invited by subsequent events is that "they" had also killed whatever was left of the last chance for containing Zionism by obliging Israel to live in accordance with the requirements of international law, and to settle its conflict with the Arabs in accordance with UN resolutions.

The U.S. Embassy in Tel Aviv was monitoring reaction in Israel and sent a cable to the State Department. It said: "The assassination of President Kennedy caught the Israeli press protest against the U.S. refugee resolution at the UNGA (United Nations General Assembly) in midstream. Articles and editorials immediately became eulogies of the late President."[103]

And then, as the U.S. embassy also reported, they expressed their enthusiasm for the new man in the White House.

One reservation was put into words by *Yediot Aharonot's* editorial writers. Lyndon Johnson would have to overcome the State Department's anti-Israel bias. "U.S. policy in the Middle East is laid down by the State Department in accordance with what suits U.S. interests as interpreted by the Department." The paper's editorial writers felt that "the issue of U.S. interests" (which Kennedy had spelled out to Golda) would "not be so much of an impediment as it had been previously."[104]

Incredibly, the expectation seemed to be that President Johnson should and would put Israel's interests first.

I think President Johnson's pro-Israel stance was determined by a number of factors in addition to his gut feelings:

- The cowboy in him saw the Arabs as the Red Indians and the Israelis as the cavalry.
- He had little or no understanding worth having of a fundamental truth—that Nasser was not a communist or even a fellow-traveller.

- He was the master of pork-barrel politics, a supreme pragmatist who realised that the Democratic Party was dependent on Jewish campaign funds and, when election races were likely to be close, on organised Jewish votes. The Zionist lobby had its price for campaign funds and votes—pay it.

- The more he became obsessed with the war in Vietnam (he knew that Kennedy had said it was not winnable), the more he was open to the argument of Israel's military hawks—that because he had too much on his plate already, he could and should leave the job of imposing stability on the Middle East to them.

- Because he had little if any understanding worth having of the dynamics of the Arab-Israeli conflict, it might also have been that he really did believe that allowing Israel to knock the hell out of Nasser was the only way to bring peace to the Middle East. The reasoning that could have led him to such a conclusion might have gone something like this... Because of the Zionist lobby's stranglehold on American policy making for the Middle East, no President would ever be free to require Israel to do what was necessary for peace on terms the Arabs could accept. That being so, there was no alternative to unleashing Israel to give Nasser such a beating that Egyptians and all Arabs would conclude that they had better make peace on Zionism's terms.

Volume 3 begins with a chapter titled *America Takes Sides, War with Nasser Act II; and the Creation of Greater Israel.* President Johnson did not, however, give Israel a green light for expansion. The truth is that Israel's attack on the American spy ship, the U.S.S. *Liberty*, robbed him of his ability to monitor and control Israel's hawks.

And they screwed him.

ENDNOTES

Chapter One: The Annihilation Myth

1 Alan Hart, *Arafat, Terrorist or Peacemaker?* (London, Sidgwick & Jackson, first edition, 1984), p. 79.
2 Ibid., p. 63.
3 Golda Meir, *My Life*, (Weidenfeld and Nicholson, 1975), p. 176.
4 Avi Shlaim, *The Iron Wall, Israel and the Arabs* (Penguin Books, 2001), p. 30.
5 Documents of the Arab League, Decisions of the Council (from the first session, 4 July 1945, to the nineteenth session, 7 September 1953); and Collins and Lapierre, *O Jerusalem!* (Weidenfeld and Nicholson, 1972) p. 78.
6 Robert Lacey, *The Kingdom* (Hutchinson & Co., 1981; Fontana Paperbacks, 1982),
7 Collins and Lapierre, op. cit., pp. 83-4.
8 Ibid., p. 198.
9 Ibid.
10 Ibid., p. 302.
11 Golda Meir, op. cit., p. 176.
12 Ibid.
13 Ibid.
14 For quotations here and what follows until otherwise noted, see Collins and Lapierre, op. cit., pp. 310–11.
15 Golda Meir, op. cit., pp. 176–77.
16 For quotations and work referred to here and what follows until otherwise noted, see Golda Meir, op. cit., pp. 178–79.
17 Paul Findley, T*hey Dare to Speak Out* (Westport, Connecticut, Lawrence Hill, 1985), p. 275.
18 Ibid., p. 273.
19 Ibid., p. 272.
20 Ibid., p. 274 (quoting *Jewish Week*, Washington D.C., 2-6 September 1982).
21 Ibid.
22 Ibid.
23 Paul Findley, op. cit., p. 273.
24 Golda Meir, op. cit., p. 181.
25 Harkabi, op. cit., p. 110.
26 Ibid., p. 199.
27 Ibid., p. 217.
28 Collins and Lapierre, op. cit., p. 384.
29 Ibid., p. 365.
30 Ibid., p. 578

Chapter Two: "Go Save Jerusalem!"

1 Yigal Allon, *The Making of Israel's Army* (London, Valentine, Mitchell in association with Weidenfeld and Nicholson, 1970), pp. 36–7.
2 Ibid., p. 35.
3 Ibid., p. 38.
4 Avi Shlaim, op. cit., p. 38.

5 Avi Shlaim, op. cit.
6 *The Forrestal Diaries*, edited by Walter Millis (Cassell & Co., 1952), p. 505.
7 Yigal Allon, op. cit., p. 42.
8 *The Forrestal Diaries*, op. cit., p. 474.
9 Ibid.
10 Ibid.

Chapter Three: Bernadotte's Assassination

1 *The Palestine Post* (which became *The Jerusalem Post*), 19 September 1948.
2 Ibid.
3 The Palestine Post (which became *The Jerusalem Post*), 19 September 1948.
4 *Yediot Aharonet* (Israeli newspaper), 28 February 1977.
5 U.S. Foreign Policy, Compilation of Studies Prepared Under the Direction of Committee on Foreign Relations, United States Senate, Pursuant to S Res 335, 85th Congress, and S Res 31 and S Res 250, 86th Congress (Washington D.C., U.S. Government Printing Press, 1966), Study No. 13 of 9 June, 1960, pp. 1308-9.
6 Ibid. 579
7 FR 1949, *The Near East, South Asia and Africa*, Vol VI (Washington D.C., 1971), p. 1074.
8 Ibid., pp. 1104-5.
9 Ibid., p. 1107.
10 Ibid., p. 1110.
11 Ibid.
12 Ibid.
13 James G. McDonald, *My Mission to Israel* (New York, Simon and Schuster, 1951), p. 184 as cited in Alfred M. Lilienthal, *The Zionist Connection II: What Price Peace?* (North American, 1982), p. 93.
14 *Ha'aretz* (Israeli newspaper), 4 April 1969.

Chapter Four: Israel Says "No" to Peace

1 Abba Eban speech, "Prospects for Peace in the Middle East", speaking on "Prospects for Peace in the Middle East", at the William Patterson College in Wayne, New Jersey, 20 Novmber1974.
2 Avi Shlaim, op. cit., p. 160.
3 Avi Shlaim op. cit. refers to *Moshe Sharett, A Personal Diary, 1953-59* (published in Hebrew in eight volumes by Yoman Ishi, Maariv, Tel Aviv, 1978). Entry for 12 October 1955.
4 Avi Shlaim, op. cit., p. 49.
5 Documents on the Foreign Policy of Israel, DPFI, edited by Yehoshua Freundlick; DPFI, Vol 2, October 1948- April 1949 (Jerusalem, 1984), pp. 126 27.
6 Avi Shlaim, op. cit., pp. 52-3.
7 Sir Alec Kirkbride, *From the* Wings, Amman Memoirs, 1947-52 (London, Frank Cass, 1976), p. 112 as cited by Avi Shlaim in *The Iron Wall.*
8 Israel State Archives, ISA, 112/18, pp. 36-9. (The Conference of Ambassadors, 17-23 July 1950, Third Session, "Israel and the Arab World.").
9 Avi Shlaim op. cit. refers to *Ben-Gurion, War Diary: The War of Independence, 1948-49* (Hebrew, edited by Gershon Rivlin and Elhanan Orren, Tel Aviv, Ministry of Defence, 1982). Entry for 13 February 1951.
10 Collins and Lapierre, op. cit., pp. 562-63.

Chapter Five: Making Nasser the Enemy, Part 1

1 Anthony Nutting, *Nasser* (London, Constable,1972), p.1.
2 Ibid., p.3. 580.
3 Ibid., p.1.
4 Ibid., p.7.

5 DPFI 1952, pp. 575–78.
6 DPFI 1953, pp. 126–27.
7 Ibid. pp. 356–57.
8 Labor Party Archive, Protocol of the Political Committee, 12 May 1954.
9 Avi Shlaim, op. cit., p. 97.
10 Alan Hart, *Arafat, Terrorist or Peacemaker?* (London, Sidgwick & Jackson, 1984), pp, 91-93
11 Alan Hart, op.cit., pp, 93-94.
12 General E.L.M. Burns, Between Arab and Israeli (London, George G. Harrap, 1962), p. 70; reprinted by the Institute for Palestine Studies, Beirut, 1969, Reprint Series No. 2.
13 Alan Hart, op.cit., pp.98–99.
14 Avi Shlaim, op.cit., p.83.
15 Burns, op.cit., p.64.
16 Avi Shlaim, op.cit., p.89. (Interview with Gideon Rafael who was with Sharett at the meeting).
17 Ibid. pp. 93.
18 DFPI 1953, companion vol., 451–52.
19 Benny Morris, *Israel's Border Wars, 1949-1956, Arab Infiltration, Israeli Retaliation and the Countdown to the Suez War* (Oxford University Press,1993), p.67.
20 Sharett's Diary, 19 October, as cited in Avi Shlaim, op. cit.
21 Ben-Gurion, *Vision and Fulfilment* (Hebrew, Tel Aviv, Am Oved, 5 vols, 1958), vol.5, p.125, as cited in Avi Shlaim, op. cit.
22 Moshe Dayan, *Milestones: An Autobiography* (Hebrew, Jerusalem, Yediot Aharonot, 1976), p.191.
23 Sharett's diary, 17 May 1954.
24 Avi Shlaim, op.cit., p.108
25 Haggai Eshed, Who gave the Order? The Lavon Affair (Hebrew, Jerusalem, Edanim, 1959). P.38.
26 Sharett's diary, 31 May 1954.
27 Ibid., 6 June 1954, as cited in Avi Shlaim, op. cit.
28 Dayan, *Milestones*, op.cit.,p.122, as cited in Avi Shlaim, op. cit.
29 Ibid., as cited in Avi Shlaim, op. cit.
30 Nutting, op.cit., p.69.
31 Sharret's diary, 26 October 1954.
32 Eshed, op.cit., p.128.
33 Ibid.
34 Sharret's diary, 10 January 1955.
35 Ibid.
36 Ibid., 27 January 1955.
37 Gideon Rafael, *Destination Peace: Three Decades of Israeli Foreign Policy* (New York, Stein and Day, 1981), p.41. 581

Chapter Six: Making Nasser the Enemy, Act II

1 Michael Bar-Zohar, *Ben-Gurion, A Political Biography* (Hebrew, Tel Aviv, Am Oved, 3 vols, 1975–77). Vol 3. p. 1126, as cited in Avi Shlaim, op. cit.
2 Avi Shlaim, op. cit., p.125.
3 Nutting, op. cit., p.125.
4 Ibid., p. 92.
5 Ibid., pp. 92–3.
6 Ibid., p. 101.
7 Ibid., p. 103.
8 Ibid., p. 91.
9 Ibid., p. 104.

Chapter Seven: No Go with Nasser for the Palestinians

1 All the quotations in this chapter are from Arafat, Terrorist or Peacemaker?, op. cit., (which was based on the author's conversations with Arafat and his most senior leadership colleagues).

Chapter Eight: Goodbye, Mr. Sharett—Victory for "Satan"

1 Avi Shlaim, op. cit., p. 127. (Conversation with Colonel Mordechai Bar-On, Dayan's chief of bureau).
2 Sharett's diary, 25 and 27 March 1955.
3 Avi Shlaim, op. cit., p. 131.
4 Sharett's diary, 4 April 1955, as cited in Avi Shlaim, op. cit.
5 Ibid., 16 May 1955, as cited in Avi Shlaim, op. cit.
6 Ibid, as cited in Avi Shlaim, op. cit.
7 Ibid, as cited in Avi Shlaim, op. cit.
8 Avi Shlaim, op. cit., p. 134.
9 Sharett's diary, 17 May 1955.
10 Seymour M. Hersh, *The Samson Option, Israel, America and the Bomb* (New York, Random House, 1991), p. 20.
11 ISA 2446/8, "Israel's policy towards the Western Powers: Conclusions of the Conference of Ambassadors", 7 June 1955; and "Summary of the Prime Minister's Talk at the Conference of Ambassadors", on 28 May 1955.
12 Ibid.
13 Sharett's diary, 26 May 1955, as cited in Avi Shlaim, op. cit.
14 Ben-Gurion's diary, 30 July 1955, as cited in Avi Shlaim, op. cit.
15 Ibid., 8 August 1955; and Labour Party Archives, Protocol of the Central Committee, as cited in Avi Shlaim, op. cit.
16 Nutting, op. cit., p. 107.
17 Ibid.
18 Sharett's diary, 12 October 1955, as cited in Avi Shlaim, op. cit.
19 Moshe Dayan, *Diary of the Sinai Campaign* (London, Weidenfeld & Nicholson, 1966), p. 12.
20 Mordechai Bar-On, *Challenge and Quarrel: The Road to the Suez Campaign1956* (Hebrew, Negev Press, 1991), pp. 39-41, as cited in Avi Shlaim, op. cit.
21 Moshe Dayan, op. cit., p. 15.
22 Shimon Shamir, "The Collapse of Project Alpha", in *Suez 1956: The Crisis and its Consequences*, edited by William Roger Louis and Roger Owen (Oxford, Clarendon Press, 1989), pp. 81-82, as cited in Avi Shlaim, op. cit.
23 Avi Shlaim, op. cit., p. 148.
24 Sharett's diary, 10 December 1955, as cited in Avi Shlaim, op. cit.
25 Ibid., 19 December 1955, as cited in Avi Shlaim, op. cit.
26 Ibid., as cited in Avi Shlaim, op. cit.
27 Ibid., 23, 25, 27 and 28 December 1955, as cited in Avi Shlaim, op. cit.
28 Rafael, op. cit., p. 48.

Chapter Nine: War with Nasser and Confrontation with Eisenhower

1 Nutting, op. cit. p. 128
2 Ibid., p. 123.
3 Bar-On, op. cit., p. 148.
4 Avi Shlaim, op. cit., p. 164.
5 Ibid., p. 165.
6 Nutting, op. cit., p. 143.
7 Ibid., p. 153.
8 Ibid.
9 Shimon Peres, *Battling for Peace: Memoirs* (London, Weidenfeld & Nicholson, 1995), pp. 121–22, as cited in Avi Shlaim, op. cit. 583.
10 Ibid.
11 Ben-Gurion's diary, 29 July 1956, as cited in Avi Shlaim, op. cit.

12 Ibid.; and Dayan, *Milestones*, pp. 218–19, as cited in Avi Shlaim, op. cit.
13 Ben-Gurion's diary, 10 August 1956, as cited in Avi Shlaim, op. cit.
14 Nutting, *No End of a Lesson: The Story of Suez* (London, Constable, 1957), p. 92
15 Nutting, *Nasser*, pp. 168–69.
16 Bar-On, "David Ben-Gurion and the Sevres Collusion", in *Suez 1956* (Louis and Owen), op. cit., pp. 149–50, as cited in Avi Shlaim, op. cit.
17 Ibid.
18 The prime and most reliable source of what happened behind closed doors in Sevres, and subsequently as a consequence of the decisions taken there, was Colonel Mordechai Bar-On, Dayan's chief of bureau. Bar-on had a degree in history and served as secretary to the Israeli delegation. As noted by Avi Shlaim, Bar-On originally wrote his detailed account of events at Dayan's request in 1957 with full access to the official documents, but he was not allowed to publish, in Hebrew, until 1991. He also published a book based on his doctoral thesis: *The Gates of Gaza: Israel's Road to Suez and Back, 1955-57* (New York, St Martins Press, 1994).
19 Nutting, Nasser, pp. 174-75.
20 Ibid.
21 Ibid., p. 180.
22 Ibid., p. 183.
23 Quoted by Ben-Gurion, *Israel, A Personal History*, op. cit., p. 510.
24 Ibid., p. 525.
25 Ibid.
26 Ibid, p. 526.

Chapter Ten: The Showdown That Never Was

1 Quoted by Ben-Gurion, *Israel, A Personal History*, op. cit., pp. 526–27.
2 Ibid., p. 527.
3 Ibid., pp. 527–28.
4 Ibid.
5 Quoted by Ben-Gurion, *Israel, A Personal History*, op. cit., p. 529.
6 Ibid.
7 Quoted by Ben-Gurion, *Israel, A Personal History*, op. cit., p. 530.
8 Ibid. 584
9 Quoted by Ben-Gurion, *Israel, A Personal History*, op. cit., p. 531.
10 Ibid.
11 Ibid.
12 Quoted by Ben-Gurion, *Israel, A Personal History*, op. cit., p. 532
13 Ibid.

Chapter Eleven: Turning Point—The Assassination of President Kennedy

1 Alan Hart, *Zionism, the Real Enemy of the Jews, Volume I, The False Messiah*, op. cit., pp. 191-193.
2 Arthur M. Schlesinger Jr., *A Thousand Days, John F. Kennedy in the White House* (London, Andre Deutsch, 1965), p. 5.
3 Ibid., p. 21.
4 Seymour Hersh, op. cit., p. 127.
5 Congressional Record, 88th Congress, First Session, 23 December 1963, p. S 7818.
6 Seymour Hersh, op. cit., p. 113.
7 Seymour Hersh, op. cit., p. 113.
8 *Herut*, 9 September 1960.
9 *Herut*, 9 September 1960.
10 Je*wish Newsletter*, 28 November 1960.
11 Schlesinger, op. cit., p. 27.
12 Seymour Hersh, op. cit., p. 43.
13 Schlesinger, op. cit., p. 30.

14 Ibid., p. 25.
15 Ibid., p. 30.
16 Ibid., p. 31.
17 Ibid., p. 17.
18 Ibid., p. 35
19 Ibid., p. 27
20 Ibid., p. 22
21 Ibid, p.22
22 Ibid., p. 40.
23 Ibid., p. 49.
24 Ibid., pp. 38-39
25 Ibid., p. 39.
26 Ibid., p. 42.
27 Ibid., p. 44
28 Ibid., p. 45.
29 Ibid., p. 50.
30 Ibid., p. 51
31 Ibid., p. 51
32 Ibid., p. 51
33 Ibid., p. 51
34 Ibid., p. 51
35 Seymour Hersh, op. cit., p. 96. On pp. 327-28 Hersh notes: "Abe Feinberg's role in presidential politics and fund-raising was initially reported in an unpublished dissertation, "Ethnic Linkage and Foreign Policy", by Etta Zablocki, Columbia University, 1983 (available through UMI dissertation information services, Ann Abor, Michigan)."
36 Ibid., pp. 96-97.
37 Ibid., pp. 96-97.
38 Ibid., pp. 96-97.
39 Ibid., pp. 96-97.
40 Ibid., pp. 96-97.
41 Ibid., pp. 96-97.
42 Ibid., pp. 96-97.
43 *New York Times*, 26 August 1960.
44 Alfred M. Lilienthal, op. cit., p. 541.
45 Ibid., p. 550.
46 Ibid., p. 548; and full text of Kennedy's reply to Lilienthal p. 855, note 16.
47 Seymour Hersh, op. cit., p. 70.
48 Seymour Hersh, op. cit., p. 70.
49 Ibid., pp. 70-71.
50 Ibid., pp. 70-71.
51 Ibid., pp. 70-71.
52 Schlesinger, op. cit., p. 383.
53 Seymour Hersh, op. cit., p. 78.
54 Ibid., pp. 79-80.
55 Ibid., pp. 79-80.
56 Paul Findley, *They dare to Speak Out* (Westport, Connecticut, Lawrence Hill, 1985).
57 Seymour Hersh, op. cit., pp. 80-81.
58 Seymour Hersh, op. cit., pp. 80-81.
59 Ibid., p. 99.
60 Ibid., p. 99.
61 Ibid. p. 141 (* note).
62 Ibid. p. 100.
63 Ibid. p. 100.
64 Schlesinger, op. cit., p. 493.
65 Seymour Hersh, op. cit., pp. 102-3; and Ben-Gurion's biographer, Bar-Zohar, op. cit.

66 Ibid.
67 Ibid.
68 Ibid.
69 Ibid.
70 Seymour Hersh, op. cit., p. 104.
71 Ibid. p. 101.
72 Ibid. p. 106.
73 Ibid. p. 106.
74 Ibid. pp. 120-21 (* note).
75 Ibid. p. 107.
76 Ibid. p. 108.
77 Ibid. p. 94.
78 Ibid. p. 108.
79 Ibid. pp. 108-9
80 Ibid. p. 111.
81 Ibid. p. 112.
82 Ibid. p. 117.
83 Simha Flaphan, "Nuclear Power in the Middle East", Part 2, *New Outlook Magazine*, October 1974; and "Symposium: The Atom Bomb in Israel", *New Outlook Magazine*, March-April 1961
84 Seymour Hersh, op. cit., p. 68.
85 Ibid. p. 109.
86 Ibid. p. 113.
87 Golda Meir, op. cit., p. 258.
88 Ibid. p. 259.
89 "Secret" State Department memorandum, "Conversation with Israeli Foreign Minister Meir", 27 December 1962, in Carrolton Press Declassified Documents Reference System, 1979/193A.
90 *Ha-aretz*, 24 November 1963.
91 Seymour Hersh, op. cit., p. 119.
92 Seymour Hersh, op. cit., p. 119.
93 Ibid.
94 Avi Shlaim, op. cit., p. 219
95 Avi Shlaim, op. cit., p. 221.
96 Seymour Hersh, op. cit., pp. 115-16 (* note).
97 Ibid. p. 115.
98 Alfred M. Lilienthal, op. cit., p. 545.
99 Schlesinger, op. cit., p. 861.
100 Ibid. p. 867.
101 Ibid. p. 867.
102 Ibid. p. 868.
103 "Confidential" airgram A-434 from U.S. Embassy, Tel Aviv, to the State Department, 17 December 1963, in Carrolton Press Declassified Documents Reference System, 1977/62D.
104 Ibid.

Index

E

F

G

H

I

J

www.ingramcontent.com/pod-product-compliance
Lightning Source LLC
LaVergne TN
LVHW020537100826
845148LV00010B/1502

* 9 7 8 0 9 3 2 8 6 3 6 6 9 *